This has to be for Val,
twenty-five years on

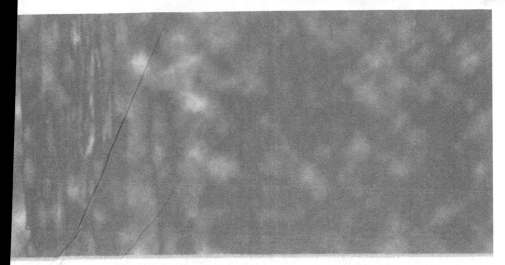

HEAT of FUSION
AND OTHER STORIES

BY JOHN M. FORD
FROM TOM DOHERTY ASSOCIATES

Fugue State / The Death of Dr. Island
Heat of Fusion and Other Stories
The Last Hot Time
The Princes of the Air
The Scholars of Night

JOHN M. FORD

HEAT of FUSION
AND OTHER STORIES

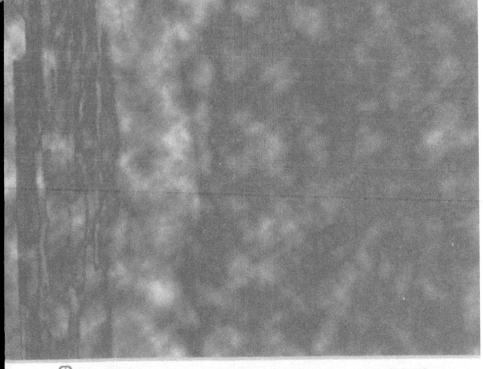

 A TOM DOHERTY ASSOCIATES BOOK / NEW YORK

HEAT OF FUSION AND OTHER STORIES

A Tor Book
Published by Tom Doherty Associates, LLC
175 Fifth Avenue
New York, NY 10010

www.tor.com

Tor® is a registered trademark of Tom Doherty Associates, LLC.

Library of Congress Cataloging-in-Publication Data

Ford, John M.
    Heat of fusion and other stories / John M. Ford.—1st ed.
        p. cm.
    "A Tom Doherty Associates book."
    ISBN 978-0-312-86939-7
    I. Fantasy fiction, American. I. Title.

PS3556.O712H43 2004
813'.54—dc22

                                        2003060675

First Edition: March 2004

Printed in the United States of America

P1

CONTENTS

The Persecutor's Tale 9

20 Questers 23

The Hemstitch Notebooks 35

Third Thoughts 43

Chromatic Aberration 49

Cosmology: A User's Manual 85

The Man in the Golden Mask 89

Preflash 103

Letter from Elsinore 125

In the Days of the Comet 131

Windows on an Empty Throne 135

Erase/Record/Play:
A Drama for Print 143

Winter Solstice, Camelot Station 193

Heat of Fusion 201

The Lost Dialogue:
A Reconstruction from Irrecoverable Sources 219

Janus: Sonnet 231

Shared World 233

Shelter from the Storm 239

SF Clichés: A Sonnet Cycle 297

Dateline: Colonus 305

Dark Sea 321

Tales from the Original Gothic 341

110 Stories 361

THE PERSECUTOR'S TALE

We were the usual sort of travelers on the Empire's high roads: unspeaking people bound on unguessable business, united only by a direction of motion. If not for the interruption of our journey, I do not think we would have noticed one another at all. I except myself, of course; but my observations are not detected by their subjects. They would be valueless otherwise.

We stopped at a small inn, with just enough rooms for our party; there were no other guests, and the innkeeper freely admitted that guests were rare. This had nothing to do with the quality of the house, which was excellent; but the city of our destination was only two hours farther by the high road, and the cars did not normally even stop.

Tonight, though, Midwinter's Eve, wet snow clogged the tracks, and ice coated the catenary, threatening to bring the wire down. It would be much better that we pause short of our goal than possibly be trapped all night in a powerless car.

There were protests, as is customary when an Imperial service performs less than flawlessly, but they quieted when the motorman assured us that our stay would be paid for by the Ministry of Transport; and they ceased when we saw the inn.

It was of the same stone as the mountains around it, with embrasures and round mock-towers at the corners; it sprawled in a manner that suggested intrigues of design but never vulgar randomness. From its leaded prism windows lights shone soft and amber and warm—from our car, in the storm, to call the effect seductive is no exaggeration.

The innkeeper met us at the car, sweeping snow from the platform, and led us inside; as he did so, a young man hitched a pair of mules to the rings on the car's front end. He handed the whip to the motorman, who cracked it once smartly, and the beasts pulled the car around a tightly curved side track—"spur," the word is—toward a small shed at the inn's rear.

The interior was as well appointed as the exterior had been. There were tapestries and paintings on the walls, intricate parquet floors with carpets in the complex southern style, simply styled furniture scarred with long use. Nothing was remotely modern, and wear showed on every surface, yet the effect was not one of disrepair but of the comfortable patina of age.

A member of our company, a centurion just returned from the Empire's northern frontier, looked in some awe at the massive ceiling beams, and commented that only far beyond his posting could trees of such girth still be found. Another traveler, an electrical engineer, pointed out the paths for wires to the iron candelabra, holes drilled with hand augers long after the beams were raised.

Our host affirmed this, showing us how the candle-holders had been altered for wire and glasslamps. We were impressed (as the innkeeper expected), and not merely with the age of the structure. The times before electricity seem to us, centuries later, as alien, feral, dark in more senses than one.

The only staff at this time of year were the innkeeper's family. His son, who had hitched the mules to the car, now ported our bags, refusing more than modest tips, though there was of course no electric lift. His daughter bustled from room to room, making down beds and checking plumbing for proper function. And his wife was preparing dinner, hot potato-and-mushroom soup followed by a cold collation of sliced beef and mutton. The bread was fresh, from refrigerated dough. Sparkling water came from a spring somewhere on the inn grounds, and the wines were more than good enough. It was said by several of us that the Empress's own chefs could have done no better on such short notice and without their army of pot-boys and scullery maids, and I believe that to be true. The family were solid gold, sturdy people, of the sort once called "the hearth-brick of the Empire."

After dinner our party, and our host, sat in the great hall before the main fire, with mugs of hot buttered ale. Snow piled against the windows, and occasionally a gust of wind made whispers and creaks and sucked sparks up the chimney, but it was not hard to forget that there was a storm outside, that we all were kept from appointments in a city leagues away. The glasslamps in the hall were dimmed and tapers lit, both in token of tomorrow's solstice and to conserve generator fuel, and the glimpse recalled of featherbeds upstairs seemed something from a dream.

The innkeeper appeared to notice that our thoughts were straying, and as he refilled our mugs he spoke of this being the longest of all nights, before the shortest of days (touching on the legends of that day), and encouraged us to use up some of the long dark hours in pleasant conversation. Thus it was revealed, gradually, who we were.

I have mentioned the frontier soldier, and the engineer, who was an instructor at a cantonment University. There was another centurion, of the famous 29th Guards, in his violet undress uniform; a young chymist, partner in a firm and of obvious prosperity; a traveling justice, robed in white, with her two clerks in black and gold. I introduced myself as a journalist, which no longer draws the disapproval it did when I was young and beardless, and tonight seemed even to impress my companions.

The last of us to speak was a spare man, gaunt in fact, in a well-

cut suit of red and black chequy, the sort that had been most fashionable in Inner Courts some years ago. His watch-chain was of
heavy silver links, his cravat of white silk. In a voice that was quiet
but by no means soft, he introduced himself as a persecutor for the
state.

There was a pause in sound and action, and then all present—
save the innkeeper—did those small, half-conscious actions that
outrun thought. The Guardsman reached toward his weapon baldric
(which was empty, of course). The frontier soldier muttered something, apparently a complex oath to some minor god. The justice
turned slowly to face the persecutor, stroking her black blindfold at
the left temple, while a clerk whispered into her right ear. I stroked
one finger minutely against another.

The first of us to speak was the engineer; he seemed very thoughtful, though I was not certain what he was thinking of. "That could
be a dangerous admission, in a company of strangers," he said, and
we waited in the pause, but he said no more.

The chymist, heedless, did. "Surely you're retired, lord sir. No active persecutor would admit the fact, knowing that one of those
present—" and then he seemed to hear the ice cracking under him,
and was silent.

For a long moment wind whistled, fire crackled on without us;
then the innkeeper rang his ladle on the kettle of ale. He said,
"Please, enough silence. It's a pleasure for me that you're my guests;
I'll not have you sleeping here displeased. My lord persecutor."

"Yes?" said the gaunt man, his eyes level and his body calm.

"You've dampened all our spirits with your revelations. Do you
not consider that . . . unjust?"

I spoke of thin ice; here was a man who danced on warm water. I
watched the justice; her tongue moistened her lips. I observed the
two soldiers; their poses told me that they were still armed, unseen.

The persecutor said, "You, sir, asked me to speak."

The innkeeper did not flinch. "To make conversation, not stop it.
I ask you . . . is it just?"

"No," said the gaunt man, quite clearly. "It is not just. You have a forfeit in mind, I think?"

"I do, lord sir. Surely you have traveled widely, surely seen things we have not. Would you tell us a tale?"

"About what?"

"About what you like." Our host faced me and said, "Of course, sir author, you know the legend of tales told on this night."

I nodded, though I knew none such. And I caught the innkeeper's look, and I scanned the hearthside circle.

One might have supposed to find us all preparing to make excuses and retire upstairs, to the safe isolation of stone walls and thick down comforters. Not at all. There was an expectance that whispered like the stormwind in the flue, drawing up sparks.

Our host dipped more ale, stirred up the fire, and I understood; we would hear a ghost story, told as such stories should be to a circle of warmth, and we would sleep well. I wondered what stories the innkeeper's children had heard, growing up in a lonely inn.

The persecutor looked long at me, as if waiting for some professional cue as to the proper forms; but we all know that tales begin at the beginning.

"There was a young person, of influence and prosperity and a devious intelligence," he said, with gathering tempo. "I'll call him a 'he,' for language's sake, but you'll understand that he could have been, might have been a she. . . .

"He came to decide that, in just one case, for just one act, he was above the law."

Yes. This was just the place to begin.

". . . but the crime, while horrid, was beyond the reach of ordinary law."

"Murder?" said the chymist, leaning forward in his chair.

"Not murder," said the frontier centurion. "For murder there's hanging, or the reaching blades."

"Or electrocution," said the electrical engineer.

"Horrid," said the persecutor, "but secret, for the young man and his lover conspired, and deeds were done in darkness, and things were thrown into deep water. With her he pursued a course of silence. It was mutual blackmail, of course."

I had seen the two legal clerks touch, earlier; now they touched again.

"And then one night he reached out for her, and touched skin, but not her skin; he felt the dead skin of serpents. He opened his eyes, and dead bare bones looked back. And he knew that the persecutor had come for him, and worse, he knew by whom he was betrayed."

The clerks drew apart. The justice moved her head from side to side, as if waiting for a whispered word from one of them.

"The young man screamed."

Wind cried.

"And when he was done screaming, however long it was, he opened his eyes again . . . and he was alone in the room."

The soldier from the frontier said, "And so he fled?"

"No. At the time, he knew better. As I say, he was very intelligent. He sought . . . redemption—"

"Good," said the engineer.

"—but he sought it as an armor of virtue, a sword of righteousness . . . a medal of good conduct."

The Guardsman swirled the butter in his ale, and adjusted his baldric and beribboned jacket.

"And he found the things he sought . . . but none of them was the thing he wanted. He had opportunities to become a dead hero, but he was not ready for that.

"And sometimes, on his cot, in the deepest night, snakeskin would brush his cheek, and the persecutor's bone mask would hover above him. And so he marched to the leaden drum."

Several did not comprehend; the Guardsman explained the phrase to mean the abandonment of a sound military career. In his voice there was something like relief.

A faint, rapid rustling came from somewhere overhead. The persecutor drank some ale and said, "Having found the honor of symbol inadequate, the young man decided to forget honor. He submerged himself in physical things—and I do not mean the fleshly lusts; sex was far too spiritual for him. I mean artifice, technology. Glass and wood and steel, the mechanical mysteries—"

"There is an owl in the rafters," the young chymist said, pointing into the dimness above. We all looked up. The owl is the bird of knowledge, legend says. And of judgment. But that is only legend. What can owls know of the sins of men?

"Indeed there is an owl," said the innkeeper impatiently. "And there is a cat. They share the mice. He's a good owl, my owl; you needn't cover your ale. Please, lord sir, continue."

"I second that," said the electrical engineer. "Could mechanical illumination dispel your young man's darkness?"

"Strange that you should say that," said the persecutor, "for he fancied once to trap the persecutor with carbon arcs and charged wires, and smokes and noise produced by chymistry. And one night his traps all erupted, and he hurried downstairs. He stood at the door to the snare room, hearing the whine and explosion, staring in at the smoke glowing blue-white . . . but he could not go in. He could not bear the thought. So, in his nightclothes, he turned and went out the door.

"There, under the moonless sky, robed all in black with gloves of snakeskin, stood a figure who looked back at him with an eyeless face.

"Then at last he fled, naked."

"It is not justice," said the centurion from the northern marches, "to drive a man mad. It is not justice, whatever law may say; it is—"

"Persecution," said the gaunt man. "And that is what it is called."

The innkeeper's wife appeared, carrying a tray of light sugared pastries, which were more than welcome.

The persecutor ate his sweetcake without haste, then cleaned his fingers elaborately on a linen napkin. He began again. "The man fled more than a locale. He fled himself. He changed his name each time it was asked, wore clothes twice and burned them, became a thousand travelers on a thousand roads."

"What," I said, "did he give as his trade, and how did he earn his way?"

The persecutor looked at me sharply; but he had examined us all as he spoke. "He had studied many things, and desperation hones cleverness. He was always one who could be here come morning and gone come night."

I nodded. So did the circuit justice.

The engineer said, "Were his trades all honest ones?"

"No. And he admitted this, in those western regions where it is admired. I think you are wondering how this could be, with persecution on him; you misunderstand. The law forbids us to intervene, or even to inform an ordinary constable. If he had been caught, I should have visited him in prison." The persecutor plucked at his clothing, removing invisible crumbs from the red and black squares. "Many persons under persecution choose to multiply their identities; very often it is the last phase of events. For when night after night the persecutor continues to appear, the subject knows, first, that he cannot escape the state; second, that whatever he may call himself, he is the same thing within . . . the evil knows its territory. And there is a third thing that he comes to know . . . that a person without an identity is dead. We all need some 'I,' even a collective 'I' such as a flag or a uniform."

The Guardsman said, "I'm proud of my uniform. And the discipline of . . ." He stopped, looked around, then was silent, embarrassed, but not without dignity.

The persecutor did not respond. He said, "In time, as happens, he came to see black cloaks by daylight, though of course only his mind put persecutors inside them. He began to wonder, obsessively, which of the people he saw in the day put on robes by night to haunt him."

"And he attacked one?" the chymist said. "You drove him to further crimes?"

"No. That has never happened."

"I wonder why," said the chymist, with what was doubtless meant to be a deep, wise irony but sounded only as petulance.

There was a pause, until the wind and the whisper of falling snow had erased the echo of the chymist's outburst. The persecutor said,

"There is no question that we drive our victims. That is the whole object. Some are driven to extraordinary measures, and this young person was one such. In the persecutor's presence, under a half moon, he—"

"Was redeemed?" I could not tell who had spoken.

"—maimed himself, in a bloody and dreadful manner that I shall not describe."

"This has been known to happen," said the justice, in a high, clear voice. Her face was tilted down, and she stroked her blindfold with the fingers of both hands. Her clerks drew back from her.

The centurion from the frontier said, "And was blood enough?" His right hand gripped his left wrist. I have heard that northern men keep a small, thin knife hidden there. "Was it enough? Finish the tale."

"The tale is finished," the persecutor said softly. "It has no proper end. No, Centurion, blood is not enough. Blood is nothing, flesh is nothing. Flesh and blood are wracked with iron, in the halls of physical justice. But iron cannot touch the spirit that sets itself above justice. Thus, I."

The Guardsman said, "Spirit," not loudly, as if he had never heard the word.

"Suppose," said the gaunt man, his face flickering in flamelight, "that a god appeared on earth, and said, 'I offer you absolution. It is a gift; there is no obligation. I forgive you, it is done.'

"A strange idea, I agree. But supposing there were such a god, what would we people do? Take the offer, no doubt. And then return to the pleasures of evil... and take it again. Steal, be absolved. Kill, be absolved. We all know the value of things that cost nothing— and if gods did make the world, they must know it too.

"So a price would have to be established. A transcendent price that one would have to try and pay... and which one could afford to pay only once in one's life."

The engineer spoke. "And in the absence of a god... when is the price paid?"

The persecutor stood up. His movements were stiff, as with cold, though it was pleasantly warm in the hall. Perhaps he had been still for too long. He went to the fire and gazed into it. "In the absence of a god, there can be no absolute. I know . . . when I see, and hear.

"And that . . . is the end . . . of my story."

The frontier soldier stood then. "Please pardon my rudeness, but I have been accustomed to a different sunset. I shall be retiring now."

"No rudeness in it," said the innkeeper. "If you rise before I, do come down to the kitchen for early tea."

The centurion bowed slightly and went up the stairs.

"I too am tired," the justice said, and rose on her clerks like crutches. "Good night to you all."

And then the rest of us followed, one by one: "Good night . . . my friends." "Good night and untroubled dreams." "Good night."

As I went upstairs, I heard the innkeeper say, "Do retire, sir, before you fall asleep; a bed will favor your back much more than that chair." And then he walked out of the hall, leaving the Guards centurion sitting straight and alone, looking at nothing.

Overhead, feathers rustled. "Who?" said the owl. "Who?"

I turned at the landing and closed the door of my room behind me.

The room was small, but very neat. A small lamp was lit on the nightstand; a bit of beef and cheese and a covered cup of warm tea were there as well. The crisp bedclothes were turned back and looked inviting. But.

I opened the inner lining of my kit bag and took out what was hidden there; put on the shapeless cloak, the skullbone mask, the long gloves of black snakeskin, and the heavy silver ring with its swirling fire opal. A tiny silver pipe went into my throat.

My step has always been light, and our innkeeper kept his doors oiled and true. I opened the one I sought without a sound.

The only light in the gaunt man's room came from the bedlamp. He was reading in bed; the book slipped from his fingers, slipped down the sheets to the floor as he pulled the blankets up. He reminded me of a picture in a book I had read as a child: a drawing in red and black of a little old woman who has heard a noise in the night. It is odd that I still remember it so clearly.

"I heard your tale," I said, the pipe in my throat buzzing and trilling.

He stared at me, as he had looked at all of us in the hall, wondering now the other side of the question; but the mask hid my face, the cloak my body, the throat-pipe my voice. And his eyes were drawn irresistibly to the opal, which blazed in the dim electric light. Perhaps, he would be thinking, I had been none of the guests; a window-peeper in the snow. Or the innkeeper, or the owl in the rafters, or a spirit in the fire. The persecuted think amazing things.

He nodded a little, but did not speak; and I said, "You seem to have learned many things, in your travels."

He found his voice; it was firm, more to his surprise than mine. "It was said that I was intelligent."

"You have recognized who pursues you."

Another nod. "Yes . . . I showed that tonight, didn't I. You're . . . myself. I—I'm sorry if what I did tonight was . . . wrong, or offended—"

I waved my unringed hand. "This has been known to happen," I said, and saw him start, and recalled that the justice had spoken those words. Well. It would not matter. "And do you then know what it is that I am looking for?"

He still clutched the sheets, and stared at his knuckles and wrists like a schoolboy looking for notes cribbed there. Then he looked up at my ring, and then at my black pit eyes.

He said, "No, I do not know." A pause. A breath. Faintly I heard his heart. "But I am willing to take whatever you have for me."

I smiled, though of course there was no outward sign. I extended my ringed hand.

He could not take his eyes from the flickering stone. He bent his head and kissed it lightly.

I brushed the ring against his bare throat, touched a trigger. The fang moved softer than a whisper. His grip on the bedclothes relaxed, and he toppled with a sigh and a rustle of linen.

His face, half-hidden, smiled childishly.

I returned to my room, disrobed, coughed up the silver pipe, and packed the things away. I wrapped myself in a velvet bedrobe and sat by the window to sip the tea and watch for dawn. On such nights I need no sleep.

The morning was bright and crystal clear; and as we all sat at an enormous breakfast the motorman appeared, with the news that the high road was cleared all the way to the city.

I cannot say our pleasure was undiluted; we could think of few finer places to be snowbound. But there were reminders of this business and that, and soon bags were brought down, and good-byes said to the innkeeper and his family (and more tips paid), and we were all standing on the trolley platform.

The gaunt man stood somewhat apart, looking down the tracks with mingled puzzlement and eagerness, talking with the trolley motorman. "Yes, sir, your ticket is valid to the city," the motorman said patiently. "Yes, these are all the bags you arrived with . . . No, sir, the service doesn't mark coach tickets with the passenger's name. . . ."

The electrical engineer listened to this as he finished a sweetcake. He licked jam from his fingers and brushed crumbs from his nose, and whistled without a tune.

"I think he's a bit mad," said the chymist. "Tries his best to ruin our evening, and this morning acts as if he barely remembers. What he did, or us, or his own—"

"He told a scary story, and it scared you," said the frontier solder pleasantly. "Who knows what he really is?"

"Maybe even a persecutor," the Guardsman added. "Anyway, you ought to spend a night awake in the dark once in a while. Good for the spirit." The two centurions resumed a spirited discussion of favorite weapons.

One of the legal clerks sat on a large bag; the other stood behind her, his hands on her shoulders. They were not looking at one another . . . but perhaps after long service to a justice one's own eyes become less essential.

I felt a hand brush mine, with a surprisingly intimate touch, and I turned to face the justice. She carried a silver stick, and wore a white silk blindfold. "My best to you," she said, in a voice only I could hear.

Perhaps it was only her custom before traveling. Surely so, for she spoke also to the gaunt man, who kissed her hand, and then touched his lips to her bandaged eyes. I noticed the white cravat was missing from his throat.

The motorman rang the bell, and the party filed aboard. I was last, and before I stepped into the car I signaled to the driver; he nodded and closed the door, and the car pulled away without me, its spidery pantograph singing a long fading note on the pristine air.

The innkeeper came out to sweep the platform. Without surprise—I wonder what could surprise him—he said, "You'll be staying a little longer, sir?"

"Yes," I said. "My appointments are postponed a little while. I shall travel on later."

"Pleased to have you, sir." He paused in his sweeping. "Did the thin gentleman board all right?"

"Yes, he did."

"He was all questions when he woke this morning, as well as waking late."

"You seem to have answered them well."

He began to speak. I believe to say an automatic "Thank you, sir," but after a moment he said instead, "My good wife and I have raised two children from birth. The questions were not wholly strange."

He leaned upon his broom, and looked with me toward the now-distant trolleycar. "It's Midwinter's morning, sir. This is the day, they say, that journeys end."

I moved a finger slightly, stroking it across another. The gesture would mean nothing to anyone not a persecutor. Only those who wear the opal ring know that it has two triggers, two fangs, two venoms.

The other brings death by convulsion, often breaking bones.

We call it Remembrance.

I have used both, according to need.

I said, "That is the legend . . . and also the day when lost things are found again."

We went inside, where the fire was warm, the beds were inviting, and the owl slept.

THE DOOR

"Go that way," said the witch, "and don't return."
And in a spicy cloud she left the scene;
The party pondered all they'd had to learn
And wondered what in Hell it all might mean.
The house was dark—had it been light before?
When down a hall, clear as the cliché day,
They saw a door, or said they saw a door,
Except for one, who said, "That's not the way."
There was a startled outburst then, because
The one dissenter fell down starkly dead;
As no one could decide whose knife it was
The company surviving went ahead.
Behind them there was nothing left to see:
No hinge or handle, and of course no key.

THE PREPARATIONS

That is no country for the naked man
And all exertions of his craft and art

Extend the faculties as best they can
And insulate the weather from the heart.
Here's wool and leather, clockwork and cold steel
The chances of survival to improve;
The map and ink, the grimly packaged meal
And merry hours each day before they move
Are spent distributing the complex load.
What can't be forecast surely can be gaffed.
You should have seen them on Departure Day:
The train lurched into motion down the road
Some cheered, some wept, and some as ever laughed
And children clapped to see the grownups play.

THE CROSSROADS

To make the walking easy, and wheels roll
Is only half a pavement's cause to be;
The other part's to silently control
Exactly where you go and what you see.
Though they'll meander, sometimes rest too long,
There is no thought to go the other way;
The impulse onward is uncommon strong,
They're set upon a course and there they'll stay,
Up to the point where two such roads present
A choice of Onwards equally displayed;
The differences would never turn a hair
And marching stumbles into argument:
Here a decision can and must be made
Yet if they could they'd not have gotten there.

THE TRAVELLER

He watched the expedition floating by
From in the park where he'd been sleeping rough;

He knew it was no use to ask them why;
He'd been there too, and he recalled enough.
But things were different once. He'd had a place
A name, perhaps a title—he'd forgot—
And one day looked across an open space
And saw something that other folk did not.
Things changed, of course, as time and distance will.
How can you tell the rootless they are lost,
Or show the flagellant the truth of pain?
There is a word for when the heart falls still.
He ate the last bit of his bread, and tossed
His only coin, and went to join the train.

THE CITY

Most pilgrims see the City as an Inn,
A Shop, a Temple, and a Trauma Ward,
A place the journey pauses or begins,
But never where the Spirit draws them toward.
The Urban Quest is darker, and disjoint,
All speed and violence, played out as fable
Instead of epic. Maybe that's the point:
In commerce, one must get things on the table.
Society requires an interplay
The City can provide, a common place
Where something like a nation can begin
Even as it inspires the alleyway,
Nothing as wide as sky or free as space,
And conurbations swallow every sin.

THE FIRST TEMPTATION

Full fifty heroes crossed the lonely mountain
And found, beyond a defile full of bones,

A cool green glade that holds a crystal fountain
Surrounded by full fifty standing stones.
One finds the right position in the middle
Of all this overly portentous stuff,
And then, as one's about to parse the riddle,
A voice will whisper, "Are you bold enough?"
It's not so much a story as a treatise,
We know damned well you should not turn away;
By definition, though, the thing you need is
The thing you're short, and will your faith betray.
The fountain still is sparkling in the glen;
You need not pause to count the stones again.

THE SECOND TEMPTATION

The years of study and the things one learns
While moving toward the sorcerer's degree
Reshape the thought, and as the spirit turns
From eager studentship to mastery
The power turns as well. Oh yes, it's real,
One can burn cities down, raise mountains up;
But as the time drips out, one starts to feel
One's spent a life to carefully patch a cup
When it was really something else that broke.
And as they understand the words the more
The less the Ipsissimi get the joke:
A chair within the garret hits the floor
And dangling from the slowly turning rope
The angled spine, unfortified by hope.

THE THIRD TEMPTATION

Who does not seek for wealth's not like to find it,
All Questers know this, and that they shall win;

They tell themselves the poor don't really mind it
As long as there's a chance they might luck in.
They know they'll meet some grossly needy person
Who must be fed, or healed, or helped along,
And if their guest's condition doesn't worsen
She'll reappear and grant a favor strong.
Sometimes the traveller will be beset,
And brings the stranger nearly to defeat
Then hearing, "We are even, let's forget,"
Finds Charity is lacking for a beat.
A little moan, a moment past redress;
A tiny bone, but vital nonetheless.

THE TOWER

Up where the air is cold and very thin
Dwell those who quite prefer to dwell alone;
If they had been inclined to let you in
They could have laid a fraction of the stone.
Some say they're mad; some others, just annoyed.
It's hard to tell; one rarely sees their faces,
The odd and arcane powers are best employed
Some distance from more habitable places.
A line of heroes always has believed
It's worth the stairs to battle, for they might
Find treasure there, so far above the town,
And fame and triumph narrowly achieved—
But one step to the left or to the right
It's seven racing heartbeats to the ground.

THE PRESUMPTUOUS

This fellowship took rivers for their way,
Since crocodiles are lazy and can't run.

These knew the rules that vampires must obey
And they were safe as long as there was sun.
Another group was firm in its belief
That balmy weather makes the troll-kind freeze;
And thousands think they cannot come to grief
As long as moss grows on the north of trees.
The afterlife is full of those who'd fix
Their fate by tossing incense at the gods;
And anytime the dealer shows a six
You're absolutely sure to beat the odds.
As someone said, it's not what you don't know
But what you do that's not precisely so.

THE AVERAGE

He had a knack for whittling things from wood
And knew one kind of berry from another;
He promised he would do the best he could
And they accepted him a Questing brother.
He sang along, though given more to quiet,
Made conversation as they neared the goal,
He found the fruits that brightened up their diet
And all agreed he was no common soul.
But when the Ogres shambled from the night
The bards will never tell you what he did:
He drew his weapon, faced him toward the fight,
Then found a ditch, and bit his hands, and hid.
By morning he was bloody as the rest
And could remember nothing of the test.

VOCATION

He never called himself a bard, because
A Bard has been to College; he had not.

He tried to be exactly what he was,
A fellow who plunked harp and sang a lot.
There was no magic in his syllables;
He couldn't heal by song, or change the weather,
Yet still he had the something-more that pulls
The party down the road, and all together.
They knew he couldn't fight, and never cared;
He sang, they stayed, they won, and lived on in
A legend of the Company that Shared,
And how much more there was than would have been
Without those words, that caused the soul to lift:
No magic needed. Time is the best gift.

THE USEFUL

She fought when needed, didn't like it much.
She couldn't sing. Her archery was good.
She mended clothing, had a certain touch
For making forage taste like human food.
The company would stop in some small grave
Of hopes, where all the locals would make plain
They thought she was a hireling, or a slave,
Or one of those who walk behind the train.
She smiled a lot, though rarely was there laughter,
She never said, "I think this way is best,"
She never spoke of life before or after,
And she had scars that were not from the Quest.
She knew that she was useful—even more,
Unlike most folk, what she was useful for.

THE WAY

The Sorcerer and Priestess lead the way
That all may know these folk are on a Quest:

The Empress and the Priest must have their say
And we all know the Lovers have the best.
The Chariot, full of fancy gear, rolls on
The Wheel of Fortune turning in its chase
While Justice, hovering, orders Death begone
The Hermit holds a lantern, just in case.
The Devil's in the bushes on the right,
The Tower to the left straight as a rule,
The Sun and Moon and Star bestow their light
And bringing up the rear there strolls the Fool.
In this wise we enumerate the Trumps,
And make paths straight, and minimize the bumps.

THE LUCKY

She always said nobody really chooses
To lean against the proper dungeon wall;
The gold behind the lath merely infuses
An accident with profit, and that's all.
She found the smugglers hunting for the privy,
And missed the deadfall for an untied shoe,
Was taken for the Thief-Queen at the divvy,
And wed a King because she dressed in blue.
A cancer took her young. It seemed an error,
The people questioned Fate, and there was weeping;
And then a neighbor kingdom brought the terror;
They stormed the palace, killed the nobles sleeping.
And long after she died, her fellows wondered:
Was she just lucky, or had they just blundered?

THE HERO

They say he never walked where he could run
And spoke with laughter, when he spoke at all;

He shone on others' lives like autumn sun
And everyone remembered him as tall.
He slew a Dragon—you can see the skin
In someone's *Wunderkammer*, saved in salt,
He did the scourges of eight kingdoms in,
And almost married—well, now, not his fault.
But wondrous Then turns into mundane Now;
He seemed content, those fading years, to be
A seller of old yarns for alehouse chow
And died in quiet, gentle poverty.
But with his life concluded, all folk knew
He could not be defeated—which was true.

ADVENTURE

It is the thing you do not find at home,
At least if you believe it isn't there;
All those who lack the fortitude to roam
Are sure they'd find it if they went somewhere:
That usurpers are balanced for a fall,
And flesh-devouring monsters stalk the night,
Or vile Vizirs hold princesses in thrall—
And who can truly say that isn't right?
The people you recall as having freed
The lovely princedom from its uncrowned heads
Were doubtless once seen differently—indeed,
They likely were considered bloody Reds.
Whether things go from bad to best or worse,
Is mostly up to those who write the verse.

THE ADVENTURERS

The path of glory leads the Questers on
Past vistas with the power to stop the breath

To nameless inns the backside of beyond
And crooked bypaths posted CERTAIN DEATH.
The taste of roasted Something-on-a-Stick,
The tyrants beaten, and the sacks of gold,
The sorcery and wild romantic schtick
Cannot prevent the bones from getting old.
Though many races don't go to the swift,
And battles only sometimes to the strong,
Far down the road they'll understand the gift
That follows having righted any wrong:
For at the end, when flesh is weak and slow,
What others only dream, these people know.

THE WATERS

If you are sure they'll part for you, they will.
Just ask the proper question and be told.
Whatever's empty, fluids neatly fill
And travel can be swift, though touch be cold.
It cuts out canyons where all things may hide
And whitely sings the traveller to sleep
Creates (or offers) space to sit beside
As it dissolves the salt of those who weep.
Do not decide what water is allowed
Or think you know the power it creates
Within a rock, suspended in a cloud
Or pent up by a dam, it only waits:
It does not care what you desire or think,
And drowns as easily as gives to drink.

THE GARDEN

A journey is a landscape with a plot,
An ordination of chaotic space;

A jungle supersaturate and hot,
The hidden turnings of a boxwood maze,
The blazing finish of a falling leaf,
The glow of fungus as the wood decays,
Or chiaroscuro snow and pines beneath
The heartless sun of February days.
A desert that has never seen a shoot
Is painted in with alkali and clays,
And even Desolation Absolute
Has Character engraved upon its face.
Locations are alike in everything
Save the mechanics of their gardening.

THE HEMSTITCH
NOTEBOOKS

Elliot Hemstitch (1896?–1954?!?) occupies a place in the literary firmament somewhere between the discount gun shop and the all-night liquor store. An unshakable believer in the principle that there are certain things a man is required to do, and after doing them throw up, he distilled the products of his experience, particularly his experience of the products of distilleries, into a series of writings that will endure forever, not least because they are not very long, use no big words, and contain a great deal of sex and shooting things.

Until recently, it was believed that all of Hemstitch's work was in print and earning someone money. (The exception, of course, is Hemstitch's unpublished first novel, the manuscript having disappeared when, during a long sea voyage, Hemstitch ate it.) This changed when the present author moved into an apartment formerly owned by screenwriter Patrick Hobby. While attempting to place cartons of rat poison, cartons containing a number of Hemstitch's unpublished notes were discovered. The find led to considerable excitement in the present author's circle, especially among his creditors. These are definitely genuine material, written with the authentic blue crayon in original Little Engine that Could and Cuddly Bear notebooks. The present author emphasizes again that the work is by Hemstitch himself, and anyone who says differently should be very careful starting his car.

The present author has plans to return to the closet corner in search of further literary material, perhaps Hitler's photo album or something negotiable with Howard Hughes's name on it. But that is a subject for another time and another book contract. Now, we are pleased to present the following excerpts from the work of a man who shot straight at life and rarely missed, especially at very close range.

FOR WHOM THE BIRD BEEPS

The furry one came into the cantina. He did not walk as a coyote should, he flowed like brown fuzzy water along the floor to the bar and held up a finger, and though he did not speak the owner poured him a drink and he drank it. It poured over his teeth and around his tongue and down his gullet and past his duodenum and into his flat coyote belly, and then he filled out and stood up straight like a man coyote does, and his eyes had the light of those who have had the very big rock fall on them, or been blown up by the Acme dynamite, or have fallen off the high cliff and hit the telegraph wires and bounced up again. When a man coyote knows these things they do not go away from him. The coyote walked out of the cantina, straight with the tire marks down his back like sergeant's stripes.

The cantina owner came over to me and put the bottle of Acme mezcal with the Acme worm in the bottom between us. "Always he comes here," said the owner, "and always he goes out again to chase the fast bird of the road. But never does he catch the bird. It is sad."

"It would be sad for the bird if he were caught," I said, and the owner smiled at me as those who understand these things smile at those who do not understand these things, and he said, "You do not understand these things. Always does the furry one chase the small fast one across the desert and the balancing rocks and the very deep canyons and the atomic test sites. Many things does he send away for from the Acme company, so that if not for him the Acme company would fail, and the Acme company people would have to take jobs in television, and would that be a good thing?"

"No," I said.

"No," said the owner. "It is what we call *queserasera*, the Doris Day thing."

"Fate," I said.

"No, that is a magazine," said the cantina owner. "You are a stupid *gringo*, but I like you. You can drink the Acme mezcal so that it goes between your teeth and past your uvula and down your esophageal tract and not get the worm stuck in your mustache. It is good that a man should do these things."

I wanted to ask him some more about the furry one, but then the cantina doors opened wide, and an old one came in, and a young one, and a not so old one in a vest, and an extremely furry one, and they began to talk of the ships that go faster than light, and I turned away, for I do not like fast ships, especially after a lot of mezcal with the worm in the bottle.

Outside, the Acme truck was delivering packages. There was an Acme rocket sled and an Acme cruise missile and an Acme compact-disc player with wireless remote, and that was all I needed to know.

THE BANANA ALSO RISES

One of the young people who tells me they will overthrow the Republic or die stands in a small clearing, looking through binoculars. He wears a polyester jacket of a color not found in nature, bell-bottomed trousers, white shoes and a matching belt. He is smiling, perhaps not knowing he does, showing teeth that are neither white nor even.

We are deep in the Republic's wilderness, a long way from its cantinas and its big malls. It is almost dawn. The young ones ask me not to describe the place too well. It is hard to hide when one wears Hawaiian shirts and Mondrian dresses with crude imitations of the

Yves Saint Laurent label sewn in crookedly. But it is how they will dress. It is what they are.

"There," says the young man in the blue jacket, and hands me the binoculars. They are not good glasses. They are of plastic, and say "Souvenir of Rock City" on the side. I squint through them, and see a line of the Republic's loyalists. All wear khaki bush jackets and baggy cotton trousers. All have epaulets with leather straps hooked through them, supporting small leather cases in odd shapes. One I know is a musette bag from the Army of Schleswig-Holstein.

The binoculars start to hurt my eyes. As I hand them back, a lens falls out.

"Our foreign aid," the young man says bitterly.

"That is not how they see it," I say. "They say you have the backing of the big stores. That you are the puppets of the warehouse discounters, and want only to plant their flags in the Republic's outlets."

The young one spits on a gila monster. "That is how all you people see the world. It is always your stores and the other stores. But I tell you we will have stores of our own one day. They may not be big stores, but the prices will be fair."

"And will they take the credit cards?" I say.

The young man frowns. "When the people are ready for the credit cards," he says, and turns away, so I can see the label on his jeans. It says CALVIN KOOLIDGE. I say nothing.

At the back of the line there is an American. He tells me to call him Brad, though the pink bowling shirt he wears says "Louie" on the pocket. He has the look of a man who has eaten radicchio and sashimi but now eats macaroni and cheese and canned tamales, which is a look that stays with a man, from somewhere a little north of his stomach.

I ask him why he is here.

"I couldn't look in the mirror any longer," he says. "Not without seeing the wrinkles. In my sleeves, my back, my knees—Oh, God, the wrinkles."

I ask him the same thing again. I have been here long enough to know that it is never the wrinkles. The ones like Brad have other ones to do their ironing.

"All right," he says. "It was Meryl Streep. But I don't blame her."

I have heard this many times too, but I believe it. For so many of them it was Meryl Streep, playing Isak Dinesen in the big film that sold many tickets. But they never blame her.

When the sun comes up there is a battle. There is no way to tell about a battle. You either know of it or you do not, and if you do not there are no words for the noise and confusion and horror that will make you know, no words that are worth the rates this magazine pays to go and get them. Maybe in the book to come later, the book with the hard covers, it will be different.

But I do have a minimum contract length, so I will tell you this: when it was over, there was much cotton on the field, getting rotten so that you could not pick very much of it. There was much polyester as well, still pressed neatly. I thought of the gingham dog and the calico cat.

The young man in the blue jacket was lying still, with one of the women in a silver Lurex jumpsuit kneeling beside him. "Is it all right?" the young man said, and the woman said, "Yes, it is fine," though when one hundred percent polyester begins to smell like that, all the fabric softener in the world is of no use.

In the camp of the rebels, they are drinking generic beer and eating sandwiches on white bread filled with the pasteurized food product of the cheese. The American has connected a guitar to the portable generator and is singing "Cielito Lindo" and the theme from *The Patty Duke Show*.

One of the rebels pulls my sleeve, a very young one in pajamas with a picture of a Japanese robot that sometimes becomes a Buick Electra. "Are you going back to America soon?" he says.

"Yes," I say, "soon."

"Tell them we know they love us, no matter what the media says," the very young one says. He is so small to know words like "media," I have no heart to point out that it is a plural noun. "I know they love us in America. I have a picture of the President's wife." He shows me the picture, which is autographed, and I nod and agree with him that it is very fine. There is no way that I can tell him that the woman in the picture is Fawn Hall.

GLITZ IN THE AFTERNOON

The mall is a cold place in the middle of the day. Those who have gone into the mall are all in the restaurants eating the burgers and the drinks that fizz, and the wide corridors are empty and the air conditioning makes them very cold then. The people in the stores are cold too, because they all wish that they too were doing the lunch break thing. It is then that a man knows whether he has come to the mall to do the hanging out, or the shopping.

Even at the cold hour there are many people in the mall. There are the women, and the children, and the skateboard ones, and the old ones with their cheap wine in the bags of paper. The elevator music is very loud and the restrooms are for those with steel in their hearts. It is much like the bazaars of the east except that the children are not for sale.

There are other men there, but there are never many. Most look straight ahead, thinking only of the thing they have come to buy, and plan a route that leads them on a true line from the trackless seas where their cars are parked to the store where they must buy the thing. Their eyes may be drawn aside by the stores that sell the good lingerie, or by the young ones who wear the high-heeled shoes, as in the videos of the heavy metal, but they do not stop. They order the good lingerie by mail, which a man may have many reasons to do, and they know well about the charge of the messing around with the a-little-bit-too-young ones in the spike heels. They go only to the store where the thing they want is, and they buy it and they go away.

That is good and clean and honest. But it is not shopping.

To shop is to go into the mall alone, carrying only the card and a little cash for food from the places that will not accept the card. A man does not know what he will shop for before he sees it, but when he sees it he will know. It may be in a window or on a table or behind a glass case, but it will call to him. Maybe he has seen it before, in the possession of another at a restaurant where the tablecloth tastes better than the food does, or in the magazine with the pages that fold out of the middle, the pages that fold out suddenly when you are trying to buy it and stick it inside a copy of the *National Review*. The thing he shops for will smell good and it will please the eye and it will probably be matte black. It will cost like a bastard. Men know this. It is why so few men shop well.

I went through the mall, watching the young ones play the games of video and shoplifting and the sales ones chasing them and the display ones setting up the Christmas decorations, for it would be October soon. There was a strong smell of bayberry, and the sharp cry that the Styrofoam makes when it is wounded. I went back and forth, past the cards and the cheese and the Benetton of many colors and the good lingerie. I went many times past the good lingerie.

I knew the thing before I saw it. I turned, already reaching for my card, and there it was, just between the two pillars that make the terrible noise when the sales one forgets to remove the tag. I have seen pillars like that in Egypt. I do not know if their sales ones ever forgot to remove the tag, but the Pharaohs were hard men and it must have been very bad when they forgot.

I went in. The sales one, who was a young one, said, "May I help you?" but she had the look that said she knew she could not help me and the clothes that asked to be helped with and the body that said if I offered to help her with the clothes she would hit me hard in the places that when they are broken do not get strong again soon.

I moved around the store. You must stalk the thing even though you know it is there. There is a chance that another man, one who already knows what he wants, will come in and make the buy before you, and when this happens you must let him do it. This is the difference between those who shop and those who only buy. If you then go back into the parking lot before him and do the small wrench thing to the brakes of his BMW, this is all right too.

No one came in. I took the thing, took it to the counter and laid it down. It looked helpless there, as the animal that shows its throat, but men who shop know this is a lie. The truth about the thing only comes when you have thrown away the store receipt and cannot return it anymore.

"Will that be cash or charge?" the sales one said. I did not speak, but took out my card of platinum and put it on the counter. The sales one shoved it into the machine, and then began what the true shoppers call the moment of truth. Either the machine will make the good beep that means your purchase is approved, or the bad beep that means you have shopped more than a man may shop. Some cannot stand the pressure, and take back the card and throw down the money that folds. In the great stores of the Champs Elysées they call it *le card cafard*, and it is a worse thing than to wear *les souliers bruns* with *le smoking*.

The machine made the good beep. The sales one put the bought thing in a shopping bag, a big one with the name of the store on the outside, so that all the other men in the mall would know that I had made my buy.

It was nearly sunset before I found my car in the big lot. It was not always so, when a man would drive all day in a car with the big fins and the name of a jungle animal. Now the cars have no fins and names like the old ones give to poodles.

When it was all over and I was home again, I sat before the box. The box was dark and quiet but I could see the numbers on the dial, and it was tuned to the channel of those who sell shoddy things to those who do not go into the mall.

There must be many reasons why a man will not go into the mall, alone as a man should with only his card of platinum and the sizes of his women. Yet I have seen the very old ones go in, though they could no longer see or hear because of the neon and the elevator music. And the young one who wrote funny, Jack Kerouac, would have gone into the mall, and when the blue light flashed for a special on motor oil, he would have bought motor oil.

I sat before the silent box, and cleaned the remote control. It was cool in my hand. I rested my finger on the button.

THIRD THOUGHTS

...and thence retire me to my Milan, where
Every third thought shall be my grave.
                              ——*The Tempest*, V. i.

Milan crumbles beneath us, say the ministers,
And so temptations speak from tropic graves.
Leaving magic is not lighter than gaining it.
The book is in the water, the staff in pieces,
The robe makes nests for magpies; yet
Milan is full of books, sticks, robes.
My umbrella hums with power, my old hat
Whispers secrets, my morning paper
Anagrams the account of a football match
Into the words that will divide thunderheads
And turn the seas to blood. The Minister
Of Finance says that we are short of gold;
The *Fiat Aurum* is simple, sand to gold.
It does not last, but sand is plentiful;
A steady flow of credit, dirt to dirt,
Until each well-provided citizen

Slips in his share, and sinks, and is no more.
The Minister of Health and Welfare says
That there are children hungry in the streets:
I could raise hospices of stark white marble
Where crystal fountains run with milk and syrup;
Those fed so never wish for better fare.
In truth, they wish for nothing more at all.
The Minister of War stands just without;
I know what he wants, and could give it him
Most easily of all: sulfur, smoke, blood.
In three hours, less, I could enchant my Milan
A citadel of wonders on the earth,
A prize past reason. There are spirits here
To be commanded, doubt it not. Yet not that one
Who did my will so lightly, nor the one
Who was my dark. Milan shall not crumble
Unless I crumble first. I thought I was wise
When I freed the spirits; it was a good act,
But not wise. Wisdom comes only now,
With knowing I would call them back to me,
With crumbling. Other states may overrun us,
I think they shall, whether with tank or bank,
General or ambassador, guided bomb or guided tour;
But we'll not crumble. I hear the Minister's children
Screaming for food by a strange device.
I require music, still not crumbling,
From viols played by hands.
Third thoughts come easily now.

VISIT SUNNY NAPLES,
Say the signs, and the beaming faces
Of the new rulers, charm of a nation.
The muscular King, marked with sea and labor,
The tan unworldly Queen, who shuns

(The tabloids say) all corsetry and shoes.
Cast off, cast off, and land in brilliant Naples!
All here is as you've seen it through the glass:
The chess games on the Palace patio,
The statue of the Old King in the square
(In coral, with pearl eyes), the nightly revels
To meet the cruise ships, fête them, see them gone;
See life through a parasol and a salt-rimmed glass.
In Naples, every day is brave and new
(Registered service mark of the National Tourist Board)
The needs of life are plucked from passing waiters—
All called Cal, a quaint local custom—
Fortune smiles all night in the Casino,
Nor does the wheel stop any perfect day.
The King and Queen will lead you in the waltz
And, from the poster and the TV spot,
Remind you, in encounters rare and fair,
A few simple precautions never did anyone harm.
Will you come, will you come, however you can,
And celebrate the nights, and drowse the days
Under the sun of universal grace,
Under the smiles of two such sovereigns
As buy up all your care? All ways lead here,
All signs, stamps, coins show the same two faces,
She wears a robe, he bears a formal staff;
There are no books in Naples.

The king of the nameless island wears
A robe of vines, a driftwood staff.
He has made a book of leaves and fiber
And written therein in his hard-schooled Italian
The names and forms of all the island's life,
All good and deadly things. The book *is* the island,
Is life itself, should one be shipwrecked here.

That has not happened yet. The king
Does not command the waves, for good or ill,
To bring in travelers or to keep their distance;
No spirit comes or goes or does his bidding.
The king is not a governor any more,
As what he likes to call the Interregnum
Ended with freedom decreed for all.
The king has no regrets. He remembers
With all his flesh the tyranny of pinches;
His soul recalls the worshipping of drunkards;
His heart conceals an unrequited—well,
The former king taught him no word to call it.
At any rate he understands rebellion,
And how one ruler's fall begets another;
The only pun he knows is "revolution."
For a while, once he was come into his own,
He played the God of Beetles, directing them
By foot and stick and stone to burrow
Where he pleased, punishing them
With death by weight or water at his whim.
But beetles lack the will for disputation
Or heart enough to mock; to be acknowledged
Sole Lord Almighty quite exhausts the game.
He built a reed canoe, and on it wracked
Red beetles among the black; nothing changed.
So he freed the beetles, just to see
What would happen. Nothing did.
They are still here. Not like the spirits.
The spirits are gone where he cannot follow,
Though now and again there's a buzz in his left ear
That he calls by a name; but there is no answer.
He hurts now, pinched invisibly again
By joints gone dry and sinews growing hard;
He understands at last what the old king

Meant by age, and though he knows surpassing well
What death is, still the scaled king,
His ancestry all muddled up, knows not
If he can die. That is all his fear:
To be trapped in a body as in the bole of a tree,
Forever. The shapeless king sits
With his back against a comfortable elm
And his book that is the island open in his lap;
He needs to put down freedom on the page
So that, part of the book, it is part of the island,
So that whoever finds the book will understand.
He knows he works the old king's magic,
The summoning of the right spirit.
Near his knee, a beetle of spectacular hue
Struggles with a pebble ten times its size;
The king smiles. He licks his pen.
He savors his dissatisfied content, and thinks
How much better it is to reign in Heaven
Than to command in Hell.

CHROMATIC ABERRATION

The end of the ancient world can be precisely fixed in space and time. It took place in the central square of the capital city, before the steps of the Great Hall of Justice, in an area twenty meters by twenty-five that had been especially cleared of wire and debris. It occurred at noon, six days after the rocket attack on the Veterans' Hospital. The sky was clear, hard like glass, a few dense clouds trapped stationary in its substance. The sun was low, it being early spring, and the shadow of the Justice Hall fell sharp as a sundial's gnomon with its point in White Birch Street. Six military aircraft flew over just then, in a perfect triangle, one followed by two followed by three, splintering the solid atmosphere with noise and contrails. Had their pilots looked down at that moment, they would have seen the city as an ordered field of white blocks mated to black parallelograms, dissected by the gray lines of streets. From that height, it was a vision not too different from the city before the revolution (I speak here only in the grossest physical sense). The geometry of a city is not destroyed by war or time, but only eroded, as memory is never completely erased, but only decays, a word here, a library there. All fires had been extinguished in the six days, and only one small one lit, there before the steps of justice. The ancient world declined that morning in the autumn glow of a bayonet heated in a brazier, and it stopped that noon in a long moist hiss.

The ancient world having stood its correction, the modern one began in a long dance of stately measures, the eradication of monuments to ancient events, dates, persons; the reform of the currency, the restructuring of the system of national health.

It was in the early afternoon, when the sun had just moved below the peak of the Justice Hall, bathing the square and all who knelt there in coolness, that the leaders of the revolutionary forces made the announcement that was both a reform and a revelation the Declaration of the Modern Spectrum. It had been established through careful historical analysis that the colors used by the ancients were, like so many ancient things, untrue to life, a fraud perpetrated by the rulers on the ruled. As the laborer toiled for money, believing that it had value, as he prayed to the saints, believing that they had power, so he said that the sky was such a color, grass another, blood another, not knowing that he was caught in a trap of perception. Finally (so ran the Declaration) our eyes had been opened, we could perceive the colors of the world.

It was said by indifferent foreign observers (and I use the term in an ironic sense) that color is immutable, a matter of wavelengths and retinal stimuli. Through this (again you will pardon the term) blindness, these ancient relics showed only that they did not understand the nature of revolution, which is to revise all things, to remake the soul. If there are modern colors—as we now know there are—perhaps they were truly not seen before. The ancient patterns blinded the eye to them, even as the modern pattern extends the range of vision, so that now we can actually see the sky, the grass, the blood.

My senses tell me that you still do not understand. Very well, I shall try to illustrate, to illuminate in modern color what ancient color distorted and shadowed. Some will call these tales fantastical and unreal; yet I say to you that the revolution itself was once only a dream in the minds of modern people; and I say moreover that the ancient world, for all its ingenuity of repair and destruction, was driven by a dream of the identical substance. Before all mechanism is the dream of mechanism, and all machines have their ghosts. This endures, no matter what.

These words summarize the credo of the revolution: What was true then, is not true now. These words summarize the credo of revolution. Thus by the subtraction of a single three-letter word is a declarative fact made into a platitude. Yet is the platitude any less valid? Can we not therefore say that the word *the* was unnecessary, that its meaning was overdetermined? Surely so. Suppose we broaden the analysis to the credo itself: subtract the word *true*, in fact subtract it twice. *What was then, is not now.* Just as meaningful, just as valid. And the word was used twice! Are we then to assume that truth can be extracted from any statement without altering its essential meaning? Continue the process. What was, is not. Something is wrong here: we have reduced the statement by half, and suffered no loss in value. This is a puzzle worthy of study, but I have no time to continue the analysis now, the immediate matter must be turned to; but please, do not forget.

The first color described in the Modern Spectrum is redor. It is a strong, heraldic tincture, without taint or compromise. Redor is the principal color of our flag; the monuments to those slain in the revolution are draped upon the Anniversary of Victory with silk dyed redor in the thread.

The revolution was entering its final hours. All the major buildings of the capital city were under the control of the modern forces. Small units of soldiers went from door to door, spreading the news of the victory and seeking out the few ancient fighters who remained in hiding. These units were armed, both for protection against unstable ancients and because the immediate correction of certain individuals had been decreed by the common will and for the common good.

One such unit was moving along White Birch Street, in the direction of the central square. The namesake trees that lined the street on both sides, spaced at exact seven-meter intervals, were still bare with the season. Many had been badly damaged by gunfire or other accidents of war. The soldiers passed the Institute for Famine Research, which had been renovated early in the revolution, and the National Theater, which was sealed. They moved between a small park to the left and a promenade to the right, and then entered the Hospital for War Veterans. It was known that many of the aged and crippled residents of the Hospital remained loyal to the ancient regime, but no corrections were planned. The Hospital was, at last report, quiet and in good order.

This report, as so many in war, was seriously out of date.

The soldiers went up a shallow ramp and passed through broad doors to reach the Hospital's main entrance hall, which was tiled, double-vaulted, with murals of parkland scenes on its walls. The main desk, of bronze and oak, was just ahead; to the right, an ornate stairway enclosed a brass-cage elevator. It was at this intersection that they were attacked by the patients. Some were armed with surgical tools, some with crutches and artificial limbs, some with only their hands. The soldiers were young and brave, but surprised, surrounded. The ancients were military veterans hardened to wounding, and what they did to the soldiers (as what they had done to the doctors and nurses committed to their care) does not bear detailed recounting. Soon the patients proceeded from the Hospital and onto White Birch Street, armed with the soldiers' weapons, armed with ancient fury.

By reports, they hesitated and milled for some minutes. Many were from the provinces, unfamiliar with the pattern of the city. Others had been wounded in ancient wars, and had spent many years knowing only the levels, lifts, and corridors of the Hospital. The openness of streets, of sky, the lack of understandable landmarks and well-remembered doors, must have confounded them. It might have been possible to have saved them, even then, but the ancient wheel of destruction had great momentum once it was turning.

It is said by some that they began to cry for justice; if this is so, then the tragedy is doubled. Others report that persons who seemed able-bodied, either malingerers or convalescents near full healing, shouted commands that imposed order and direction on the patients. Whatever the cause, they began to move—in good order, as the soldiers they had been, not a rabble, not a mob—past the Hospital gates, to White Birch Street, and then to the right, toward the Great Hall of Justice.

The Hall dominates the square. To the left as one faces it is the Exposition Park, which was once public grazeland and was later used for fairs and public display. To the right was, at one time, the Basilica of the Apostles, a domed cruciform building whose promenade was lined with life-sized statues of the Twelve Collaborationists. The statues had, however, been renovated in one of the first revolutionary incidents, and the fragments allowed to remain as a symbol of either rebel atrocity or the inevitable triumph of the revolution. (A few bits were secretly removed by the ancients, though powerless dust is all that they were.) Both the Basilica and the promenade have been removed without trace since modern times began, but at that moment they existed, one solidly, one only halfway in memory.

At that moment the Great Hall of Justice was occupied by one hundred seventeen revolutionary militia under the command of one rebel Colonel (formerly a Lieutenant of the national guard) and a Modernization Officer (formerly a waiter at the Regency Hotel). The defenders were ranked on the steps, behind barbed wire, armed with rifles and two tripod-mounted machine guns in sandbagged emplacements.

There is no doubt that the revolutionaries fired the first shots, single shots from individual rifles. They had no communication of the incident at the hospital, and at long range of engagement they could not identify the dress of the approaching force. (Some of the patients also wore pieces of their former uniforms, an ancient custom of remembrance, adding to the confusion, further underscoring the self-destructive essence of the ancient world.) The patients returned fire. And then it was war, and there was no recourse.

The patients advanced, under fire. They took losses; they inflicted them. And then, just as the two sides were close enough for recognition, the patients charged.

The revolutionary forces could now see who was attacking them. It is said that some of the old and young soldiers were related by blood; this is true in spirit if not in fact. But the modern forces knew their duty was to defend the Great Hall of Justice, and this they did. They fired, and fired, as many of the attackers and not a few of their own number fell. Uniforms and bandages were stained with blood and bone and brain. Flesh limbs and wooden ones were shattered. The wire was crossed in the traditional manner: by using men, dead or about to be, as bridges. The sound of guns in the long moment of that charge has been compared to hammering, to forging, and to bells, and stone broke like crockery, but no one who was there can recall a single cry of pain, nor of triumph, not one human sound at all. Only the guns, and the stones, until all the sound stopped, and the last charge of the ancient world was over. The last old soldier had fallen barely an arm's reach from the defending line.

There was, in the remaining seven days of the ancient world, discussion of a memorial to these people, who died in the pursuance of their faith, but on reflection it was seen that modern children, on seeing the monument, would ask why it was there, who it memorialized, what they had done; and there were no longer any answers to these questions. Instead, a scroll was prepared, bearing the names of the patients; then the paper was thrust into a brazier alight on the steps of the Great Hall of Justice. It burned with a redor flame.

In the course of examining the bodies for the preparation of the roster, it was discovered that one-seventh of them had died not of wounds but of heart failure, and one in four was blind. Are you moved, despite the futility? I am.

Words are inadequate (the poor craftsman curses his tools) to describe the loveliness of our coastal regions, but words are what I have available. From the Western Delta to Fox Point Light is a map distance of seven hundred forty kilometers, the major landmarks being, in order west to east, Guise Inlet, Nine Wreck Head, Paradise Shoals, and the Great Palisade. The actual distance cannot even be estimated, as the shore is looped and involuted with inlets, coves, and pools. A thousand things have hidden along that shore in ancient times: smugglers, pirates, hermits from time, though all are gone now. The coast is rocky, swept by wind and water, and life there can be hard, yet when the sun is low through mist, or the moon looks palely upon a quiet sea, one might never look upon another scene and still be content to live in those memories.

Angeyel, the second modern hue, is a delicate color, of great beauty in deep concentration; but it is best appreciated in subdued light, as the strong light of full day tends to wash it out, to destroy it.

There was a woman who lived by a tidal pool, who though she had no formal training had made the study of the pool's creatures her life. A few of the older folk in the nearest town knew the woman's name, but they never used it. She was called Sea Angel, after a variety of small shrimp that she found especially beautiful and fascinating, and bred in dishes, and made into a delicately flavored soup.

The water and her garden gave her food, and she sold rare shells washed up on the shore to buy books and equipment for her work. She had a fine optical microscope, and many hundreds of prepared and fixed slides, racked and elaborately catalogued. There was only one other thing that she desired, and on certain nights, a small boat would cross the pool from the fishing town on the other side, and return only with the morning.

One of those who made this late voyage was called Knotsmith, because of the fineness of his craft in weaving nets. Sea Angel was delighted by the skill of his strong slender fingers, and Knotsmith in turn admired her studies by the pool, for he was in fact of modern mind, and early on became a leader of the revolution.

Knotsmith often asked Sea Angel to join in the modern movement, but she, not understanding, would only laugh and say, "I am an uneducated water-widow who knows nothing of these matters. I live in the drops of water beneath my strong glasses; I live within shells from the strand."

The battles of the revolution did not reach Knotsmith's village or Sea Angel's pool. Knotsmith made the night voyage rarely now, kept away by the needs of the war; but when he did return Sea Angel was pleased to see him, and tell him of her discoveries in salt water. Once he brought her a book from a distant nation, describing the very tiniest of water life, creatures Sea Angel's microscope could not reveal; he told her that in the modern world she would have the device for this perception, and any other equipment she might desire.

Sea Angel smiled and thanked Knotsmith for the book, and placed it on her shelves with the other books and files and specimens, but to his sorrow she still did not understand, did not take the lesson that the modern world could see things the ancients could not. She saw still in the ancient manner, which is to say, she could not see at all, but felt her way blindly through halls of memory.

On a night not long before the final triumph of the revolution, Knotsmith came to Sea Angel's house by the water. She saw that his wrists were puffy and sore, discolored from scratching them.

Sea Angel scraped at Knotsmith's swollen skin with a small knife, then spread the scrapings upon a glass slide and examined them through her microscope.

"You have been fishing in strange waters," she said.

"What—do you mean?" Knotsmith asked.

"The itching is caused by mites in your flesh. From their form I am certain that they are sea mites, but they are a kind I have never seen before. Where have you woven your nets, Knotsmith?"

Knotsmith said, "The modern world is wide," and would say no more. Sea Angel spread a balm on his wrists, and turned the lantern down.

Knotsmith departed earlier than his custom, rowing back across the pool well before dawn. When the lantern on his boat was only a flicker on the dark water, Sea Angel put out her own boat, a gift from a fisherman friend. She fastened on the small motor her shell-money had purchased, and went out to sea.

Just at dawn she saw a ship. It mounted cranes, and its deck was piled with crates. Atop its pilothouse was a curious bristling of metal rods, bright in the rising sun. Sea Angel looked through her binoculars, and saw that it flew the flag of a nation half the world away.

Then she turned her attention away from the ship, and lowered her sampling bottles into the sea. She opened a tin, and cast a handful of her namesake shrimp on the water, then shook out her small fishing net. If the mites were in the water here, if she could catch a fish, she was almost certain to find them.

She put on a broad-brimmed hat to shade her eyes from the blinding sun, and sat quite still, the net in her hands, watching her bait. A little while later, she heard the sound of motors; it did not come from the freight vessel, and she turned to look.

A fishing boat was approaching, but alone, not part of the fleet. Men in uniforms stood at the rail, and in the prow stood Knotsmith, in a uniform with metal on his shoulder and his sleeve. Sea Angel watched as the boat drew close to the freighter, pulled alongside and was drawn fast.

Idly curious, she looked again through her binoculars, and saw Knotsmith going aboard the freighter. After him went a soldier, carrying a bundle of a peculiar color.

There was a ripple on the water, and Sea Angel cast her net; she brought up a pair of small fish that landed flopping on the bottom of her boat. She lowered them gently into a bucket of water, started her boat's motor and turned toward her pool and her house, the other ships all forgotten.

It did not take long for her to find the unusual sea mites in swabbings from the fishes' gills. She sat down with her notebooks, describing the discovery in detail.

As she was writing, a slip of paper she had used as a placemarker fluttered to the floor. She picked it up, struck by its color. It was a note of modern currency, given to her by Knotsmith. Enblu, he had called the shade. It was just the color of the bundle the soldier had carried aboard the ship. She put it back in the notebook and thought no more of it.

After some time, she heard a weary splash from the bucket with the fish in it. "I am sorry, I entirely forgot you," she said, picked up the bucket, and carried it to the shore of the pool.

The fishing boat was just coming in to shore. The crates from the freighter were stacked on the deck. Knotsmith had jumped over the rail and was wading through the shallow toward Sea Angel; some of the soldiers came after him.

"Thank you, fish," she said, "find your way home safely," and cast them in a long low arc toward deep water. They splashed, and leaped, and were gone.

"Sea Angel," said Knotsmith, the rest of his words trailing away as a boat vanishing into fog.

"Good day, Knotsmith. I know now where you have been weaving your nets."

"Of all the greetings you might have spoken," Knotsmith said, "I wish you had chosen any other than that."

"I don't understand," said Sea Angel.

"That is the difficulty," Knotsmith said, "you do not, you have never understood, and now your speech repairs me...." He made a gesture, and the soldiers moved toward Sea Angel. "You have committed a terrible and ancient error," Knotsmith said, "and you must stand corrected."

"I am sorry that I do not understand," Sea Angel said, "but there are things which I know—" and she broke away from the soldiers and ran for the sea, flying from the strand like a bright leaping fish. But Knotsmith spoke an order, and the soldiers fired with revolutionary precision, and Sea Angel fell dead on the shore, neither quite in the sea nor out.

The soldiers set fire to the house, and then they and the man who led them got into their boat and went back across the pool, the first time that anyone had ever sailed from Sea Angel's shore at twilight.

In the morning there came several small boats from the town, but the fire had been thorough, and the night tide had come and gone. The books and files were scattered, the slides for the microscope smashed to powder, the knowledge all disordered, and there was nothing to take back or preserve or remember, only traces left for the imaginations of those such as I.

Lie of the ground is important militarily, both for its direct physical effect on combat and the supplying of combat, and for its function as a framework for the conduct of the war. River lines, defensible passes, the possession of hills and encirclement of cities; these are the syntax that structures the speech of guns. And when the guns have spoken their part, it will be the rivers and the passes, the hills and the cities, that column and paragraph the memories of those who were there. It is the ordered vision that persists.

The next modern color is known as lowgre. It is a strong, deep color, a color for arms and armor. It is the color of the uniform worn by all soldiers in the modern army.

The General of the Fourth Brigade of Armor had first seen war as a boy, smuggling ammunition and medicine to the rebels in the hills. He was a small boy, and wiry, dressed in uniform trousers with the legs rolled up, sneakers, and a shapeless army blanket; all of these he stole from the depots of the national guard. The blanket served him as overcoat and sunshade and tent, as carryall bag and camouflage. The hill country was a language he spoke fluently, as anyone living among an enemy must use the enemy's language in the prescribed manner, especially when one has dangerous things to say. At the first step of a sentry he could throw himself to the ground, the blanket settling upon him, and become invisible, a patch of moss or an overgrown boulder upon the hillside. There was a saying among the rebel fighters: "Never shoot the earth, it's friendly." The boy, and the others like him, may have given rise to this proverb, or perhaps it was an expression of solidarity with the land, or more mundanely a warning against wasting precious ammunition.

Due no doubt to these early habits, the boy who would become the General of the Fourth Brigade never adopted the habit of uniform dress. He would wear military clothing, which is after all utilitarian, but old, odd, mismatched pieces, sometimes from the ancients' uniform. He was the despair of his training leaders, and later his supply controllers, and in the ancient forces would surely have ended in prison or disgrace, just for the look of him. But modern times were dawning, and the great leader within the poor costume was recognized and allowed to develop.

For he was indeed one of those whom soldiers will follow, though it be to death, or utter annihilation; and even in ancient times it was understood that this power is not made or created, it simply is.

When he was a Colonel of the revolutionary forces—no longer rebels, but a genuine army, in a true war—he led a surprise assault on a stronghold of the national guard, striking like lightning at daybreak, using trucks and motorcycles as if they were tanks and planes. The garrison surrendered in less than an hour.

The commander of the guard camp was a strutting small General who wore a black tunic, hung with his shining minor medals. He was brought to the Colonel with his tunic and trousers unbuttoned, with a rope around his neck. The little General knew that he must stand corrected, and he did not argue for his life; he asked only that his soldiers not be killed outright.

This was a brave and noble thing to say, though without understanding. When the Colonel heard it, he ordered the rope taken from the camp commander's neck, and that the General stand his correction by gunfire. It was an ancient custom that there was a difference.

The Colonel's men gave him the General's fine black tunic as a prize of war. He removed the medals and put it on; the General had been a small man, but the Colonel was slender. The sound of the correction was loud in the camp, drowning out small cries that came from closed rooms; for though the Colonel had insisted that the defenders not be repaired, information was required. Balance was required. The repair of human beings is terrible to watch, but it brings information, and balance. And many of these repaired need no more suffer to watch anything.

When the leaders of the revolutionary forces heard the story of the capture, and saw the Colonel in his black coat, they knew that they were in the presence of, not a man, but a legend. "Since you are wearing a General's stars," they said, "you had best be a General." And in the next moment, there was a Fourth Brigade of Armor, and the Colonel was its General, though the entire armored contingent of the revolutionary forces was two old automobiles with boiler plates welded to them.

This would change.

In the last weeks of the last campaign of the revolution, the Fourth Brigade had twenty tanks and fifty armored cars and support vehicles, and the General was still wearing his black coat to lead them. Then the leaders of forces called the General in for a conference, and gave him a uniform, well-tailored to his measurements. It was colored lowgre, of course, in strong and striking value, almost as dramatic as the tunics the leaders themselves wore.

"The revolution is nearly over," the leaders said. "The image we cast now will be the image that shall remain with us in modern times. This uniform is part of that image. You see that we all wear them; this one has been made for you to wear."

"I've never needed such a thing," the General said.

"There are other needs besides your own," the leaders said. "Think of the soldiers who follow you."

"They gave me this coat," said the General.

"And is it the coat they follow," said the most astute of the leaders, "or you?"

"You aren't people who bear arguing with," the General said, and without another word took the new uniform and put it on.

The General's aide-de-camp, a woman of the town where the General had been born, saw him on his return to the Brigade and said, "That is a fine new uniform."

"Your perceptions have always been accurate," said the General, and no more was spoken of the matter.

The Fourth Brigade of Armor was on the move, ordered from its camp near the town of the General's birth to the capital, along the roads and half-roads, through the woods and glades. The General was at the head of his column, as always, dressed in his new uniform.

In the General's eyes, there was a movement, in the heavy growth to the side of the trails. "Look there," he said, and pointed.

"At what, sir?" said his aide.

"I saw a boy," the General said, "wearing a blanket on his back."

The aide looked into the brush. She was sharp-eyed, having herself been a scout for the revolutionary forces when only a child. "I see nothing," she said. "It could have been an animal."

"Yes, it could have been," said the General, and pointed ahead, the signal for the column to proceed.

Not long afterward the General waved his vehicle to a halt. "Look, look now," he said.

"I see nothing," said the aide.

"Could it not have been a boy?" said the General, "in sneakers, and pieces of a captured uniform?"

"The people of this area are all modern of thought," said the aide, "but if you wish me to take a patrol, I will do so."

"No," the General said, "your perceptions have always been accurate. We shall continue to the capital, as ordered."

In only a few more minutes the General stood up in his vehicle, pointing and staring into the trees and the moss and stones he knew as well as he knew the words for trees and moss and stones. "There again—there again! Crouching against the soil—do you see?"

The aide hesitated. Then she said, "What might I see, sir . . . if I were to look in the right place?"

The General looked at his aide, and smiled faintly. "Give the order to button up," he said. "We're going into the brush."

And the Fourth Brigade wheeled to the right, plunging into the rough country, the half-roads and possibilities of roads, through the gullies and roots and pale thick mist. Every soldier of the Fourth knew that their orders were to move to the capital. Every soldier of the Fourth followed the General without a moment's pause.

The going was difficult; indeed, this was the same terrain in which the revolutionary forces (during their days as rebels) had so often ambushed the national guard. But the General led them through as if he were leading close friends on a tour of his home. Which, of course, he was.

"General," the aide said gently, and offered him a sip of tea from her flask.

The General drank, without taking his eyes from the country. "I see where he has gone," he said. "Through here, and over that large rock, and vaulting between those trees so as to leave no footprint nor ground scent. . . . Yes, I see very clearly now."

The aide waited for a little while. The Fourth Brigade was becoming dispersed, and a support vehicle broke an axle and had to be abandoned. Still the soldiers of the Fourth pressed on after the General's lead.

Finally the aide opened her mouth to speak, but instead her eyes widened, and in place of whatever she might have been about to say, she said, "Commandos, sir. Ahead, to the right. Commandos of the national guard."

And then, before anyone could say anything more, there was the pop of gunfire and the rainlike rustling of bullets through the leaves, and the Fourth Brigade of Armor was at war with the ancient army. Had things been one way, the Fourth might have been lost, its great vehicles immobilized by the terrain amid the swarm of commando troopers; but this was the General's land and way of war, and things were not that way but another. Again he transformed the equipment under his command into what he needed, using his tanks and cars as if they were bunkers and helicopters, and in the space of half an hour the guardsmen who had been on their way to brutalize the General's home as of ancient times were themselves alive only in history.

The Fourth Brigade cheered its General upon the field of victory. And then a strange thing happened. The General looked down, into the face of one of the dead ancients, and said, "Do I not know this man? Was he not a rebel with me, in the hills when we were young?"

"He wears the uniform of the national guard commandos," said the aide, pointing at the dead man's black tunic. The General nodded and turned away, saying, "Certainly he does. Come, now, we may be needed at the capital."

The Fourth Brigade reached the capital city in good time, encountering no resistance. When the column was in sight of the downtown buildings, a messenger from the revolutionary leaders approached the General.

"There is terrible news, sir," the messenger said. "A team of commandos from the national guard has attacked your birthplace; there are reports of grave atrocities."

"How can this be?" said the General's aide.

The messenger said, "They attacked from out of the hill country. The press has been notified; they are going there to report the horror to the world. The ancients have hurt themselves badly by this."

The General looked past the messenger. He seemed to see something very clearly, though his aide saw only the buildings of the capital. "Come with me," the General said, and they left the Fourth Brigade to rest, and followed the messenger to the headquarters of the revolution.

The aide waited in a bare room while the General spoke to the leaders in their inner chambers. She was used to the open air and felt uncertain in the windowless room; she felt as if she were in an empty, dead cell, surrounded by busy cells crowded with unknown machineries. When the General came out again, he took his aide gently by the arm—this startled her, as he had never touched her in any fashion before this—and led her out of the headquarters. In one direction was the city, in the other the forest where the Fourth Brigade was encamped.

The General pointed toward the encampment. "Do you see a boy," he said, "a boy in sneakers with a blanket on his back, who runs through the hill country as only a rebel hill boy can know how to run?"

"No, sir," said the aide, in an uneven voice.

"If the boy were not so dressed . . . if he wore another sort of uniform, would you see him then?"

"Sir, I see no boy," said the aide, nearly in tears because she did not see or understand.

"You do not see the boy, and your perceptions have always been accurate," the General said, "therefore the boy does not exist. . . . Yet still I see him."

And with that the General of the Fourth Brigade of Armor drew his pistol, pressed its muzzle to his chin, and splashed his brains into the clear, clear sky.

There is a statue of the General in the town where he was born, the town that he saved. An ancient library was renovated to make space for it; bits of the rubble are still preserved by the citizens. The statue is not large, though it stands upon a high plinth; the figure is in fact exactly the size of the General in life. It is important that art should tell the truth.

The General stands with his knees slightly bent and his arm outstretched, his metal finger pointing forward. The statue is all one color, the General's face and hands, his boots and weapons, all the lowgre of his uniform. The pose is dynamic yet very natural.

Everyone knows what the figure illustrates: the General is leading his brigade forward to victory. But no one asks what his finger is pointing at. Even the children do not ask what it is that the General sees.

And perhaps it is best that they do not.

Truth, it was said in the most ancient times, is an absolute. The later ancients, troubled by the ease with which the absolute would shift on the plate under the stab of their forks, swung to the opposite asymptote, deciding that truth was a purely relative condition, dependent on external factors that entirely evaded quantitative measurement. But with modern study, the same study that gave us the reality of color, we know that much is discoverable to any desired precision, in any number of parameters, except for the parameter used to take the measurement; as a physicist would say, we may know the position by rendering the velocity unknowable through the detector's impact, or know the velocity at the cost of the position. It then simply becomes a question of deciding which part of your subject's nature is of no importance, and then (figuratively speaking, of course) beating it out of the population.

The fourth shade of new light, enblu, is a moral color, a color of truth and straightforward dealing. Our currency is enblu, and the greatest care is taken to ensure that its inks are of the truest, clearest hues possible to modern technologies.

The Controller of the Currency reached within his coat, producing a large bronze key. "This is the only key to the counting room," he said, unlocked the wired-glass door, and entered. After him came two of the leaders of the revolution, and four counting clerks in smocks and gloves.

Around them was downward lighting, soft so as to spare the clerks' eyes, and steel tables covered with neat stacks of freshly cut notes. Through the floor was a gentle thrum, transmitted from the coin-minting floor below; a high whine penetrated from the printing presses a few rooms away. There were neatly pigeonholed forms and tools and office supplies around the walls, and white-surfaced tally boards, neatly gridded, neatly written upon in cleanly erasable marker.

"All of the notes pass through this room?" one of the leaders said.

"Every one," said the Controller of the Currency. "The ancient problem of diversion has been reduced to the vanishing point through our redesign of the system of corridors and locked doors."

"Vanishing point?" said the other leader. "What precisely does that mean? A tiny amount, or zero?"

The Controller of the Currency picked up a pen and drew a figure, like an elongated S, on one of the tally boards. "The integral," he said lightly. "A quantity smaller than measurement allows, but a quantity nonetheless." The Controller had been a mathematician, in the ancient world.

"What sort of nonsense is that?" said the leaders, who were modern men. "Either all the notes are accounted for, or they are not."

The clerks looked uncertain.

The Controller said, "We count. We check. We count many times; when the blank paper is delivered, when the serial-numbering apparatus is started and stopped, when the notes are cut, in this room where they are stacked and bundled. We are even researching a method of weighing the ink before and after the presses are operated, though variations in humidity make this unreliable." He did not mention the spectroanalysis machines, which, being calibrated to the ancient colors, had been removed from the offices and were undergoing torture until they should tell the truth.

"And?"

"And still we are people. Still there is a possibility of errors going unchecked, regardless of the number of checks. As I say, vanishingly small—"

"I believe I understand," said a leader. "You are imposing a mathematical abstraction upon the reality."

"I am saying," the Controller said firmly, "that errors are never zero. Zero is itself a mathematical abstraction, that can never be imposed upon reality."

"Have there been repairs and corrections? You may ask for them, you know. If you like, we will authorize you a standing repairman."

"A clerk stood corrected some weeks ago, for removing a few notes in his clothing," said the Controller. "He was not a clever thief, however, and his correction merely stopped a known loss. We have, as I told you earlier today, no known losses. That is the problem."

"It is time we moved on," said one of the leaders of the revolution to the other. Then he said to the Controller, "We will accept that you are trying to solve the problem of missing notes. This plan of weighing ink sounds promising; if you require humidity-controlling equipment, you know the proper channels of approach."

The Controller led the leaders from the building. The Currency Office was an almost painfully rectilinear structure, everything in it—work cubicles, tables, pigeonholes, the empty spaces where the spectrographs had been—being built to the space-efficient perpendicular; the staircases came closest to rebellion, but only to the extent of forty-five degrees. The revolutionary leaders went out the square doors, down the square steps, walking with square shoulders and a precisely parallel gait. Then the Controller returned to the counting room, where the clerks were still standing at attention, cubical beads of sweat on their flat foreheads. The Controller erased the sign of the integral from the tally board and said to the clerks, "You may begin now."

The clerks completed their counting in the early afternoon. The Controller of the Currency thanked them, locked away their tally reports, and saw them out of the Treasury Building. Then he admitted a second set of clerks, who repeated the counting process on the same stacks of notes. Long after dark he locked these out as well, and then compared the two sets of reports himself. Nothing was missing, of course. The Controller sighed. Nothing could be missing, he thought, resting his face in his hands. His eyes hurt so much. Still his mathematician's soul rebelled at absolutes, and he knew well enough that no absolute would satisfy the leaders anyway.

The Controller was not an economist, but he understood the leaders' concern. The ancient world had nearly destroyed itself playing games of paper wealth, creating a system no nation could stabilize but any could capsize; mutually assured fiscal destruction. The modern world had to make certain that its currency could not be used as a weapon by the forces of reaction. That was the leaders' concern.

It was the Controller's concern as well; he hoped that the leaders knew that. Halfway between sunset and dawn he locked the door to the counting room and walked home, enblu afterimages burning his eyes.

Early the following day, another leader of the revolution arrived at the Treasury. "Does the currency travel of its own volition?" he said. "It does not. You must stop this hemorrhage of our economic lifeblood." As he spoke, he knotted a skein of cord in his slender fingers.

"What is blood?" said the Controller wearily. "Only seawater."

The leader gripped the cord in his hands. "You do not seem to understand our concern," he said to the Controller.

"Perhaps I do not," the Controller replied, and though the leader continued to talk, the Controller did not hear him.

Eventually the leader left, and the first shift of counting clerks was replaced by the second, and finally the Controller was left all alone in the Treasury Building, looking at a piece of paper from the teleprinter in his office.

The paper called for the Treasury to transfer several hundred ounces of the ancient metal locked in its basement vaults to an account in a distant nation, in exchange for some of the enblu notes that lived in numerical symbiosis with the metal, balanced on the other side of an equal sign.

Tomorrow, he knew, the leaders would ask him to again examine the procedures of accounting, to discover how so many of the notes could have found their way to that other nation.

The Controller of the Currency did not know how the notes escaped, and he had tried, tried very hard, to trace their route. Nor did he know who it was that possessed the notes, but desired the ancient metal more. He had, more than once, asked the modern leaders if they would suspend the exchanges, draw a stroke through the equation; they would not. They told him he did not understand.

And being no economist, he did not. He sat in the counting room, all quiet and alone, seeing no more than an ancient could. The minting and printing presses were all shut down, and the stillness droned in his ears, like a pounding heart buried beneath the floorboards.

A note fluttered up from the counting table, and was caught in a draft of air; it flew past the back of the Controller's hand, its edge flicking along his skin. The crisp paper cut him, and he bled.

The Controller flexed his hand. The film of blood smeared, and his sweat entered the cut, making it burn with salt; in the fire there was light, and clarity.

Large industrial fans were mounted on the minting floors for relief from the heat of work. The Controller of the Currency moved two of these into the note-counting room. He locked the door behind himself and switched the fans to their highest speed.

Notes stirred, as if awakening from a sleep; they arose, they flew, beating their sharp wings upon the turbulent air.

The Controller of the Currency watched the rising storm, feeling a joy he had thought lost to him forever. He began to undress, hurrying, fumbling as a boy eager to be a boy no longer, and as frightened. He threw his clothing into the wind, and then he threw himself.

He was struck by flying paper, and was cut, and the wetness upon his body (of blood and ink and other things) made the notes adhere, so that the Controller grew scales, was leafed as a tree, as the leafy man of ancient legend. He became dizzy with the loss of blood, and nearly fell, but the wind bore him up. Notes covered his face, and there was darkness, a blindness the color of wealth and as finely engraved as the surface of human skin. He could not see, but sometimes one has seen enough. Sometimes.

The sheath of currency stiffened, grew heavy. As it brought him finally down, the Controller knew that he was now one with it, inseparable. They would never disengage him from his work now . . . they would never complete their count, unless it numbered him in the telling.

To organize and record large quantities of data before the printing press, the extreme ancients created what they called Memory Palaces: furnished rooms of the mind in which each fixture, each detail, recalled some fact. The palace builder could at liberty walk through his creation, into the room where (say) the philosophies of sunlight and reflection were archived, a long bright gallery open to the sky along the solar path of the equinoxes, and in every sill and stela read a line of the accumulated text.

This seems illogical, which combined with its ancientness is to say insane, to the modern; but this is because we are immersed in the printed word. Movable type is a sort of standard builder's brick for knowledge, which anyone may use to brick thoughts up in lasting fashion, for everyone. This was the failing of the Memory Palace, truth to tell; only the proprietor had access. No one else could enter, no matter how much light they might have brought, how blinding the glow they held.

Continuing along the spectrum, we come now, suddenly and lightly, to eindi. This is a trivial color, a color of the fashionable moment. Some have said that modern times have no place for eindi, but this is shortsighted. Humanity's concerns are not all grand in scope; to ignore our trivialities is to deny a crucial part of that humanity. Some portion of each of us is colored eindi; it is part of our spectrum.

At the end of the Night Physician's rounds, when she was nearly overcome with weariness, she would climb five flights of stairs, past the operating theatres, the examining suites, the patient rooms, to the hospital solarium, a long, rectangular room with skylights and long windows. From there she would look into the eastern distance, toward the soft line of dawn. As she stood in the unlit room, among the night-shapes of tables and chairs and plants, the dawnglow seemed to bathe her in coolness, quench her hot grainy eyes, as a man in the heat of sunlight might be soothed by shadowfall. She never sat down, but sometimes she would drift into something like sleep, standing up, eyes open, until an edge of sun showed itself and dazzled her, or an orderly wanting to sneak a cigarette came in and, seeing her, hurried out again.

Then, stirred again into slow motion, she would go back down the stairs—never the elevator—and sign herself and her equipment out of the building, put a woolen serape over her hospital tunic (whatever the weather, though the mornings were always cool) and board a shuttle bus, one of those that endlessly courses the city, day and night, like the motion of those small memories of distant pains and pleasures that are invisible until they appear to transport one away with them.

The Night Physician's apartment was in a new building, gray and blank, its walls constructed at oblique angles so that something kept the eye from banal madness. The apartment was very clean, though books and papers and medical journals littered it; this litter was not confusion, but the Night Physician's method of keeping information accessible. She would make a small meal, read a journal while eating, and then retire to her heavy-curtained bedroom, where the soft deep carpets had never known another footstep but her own.

On a particular morning, the Night Physician's reverie was interrupted by a man's voice saying, "Do you think the dawn is so beautiful because it is so evanescent?"

The Night Physician turned. A man sat in one of the solarium armchairs. He was dressed in linen, and his eyes were sunken and his cheeks were darkly hollow. The Night Physician looked around for someone else the man in linen might have been speaking to, but there was no one else. "Who are you?" she said.

"A patient here," said the man in linen. "Who are you?"

"A physician here," the Night Physician said. "Patients should not be here at this hour."

"Ah, but I am a very special patient," the man said. "I will never leave this building . . . not alive, I mean."

"This is a certainty? You have been told?"

"As certain as the sunrise. It was sunrise we were discussing. Do you agree, it is the dawn's death in daylight that makes it so exquisite a phenomenon?"

"If you are a patient, you should not be here," the Night Physician said, "and my work here is over, and I must be going home."

"I shall be here again," the man in linen said.

And he was, for the next several nights, speaking of death and dawn in the same short breath. The Night Physician considered calling the orderlies to replace the man in his room, in his bed, but she never did. Properly he should not have been in the solarium, but he was causing no disturbance to the hospital by being there.

She had the vague, curious feeling that if she were to call for orderlies, they would arrive to find her alone in the solarium, looking at an empty chair. At least, she had this feeling at first; with each night that passed, the reality, the solidity, of the man in linen became more apparent.

Yet he *was* a disturbance, a source of disorder, in a place that should know no disorder. The instruments on a surgical tray are always laid out in a certain fashion; when the fingers reach for a hemostat they do not find a sponge. The controls of the anesthesia equipment always turn in the same way. Dosages are specified in common units, in common terminology. It is well to be ruthless about certain things.

She examined hospital records, to see who he might be, but without knowing his name, or at least his ailment, there was no way of being certain. The staff must know, she thought, but she was the Night Physician, and as such had little contact with them.

In the hours between her work and her silent trips home, the Night Physician moved through the hospital corridors and chambers as, when a student, she had probed the connections and organs of her dissection cadaver. In the basement was the hyperbaric chamber, brought dismantled from its country of origin and reassembled plate and bolt and valve according to detailed written instructions, its purpose to drive out the terrible anaerobic infections of the wild country (which eat flesh alive, and induce visions) with pure oxygen under high pressure, drowning alien life in the substance of life. Here also was the radiology unit, where invisible energy was used to search and renovate.

On the first floor were the file and record rooms, neat racks of little spaces where every patient in the hospital's history was preserved, from admission to treatment to departure (by whatever means), a four-dimensional cross-section of the universe. There was also a laboratory with every instrument of research, even spectrometers; health care being a priority of the modern government, the hospital's machines were the first to be tortured into proper functionality.

On the second floor were the examination and treatment rooms, equipped for minor surgery including ophthalmic laser and electric cautery. Neither of these tools was used for enucleation (that is, the renovation of an eye for the good of the whole patient), that being done with a small scalpel with a curved blade. The knife was not heated for such use, though of course it had been sterilized, in the hissing autoclave.

The third, fourth, and fifth floors housed patients, in their rooms, in their beds, by day in the light that pleases the eye open to receive it, by night in the darkness that blankets all pain, that even those without eyes can feel.

It was on the eleventh night (the fifteenth in absolute terms, since she had rounds only five days in seven) that the Night Physician threw her serape over the shoulders of the man in linen and led him down the stairs and out of the hospital. And so her bedroom knew a second set of footsteps, though they made no sound.

When she awoke, the man was gone. She did not see him that night, or the next, but on the third night he appeared, and with only the smallest exchange of words he again wore her serape from the hospital.

On the next such morning, the Night Physician said, "Why do you do this?"

"It is merely a thing I wish to know, before I depart forever," said the man in linen.

"Surely you must have known it before this."

"But not with you. Not with . . ."

"Yes?"

"All of us are different."

There was a silence.

"I wonder if I have proven adequate," the Night Physician said. "I am very tired at the conclusion of my rounds."

"You are more than adequate," said the man. "You are all that I had hoped you might be."

"Still, there is something I would like to know, while you are still here," the Night Physician said. "Would you meet me before my rounds begin, while I am still fresh?"

The man hesitated, then said, "Of course. But I have a roommate at the hospital—"

"I know of a room that will be empty," the Night Physician said, and gave him the number. "I will trust you to be there tonight."

"I am a committed man," he said. "What else have I but trust?"

That afternoon the Night Physician's clock awoke her hours before her usual arising time. The man in linen was gone, the print of his head on the pillow still warm. The Night Physician dressed and packed her equipment, and then went to the hospital, where she spent the late afternoon in the office of patient records.

Not long after dark, she tapped at the door of a room in an empty ward. The man in linen was sitting on the edge of the bed. He smiled and said, "I told you I was trustworthy."

Two muscular orderlies entered the room, and before the man in linen could do anything, the orderlies stripped off his tunic, pinned him down to the bed, and fastened straps around his wrists and ankles. The man protested. The orderlies ignored him and went out of the room without having spoken a word.

The Night Physician entered, placed her kit on the bedside table and began to unpack her tools. The man in linen began to wail and moan. "Others have called out," said the Night Physician. "These rooms are quite proof against sound."

"What are you going to do?"

"I am the Night Physician," she said. "You know that, and you know what it is that I do on my rounds. You said when first we met that you were one of my patients."

"A lie," the man shouted.

"You are a trustworthy man." She took the rubber mask and the small steel bottle from her bag. "What else do you have, in your hopeless condition?"

"No, no! I did it because—"

"I know why you did it. I think many of my patients have desired to do it. You are only the first to find the courage."

"But I am not one of your patients," the man in linen cried, "it was a lie, I am not, I am not!"

"You have become one," said the Night Physician, pressing down the rubber mask over the face of the man on the bed. "Do you not know that some diseases are contagious?"

The man strained at the straps that bound him to the bed, and might have broken free, for they were designed for persons in a weakened state from disease or recent repair, but they held, and soon he ceased to struggle.

The Night Physician removed the mask and went on to the completion of her rounds. Then she slowly climbed the steps to the solarium and waited, alone, for the first light of morning to fall softly upon her, as upon I or you.

Tell what was in the past, the saying goes, and what is in the present will surely make sense. Yet if the ancients saw their world through compound prisms of lies—as we know that they did—then what shall we say that past was? Is not the sitter a part of the portrait, the occupant of the house a component of the home?

The last of the new shades, the distant end of the accurate wavelengths, is goviolet. Goviolet is the color of our hopes, our dreams, our imaginations of tomorrow. It is not a color that lends itself to commonplace uses—an article of clothing, the wall of a room—because of this quality of reflecting not what is, but what could be.

The Artillerist and the Architect had grown up in nearby houses, in a part of the capital of moderate prosperity—enough to insulate their families from both the agonies and the corruptions of the ancient world. They attended the same school, used the same playground, even (through one of those complicated circumstances of linkage that bears no investigation) found themselves at the same large family functions, identically bored.

As children, their play was a curious reversal of their later careers: for it was the young Artillerist who built fortresses, of blocks or sand or snow, and the young Architect who found ingenious ways to bring them down.

Their fascinations were the world and one another. Their families did not disapprove; this is not one of those stories. It was commonly thought that they would, in time, form a linkage. The young people may or may not have thought this themselves; it is true that they went together on the search for secret things, but they did not ever reach the brightest dark place.

And when they parted company, one to study construction at the University and the other to enter the Engineering Academy of the national guard, it was not with a thought of meeting again, or of not meeting; it was the evening of the day and that was all.

But of course they did meet again, or there would be no story.

The first time was during an inter-university competition, a ritual of the ancients believed to enhance learning though formal conflict. There were sporting events, tests of computational skill (as if anything were proven by the position of a ball on a field or the rapid working out of equations with solutions already known) ... and, in the case that concerns us, a battle between the Engineer cadets and the students of Architecture.

The battle took place in the Exposition Park, directly across the city square from the Basilica of the Apostles and diagonally adjacent to the Great Hall of Justice. The Architects were given a large fresh hen's egg, and a certain quantity of materials to construct a defense around it; the Engineers had a quantity of explosives and other matériel to attack the bunker and break the egg.

The bunker the Architects built was a squat pyramid of earth and wood and wire, the goal egg buried within it. The cadets' devices reached and arched and crouched around the pyramid, fencings of destructive potential.

The field was cleared. The audience became quiet. Then a pistol was fired into the air. Circuits were closed, the attack began. Sprays of pellets scarified the pyramid, jets of flame and molten metal chewed into it, a wave of liquid fire engulfed it, burning the lower wooden scaffoldings to crumbling charcoal so that the earth heaved and subsided. Oily smoke obscured vision of the scene, and for long minutes there were only flashes and sounds in a dark cloud.

Then the battlefield fell silent, and the smoke cleared. The students and the cadets moved in, to count the dead.

Under close supervision to avoid any trickery, an Architect—our

Architect—moved a set of baffles and in a moment exposed the egg. This clever design drew applause. The Architect lifted the egg in a gloved hand, and displayed it unbroken.

"But it is hard-cooked," the Architect announced. "The bunker was designed so that the heat of the first attacks cooked it, hardening it against shock."

The applause rose. Then, quite suddenly, there was a whistling, screaming sound from high overhead, rising in pitch with the approach of the source in a catenary arc.

Some of the people on the field beneath the screaming missile dove for cover; some stood entirely still. Before there was time for any considered action, the missile struck the ground with a very small pop.

Only a pop, for the device was only a length of cardboard tube, with tin fins notched to whistle through the air.

From behind a greenskeeper's pavilion at the edge of the Park there came an Artillerist—our Artillerist—carrying a pail. She dumped water over the fizzing skyrocket. Then she pointed at the egg, which was still in the hand of the Architect. But in the stressful moment, his fingers had closed upon it, very hard.

"It's broken," she said, which it surely was. "We win."

The audience began to laugh, and to applaud. The team of Architecture students began to protest. Then our Architect was stopped still by the shock of recognition, and he entirely forgot his surroundings and ran to embrace the Artillerist.

In the years that followed this incident, the two would cross paths many more times. This might have been considered unusual in those ancient times, when little was understood of the dynamics of history. It is possible that this particular dynamic was responsible for the Architect's modernization of spirit; whatever the precise cause, it is true that he began to hold revolutionary views, and fell therefore into deep disfavor with the powerful ancients who had once been pleased to purchase his services.

It happened one day that the Architect was in the National Library, in the great vaulted Hall of Maps, and heard a step behind himself. He turned, expecting one cannot say what, and saw the Artillerist, who now wore the uniform of a Colonel of the national guard.

The Hall of Maps was memorable for its surface detail. The walls had vertical wainscot of book-matched, strongly figured oak, and above that the arched ceiling was hexagonally tessellated, a decorative brass boss in the center of each cell. The map cases that filled the chamber were also hexagonal, for closest-ordered packing. The map librarians disapproved of this arrangement, as it defied standard grid numbering for the location of a particular tube. It introduced, they said, a fifty percent error. Yet the meticulous grandeur of the hall, and the tactile satisfaction of the hexagonal wooden map tubes in their carefully carpentered racks, overrode such delicate objections. Besides, the mystery extended only to the boxes. A map, once uncased and unrolled, is either the one you are seeking or it is not; the batteryworks near Fox Point Light are not going to pretend they are a hill-country forest. Maps are not given to irony.

The Artillerist looked at the diagrams spread out before the Architect and said, "The Great Hall of Justice is a fine building."

"It is a parody-Palladian heap without a single line in proportion," said the Architect, "but it is strong and defensible."

"It may be built of stone, but if charges were to be placed here and here and here"——she indicated locations on the elevation drawings—"it would become so uncertain of support that it would have to be abandoned."

"Wrappings of wire would ablate your charges."

"Shaped charges would turn your wire into molten cutting torches."

"You would never reach the steps to plant them, given only a few soldiers upon those steps."

"Those steps are too shallow for effective ranked fire, and the statuary in the square—especially the figures of the Apostles—create many blind fields. What do you mean to do with this information?"

"I will take it into the hills," said the Architect, "where there are people who will know what use to make of it . . . for whom the nation's justice is already so uncertain of support that it must be abandoned."

The Artillerist was silent for a little while. "You should not have told me that last," she said, "for it will be very difficult for me to keep it silent."

"I do not care if you keep it silent," said the Architect. "It is a thing that needs speaking."

"Nevertheless, I shall say nothing."

"I do not care."

"That is not the truth," said the Artillerist. "The truth is that there is nothing in the world that you do not care about, in one way or another."

"I built houses in the hills, for the wealthy and powerful," said the Architect, very softly, "and they are beautiful houses, and they shall be destroyed in the times to come."

The Artillerist said, "One cannot make an omelet without breaking an egg."

The two of them touched hands, and then the Architect gathered up his papers and left the Artillerist alone in the library hall, and that too was the end of a day.

They did not see one another again for all the years of the revolution. That is to say, they never saw one another face-to-face; but from time to time the Artillerist would examine a revetment or empty bolt-hole that had resisted her efforts to an exceptional degree, and the Architect would walk through the broken and smoldering renovation of a modern construction, and they were in each other's presence.

In the course of the war, the Architect became an adviser and confidant to the leaders of the revolution, in a curious modern version of his old relations with the ancients. He was asked by the leaders to help plan the modern housing and public buildings that would be raised once the ancient world was dust. So it happened that in the last hours of the revolution the Architect was in the capital city, examining what had survived the fighting and what had not. He was in White Birch Street, with his pad and his pencil, when he saw a face in a window, and as on another battlefield he was taken in his depths by recognition.

The Architect walked up the ramp to the building, which was strangely empty of life and wildly littered for a hospital. He approached the main desk, which was untenanted. He turned right, climbed the stairs encircling the elevator. He knew the layout of this building exactly; he knew the plan of every major structure in the city. He went through the seventh door on the right-hand side of the hallway, and found the Artillerist.

She was sitting up in bed, near the window. She wore a linen tunic, buttoned at the shoulder, and her lower body was wrapped in cotton sheets. "You will pardon me for not getting up," she said, through lips that the ancients with their inaccurate vision would have called colorless.

"Let me help you," said the Architect.

"Not much chance of that now," said the Artillerist, but she allowed him to move her into a wheeled chair, and when he began to weep at the sight of what the sheets had hidden, she said, "Triumph of construction over assault. Else I'd not be here."

There was the sound of gunfire from the city square, and the Artillerist added, "But the assault was potent too, or I'd be elsewhere. You've noticed all my roommates have gone." She rubbed her eyes, though they were only tired with looking from the window; a small folding binocular was upon the sill. Blindness produces a bitter depression, all the more when it is blindness caused by war, for the last image, the last deeply burnt memory, is of the bayonet and the enemy who holds it.

Then there was a whistling from the sky outside, and the building shook. The lighting failed, windows broke, beams fell. The smells of plaster dust and ozone mixed with those of disinfectant and old wounds.

"Is this how it ends?" said the Architect, who could predict a building's whole fate from an echo down its corridors.

"Must you hold me so tight, is that your idea of reliving history? Besides, those are no work of mine. If they had been my rockets, we'd be omelets by now."

The Architect eased the Artillerist in her chair down the quaking flights to the ground floor. In the lobby, amid the mess, the Artillerist gripped the wheels of the chair. "Listen," she said. "The firing from the Plaza has stopped. And do you hear the whistling? Not my artillery, but rebel—"

"We must hurry," said the Architect. "The ceiling will give way under another impact."

"The second salvo should arrive just now," said the Artillerist, and rolled herself away from her companion.

Both of them were right. Plaster and metal and wood fell. The Architect was blinded by dust and smoke; when his vision cleared, the Artillerist had disappeared. He called to her, and listened through ringing ears, but heard no answer; then he saw her hand, protruding from a heap of debris. The Architect had been here before, many times; it had been a long war. He knew when there was hope, and when not, and there was not, and he could not bear to touch the hand knowing this. He staggered from the building.

He felt hard body blows, and supposed that he must have been deafened, since he had not heard the shots. He looked up at the soldiers, and was confused for a moment, then realized that his uniform was covered with plaster and splinters, unrecognizable. The soldiers had misperceived him, fired upon the fallen ancient dust, the bits of broken Apostles.

He turned to go back into the building, wanting now to hold the Artillerist's hand, but he felt more bullets strike him, and his legs would no longer hold him up.

"Was there ever such a love as this?" the Architect cried out, and in his voice there was the terrible sound of a soul that knows it has lived too long, if only by a few minutes. And then the story—all the stories—were over.

You will understand that I am no longer young, and if my tales seem vague and discursive, it is only from a desire to present all the information necessary in the most usable fashion. Of all the changes modern times have brought, I think perhaps the most important is the insistence upon diagrammatic clarity in the arts, the presentation of clear moral truths, rather than murky pools in which the patron must fish blindly for meanings. This ancient tactic led to acts of outright madness, such as the reading of secret messages from text, say, in the last word before a line break, or the first word after. Such people might stare until they burned their eyes from their heads; and would that be unjust, unmerited, undeserved?

It was this lack of emotional clarity that caused the ancients to repair others for what they had lost in themselves, to renovate that which they found empty, to wander the streets hollow-eyed, looking for the place where their former joy had been concealed. To frame one more story, it was as if, having refused to pay the piper who lured their rats away, their children were taken from them as well.

But modern vision shows us that the children were never gone at all. They were there, in front of everyone—but reflecting a light of colors that ancient eyes simply could not detect. The empty places were filled with light unknown. The joy was before them, but they were blind to it.

Blindness is not just blindness, you see. You see, you see, you see, you see, you see.

COSMOLOGY:
A USER'S MANUAL

$\propto$

First Cause, the Word, Big Bang—what name you choose,
One bright note sounds. A symphony ensues.

ANTHROPIC PRINCIPLE.

If we, who love the light, had never been,
The stars would find new shoes for dancing in.

BOUNDARY CONDITION.

Beyond, no fusion burns to light the stars;
The waves will not collapse, the joke won't parse.

CAUSALITY

First one cuts down the tree, then hears it fall—
It seems we don't need this one, after all.

DARK MATTER.

Our sight and hearing span the spectrum, yet
Most of the universe plays hard-to-get.

EMISSION LINES.

The stellar fires are profligate indeed,
And what they throw away, we glean and read.

FERMI'S PARADOX.

Hello out there! We're here! Do come and play!
Don't mind what our old broadcast quanta say.

GRAND UNIFIED THEORY.

You hold the chalk, and I'll apply the glue;
Oh, dear, that's loose again. One's never through—

HUBBLE CONSTANT.

The galaxies rush on; the redshifts climb,
And loneliness increases over time.

INFLATIONARY UNIVERSE.

When it was new, the cosmos moved right quick;
Then (sound familiar?) things began to stick.

JEANS, JAMES.

"Like a great thought," he said, but did not cease
To search and blueprint its machineries.

KEPLER, JOHANNES.

He wished elliptic orbits to prove wrong,
Yet still proposed them. Reason's whips are strong.

LORENZ CONTRACTION.

If you will not stand still, while I do so,
I shall see you diminished as you go.

MICROWAVE BACKGROUND.

The cosmic egg-shell cupped against your ear,
The rush of the dark ocean's plain to hear.

NON-EUCLIDEAN GEOMETRY.

It's not that he was wrong, the clever Greek;
But where bare Beauty's seen from, so to speak.

OPEN/OSCILLATING UNIVERSE.

So will it stop, or not? The answer tells
Much less about the stars than of ourselves.

PLANCK EPOCH.

One flash when gravity was consummate—
No era spans less time, or greater weight.

QUANTUM LEAP.

The particle is here, and then is there—
But never in between. How does it *dare?*

RELATIVITY.

One clock stayed on the ground; its double flew.
And *it ran slow.* So, then. The mad thing's true.

STRING THEORY.

The particles extend like tightened strings,
And when their frets are plucked, they chord all things.

THOUGHT EXPERIMENT.

First conjure up that one you love to please.
Now, once again, with quarks, or galaxies.

UNCERTAINTY PRINCIPLE.

Position, yes, or speed, but not the two:
To learn, to see, must be to alter, too.

VIRTUAL PARTICLES.

Some facts (see Heisenberg) we cannot know,
So mass can rise from void, and back there go.

WAVE FUNCTION.

Reduced to mathematics, matter's germ—
"Reduced?" What an unfeeling, thoughtless term!

X-RAY ASTRONOMY.

Beyond the atmosphere, a higher light
Proclaims unique new glories of the night.

YANG-MILLS THEORY.

All sterile are Narcissus and his twin:
When symmetries are broken, things begin.

Z_0 PARTICLES.

Too massive in thin space to ever thrive,
Yet, *rarae aves*, dinosaurs survive.

$$\Omega$$

Heat death or cold, in randomness or Cause,
It is not how it ends, but what it was.

THE MAN IN THE GOLDEN MASK

We now return the reader's mind
To Paris, and the tavern *L'Ermitage,*
Where four companions, having drunk and dined
As in their old acquaintance, in *L'Age*
D'Or, wander the cold December street.
Reunion joy should be complete,
But melancholy chill of night
And troubles elsewhere spoken of
Weighed down the hearts that should be light
Though they strode boldly, glove in glove.
They saw a man, across the road,
Entirely muffled in a cloak,
All black in fog, bent as with load.
D'Artagnan cleared his throat, and spoke:
"What dreadful errand sends you out
Without companions or a lamp?
The night is cold, and dark, and damp,
Bad spirits well may be about."
The stranger turned, and showed his face—
Or rather, what stood in its place;

A mask of shiny golden stuff
With curling brows and tilted eyes,
A pointed nose quite long enough
To service as a dagger-case.
"My errand, sirs, brooks no delay,"
He said, in crisp but civil voice,
"I ask you to unbar my way
Or else defend the pass—your choice."
Said Porthos, when he heard the masked man speak,
"A Gascon playing Scaramouche? *Pardieu!*
It quite out-Hectors Hector. D'Artagnan,
This fellow is your countryman. Have you
A friend who so affects a gilded beak,
Or carries comedy so boldly on?"
D'Artagnan paused before he made reply.
"Perhaps," he said, "I have done—on the boards.
Porthos, stand back, and let this man pass by:
Pray, sir, forgive my friend his friendly words."
Porthos declaimed, "This from a Musketeer?"
But Athos softly said, "No quarrels here.
I ask you to pardon my comrades. We've been
Renewing acquaintances dormant for years,
And wine and good fellowship—" "Quiet your fears,"
Said the man in the mask. "They may say what they've seen,
Or heard, or imagined. I've no fear of words,
And honest men's voices sound lovely as birds
In a winter of lying, and rumor-as-fact,
All the hypocritations that others call tact—
But I *do* ask your pardon, Monsieur, for I see
The light in your look that is nobility:
A gem of first water one finds less and less,
And that most distinctly among the *noblesse.*"
"What mission, friend, can make you offer us
Odds so unequal, on so poor a night?

Unfold your errand; if it strikes us right,
You will not want for ready company."
The stranger said, "Well spoken, sir. I must
Lose no more time, so kindly follow me
As I explain, and if you find it just
We'll see some entertainment presently."
So off they went along the bitter street;
Porthos called back, "Ho, lackeys, mind your feet!
Tread lightly as you travel, lest you fall
Upon an unexploded Gasconade."
The masked man said, "Ah, ace Picard, well played.
And now my tale. There is a Chevalier
Who dines some streets away, alone tonight,
As is his habit; but I fear he might
Take harm this special evening. If I may
Divert the danger, justice will be served.
You see, this nobleman has well deserved
His country's honors, having grown full old
In battles, being wounded many a time;
But honored scars, and this inclement clime
Give him small leave to walk, and none to fight.
I wear this mask therefore, because the sight
Of my plain face, as we are friends, might move
The Chevalier to guess he is at threat;
And, in his noble pride, to disapprove
Of any plans of aid that I might set."
Athos said then, his voice a quiet knife,
"Who can propose such base ignobleness?
Be he a prince or minister, my life
I swear for his: honor demands no less."
"His name is Monsieur Josserand,
Un gentilhomme, you understand,
But noble not in line or grace;
He rakes the bounty of his land,

Trades it for gold, and gold for place.
Chevalier's ribbons he would gain,
But since the Grand Chévalierie
Just now contains no vacancy,
He must make one by *coup de main*."
Porthos put in, "Yes, that is fine,
But he has not a noble line!
The rules are very clearly stated."
"Yes, now the task is complicated,"
The masked man said, "and when you know
The shape that stands above the foe,
And understand the game at full,
Your promises I will annul.
The center-scheme of Monsieur Josserand
Is bags of gold for Cardinal Mazarin;
The Minister of State shifts papers well,
And, for some tens of thousand *louis d'or*,
Will make him nobler than he was before.
The times are strange, my friends. One cannot tell
Who owes position to the Cardinal,
And if you are his men, then that is all
I have to say: let's go our ways, or fight."
"Of course we'll fight!" said D'Artagnan, "but not
For Cardinal or Nobles, but for right
And honor, as a worthy battle's fought!"
"You have the right, friend Gascon, and I ought
Have fought it single 'gainst whatever foes;
Yet welcome valiant fellowmen, because
I tire when fighting more than ten; because
I'm melancholy when alone; because
Time's rapier scrapes me at the bone; because
I am no longer young as once I was."

The landlord of the inn that housed the plot
Opened his door, and near fell on the spot

To see a shapeless cloak and pointed mask
Confronting him. "Forgive me! I'll not ask
For any names; your gold has spoken clear:
Do as you please; my staff are sent away,
Your guest is here, but nothing has he learnt;
And nothing shall disturb the Monsieur's play—
Although I beg you leave the walls unburnt—
I hope you shall be very merry here."
Aramis said, "The field ought to be clear."
He called the lackeys to him, and wrote out
Some lines upon a paper. "Look about
And find the chair that brought the Chevalier;
You must be chairmen for an hour or so.
Take up the Chevalier, and bear him post
To Abbé Scarron's house; give this the host:
It will explain the stratagem. Now go."
The cloaked man said, "Most wisely rused, Abbé."
Aramis said, " 'Tis good of you to say,
But ere we start, Monsieur, just one more word—"
"I know my voice is one that you have heard,"
The masked man said. "I would have Monseigneur
Believe his secret is entirely sure
From gratefulness for his assistance, and—
Well, not all happy prospects end as planned.
There is not much that anyone can tell;
The bridegroom was a soldier, and my friend,
He died all nobly, fighting as he fell,
The lady is his widow. There an end,
Except to say: when I this tale allow,
I say a Capuchin performed the vow."

A little distance from the inn, a crowd
Of rough-dressed men was standing, grumbling loud
At waiting, and the icy element,
And at their pay. But Monsieur Josserand

Advised them patience. He'd already sent
The biggest and best-muscled of his lot
Into the inn alone. "I play my hand
The better playing close," the Monsieur thought,
"And if the big one kills the Chevalier—
No service means no pay for those still here."

The swordsman shoved inside the inn, to see
A big man, seated still, and awkwardly
Trying to doff a boot. He moved as if
His muscles and his joints were frozen stiff.
The swordsman said, "Monsieur le Chevalier?"
"Ah, there's a waiter! Come this way,"
Said Porthos, tugging at his shoe
As if it were attached with glue.
"Come give some service! Are you dead?
I'll have some mutton, bread, and wine."
The swordsman spoke with venom fine,
"The mutton, sir, is in your head,
And wine's not what I come to draw."
"What?" Porthos said, "I fear my hearing's bad,
This inn, however's, bad as e'er I saw:
Assist me with this boot, now there's a lad."
The bravo growled and said, "You'll have my aid
In one way only; that's by surgery.
Monsieur must be let blood for his disease;
The purest physic. Be you not dismayed,
Sir will but briefly feel the remedy,
And then have an eternity of ease."
But as the swordsman steadily advanced
Upon his seated foe, it somehow chanced
Porthos's boot came off with violence
And quite escaped his grasp, to tumble hence
And catch his bold companion in the face.

His nose began to bleed. He slacked his pace.
"Doctor, a thousand pardons!" Porthos said,
"Let me return your care after my health;
We must now keep your feet above your head,
Lest you should swoon, and haply bruise yourself."
He reached out, unconcerned, and firmly grasped
The swordsman by the ankle; then he clasped
The sword—"You'll hurt yourself!"—and quite upended
The man, and held him flailing and suspended.
"Again your pardon, sir! I'd no intent
To knock your pate upon the floor like that;
This beastly gout does leave a fellow spent
Of his good powers. Let me find your hat
To cushion you against such fearful shocking;
Don't struggle so! Wouldst bleed upon my stocking?"

When Josserand heard nothing in reply
From his first henchman, he decided, "I
Was wrong to trust a solitary man;
Men unobserved turn coward, if they can.
These two look sturdy. I'll dispatch the pair,
Their wage for my blue ribbon's only fair."

The pair of bravos felt no great surprise
To find two men within instead of one
One said, "Now we know how our master lies,
We'll make him pay us triple when we're done."
Athos spoke then. "Good servants, pleasant night;
Your duties here are bounden to be light.
For I am old, and my friend is a priest:
And neither of us wants too grand a feast;
But we shall drink a bit, and then some sup;
Go to the cellars, bring some bottles up."
The henchmen paused on hearing Athos's tone;

One said, "What matters it he's not alone.
They'll dispatch straight. But I've a jest in mind:
Let's go downstairs and bring their final wine."
The other said, "You're right. 'Twill not be hard,
And make them drowsy, put them off their guard."
Any old soldier knows a porter's way;
They brought the wine, and glasses on a tray.
Athos toasted Aramis, and sighed.
"It is near midnight. Do you hear the chimes
That call the ghosts with whom we used to ride?"
"Ghosts soon enough," one of the bravos said,
"Let's now be quick, and strike these slow men dead."
Then Athos fixed them with a steady eye
And said, "We are most grateful. Stay a bit:
My friend believes he caught the scent of pie
Out of your kitchen. Bring us some of it."
His voice was calm, so easy in command,
That ere the bravos quite could understand
Just why, they had gone through the kitchen door.
"This is not what our master paid us for!"
"But here's the pie. It is not much to ask
That they should eat their last. A little later,
When they are in a full and slow condition,
How much more easy will be our commission."
And so they put on aprons and played waiter;
They watched their victims slice and eat the pie,
Noting the rapiers quietly set by,
And made to ready their own weapons—when
Count Athos wiped his lips and spoke again:
"A good house, goodly serviced, by this light!
But now my friend and I would contemplate;
Bring that tobacco here. Then you may wait
On your own pleasures. Leave us, and good night."
The hirelings gnawed their lips. Aramis said,

"We are grown men, and we can find a bed
Without assistance; let your minds be free.
Here are ten *louis d'or* gratuity."
After a moment meeting Athos's look,
The two men doffed their aprons, bowed and took
The humidor, the money, and their leave.
Aramis said, "My friend, I do believe
Those two were gentler than their looks let on."
He glanced outside, the way that they had gone,
And from the dark he heard a dazed voice say,
"They had a quality I would obey."

"The man is an invalid!" Josserand thought.
"Can't anyone trust what his money has bought?
He must have a comrade—a hireling or friend,
To reload his pistols and help him defend.
First one, and then two, and they still are alive:
We'll see what the pair of them do against five!"

The first man waved to the other four;
He held aside the tavern door,
And just as softly drew it closed.
He saw a man who deeply dozed
Upon the table, limbs askew,
No weapon held in open view.
He said, "A valiant man, no doubt,
But he has fought himself quite out;
The fish is landed, plain to see,
Gold should not come so easily."
The man sat up and gave a yawn.
"You have it right," said D'Artagnan,
And in one instant he was on
His feet, his rapier fully drawn;
"Gold is too dear for such a gift.

It wants some labor. Start the shift."
The bravos drew their rapiers, and ducked;
D'Artagnan gave example to instruct:
"Watch close, for this is how a pass is held.
Look well, Sir Ass, and Monsieur Quelque-Chose;
But care that you do not observe too close,
For he who thrusts too soon is soonest felled."
And it was done as he had prophesied;
A henchman shouted, drove his blade, and caught
Eight inches of Toledo in his side.

"Again no word comes back! Were five too few?"
Josserand fretted. "Now it's eight men lost.
A dozen now to pay, and the landlord's due;
I dread to think how much this night shall cost."
So he sent forth all of his company,
Keeping a careful distance back to see
What sort of tiger laired inside the inn;
And in a moment more, he could begin
To hear a melee brewing. "That's the way
To conquer: by the numbers. Chevalier,
Your count is up, and if by chance you may
Some cut it down—that's fewer fools to pay."
Josserand smiled to hear the sport
And, satisfied his plans went well,
Imagined how he'd look at court
And framed the battle-tale he'd tell
When suddenly a window burst
Expelling henchmen like a sneeze
Two had already met the worst;
The third expiring with a wheeze.
Then there was silence, full and cold;
No one was groaning anymore.
His prospects once more made him bold;

He swaggered through the tavern door.
What he saw brought his coward back:
For men lay dead at every hand;
Their limbs were bent, their jaws were slack;
Monsieur was nigh too weak to stand.
When all at once there came a sound,
Like nothing real, and nothing good;
From nowhere and from all around—
And then four of the dead men stood
"I am the ghost," Athos intoned,
"Of days that are too gone to save;
Of fertile land you may have owned,
But husbanded into a grave."
"I am the ghost," said Aramis,
Of this fair day and this cold night
The depth of your dishonor is
Too great to reach a morning's light."
D'Artagnan said, "I am the ghost
Of all your days that lie ahead:
Their number's nought. Now ride you post
To fall in company with the dead,"
And with his rapier's point he snuffed the light.
Then Porthos rose to his gigantic height,
And thundered in a voice like Roland's horn:
"I am the little crippled one you scorned!"
Then Josserand let fly a strangled scream,
Turned stumble-toed, and stared into the beam
Of a small lantern held without the room;
There stood the stranger with his mask a-gleam
His black cloak spread out like a wingéd Doom.
"Is this the night the Devil wanders free?"
Said Josserand, "But what else can it be?
What purpose can you have in killing me?"
"What purpose, sir, in killing what is dead?

Your reputation's bleeding by the minute
Your honor seeks a hole to hide its head
'Twould be too kind to slip the dagger in it.
You planned by tricks to crush a better man
But other better men were not asleep;
These fell upon their watch. I bid you then
Begone, or join the merry midden-heap.
My sword is keen to bring into the light
Your liver's color—though I know it white.
Draw, scoundrel, if you would survive the night!"
Throat gurgling like a bunghole, Josserand drew
And stood there, but the masked man's rapier flew
Like ravens in the flock; and with his play
The golden mask made verse extempore:
"You have no plumes, and now you have no hat;
The epaulette whose honor you abuse
Is gone—but 'twas ungloried, what of that?
And now the damp will penetrate your shoes.
What, corsets sundered? How your guts explode!
You must to Belgium, sir, to buy new lace;
One half a beard? But that is not the mode:
A moment—there, that balances your face.
This cloak will turn the north wind nevermore;
This coat would bring a tailor to despair;
Alas, it seems your pants are on the floor
And now you are as well. You must take care,
'Tis cold to be turned out disastrously
Turned out as now you are—yet shall it be."
And with a dozen slaps of sword on bum
The knave fled to the darkness whence he'd come.

The Musketeers laughed heartily at this,
And wiped the ghostly chalk off of their skin;
"See how the wicked flee," said Aramis,

"Where no man doth pursue—and so amen."
"But where," said Porthos, "is our gilded host?"
They all were quiet for a little while,
Then Athos said, with just the slightest smile,
"I wonder if he could have been a ghost?"

The morning next, D'Artagnan shook awake
Called by a messenger, who brought a basket
With wine of Anjou, biscuits, Christmas cake,
A letter bearing just the Gascon's name.
"A man gave me commission, and I came.
The monsieur's name? I did not pause to ask it."
D'Artagnan sat down hard upon his bed
And opened up the letter, where he read:

Monsieur was quite correct; it was on stage
That once we met—and it was years ago—
But that is an illuminated page
In memory, though then I did not show
Appreciation. There my fault does lie
Alongside one that points plainly ahead:
"A well-placed point," you said. I gave it naught;
You will imagine what my choler thought;
Had I not been so angry then I ought
Have seen it as a praise disinterested.
And once again I pay the favor back
So meanly as to earn contempt of men
I here salute my equal in attack
(Your wrist is iron now as it was then)
A shining plume above a world so black:
Yours from Hercule-Savinien
De Cyrano de Bergerac—
Live boldly, brother, till we meet again.

PREFLASH

Exterior, hospital, day. Fischetti pushes Griffin's wheelchair out the door and to the street. Pietra Malaryk is at the curb, leaning against her Chevy wagon, a brand new Arriflex under her arm. Malaryk smiles as Griffin looks up; she hands him the camera. "Welcome back, A.D.," she says.

Griffin checks the Arri. It is a double to the one he lost in the accident. There is a 400-foot magazine of Ektachrome Commercial already loaded; the battery belt is in Malaryk's hand.

Griffin stands up, aware that Fish and Malaryk are both waiting for him to fall down again. He doesn't. He says good-bye to Fischetti, and Fish nods and wheels the chair back.

Griffin shoulders the camera. The balance is strange; it has been eight months since he has had a camera on his shoulder, since the accident. That is a long time not to be whole.

His vision is still blurry, with flashes of phosphene light, but he frames Fischetti pushing the chair, small against the face of stone and little windows, and he presses the trigger.

"How is it, A. D.?" Malaryk asks. Malaryk is as good a camera-man as Griffin ever was and will know that he is lying when he says it's perfect, but that's what he says anyway.

They get into Malaryk's car. Griffin shoots through the window until the magazine is gone. People on the street see the lens and smile and wave, and make obscene gestures. The sun makes darting afterimages in Griffin's eyes.

It was explained to Griffin that his skull has splintered internally, spalled like concrete, and the bone chips in his brain cannot be re-moved without either killing him or turning him into a vegetable, probably a cabbage. Griffin, not wanting to be either dead or dead-and-breathing, therefore agreed to sign the malpractice waiver. They did not operate, he would not sue. There is no one to collect the money anyway.

As they drive through the sunlight, a good place for cabbages, Griffin puts the Arri down and turns to look at Malaryk. She is wearing the standard bush jacket with pockets full of photo goodies, over a deep-cut cotton blouse.

This is what she is wearing down the right side of Griffin's vision. Down the left she appears in grainy black and white, lying on a bed, wearing a bathrobe over underwear. There are dark stains on her skin and clothing, and something blurred. Griffin thinks that if he were editing this film he would slow it down for a better look, and it slows down. The blurred object is a crowbar. A man dark against vertical strips of light is swinging it. There is a barely discernible line between the color frame and the monochrome that wobbles when Griffin tries to focus on it.

Griffin puts a hand to his temple. There is brilliant light like a lens flare, and then the black-and-white film is gone.

"Are you okay, A. D.?" Malaryk says.

He demounts the Arri magazine and labels it, so she will know he's all right.

"So what'cha going to do?" Malaryk says. "Been awful quiet in the pool without you and Carrick."

"Got some offers to do music videos."

"Music videos. You?"

"I can't go into the bush anymore, Pia. Who'd buy me a ticket?"

"Music vidiocy. You. The whole thing's dying."

"Everything dies," Griffin says.

When Griffin was nineteen years old and independently wealthy, he was sitting in a Miami bar chain-smoking Russian cigarettes. The TV was showing a half-hour news special on the Salvador war. Nobody was watching it.

A guy came into the bar. He looked like a street bum: dust all over army-surplus clothes, week's beard. There was a still camera around his neck; as he pushed up to the bar, Griffin saw it was a Leica. Thousand-buck camera with a thousand-buck lens around this bum's dirty neck. Griffin had only paid eight hundred cash for the suit he was wearing.

The guy with the camera ordered a Black Bush with water on the side. He looked at Griffin. "So what do you do, kid?"

Just like that.

"Oh, a buncha shit," Griffin said. "This is one of the things I do." He lit a fresh cigarette with a five-dollar bill. "So what do you do, man?"

The grubby guy pointed at the television set. The camera was bouncing through the jungle, following a squad of soldiers. One of the grunts got hit, went down. The camera spun, paused over him—just a glance at the soldier, but enough to tell you he was dead.

No. More. Enough to be a little ceremony, an amen over his death.

Griffin felt a pain in his hand. The cigarette had dropped from his lips and burned him. He looked around, saw that everybody in the bar was staring at the TV.

"Shot that two days ago," the guy said. "Film beat me here."

This guy had done that with fifteen seconds of film? On a fucking television set?

"My name's Carrick," he said. "If you're Griffin, somebody told me you were good."

"I—yeah," Griffin said. "Yeah, I'm good."

"Fair enough. How'd you like to be good *at* something?"

Griffin was in the hospital four weeks before he was conscious. For another four after that he couldn't move, couldn't feed himself, couldn't do any of the stuff that adults are supposed to do for themselves. He could think, naturally. And he could talk. He could scream, too, but no one listened to that so he didn't do it for very long.

"So how come you guys go down to wars and get shot at?" Fischetti said, easing a bite of mashed potatoes into Griffin's mouth. "I mean, it ain't like somebody was givin' you orders."

Griffin chewed and swallowed as if he were thinking hard, which he wasn't. "It is, though, at least at first. You start out by following somebody."

"A. D., this is Suzy Lodi."

Griffin is being introduced to a tall, thin woman in a straight-lined silver-mesh dress. He braces himself for the sight of her death, as he has learned to do since leaving the hospital, rehearsing the possibilities. Suicide, he supposes, or a fast car full of hamburger, or the ever-popular cocaine heartburst. Can he really be the only one who sees this? He has imagined cutting people open, looking for the hidden cameras.

Griffin looks up, at large eyes, a pointed chin, a look of vulnerability.

There is no film.

After a moment Griffin catches himself straining to see, and pulls back from the edge in an almost physical sense. No film. It is as if a terrible beating has suddenly stopped.

"I've been looking forward to meeting you," Suzy Lodi says. Somehow her voice retains most of its recorded quality: the depth, the energy. She is like a clean mountain waterfall rushing through the coked-out, juiced-out, smacked-out people in this five-thousand-dollar suite overlooking . . . Griffin cannot remember what city they are in. Maybe Paris. Jesus Christ in Panavision, she is beautiful. Is she straight? Her first album had a single called "Preference Me" that was Number Eleven until somebody decided it was obscene, which drove it to Number Three with a bullet.

"So," Lodi says, "you know what they say the A. D. stands for?"

He knows. In movies it means Assistant Director, in print Art Director, in history books the godless are trying to replace it with C.E.

But when people talk about Griffin it means Already Dead.

The A. D. actually stands for Absalom David, because Griffin's mother was an illiterate who couldn't keep her Bible stories straight. There were no books in Griffin's house. There was no newspaper. There were magazines, if they had enough pictures. And there was television, most of the hours of the day. Dody Griffin's entire print vocabulary was of products whose names were written large on the glass while an announcer spoke them. She could read Dial and Oreo and every major brand of beer.

When A. D. Griffin was fifteen, he came home to find that his mother had mistaken a bottle of ant poison for cough syrup. She was sitting half upright, her lap full of vomit, in front of the cartoon adventures of Rambo.

Griffin found the car keys, loaded the old Buick with what he thought he could hock, and drove off.

Suzy Lodi leads Griffin into another room of the suite and points to a man all in black, five feet and a couple of inches tall.

"Jesse Rain. My lyricist. Also my manager."

Rain has black hair just to his collar, and his clothes are entirely black: denim jeans, silk shirt, boots and hard-worn leather jacket. A black scarf wraps his throat. He is drinking Perrier from the bottle.

Rain's face is hard and planar, like a cliff, his cheeks hollow and gray with beard stubble. He wears black Wayfarers and a ring carved in one piece from some smooth black stone. Griffin thinks of a Karsh photograph; he expects the film of Rain's death to look like double vision, monochrome both sides.

But there is no film.

The relief is less than with Suzy, but it is still there, and cool, and pleasant.

Rain sips his mineral water, looks shade-eyed at Griffin. "Hello, A. D. You're interested in shooting some tape of Suzy." His voice is very measured, like an actor speaking blank verse.

"I don't work in tape," Griffin says. "Only film."

"Film, then."

"Aren't you going to ask why?" Griffin is aware that he is staring, but there is no film. Not of Lodi, not of Rain. He looks at another partygoer, just to make sure, and indeed there it is, perforated ulcer, hemorrhage until Griffin's fingers against his temple break the frame with light. But not of Lodi. Not of Rain.

Jesse Rain says, "Do you ask why Suzy sings with words?"

"You got me."

"I think I might," Rain says seriously, and Griffin doesn't know what the hell he means by it. "But I'll want to see a sample first. One of the songs from Suzy's first album, *Middle Distance*. At our expense."

"If you're going to pay for it anyway, why don't we just—"

"It isn't that I don't trust you," Rain says. "It's that not everyone can shoot Suzy Lodi."

"See these?" Carrick said to Griffin, holding up a yard of sixteen-millimeter in a cotton-gloved hand. "Edge numbers. That's what it's all about. We're all doing edge numbers, dancing right on the sprocket-holed brink."

"I know how to edit, for chrissake."

"Sure. Bet you've read every word Comrade Eisenstein ever wrote, all 'bout how it don't mean a thing if it ain't got that montage. *Look here*, A. D. me lad." He swept his hand across two dozen lengths of film hanging in a cloth-lined editing bin. "You can pick up a piece of film and look at it and say, 'Yeah, here's where this one fits.' You can put it together with your *hands*, understand? On tape, well, there's a time code in there somewhere, say the magic word SMPTE and it all fits, but you can't see the codes. You can't see *anything* on tape, because there *isn't* anything on tape but some oxide particles with a religious orientation. Tape is attitudinal, A. D., but film grabs that hot raw light coming through the gate and makes something out of it."

"That's bullshit."

"It sure is, A. D. . . . but it's *my* bullshit."

The space between the accident and four weeks later in the hospital is dark. Not totally dark, and not empty. There are half-lit shapes there. Griffin thinks—believes—that he could enter the darkness, see the things close, touch them, know them.

The thought terrifies him. The faith is worse.

Suzy Lodi wears black, against an overexposed white background. Her tight leather dress is an inkblot, her bare arms enveloped by light like fog.

> Put the wires into my nerves and brain
> Wash my body down with Novocaine
> If the treatment doesn't ease the pain
> Pull the plug and start again

> You've got to cut wide open, rub salt in your soul
> You've got to crawl through fire, naked on the coal
> You've got to breathe deep water, draw until you drown
> You've got to reach for heaven, pull the temple down

As she moves in front of the reflective front-projection screen, the light absorbs her limbs, gives them back. She is dancing, but dancing with nothing.

> Drive the nails into my hands and feet
> Daily paper for my winding sheet

If the hammer doesn't wake the street
Draw the stake, resume the beat

You've got to cut . . .

Jesse Rain stops the projector, turns up the room lights, taps his black ring on the black tabletop. He takes a sip from the glass of Cold Spring at his elbow, and smiles. Without the sunglasses, his eyes are colorless, like spring water. "I like it very much. There are nine songs on the new album. What do you feel like committing to?"

There is something in the way Rain says "committing" that makes Griffin think of distance.

Griffin and Carrick and one of the BBC guys were out in the Guatemalan bush when a bunch of Green Berets stumbled over them; no officers, just a couple of shot-up fireteams looking for home and mother. They said there were Cubans behind them, at least eighty thousand of them reinforced with tanks and planes and Erwin Rommel and Genghis Khan.

There were some gunshots. The grunts, not all that paralyzed, shot back. Finally Carrick said to Griffin, "Enough of this shit, I am not getting killed by these wieners," and he picked up his camera just exactly like John Wayne hefting a machine gun; yelled, "Okay, men—*let's make movies!*"

They all got up and followed him, the grunts shouting and shooting, until they crashed into five Cubans with a disassembled mortar. The Berets killed them all. One of the soldiers got the Bronze Star.

"Remember," Carrick said to Griffin when all the noise was over, "use this power only for good."

"I hear you've got a contract," Malaryk says. They are sitting in the TWA private lounge at Kennedy, over margaritas and bowls of little pretzels. In half an hour Malaryk will take off for the Persian Gulf. Another ship has been sunk. What goes around comes around.

The lounge is a long curved room with a cathedral ceiling and ruffled white curtains hiding its windows, since the people here pay two hundred bucks a year to forget that this is an airport. Griffin keeps looking past Malaryk at the high drapes, because when he looks at her he sees a crowbar crushing her skull, over and over in coarse monochrome, lit by high thin windows.

"We're going to do three off the new record, *Windwriting*. If those work, Jesse Rain wants to do a full video album."

"That's nice," Malaryk says, and Griffin can hear that it isn't quite a lie.

"Beats staring at the ceiling."

"Doug Leibnecht said that any time you want a field job——"

"Tell Doug I said thanks."

"You tell him," Malaryk says, bitterness on the soundtrack. "I've got work to do."

They have another drink on Malaryk's network, and then her plane is called. Griffin puts a hand behind his head and pinches, and through light, light, light, kisses Malaryk. How does he tell her to frisk guys for crowbars before letting them into her bedroom?

He aches for her himself, eight months is a long time not to be whole, but the face of the man with the iron is blurred.

There is the usual American pantomime of security. One of the toy soldiers at the checkpoint will die in a hit-and-run by Washington Square Park. The other has her respirator switched off by a man who is not wearing a doctor's coat and is grinning as he pulls the plug. Who knows, maybe both the killers are international terrorists.

Griffin watches the plane go, comforted in knowing it cannot crash.

"Some days I think it's all going to come back to us," Griffin said to Carrick once between firefights. "The detachment, I mean. Keeping distance has to have a price."

"Molto wrongo," Carrick said. "Nobody ever paid for keeping a distance. Nobody ever got shot who wasn't in the line of fire."

"But you've always been as close as anybody."
"So I'll get shot," Carrick said.

Griffin's crew has responded to the decline in the promoclip market. They have met the challenge of spiraling costs, of the American drive to find a better way. They have come to Toronto to shoot.

> Once you played with line and color
> Threw the paint against the wall
> And your scribbled name was hanging
> Under hot lights in the hall
> But now the studio's empty
> And the gallery's closed
> And you can hear the doors are slamming
> No matter where you go
> Fashions you thought you were in
> Gone before you quite begin
> Tell me how long have you been
> Alone

There is something in Suzy Lodi that does not want to be filmed. It is easy to ignore this because she is so beautiful; there is enough for the camera there, and all the directors before Griffin have been satisfied with it, content to dance with her image.

Griffin has instead used long lenses and tight apertures to stretch the field, to go deep. For a softly bitter little ballad someone else would have shot in black and white, with smooth slow camera movements. Griffin has used a series of jumping still frames in hypersaturated color.

> Once you drew and cast the numbers
> Dealt the red upon the black
> And no matter how you lost it
> One more play would win it back

But now the pot of gold's empty
And the banks are all closed
And no one's got a dime to lend you
Just look how much you owe
Take your chips and cash them in
Leave the table, you can't win
Tell me how long have you been
Alone

Red paint and green felt and empty blue skies tear holes in the
retinas, blacks and whites are slabs applied with a palette knife; there
is no relief anywhere. Not even in Suzy Lodi's voice, calm as it is.
The reviewer for *Rolling Stone* says, "When she asks 'how long have
you been alone,' there isn't any doubt who left the guy."

There was a time for conversation
In your educated way
There was an audience just waiting
For whatever you would say
But now the words are so empty
And your mind is so closed
And you believe there's someone listening
But you don't really know.
Razor wit can cut too thin
Voices fading in the din
Tell me how long have you been
Alone

The single goes platinum in eleven days. The following week there
is a rumor that returns of engagement rings are up thirty percent.
But there are always rumors.

In the seconds before the darkness, Griffin was looking through his
viewfinder at four Iowa Nazis in brown shirts with stars 'n' stripes

armbands. Griffin was behind what was being called a safety line; the Iowa Nazis agreed that they would not cross the line if the counterdemonstrators and the press and the cops did not cross it.

What the Nazis were doing today in the public eye was killing pigs with spears. A boar hunt, they called it, and issued a statement with some crap about the bold traditions of the Teutonic Knights. One of the countermarchers had a sign reading ALEXANDER NEVSKY HAD THE RIGHT IDEA. It also seemed to be related to a manhood ritual from South Africa, another land of Right Ideas. Griffin felt flashed back to the good old days: he was shooting *Mondo Cane* in the corn belt.

The four he was watching had rifles. This was supposed to be all right too. As the film wound out, one raised his gun.

Griffin's Arriflex exploded next to his temple, into it. He plunged into shadow.

Griffin's clip for Suzy Lodi's "Paper Corridors" has been blamed for an increase in draft evasion, despite that the song has nothing to do with the draft. Griffin has been accused of using subliminals. His reply is that "subliminals are bullshit," which has been quoted—at least, all but the last four letters—in most of the national journals.

"Have you ever thought . . ." Griffin says to Jesse Rain one quiet afternoon, not really knowing how to say it, ". . . of writing Suzy something political?"

"Do you mean something polemical?" Rain picks up a guitar, begins knocking out the bouncing chords of sixties beach rock. He sings:

> So keep your eye on the Russians
> 'Cause I think that they're gonna invade now
> You've got to hide in your shelter
> Till the fallout has gone and decayed now
> Now every girl loves a soldier
> So I sure hope we're gonna get laid now
> And we'll have guns guns guns
> 'Til atomics blow the Commies away-y-y!

"On Suzy's first EP," Rain says as the ringing dies, "I gave her a song called 'An East Wind Coming,' all about Chernobyl. I put everything I had into it. It bored people blind."

"Did that make it not worth doing?"

"Yeah," Rain says. "It did."

After the four weeks of coma following the accident, the first face Griffin saw was Fischetti's. The second was Malaryk's. He had expected to see Carrick, but Carrick was dead. He had been blown out of the sky leaving Yemen. Yemen, for God's sake.

Griffin did not weep until Malaryk had kissed him and gone, and then he began to cry uncontrollably. His arms would not respond properly, his hands were no goddamn use at all. Fish came in and dried his face without saying a word. Griffin understood that none of this was new to Fischetti. He wondered how Fish kept distance. How far the distance was.

The line of those waiting to enter Club Glare is half a block long in cold Manhattan drizzle. Jesse Rain, Suzy Lodi, and Griffin walk past the line to another door and are admitted instantly.

The club's sound system is loud enough to ignite paper. Its lighting carries enough wattage to give a small African nation all the blessings of civilization.

The DJ in the glass booth overhead goes by the name of Wrack Focus. She reminds Griffin of Ming the Merciless in red leather. She is tipped to Suzy's presence, makes the announcement—the applause almost drowns the music—and puts on Griffin's clip of "Paper Corridors." It was shot in darkened government buildings in Ottawa, using preflashed film; the raw stock had been briefly exposed to light, making it more sensitive. There is a cost in haziness, but they can shoot in darker corners.

Griffin and Lodi and Rain get a table with a good view of the crowd and vice versa. Griffin and Lodi order Roederer Cristal. Rain gets straight Perrier, without even a twist.

Griffin looks at the giant video screen. But he's seen that. He looks at the crowd. Film flips by, death death death. He looks at Suzy, and she is calming at first, and then—

"I'm going upstairs," Jesse Rain says. "See you when."

" 'Night, Jess," says Suzy.

"He's going to sleep up there?"

"No. Talk to somebody, I think. But that's the last we'll see of him tonight."

Griffin cannot think of a stranger place to do business than inside this jukebox, and he has seen business done where revolutions per minute referred to the transfer of power.

"Is everything all right, Miz Lodi?" says the voice of a BBC announcer. Griffin looks up. There is a seven-foot Haitian in a Club Glare T-shirt looking back at him.

"Just fine, Robert. A. D., this is Rather Rotten Robert. Robert's job is to break the arms of anybody who hassles us, right, Robert?"

Robert smiles, showing more gold than teeth, and says in the perfect Oxbridge purr, "That's quite correct, Miz Lodi."

Through his left eye Griffin sees the huge man kick a .44 out of a zipunk's hand and then throw the zipunk out the door one-handed; as Robert turns, a bald girl with fishhooks in her lips picks up the big pistol and fires it twice, punching Robert's heart out of his body, taking off a corner of his skull. Rather Rotten Robert says, "Oh, now, why, lady," and then there is blue light, neon through a beer bottle.

"May I bring you another bottle, sir, madam?" Robert says.

"I think we're going early tonight," Suzy says. "Would you call the car?"

"Certainly, Miz Lodi."

Griffin looks at Suzy Lodi, and there is no film. It has been a long time not to be whole. They go out past the line of those who cannot enter, and for once what those people are thinking is right.

It's never like one expects, but even more so tonight. No torn or thrown clothing. No dominance or submission beyond a little friendly no-I'm-on-top. No kinks and very little perspiration; as clean as a really good porn film. Just the sweet uncomplicated joy of an exchange of tenderness between two people who don't give a damn for each other.

Griffin goes home early the next afternoon to find a message on his answering machine from Malaryk, in town again and wanting to talk to him, and he doesn't even feel guilty.

There is a knock at Griffin's door. Standing in the hall is a man in a bulky coat, a hat half across his face. He looks straight at Griffin, and the face is empty of anything like expression. The medium, in this case, is the message. Griffin turns away before he looks any closer.

"Are you fully recovered from your injury, Mr. Griffin?" the man says, and again it is not the words but the tone.

"I'm doing all right."

"Very glad to hear that, Mr. Griffin. Glad to see you've found productive work. You are enjoying your work?"

"Sure."

"No desire to return to your former job?"

"This pays better."

"Yes," the man says. "I'd keep that in mind. Should anyone make any sort of counteroffer to you—do remember the difference in pay."

Griffin stares. He can't help it, perhaps. The film rolls. Griffin sees the man being knifed in a narrow street, buildings with an East European look. The camera looks down on him as he lurches, holding his stomach in his hands, bumps against a street sign.

"Be careful on Kalininstrasse," Griffin says.

"I hope you're listening to me, Mr. Griffin," the man says in color right frame, while in left frame he falls and makes a splash in his own blood. The man is puzzled. He is used to people being afraid of him, and to their standing up bravely to him, but Griffin's response has him stymied.

"You too," Griffin says, and looks, and looks, until the man turns around and goes.

Griffin shuts the door, and manages not to vomit until he reaches the bathroom.

> One look away
> One voice that won't stop screaming
> One wish that keeps on coming true
> One lonely day
> One night of lucid dreaming
> One coded message coming through
> Breaking through to blue

Malaryk keeps looking at the bar television during the Suzy Lodi clip. She is fascinated, so much so she keeps not telling Griffin what it was that was so important this morning.

> One barren place
> One scent that always lingers
> One introspective point of view
> One hidden face
> One hand with seven fingers
> One wired instruction what to do
> Breaking through to blue

"—but I think I got tape of somebody's missiles in somebody else's cargo holds," Malaryk says suddenly. "I held the camera on the stenciling, and the bills of lading, and if they're all readable—"

"Pia," Griffin says, "has a man—"

The crowbar falls and falls and falls before the thin windows.

"A man what?"

"Be careful," he says, and leaves her, no doubt wondering.

Griffin knows he must have film of Carrick somewhere. He knows that he shot it, as tests, as jokes, as remembrance, for any reason except the one he has in mind now. Tape will not do. Tape is attitudinal, a cool medium at a safe distance.

He finds a reel, jams it onto the editor spools, slaps off the lights and begins to crank.

There is Carrick, moving, living in the light. This is Guatemala film.

And down the left side of Griffin's vision, Yemeni film. The crew is getting out, a Hercules is waiting to take them home.

They crowd aboard the Herc, it takes off; there is a round of gallows jokes and straight shots of whiskey, the plane reaches altitude.

There is a bright light as if the film has broken, the lamp unconfined through the gate. And then nothing.

Griffin runs the film back, slows it down. The light contracts to a sphere, to a point. It goes out, leaving a knapsack in a seat. It was all over in three frames, one-eighth of a second. No one felt a thing.

Griffin stops the projection again, counts the passengers. There are twelve. He turns back to the boarding, counts again. Thirteen. The one with the knapsack in his hand does not take a seat. He drops the bag, turns as if going after more gear.

Griffin stops the film. The man's face is blurred with motion, but Griffin has seen it that way before. In Kaliministrasse. And behind a swinging crowbar.

In the next-to-last frame before the fogged footage, the Iowa Nazi raised his automatic rifle. Bits of film camera crumpled into Griffin's head. But the man with the rifle did not fire it. Griffin had filmed men shooting rifles on four continents, including directly at him, and this one did not.

Griffin wonders who was standing next to him, behind the safety line. But he has no film of that.

He looks at the telephone. He knows the digits that in the right sequence will connect him with Malaryk. But what after that?

The phone rings.

Griffin picks it up.

"A. D.?" Jesse Rain says. "Couple of things I'd like to discuss with you."

"Get the hell out of here, Griffin," the high-school principal told the fifteen-year-old. "I don't know what you bother to come to school for."

"Because I run your audio-visual department better than that drunk Haley ever did, and you don't have to pay me."

The principal swung the yardstick in his hand at Griffin. Griffin grabbed it and snapped it in half. He ran. He'd been told to get out, after all.

He ran home, because that was the only place he had to run. When he got there, he paused, and thought, and gathered, and kept on running.

Rain takes Griffin to Club Glare, and upstairs. Here the floor hums with the sound for those below, and sometimes the light flashes through the windows like lightning, but they are isolated. Rain looks down at the dance floor, the keystoned video screen. They are above even Wrack the DJ.

When they sit down, Griffin has a pint glass of Guinness at the proper temperature, Rain one of Vichy water.

Rain says, "What do you see when you look at me, A. D.?" The words rhyme so that for a moment Griffin thinks it is a new lyric for Suzy. Then he hears them properly. After a moment, he says, "What am I supposed to see?"

"You're an artist. I'd hoped you could tell me."

"I make movies."

"You know it's more than that," Rain says. "You work with light. While some of us . . ."

Rain's lips are moving. Griffin cannot hear the words, if they are words; only a soft whistling. Rain dips two fingers into the straight-sided glass. There is a flare of light from his ring, with star-filter points.

The water glass is empty, and a black-furred mouse clutches the back of Rain's hand. It runs up his sleeve, perches on his shoulder.

"Look hard at the mouse," Jesse Rain says. "See anything?"

Griffin looks. The mouse looks back, curious little eyes. There is no film.

"I'm, going to throw him under a truck when we're done here," Rain says. "Anything yet?"

No. The mouse licks Rain's ear.

Rain says, "I know your work. You know mine. Technique."

Griffin looks Rain straight in the colorless eyes. Rain feeds a peanut to the mouse, says, "A. D., can you see me?" to the beat of the Who song.

No. Lightning strikes in Griffin's brain, and he pulls at his drink. So this isn't how Carrick did it after all. Griffin had thought—but no, this is different.

Rain says, "It doesn't have to hurt. It can be more fun than anything. You just need to work on your technique." His face is a test card and his voice is a click track. The mouse snuggles down on Rain's shoulder. Surely a mouse has to die. Everything dies.

Rain says, "Did she act like a puppet? Was there any lack of spontaneity?

No. Griffin's crotch tightens at the thought.

"Technique." Rain stands up, the mouse crawling into his jacket. He says, "Let's go. I can only stand so much of this place."

They descend into the noise, and Rather Rotten Robert clears a way for them. Every time Griffin looks up he sees the bullet opening Robert's skull, so he looks mostly down. On the street there is still a line of people waiting to be approved for entry; a glance shows Griffin clips of stopped hearts and fried brains and overturned cars and a boat propeller taking hungry bites. Griffin touches his jaw joint and the film breaks, white light through the gate, painful but clean.

Rain says, "This way. Easy now—you get thrown in the drunk tank and you're in for a long and visionary night."

The neon blurs and goes out. Griffin realizes he is being bundled into a stretch limo. Plush and leather caress him, dark glass soothes his eyes. Rain puts a cold beer into Griffin's hand and he suckles it.

"Where are we going?" Griffin says finally.

"Where do you want to go? Remember we have a clip to shoot in the morning. Want to do it in Paris? We'll pick up Suzy, be on the jet by two. Suzy likes Paris. That's where she met you, remember?"

"Take me up to East 92nd."

Rain twists the cap off a bottle of Evian. They drive north.

Griffin sold the family car, which he wasn't licensed to drive anyway, and pawned the household goods. The hockshop had a sixteen-millimeter movie camera, a Canon Scoopic. Griffin bought it, and a reel-to-reel tape recorder. "Nobody uses this stuff no more, they all make videotape," the pawnbroker said. "Who you gonna be, Cecil B. deMille?"

"Herschell Gordon Lewis," Griffin said, but the pawnbroker didn't get it.

Four years later A. D. Griffin was producing, directing, scripting, and lensing hardcore for the inner-city markets and the occasional softcore splatter for the drive-ins. He had a before-tax income of thirty thousand dollars, and an after-tax income of thirty thousand dollars. He had neither a credit card nor a checking account, and had never written a ledger entry in his life. Most of the people he dealt with thought he was just a runner for the real A. D. Griffin. He didn't care. He had everything.

He thought he had everything, until Carrick showed up. What goes around comes around.

Fischetti's fingers dug deep into Griffin's back, working out the pain, putting Griffin's mind back in touch with his vacationing limbs. Griffin thought about things in order, said, "You know who Eisenstein was, Fish?"

"Sure. He was a Jew that built atom bombs."

Rain's limousine lets Griffin off at the steps to Malaryk's brownstone. It has begun to rain. Rain says nothing as Griffin leaves the car. When Griffin turns back for a moment, the limo is gone.

He climbs the stairs to a high double door, wire in its glass panes. To his right is a column of glowing doorbell buttons. Malaryk's is the third up. Griffin glances up, through the rain.

The building has high, narrow windows.

Griffin stops. Either he can change what is happening up there, or he cannot. Either he has been seeing the truth or he has not.

If a man cannot trust himself, trusting God is a small consolation. Griffin looks away from the door, high crane shot of the sidewalk below.

There is a young couple, teens, walking past, drenched, nuzzling, not feeling the rain. In Griffin's left eye the boy kills the girl with a potato peeler. The state electrocutes him. What goes around comes around. She is wearing an oversized T-shirt, plastered to her breasts with rain. It reads CHOOSE LIFE.

Griffin spins around, panning over the lighted doorbells. He stumbles down the steps. Water splashes on his shoes.

A man comes out from between the buildings, coat turned up against the rain. He is whistling to himself. He might be on his way to the corner for a paper. But he is not. Griffin stares at him, and stares, watching the film of his death over and over.

It isn't enough.

The man has a chalk mark on his shoulder now, a broad white M. All around him are scrapings and thuds and footsteps. Hands reach up from sewer gratings. The underworld pursues the murderer, for if the police cannot, who else is left?

Griffin tilts up. The sign on the lamppost no longer reads Kalininstrasse. Beneath it the man is just as dead.

So.

Griffin takes a few squelching steps. He sees a little man in a long black coat, just ahead. The man snaps his arm out straight: Griffin barely sees the blur of black fur before it disappears beneath a passing truck. He can hear the crunch of tiny bones.

The man in black walks away. Griffin turns another way. So much water.

He will bind Suzy Lodi in black cloth and soak her with water, so that her movements are struggling and slow. Filters and lighting will show each drop in high contrast as it rolls down her face, her body to the pool that rises, black as oil, past her hips. In the last bars of the song it will reach her chin, and still rise, until there is only a silver ripple on darkness. Jesse Rain will write a lyric, and it will sell a million pressings. Kids will drown and not be missed. Double platinum.

A siren shrieks. The cars pull up, the cops pile out. So someone did hear something, say something. Down left frame, one of them is shotgunned in the face by a stocking-masked bandit, another hangs himself dressed in women's lingerie. Fog and darkness make the right frame seem as colorless as the left, except for the red and blue flares of light. Griffin saves the image for a future video. There will be music.

Griffin turns his back.

A little farther on, Griffin's transportation is waiting, calmly pawing the pavement with its eight-inch claws. It turns its head, and dips it, clicking the eagle beak, as submissive as such a creature might ever appear.

Griffin climbs on his namesake's back, running a hand over the feathers of the head, the stiff but smooth fur on the huge shoulders. He is taken into the night sky, the bank over the city smoother than a gyrostabilized helicopter mount. It's more fun than anything.

The street where they are clustering around death is only one square of an endless dark grid, and at every point of the grid there are police, firemen, ambulances, light sparking hopelessly against the night.

So he doesn't have Carrick's gift, so what. He has his own, and Rain has shown him what it's good for. Griffin will go back now, to the people he can stand to look at, because they have nothing inside them.

Regret dies last. But everything dies.

LETTER FROM ELSINORE

Just days ago we sat upon this rock
Watching the ignorant armies marching past
With the scholar's sense of knowing more than they.
Now you are in England
And the soldiers somewhere as grave,
And I seem to know nothing at all.
Oh, I can name you stones, plants, stars,
By Agricola, Linnaeus, and Tycho;
Words I know, objects, machineries, but
    mechanism
Has ceased to be sufficient for events.
I still do not believe in ghosts, say I.
A lamp burns blue from gasses in the flame,
Light blooms in unstruck conduits of the eye
And the shape-seeking mind gives it shadow
    substance:
I saw a phosphene with a silvered beard.
It was easier for the others: they believed.
Unpolished by the wheels of Wittenberg
They roughly knew that death sleeps not

When trouble wakes it. We were so very cold.
What did you see by darkness, then? Your mind
Had always a good eye, and your soul
Always a muted voice. Some recollection
Was it, some fatherly advice
On power, trust, and counsels in the court
Rose up to haunt you, and you called it Father.
Why there I have deduced it, QED.
I will believe that men are stricken mad
When I can think naught else, as I believe
That they are dead when I do see a corpse.
Recall that night in the days of our study
We went up to the tower in Wittenberg
Because the old professor, Johann Faust
The wondersmith, the one who could not choose
If God had mercy, promised us a wonder.
Shortly he gave it, with his body and crossed timbers
And a thunderclap. Demons, you said,
Had rent him. I never thought you
More than metaphorical. Surely
Something in an alembic had gone wrong,
A spark touched to a firework, perhaps
Those strange heavy metals he said were Philosopher's
    Stone.
He swore he could wall Germany with brass
And all knew he meant cannon: Gustavus Adolphus
Taught the world that trick. You and Rosencrantz and I
Looked on Faustus in pieces among his instruments:
Thence Ros went off to form that fond attachment
To Guildenstern with his horrid clarinet,
Flowering Narcissus. You said demons,
Meaning more I think now than I thought then.
I confess to this air that I saw first and mainly
Anatomized Man, in exploded view,

And wondered which of all those riven vessels,
Those open hollow parts, had spilled his soul.
There's a mystery wants answering.
You did not stab Polonius in the brains,
Nor heart, nor anything particularly.
(The doctors never thought to open him;
A lung, the liver portal veins, I'd guess.)
You did not stay to see the transference
Of wounds. Your thrust went further than you know.
Here is where we define Horatio's courage.
If I put this message to paper and ink
Instead of casting it on water after you
Would I tell you, reasonable friend,
How Ophelia's reason cries out in its sleep?
They gave me charge of the distracted maiden,
Thinking her safe thus, I suppose;
How flattering to my mind. Though safe she was,
Not just because she was, in my faith, yours,
But out of simple fear. Not simple. Mine.
I think she knew it. It was she who kissed
My palms as if they smoked, then ran, light-foot,
Trailing blossoms, laughing. Laughing, laughing.
There was never such laughter at Wittenberg,
Nor demons either. And now the girl is tended
By some old hen who fears to go near water.
Does any of this matter to you, damn it,
Who turned her aside for reasons I trust are good,
Who'd have her without taking her? At school
You thought on sex. I heard you through the walls.
Of course it's not a cloud of autumn light;
It's awkward and it's noisy and it's humid
And leaves you feeling half like Jupiter
And one-third set to vomit. Do I shock you?
Oh yes, friend, women have delighted me,

As, I should hope, I them. Consider it
Research, hands on the openable book,
Affording here and there to the caring student
A subtle proof that flesh can be in earnest,
A glimpse of Time and God.
No. No. It is my faith to understand,
Not to disprove, your motives. I would know,
And now that I am here, I think I do.
My parents' house had walls and doors and roof,
Elsinore none of these. The place is open
As diagram in book; here read the legend:
A represents a whispering-gallery,
B indicating a confessor's alcove,
C shows a hanging that provides concealment,
And D a hollow underneath the stairs.
This is no house, it is a theatre,
A cockpit in continuous performance,
All actors, all audience, no interval.
You hurt me when you would not take my oath
Of silence, but you did not mean to do:
You only knew your ground, this listeners' kingdom,
Where intimacy's the rarest paradox.
I wonder if this place does wound the mind,
Echoing nights with auditors and ghosts
(Memories, I mean, the ghosts I will acknowledge)
Toxic with stone-dust, lead in wine and paint,
The moldy wheat that dements villages?
Is it the time, near war, too near to death,
The witchfinder's needle bearing down,
Demanding, scream or be burned alive?
I learned in Wittenberg, I learn here
To watch men die and women suffer
With the same Apollonian detachment I kept
For the droppings of unidentified wildlife

And tumors in jars, driven by the passion
Of glands undiscoverable by knife, and the thought
That the world might not be left
So bad as when one entered;
If demonless Wittenberg and haunted Elsinore
Were brought together in some essential coitus
Would the child be good?
Gone friend, what do you dream
What my philosophy dreams of?
Words fall in water, and the world shall end
No different for Horatio's tenancy.
Down yonder hill two clowns are digging holes
For dead men. Every doctor knows
Whence comes his study-matter; I'll go there
And see if spades have brought up interest.
There's motion, out to sea. A pirate sail,
Black sheet on silver water. That's a legend:
Of grief and trouble come to royal fathers,
Trouble and grief come unto princely sons.

IN THE DAYS OF THE COMET

DISPATCH 135, OORT CLOUD SURVEY

Camfield is dead, and this ship is very quiet now. I have tried to be hopeful in the recent dispatches. We were; Camfield certainly was. Prions are not supposed to kill people anymore, but they can, and they have. Which is part of the reason Camfield was out here in the first place.

He was a teller of jokes and he played the guitar very well—these are valuable things when you are doomed to spend years aboard a cantankerous old ship. Several installments ago, I described the lab accident that infected Camfield, and I have received numerous messages calling the events absurd. This is true. In addition to myself, the organic Petrovna and the Neumann Thucydides saw the incident, and we all laughed until we realized Camfield was hurt. Petrovna, at least, can forget, although I do not think she will.

The prion has been decrypted and entered into the antigenic database, so no one should ever again die of Agent Op-1175s/CFD.

Which is the story, but not its point.

At the cusp of this millennium we discovered that it was not hard to manufacture prions, and not that hard to custom-twist them. It took longer for our twists to be meaningful, but now organic humanity can don an armor of proteins for defense against a hostile Universe. Rather like viruses. Draw your own conclusions.

If one could find the right message, a prion would make a wonderful interstellar, even intergalactic, postal card: immune to temperature, pressure, radiation, and time. The ideal pony for the express would be a comet, packed with messenger proteins, flung into a hyperbolic orbit, to seed any worlds at the far end with its cargo.

One could write one's name in the evolving life of a planet. At exactly the right moment, one might even begin the process, dropping a bouillon cube into the primordial soup.

Assuming that no one at the other end is quite as evolved, and quite as dependent on delicate higher neural functions, as we are.

So here we are, myself, 29 (down from 30) organic crew, and eight Neumänner, combing the comets of the Oort for prions. We have found a lot of prions, and there are a lot of comets left. You've got mail, as we said when I was organic.

Maybe. Or maybe one of the 48 published theories of spontaneous prion formation in comets is correct. It is the Neumänner who are most insistent on deliberate seeding. Perhaps it comforts them to think that, just as we built them, somebody built us. How human of them—but, as their namesake said, adequately describe any activity, and a machine can perform it.

In Camfield's last hours he was afire with fever, his whole body trembling, but there was a clarity in his speech that was at once heartbreaking and terrifying. Fischer, Chiang, and the Neumann Hypatia were tending him. Abruptly he calmed, fixed Chiang (and me, unavoidably) with a direct stare, and said, "I see the Martians now! They are flat, and they roll!" He shivered then, and I heard his heart stop.

The exclamation points are not added for drama. He was excited by what he saw, transported by whatever the alien messenger in his brain was revealing to him. Camfield was born on the Moon, not Mars, so we cannot explain away the vision as *Heimsucht*.

We cannot, of course, positively explain it at all. But we must examine the possibility that, eons ago, Op-1175s/CFD fell on Mars and began life there, which was later carried to Earth by a planetary blunt trauma.

Thucydides carefully wrapped and sealed Camfield's remains for storage until we return to the Moon, eight years from now. When he was done, Sid paused for two full minutes (exactly—we are like that), just looking at the bundle.

This kind of behavior is by no means strange for a Neumann (one can adequately describe a thoughtful pause) but I asked Sid what he was thinking. He waited fourteen seconds longer—which was purely theatrical of him—and said, "I will miss Camfield. He was always interesting to be with, even when nothing was said. And has he not left us with a fine and difficult question?"

Camfield gave many gifts to his shipmates and his ship. The question—and it is fine—he gave to all of us.

Autonomous Exploration Vessel *John M. Ford* was one of the first private citizens to undergo cortical shift, first to a netlinked mainframe, passing through a series of mobile installations to an AEV hull. In addition to his fiction and his work on the Oort Survey, he is developing *The League of Steersmen*, a history of the AEVs.

WINDOWS ON AN EMPTY THRONE

THE UNIVERSE

The stars revolve above the land;
The land is centered on the King;
All power flows from one strong hand;
The King ordaineth everything,
Each angel moves his satellite
(The Sun needs eight, by hours, to swing)
The Moon keeps watch on traitorous night
The King observeth everything.
The crystal spheres dance in a ring
The brazen gears cannot be stopped
But hear the tiny stuttering:
A feather falls, a stitch is dropped
The angels bend their heads and sing:
The King is dead, long live the King.

JUDGMENT

They say it was a little pin
That augered through his castle wall;
The vein with age and care worn thin
The blood was let, and that was all.
The siege was fought both hard and long
On this the doctors are agreed;
Their care helped keep the good man strong
Until the ordained time to bleed.
Examinings of fingernails
The closely studied pot of piss,
These small undignified details
And hard-won learning come to this:
They did all that their art could do
And pray they shall continue to.

THE TOWER

No one likes to look too long at towers,
Slender, Heaven-taunting peaks of stone;
They show a light at dark unseemly hours
And whatever would live there, lives alone.
Why should a narrow garret seem so frightening?
Is it the fear of heights or just the climb?
Groundlings, should the spire lure the lightning,
Can just be glad they missed the bolt that time.
Does someone have converse with shadow voices way up
    there?
Hidden wisdom floating on the insubstantial air?
Is there someone running down the endless spiral stair,
Coming from a casting, gone to tell a king Beware?
The tower is empty, the crystal is clouded;
Such warnings come late, or unheard, or just doubted.

THE HANGED MAN

A quarter of an hour before the rope
Would have stretched to infinity, the messenger came:
All men are pardoned in the late King's name.
A thing beyond anyone's grasp; not mad hope
Contained it: the guards tumbled the man down
He heaved on the street as the crowd, uncertain, stared:
A King dead for a thief spared,
A tale they all knew, but no one found
The connection with the events they saw;
They grumbled and shuffled in the dust-hazed thought
That this was not how the world ought
Treat those with faith in the power of law.
Redemption caught the man sudden and strange:
He cut a purse quickly, in fear he should change.

THE WHEEL OF FORTUNE

The Fourth Minister was a man of conviction:
The Law is a guide through all follies and fogs.
What is phrased in the statutes' eloquent diction
Will keep the world true, though the clouds drip frogs.
He fined those employers who gave their apprentices
Liberty on the King's death; to reward ill times
Is to praise sedition. A few present sentences
Are salt in the soil of tomorrow's crimes.
As the King's knell fades, someone pounds at the
    Minister's door
And with no leave, unkempt constables barrel in:
There are boots on the carpet and iron-shod pikes on the
    floor,
A man shows a writ, on his lips fresh spit and a grin;

The Minister feels the world slip like sand in a fist
Where now is Law? How can the rope so twist?

JUSTICE

With a quill pen dipped in the city's grief
Destiny is marked in an angular hand:
This stroke is freedom for a gallows thief
The next one is death for a less guilty man
Who thought the right word would unbolt his door:
Which it will, for a moment, six heartbeats, no more
Enough for some blood to be spilt on a floor
That has weathered a thousand such showers before.
The door opened last for a voice with no face
Did the prisoner know someone some way inclined
To—the kind of thing one would expect in this place?
Now the scratch of the pen (which like Justice is blind)
Means someone kills someone who knew something, such
That nobody left is left knowing too much.

THE HERMIT

The general had never given in:
So when the doctors said there was no cure,
And had their money sent by messenger,
He turned his crumbling face into the wind.
He had been the King's hand, when he was clean and
    strong,
Fought at the side of stranger and of friend,
But even enemies are other men:
He thought he knew aloneness. He was wrong.
So when the King died, he stood upon the road
Where the cortege would pass: if they drew sword
And killed him, well. He could die with his lord.

But all eyes watched the carriage with its load.
Abandoned again, he bowed, and tugged the hood
That spared men's eyes—and saw his flesh made good.

THE LOVERS

The King's Life Guard are holding tournament,
A hallowed custom for unstable hours;
Mock battle occupies the knightly powers
Until the warrior energies be spent.
One captain lays about him with a will
Crying with arms what voice will never tell;
When he was young, the King was young as well
And something happened Death itself can't kill.
It was not the love the world shows
And plain men must work if they'd live
Hearts alter course as the wind blows
And passion is borne in a sieve;
He only knows what the queen knows
And there is no comfort to give.

THE CHARIOT

From fleshpot straight to throne the heir approaches:
The King is dead, all cry, long live the King!
No time now to remember old reproaches;
The prodigal already wears the ring.
The dispatch from the castle found him drinking
(To not would have surprised his father's men)
He read their letter, spent a minute thinking,
And laughed aloud, and did not laugh again.
The boy adored his father as a master
And loathed him as a mortal ten times more;
And soon, he thinks (and whips his horses faster)

And too late, he'll know what it all was for.
He lifts the reins: let all the city see—
His name is Phaëthon; they know his mystery.

THE PRIEST

The forms observed in this regretful day
Are many, and older than kings and queens;
There is much reassurance in the way
Remembered words are said, and calm by means.
A certain garment worn precisely so,
Familiar constellations of lit sconces,
The congregation must already know
How they are called, and all their right responses.
There are no alterations in the text
Who knows how soon we'll play the show again?
Is not one ruler very like the next?
Alone, the priest must find, in the hour when
The candles are out, the vestments laid aside,
A private word, for the man who private died.

THE PRIESTESS

In a flash of green on a distant peak, a woman
Hears the knell fading on the smoky breeze;
She sees the city whole, a scab of all things human
And nothing but, no open ponds, no trees
Uncarpentered, unburnt. They stretch their ways
On wheels, on radiating stone-paved lines
That smother soil and untune ancient leys.
She turns, making no sound among the pines.
This morning she found henbane and a knife
And words: *Great Lady, you have willing hands.*
Who still believes that life is cut from life?

It was the soul's corruption made the land's.
Not just the whine of saw her sleep disturbs
But nightshade, foxglove, tansy, bitter herbs.

THE EMPRESS

The years can lower grimly on a queen;
Heavy the habit majesty must wear,
She must be fair as frost when daily seen
And riot nightly till there be an heir.
But cords that mortal wit cannot untie
Are in a stroke dissolved, the story goes.
A moment's task to lay the scepter by,
A minute more to change to darker clothes.
All hearts are with her, now the king is dead;
The city is in royal mourning, but
What was a man is on the loveless bed,
The windows to her truest self are shut.
Extraordinary burdens she has known
And borne—but not alone. But not alone.

THE JUGGLER

After they hanged her father, she had eight cloth balls
And the skill to keep six airborne in cascade;
Once she saw a rich man by the castle walls;
She did her act. He smiled. He even paid.
She lost one beanbag, scrambling from the place
(When you're small on the street, gold's hard to keep)
Her birthright for a coin—with the rich man's face—
She held it hard, and wept herself to sleep.
When word was passed that the old King had died
She floated seven till the sun went down
And for the third time in her life, she cried.

She dreamt of a gray bird over the town
It wheeled into the sun and vanished. Then
She woke to find the lost thing hers again.

THE FOOL

He once drove out a foreign lord
By eating with the unclean hand;
The diplomats just laughed. And word
Trumped sword in the disputed land.
But when the shadow that protects a clown
Deepens to darkness, then it's time to shift:
So, bindle packed, he slips the sleeping town,
Pausing to leave one ball—the King's last gift.
One last jest's under covers in his bed:
When the most noble knights he'd caused offense
Break in, they'll stab his concertina dead;
With feathers and rude noise the matter ends.
The dawn road's for the light step made
Before the final laugh can fade.

ERASE/RECORD/PLAY
A DRAMA FOR PRINT

[The curtain is up as the audience enters. There is a small table upstage right; on it is a large reel-to-reel tape recorder, the reels facing the audience. Behind the table is a stool, high enough so that the person in it will be clearly visible, and a stand microphone at the appropriate height for that person. A lectern faces stage left.

[Aside from this, the stage is completely empty; there is no backdrop, so that the rear wall is visible, and some of the equipment overhead dangles slightly in view.

[As the audience finishes finding their seats, DR. GORDON enters. He is in his late forties. He wears casual trousers and jacket, no tie. His shirt has French cuffs with cufflinks. He sits on the stool and adjusts the microphone. As the house lights go down, a spotlight illuminates him. The recorder clicks loudly without being touched, and the reels of tape begin to turn.]

DR. GORDON
(facing the audience directly)
Is that working now? The power's been much more
reliable the last couple of months, but . . .

INTERVIEWER
(a disembodied voice from somewhere above the audience)
Fine, thank you, Dr. Gordon. I have a battery-operated
recorder, but—

DR. GORDON
—but you can't get batteries at all here. Yes. Shall we go on, then?

INTERVIEWER
Your actors—

DR. GORDON
Players. We don't call them actors, or myself a director.
(a beat)
It's a way of defusing criticism, if you like.

INTERVIEWER
What do you prefer to be called?

DR. GORDON
Doc.
(getting no response)
I have an M.D. in psychiatry. I'm a licensed therapist. In fact,
twice licensed. I had to be recertified, afterward.

INTERVIEWER
The players were all in the same camp, correct?

DR. GORDON
(looking at the audience)
That's right. Camp Eighteen.

INTERVIEWER
Everyone knows where they were?

DR. GORDON
We know where everyone was released from. There were some
movements between camps. . . . (he shrugs) So yes, everyone knows
who wishes to know.

INTERVIEWER

Some don't wish to know?

DR. GORDON

Oh, some, always. But most consider it . . . a kind of family name. You may have noticed people wearing their numbers on their clothing.

INTERVIEWER

Yes. I'd seen that.

DR. GORDON

There were twenty-five camps. It's been decided that each of the first twenty-five days of Liberation Month will be the corresponding number's day to celebrate.

INTERVIEWER

Do you expect them to celebrate?

DR. GORDON

I expect them to celebrate as though they had never before in their lives had cause for celebration. *I* certainly intend to. I'm a Nine, by the way.

INTERVIEWER

So they see their status as . . . inmates as a matter of . . .
(a pause)

DR. GORDON
(humorously)

Lose your script?

INTERVIEWER

Can you fill in the blank?

DR. GORDON
(coldly serious)

That's a dangerous thing to ask around here.
(light again)

You said "matter of," so you probably meant to say "a matter of pride." But I don't believe it's that. A matter of fact, certainly. A matter of history, it is to be hoped. A matter of identity . . . such as it is.

[WALTER, MARK, PARIS, ADELINE, VIRGINIA, and HOWARD, the six PLAYERS, enter downstage left. They are all around thirty.

[WALTER is handsome, and carries himself with confidence. MARK is a large man, who moves carefully though not awkwardly. PARIS is slight, attractive, graceful. ADELINE is angular of face and body, and occasionally shows a little stiffness in movement. HOWARD is rather short and self-conscious. VIRGINIA is strong-looking, precise, a bit wary.

[They carry seriously thumbed playtexts and are dressed in rehearsal clothes: jeans, sweatshirts, sneakers. All wear long sleeves. WALTER has a small badge showing the number 18.

[They glance briefly at the backstage hardware. MARK stumbles, does not fall, clutches his script to himself; the others look at him, without hostility. They sit down, apparently at random, facing DR. GORDON.

[DR. GORDON turns ninety degrees on his stool to face them over the lectern; as he does, the light on the tape recorder fades, leaving its meters glowing in darkness. DR. GORDON takes a script, as well-worn as the others', from his pocket.]

"There are only two immutable rules of play," Dr. Gordon said. "One: Inviolability of Text. You may neither omit lines, nor add your own verbal material. You may speak the lines with any tempo or inflection you think right, pause as you choose, but no cuts, no ad-libs. You may *do* anything you feel is right while speaking, except as defined by Rule Two.

"Rule Two: The Cut Rule. Physical contact is allowed, up to and including *simulated* acts of violence. You all did very well in Fake

Fisticuffs 101, by the way." The players grinned and nodded; Paris laughed softly. "But anyone involved in a contact situation who doesn't like the way it's going can stop it at once by yelling 'Cut!' "

Adeline said, "Are we chicken if we Cut?" The tightness of her voice concealed any meaning.

"Damned if I know," said Dr. Gordon. "The other thing is that only a player who's actually been touched in the scene can Cut it. That includes me." He smiled, riffled through his copy of the text. "Okay, I know you're all anxious to perform, so let's start."

The players stood up, opening their scripts.

Dr. Gordon said, "Act One, Scene One: A Wood near Athens. Enter Theseus and Hippolyta, with Attendants. That's Walt and Ginny; the rest of you, strike poses in the rear."

"Attentive poses?" Mark said.

"How about classically Greek?" said Paris.

Dr. Gordon said, "Statuary, that's good. Want to illustrate, Paris?"

Virginia said, "Shall I have a bow? Like Diana?"

"Why not?" Dr. Gordon said, and Virginia slung an imaginary longbow and quiver while Paris demonstrated positions of marble ballet.

Walter held his textbook loosely at his side, and looked straight at Virginia. "Now, fair Hippolyta," he said, "our nuptial hour draws on apace; four happy days bring in another moon: but O, methinks . . ." He paused, but he did not look as if he had forgotten the line. He said, low and slow, ". . . how slow the old moon wanes." He took a step toward his bride-to-be. "It lingers my desires, like to a step-dame or a dowager, *long, withering* out a young man's revenue."

"Four days will quickly steep themselves in night," Virginia said, quite crisply. "Four nights will quickly dream away the time. And— *then*—the moon, like a silver bow new bent in heaven—" she unslung her own invisible weapon, reached for an arrow—"shall behold the night of our solemnities." She concluded with an arrow nocked, casually aimed at what definitely was not Theseus's heart.

Theseus shrugged with both hands in the air, turned to Dr. Gordon. "Go, Philostrate," he said, cocking a look at the book in his hand. "Stir up the Athenian youth to merriments. . . ."

[DR. GORDON nods and turns back to the audience; the light on the PLAYERS dims and they freeze into tableau as the tape begins to roll.]

INTERVIEWER

Your players don't memorize the script?

DR. GORDON

They memorize as much as they please. They're not going to face an audience who are programmed to think that scripts break the illusion; they're each other's audience, and the illusion they create is their own.

INTERVIEWER

So they're not going to perform before an audience—

DR. GORDON

Is that what I said? (without pausing) Memorization is a great mumping boogeyman that hangs around the theater, scaring people away. It's necessary to meet it face-on, go a few backalley rounds with it. I can do all of *Hamlet* and *Lear*, all the male parts in *Guys and Dolls* and *A Funny Thing Happened on the Way to the Forum*, including the songs—(he hums a bit of "Comedy Tonight," then abruptly leans forward and speaks in a quiet but almost threatening tone).

And I have no more idea of what I've been doing for the last five years than any of *those* people do.

[He turns back to the players and the action resumes as before.]

"Hippolyta." Walter extended a finger; he delicately turned the point of Virginia's arrow aside, took a step closer. "I woo'd thee with my sword . . ." He put the finger on her shoulder. She tilted her head to look at it resting there. ". . . and won thy love . . . doing thee injuries."

Among the attendant statuary, Adeline turned her head, took a silent step.

Walter said quietly, "But I will wed thee in another key, with pomp, and triumph, and with revelling."

Virginia let her bow fall, raised a hand as if to brush Walter's hand away like an insect; but she just put her fingers on his.

Adeline took two long steps, said sharply, "Happy be Theseus, our renowned Duke!"

"Thanks, good Egeus. What's the news with thee?"

INTERVIEWER

Egeus is a man?

DR. GORDON

Apparently. A parent, anyway. (He pauses, as if waiting for a laugh that does not come.)

Egeus has a daughter, Hermia. Hermia is supposed to marry Demetrius, a nice young Athenian manly fellow of a lad, but Hermia's fallen in love with Lysander, another nice young etcetera, who's so equal in virtue to Demetrius that for four hundred years nobody's been able to tell them apart without a program. But it *does* matter to Hermia, and Athens has this serious parental consent law—Shakespeare didn't make this up, by the way.

"I beg the ancient privilege of Athens," Adeline said, her voice rising to a cackle, her hands in claws, "as she is mine, I may dispose of her: which shall be either to this gentleman . . ." Egeus spread wings over Mark. "Or . . . to her *death*, according to our law, *immediately* provided in that case." She took a step toward Paris as Hermia; Paris spun to face Duke Theseus and dropped to her knees.

Walter/Theseus reminded Paris/Hermia coolly and impassively that the law of Athens was, after all, the law, and parents were to be obeyed. He looked into space, not at the quietly pleading Hermia;

but he didn't miss Hippolyta's recovering her bow and selecting another arrow. In what might have been a conciliatory voice, he offered Hermia an alternative to Demetrius or Death: a convent and a vow of chastity. Hippolyta shot the arrow squarely between his feet.

INTERVIEWER

How long does it take to teach them to play like this?

DR. GORDON

It isn't necessary to teach people to play. It's with time and society that they learn play is foolish, a distraction from the goals of wealth and empire. It's necessary to *un*teach that.

But to answer your question, we spend three weeks on improvisation games and independent reading before running through the play together.

INTERVIEWER

Before a full rehearsal.

DR. GORDON

Before we read together at all. I *do* mean what I say. "Rehearsal" implies that it doesn't really count, and for our purposes *everything* counts. As for "full," no, we don't do little bits here and there. If you ate a bean yesterday, a carrot today, and a little piece of beef tomorrow, would you say you'd had stew three days running?

The two male suitors, Mark as Demetrius and Howard as Lysander, had stepped forward to flank Hermia. Mark said "Relent, sweet Hermia, and Lysander, yield thy crazéd title to my certain right." There was nothing very certain in his voice, and something a little crazed. Howard paused with his mouth open, looking up at the other suitor, a full head taller than him: he swallowed and said "You have her father's love, Demetrius. Let me have Hermia's—do *you* marry him."

Demetrius scratched his head and looked at Egeus, as if seriously considering the offer. Egeus fluttered and squawked. Theseus reiterated that the law was the law and Hermia was up against it; then he departed with the court, Egeus, and Demetrius, who followed his future father-in-law rather like a large bumbling puppy. He paused to throw a big smooch at Hermia, who wiped it off her cheek and scraped it from her delicate fingers like a stranger's snot.

Hermia and Lysander dithered in romantic silence for a minute or so, looking at each other, and here, and there.

Dr. Gordon said very quietly, "You may use the books."

Howard said, "For all that I could ever read . . ." He froze for just an instant, then went on: "Could ever hear by tale or history . . ." He looked up from the book, straight into Paris's eyes, and there was a sudden light in his face. "The course of true love never did run smooth." He looked down again, and then, perhaps too fast, said, "But either it was different in blood—"

"O cross!" Paris said, "too high to be enthralled to low."

Howard was still half-paralyzed. "Or else misgraffèd in respect of years—"

"O spite!" Paris's voice was sharp but not raised, a quiet ache. "Too old to be engaged to young."

"Or else it stood upon the choice of friends—"

"O . . . hell to choose . . . love . . . by another's eyes."

They went on for two dozen more lines, but there was nothing more to compare to that first shock. No one else moved at all.

Then Adeline stumbled forward. Howard said, "Look, here comes Helena," and she plunged between the two of them as if she saw neither.

Helena was in love with Demetrius, of course—how else should it be a romantic comedy?—and her distraction was not much reduced on hearing of Hermia and Lysander's plan to elope on the following night. Left alone on stage, Helena decided, "I will go tell him of fair Hermia's flight," to prove to Demetrius Hermia's lack of affection for him. In her closing lines, "Herein mean I to enrich my pain, to have his sight thither and back again," there was a distinct touch of Egeus's vulture cackle.

INTERVIEWER

It must be confusing to have each act—*player* perform so many parts.

DR. GORDON

Sometimes it is hard to tell who is who, yes.

"Is all our company here?" Paris stood in the center of the stage, book in both hands, while the others shuffled in from all around her.

Howard came in with long, Rudy Valentino steps; he struck a profile and sat down hard. "You were best to call 'em gen'rally, man by man, accordin' to the scrip."

Paris gave Howard a doubtful look. "Here is the scroll of every man's name which is thought fit through all Athens to play in our interlude before the Duke and the Duchess, on his wedding-day at night."

"Fir-r-r-st," Howard said, "good Peter Quince, say what the play treats on, then read the names of the actors, and so grow to a *point.*"

"Marry, our play is—" she squinted through imaginary eyeglasses—"*The Most Lamentable Comedy*—" another squint—"*and Most Cruel Death of Pyramus and Thisbe.*"

"A very good piece of work, I assure you," Howard said, "and a merry."

The other players gaped at him.

"Now, good Peter Quince, call forth your actors by the scroll. Masters, spread yourselves." Howard stretched out his arms, bowling Virginia over; his left fist landed on Mark, who looked at it as if it had fallen from the sky.

Paris/Quince said, "Answer as I call you. Nick Bottom, the weaver."

"Ready!" Howard sprang up. "Name what part I am for, and proceed."

"You, Nick Bottom, are set down for Pyramus."

"What is Pyramus? A lover or a tyrant?"

"A lover," Paris said, "that kills himself most gallant for love."

Howard mused. "That will take some tears in the performing of it."

INTERVIEWER

How many died?

DR. GORDON

One in four.

INTERVIEWER

In absolute numbers—

DR. GORDON

In absolute numbers *what?* Would ten thousand adequately horrify? A hundred thousand? Or do we only count graves in millions now?

Suppose you had a mother and father. A brother and sister. One of you dies. Does that matter?

INTERVIEWER

But the figures—

DR. GORDON

They were never meant as death camps. There was a sincerity—a kind of sincerity, at least—in the word "Re-Education." Re-education through good will, firm ideology, and the drug LX, of course.

We believe that no one died in the first six months. We have a few paper records from that period, and because we do not trust them, we have opened the graves. As I say, if any prisoners died in the first six months, the bodies are well hidden.

Mark, as Snug the carpenter, said "Have you the lion's part written? If it be so, pray give it me, for I am . . . slow of study." He put a finger to his mouth.

"You may do it extempore," Quince said kindly, "for it is nothing but roaring."

"Let me play the lion too," Bottom shouted. "I will roar, that it will do any man's heart good to hear me. I will roar, that I will make the Duke say, 'Let him roar again, let him roar again!'"

Walter, who was currently Snout the tinker, gave his head a tilt of ducal disapproval.

"And you should do it too terribly," Quince lectured Bottom, "you would fright the Duchess and the ladies—" Virginia showed a bit of surprise that a mere lion should worry Hippolyta—"that they would shriek; and that were enough to hang us all."

"That would hang us all," the players chorused, nodding among themselves, "every mother's son."

INTERVIEWER

Have people been hanged for bad acting?

DR. GORDON

(offhand)

Some have certainly 'scaped the noose by good acting. And those who own the rope and the scaffold have certainly hanged those who have frightened them.

INTERVIEWER

There were tribunals, after the liberation. Executions.

DR. GORDON

Hangings, necks broken, drawers soiled, slow writhing strangulations, bodies mutely protesting the deaths of their brains . . .

There were one hundred forty-seven public executions. Forty had refused to take LX, and freely confessed their actions. Another eighty had not taken the drug, but tried to pretend they had; a grave mistake. Four were cleared of having been in the camps at all, though a bit late. The rest were LX subjects, convicted on circumstantial evidence. It was a while before we understood the real difficulty of telling Group A from Group B.

INTERVIEWER

A and B?

DR. GORDON

We could say Guards and Prisoners, but some did more than guard. Torturers and Victims, but not all tortured and some fought back. Tyrants and Lovers . . . sometimes, perhaps. There are no words to mean what we want to say; so we say Group A, Group B.

INTERVIEWER

Nonjudgmental.

DR. GORDON

Judicious.

INTERVIEWER

And the difference . . . ?

DR. GORDON

Oh, Group B is the majority party. The ones who own the rope now.

The Athenian workmen sorted out the rest of their roles and agreed to meet in the wood the following night for rehearsal. They went out by their several exits.

"End of Act One," Dr. Gordon called out. "Coffee break."

Virginia had brought in her milk ration ("Go ahead, I never drink the stuff.") and Mark a box of vanilla wafers, so they sat around the stage sipping and nibbling in great content.

Howard said, "The fairies come on next, right?"

Dr. Gordon said, "That's right. Walter is Oberon and Paris is Titania. And Virginia's playing Puck. The rest of you will fill in as Titania's fairy court." He nodded slightly at Howard. "When you're not otherwise engaged."

Mark said, "Should we have something, for the fairy parts? Some kind of costumes or something?"

Dr. Gordon said, "Do you want them?"

Adeline said, "Not whole costumes."

Howard said, "No. But you mean, say, hats when we're the fairies?"

Mark took the empty cookie box and put it on his head. Walter laughed out loud.

Dr. Gordon said, "It's a lovely improv, Mark, but I don't think it's very elfin." He leaned on the lectern. "Let's think about this. How do you see fairies?"

"In my mind's eye," Walter said, with a small silly grin.

"Small. Tiny," Virginia said.

Mark said, "That leaves me out," and they all laughed.

"Fairies," Paris said, in a barely audible grumble. "Sugarplum . . ."

Virginia said, "They *are* supposed to be little. The play talks about them hiding in acorns."

Walter said, "The characters talk about a lot of things that actors can't really do."

Adeline said, "We *could* play small," and stood on tiptoe, her hands arched at shoulder level, peeping over something.

Virginia said, "More than that. They can be invisible. They're light, and graceful. They can *fly.*"

They were all silent; and then they were all looking at Paris.

She looked back, turning her head rapidly from one to another. Then, furiously, she tore the laces of her sneakers loose, kicked them across the floor, and sprang up to stand on one foot. "Is this what you had in mind?" She whirled, leapt to the other foot. "Is this elfin enough for you?"

Walter looked at his own shoes for a long moment, then pulled them off, stood up, flexed his feet. "Yeah. That's good."

Paris stopped, nearly stumbled. Hands were raised to catch her, but she did not fall. Her left foot came down with a bump. "And suppose . . ." she said hesitantly, "the workmen, the players, wear work shoes. Heavy ones."

Adeline said, "Clogs, maybe, so we can just kick them off to change."

Dr. Gordon said, "And the Athenian nobles?"

"Sandals, right?" Mark said. "The Athenians wore sandals."

Dr. Gordon said, "There is a property room down that hall, the heavy door on the right. I would you would make free with it."

Paris hung back as the others went down the hall. She turned to Dr. Gordon, opened her mouth.

"Sssh," Dr. Gordon said. "When you're sure of what you want to say, tell them. That's the whole idea."

INTERVIEWER

Tell me about the drug.

DR. GORDON

Lethe Experimental. LX. Sometimes called Compound Sixty.
Administered by intravenous injection, it produces brief nausea,
and drowsiness and disorientation lasting between one and three
hours. By intramuscular injection, the effects are subdued but
prolonged. LX readily crosses the blood-brain barrier.

INTERVIEWER

And its main effect?

DR. GORDON

I assumed that was the part you already knew. Lethe
Experimental causes a loss of long-term memory. It seems to act
as a kind of phage, attacking memory RNA.

INTERVIEWER

How far back does the memory loss go?

DR. GORDON

All psychoactives have drastically different effects on
different people. LX is certainly no exception. Further, the
doses—and circumstances of doses—were different in almost
every case.

Think of raindrops on a train window . . . how they find their
own, unpredictable paths; some split off early, some cross the
entire pane. That is Compound Sixty in the human brain.

INTERVIEWER

Then—

DR. GORDON

I'm answering your question; it's not a simple answer. You *know*
we've lost the camps, and they were in operation for five years.
Some people have had their internal time completely reset to
sometime in the past; others know the correct date but have no
useful recollections since adolescence. Most who were college
students remember nothing of college—you can read what you
like into that. I had to take a recertification test for my medical
license, and I'll swear I did *better* on it than I would have before,
though I'd spent several years in practice.

We have only a very few cases of people forgetting their
names—we think those may be, you'll pardon the expression,
natural amnesia rather than drug effects. But most people have
lost the memory of parents, siblings, a spouse, children—rarely a
whole family, but almost always one or two people.

INTERVIEWER

Could some of that reflect wishful thinking? The desire to
forget someone?

DR. GORDON

(He considers his response for a long time. When he finally
speaks, it is with a distance that approaches contempt.)

The data do not support that hypothesis.

Virginia adjusted the rolled cuffs of her jeans, loosened her shoulders, and glided barefoot into center stage, where Adeline, shoeless as well, was busily miming what looked like mail sorting. Beside her stood a tall hat rack that the players had seized from the prop room, to stand in for the fairy forest.

"How now, spirit!" Puck said, in a voice that really did not seem to be Virginia's; too high, too careless.

"Over hill, over dale," Adeline chanted, "through bush, through briar, over park, over pale, through flood, through fire," and explained in verse her fairy duties before Titania Queen of Spirits should arrive. "I must go seek some dew-drops here, and hang a pearl in every cowslip's ear." She unslung an apparently massive burden of dew from the bare tree, shouldered it.

"The King doth keep his revels here tonight," Puck said, "take heed the Queen come not within his sight: for Oberon is passing fell and wrath, because that she as her attendant hath a lovely boy, stol'n from an Indian king—"

"*Cut!*" Paris said, a fully contained shriek.

"You can't," Dr. Gordon said, smoothly, firmly. "You're not in contact. Puck, go on."

"She never had so sweet a changeling," Virginia coolly went on, explaining that Oberon wanted the child, but Titania would not give him up; there was Trouble in Fairyland. "But room, fairy! Here comes Oberon!"

"And here my mistress," Adeline said, her voice all there's-a-fire-in-the-woodpile-*now*, "would that she were gone!"

Adeline's fairy ducked and doubled back behind Paris as Titania. Paris seemed composed now, standing straight. Walter, as Oberon, strode in from the opposite direction. Dead center, Puck cocked an elbow and leaned nonchalantly against the hatrack.

"Ill met by moonlight, proud Titania."

"What, jealous Oberon? Fairies, skip hence; I have forsworn his bed and company."

Puck looked from one fairy monarch to the other, shuddered, and held up the playbook to hide her face.

It got worse. Oberon and Titania's quarrel, to hear them describe it, was turning the whole natural world sidewise and shaking it: fogs, fevers, rotten corn, early winter. "And this same progeny of evils comes," Titania said, "from our debate—from *our* dissention: we are their parents and original."

Puck turned her head, like a spectator following a tennis ball in play.

"Do you amend it then," Oberon said, with a bad imitation of indifference. Then he said, "Why should Titania cross her Oberon?" with an even worse imitation of sweetness. "I do but beg a little changeling boy . . ."

Paris spat back at him, speaking of the child's mother, a priestess, and a friend, of Titania's—"But she, being mortal, of that boy did die," she said, all cold metal. "*And for her sake do I rear up her boy. And for her sake I will not part with him.*"

Oberon took a moment to absorb this. "How long within this wood . . . intend you stay?"

"Perchance till after Theseus's wedding day," she said idly; then, almost offhand, "If you will patiently dance in our round, and see our moonlight revels . . . go with us. If not, shun me, and I will spare your haunts."

"Give me that boy, and I will go with thee."

"Not for thy fairy kingdom. Fairies, away!" She turned to go, then turned back and smiled thinly at Oberon. "We shall chide downright if I longer stay."

Titania's court departed. "Well, go thy way," Oberon muttered. "Thou shalt not from this grove till I torment thee for this injury."

Puck turned, still holding the book in front of her face, and began to slink after Titania's train.

"My gentle Puck," Oberon said crisply. Puck froze. "Come hither." She did.

The Fairy King told Puck of a flower whose nectar had the power to make a sleeper fall in love with the first thing seen on awaking. He ordered Puck to bring a flower to him.

"I'll put a girdle round about the earth in forty minutes," Virginia said, and was gone, with a *whoosh* of takeoff.

Oberon explained his plan to twist Titania's mind. "But who comes here? I am invisible—" He took a step back and put his own script in front of his face.

Mark, now wearing Demetrius's sandals, shuffled in, apparently alone. He turned, revealing Adeline as Helena clutching the tail of his shirt, dragging after him on her knees.

"I love thee not," Demetrius said, "therefore pursue me not." He turned this way and that, Helena remaining firmly attached. "Hence, get thee gone, and follow me no more!"

"You draw me, you hard-hearted adamant," she said, and jumped up to hang on his shoulders.

Oberon lowered his book long enough to display a broad, malicious grin; then he hastily raised it again.

"Do I entice you?" Demetrius said. "Do I speak you fair? Or do I rather not in plainest truth tell you I do not, nor do I cannot, love you?" He twisted his shoulders, trying to shake Helena off—but instead he threw her off; she landed hard on her shoulder and hip, with a groan.

The players stared. Dr. Gordon held out a hand, and they did not move.

Adeline threw her arms around Mark's legs and hugged. Mark went down on first backside then back. He waggled his head.

Adeline crawled on top of him. "And even for that do I love you the more," Helena said. She grabbed him by the shoulders and shook him furiously, bouncing his head on the stage. "Spurn me!" *bonk* "Strike me!" *kabump* "Neglect me!" *wham* "Lose me!" She fell on him, exhausted. "Only give me leave, unworthy as I am, to follow you." She slithered off.

Dazed, Demetrius sat up. "Tempt not," he said dizzily, "th' hatred of my spirit . . ." He stood uncertainly, then said with gathering speed, "for I am sick when I do look on you." He turned his back, bent over, made a dreadful noise.

The other players were folded double with silent laughter.

The mismatched lovers went on for a while longer, until Demetrius fled, and Helena resumed the chase.

INTERVIEWER

You insist that they make no changes at all in the dialogue. But cutting and altering plays—particularly Shakespeare—is very common.

DR. GORDON

Aye, it is common.

(a beat)

Tampering with someone else's construction is a liberty many take, but to me it is a privilege one has to earn. You have to know what you're doing, at least well enough to argue the point.

My people aren't theatre people—at least, not before the suffered sea-change of Compound Sixty. So the rule is that they read all of the words. Even if most of them roll off their tongues and are lost in the air, a few will bounce. Resonate. Explode in the mind. And they can't, *I* can't, tell *which* words, before the moment.

INTERVIEWER

You see play therapy as a kind of discovery process?

DR. GORDON

Learning is a big enough word for it. Someone once said, "joy is the light that shines into unsuspected chambers of the heart."

INTERVIEWER

So learning the truth makes people happy, you would say.

DR. GORDON

What *I would say* is that denying people the truth makes them frustrated: and frustrated, ignorant people are not happy.

Puck returned from her travels bearing the flower of enforced love. Virginia's hand was arched, two fingers above, the thumb below: unmistakably gripping a hypodermic syringe. She placed it on her script held as a tray, handed it to Oberon, then made as if stripping off rubber gloves.

Oberon picked up an invisible syringe, examined it with narrowed eyes and a flat, clinical smile. He then passed back the tray, and told Puck to administer the flower juice to the young Athenian fellow she would find elsewhere in the wood.

"Fear not, my lord," Puck said, "thy servant shall do so." She snapped the script under one arm, saluted, turned smartly, and marched off.

Still examining the hypodermic, humming faintly to himself, Oberon departed as well.

Titania and her fairy court—all the players except Walter as lurking Oberon—entered. After a long yawn, Paris/Titania ordered her host to sing, dance a turn, and then go hunting the creatures of the night. "Sing me now asleep; then to your offices, and let me rest." She curled up on the floor at the rear of the stage, and the others sang her to sleep.

"Hence, away!" Adeline said just above a whisper. "Now all is well: one aloof stand sentinel." She waved the rest away, then crouched, hands folded on one knee, at the edge of the stage.

Hands swept in from the darkness beyond. One sealed the fairy's mouth; others, disembodied in the dim light, pulled her out of sight.

Oberon came in, daintily wiping his hands, scraping a foot clean on the ground. He knelt by sleeping Titania, drew out the syringe. He spoke softly, kindly, even lovingly. "What thou seest when thou dost wake, do it for thy true love take; love, and languish, for his sake.... Be it ounce, or cat, or bear, pard, or boar with bristled hair, in thy eye that shall appear when thou wak'st—it is thy dear. *Wake*—" he enclosed her face and neck with his arm, stabbed into her throat; she kicked once and was still—"when some vile thing is near."

Oberon stood, backed away, watching to left and right, and disappeared into the night. A moment later, Titania too faded from sight.

INTERVIEWER

You said the camps were not intended as death camps. How did they get that way?

DR. GORDON

One life at a time.

INTERVIEWER

You said no one died for the first few months.

DR. GORDON

As far as we know. (smiles) Whatever that means.

(a beat)

Do you want me to guess?

INTERVIEWER

I'd like your opinions. Your theories.

DR. GORDON

Hypotheses. There's a difference.

All right. First, I think re-education didn't work. LX doesn't turn people into blank slates; it's unreliable, as close to random as doesn't matter. I think someone got frustrated, and took out that frustration on someone else. Then, in the calm after the storm, whoever did it wished it hadn't been done.

Compound Sixty can do that. Can make it didn't happen. And once that was realized, well then, why stop? How many wishes would the genie in the bottle grant?

INTERVIEWER

More than three.

DR. GORDON

It wasn't really three, in the original story, you know. Aladdin had as many wishes as he wanted.

He did, however, eventually have enough, and set his slave free.

INTERVIEWER

And lived happily ever after?

DR. GORDON

No. Not in the original. Muslim stories always end, "they lived happily, until Death came for them."

(he sighs)

Then there's Hypothesis B. No time of innocence. Just the knowledge, just the will, just the act. And soon it was all there in memory: whether 'tis nobler in the mind to suffer the slings and arrows of outrageous fortune, or to take arms against a sea of troubles, and by opposing . . . end them.

Lysander and Hermia entered, hand in hand. "Fair love," Howard said sweetly, "you faint with wandering in the wood, and to speak troth . . . I have forgot our way."

Hermia stopped and stared at him.

Howard shrugged, spread his hands. "We'll . . . rest us, Hermia," he said, squeezing the words out like toothpaste, "if you-u-u think it guh-guh-good? And, uh . . . tarry. For the, uh, comfort. Of the day."

Paris tapped her foot. "Be it so, Lysander." She sat down. "Find you out a bed; for I upon this bank will rest my head."

Lysander dropped quickly to his knees, began brushing the ground to receive Hermia's head. "One turf shall serve as pillow for us both," he said.

Hermia sat straight up.

Howard said, "One heart, one, uh, bed, two, er, bosoms, and one troth—" He was stopped by Paris's forefinger pressed hard against his forehead.

"Nay, good Lysander; for my sake, my dear . . . lie farther off." She pointed with her other hand. "Do not lie so near."

"O take the sense, sweet, of my innocence!" He raised his hands, palm up—and flopped forward, his head landing in Hermia's lap. Somewhat muffled, he went on: "Lff tks th' mnng'f lff's cnf'renth."

She stuck her fingers in his ears, lifted his head and shook it.

They finally agreed on an acceptable distance between bunks, and slept.

INTERVIEWER

There is, of course, some corollary evidence.

DR. GORDON

You mean the Castillo Diary.

INTERVIEWER

Yes.

DR. GORDON

Twenty little pieces of paper torn from an examining-table roll, written on with shoe-polish ink and a split fingernail for a pen, crumpled and stained from their hiding places. It names sixteen persons guilty of rape, torture, murder . . . and so forth, and so on.

INTERVIEWER

Do you believe it's a fake, as some claim?

DR. GORDON

I believe it is absolutely genuine, and that everyone it names is guilty. Do you know why?

INTERVIEWER

Tell me.

DR. GORDON

The mistake. If the diary were deliberate false evidence, it would be complete and precise in its descriptions, so that we could readily identify everyone named. And one or two of those people would be immediately proven innocent—dead elsewhere, cleared by other documents. So if it *were* false, it would in fact be mostly true, but its slight falsehood would free the truly guilty— isn't that a lovely paradox?

But. While Castillo named names and crimes—you've read it; will you ever forget the acts of James Edward Sloan?—there is nothing to pick out one man named James Edward Sloan from any other, and when you hang a name, a man's neck breaks.

The diary is real because it is useless: Castillo did not realize what it would have to prove.

INTERVIEWER

Yet three of the names were tried and executed. And five more committed suicide.

DR. GORDON

What's in a name?

Puck appeared, pacing, hands behind her back. "Through the forest have I gone, but Athenian found I none on whose eyes I might approve this flower's force in stirring love. Night and silence——" She nearly tripped over Lysander. "Who is here?" She examined the body, picked up one of Howard's feet by its sandal strap. "Weeds of Athens he doth wear." She wiped her forehead with a *whew!* gesture. "This is he my master said despiséd the Athenian maid—and here the maiden, sleeping sound, on the dank and dirty ground."

She raised Lysander's wrist, took his pulse, gave the injection without any fuss but for one comic twitch of Lysander's legs. "I must now to Oberon," Puck said, and ran off.

Demetrius came on, breathing hard, looking back over his shoulder. He turned—and saw Helena in front of him, in the pose of a football tackle.

"Stay," she said, "though thou kill me, sweet Demetrius!"

They exchanged a few brisk words, and then Demetrius executed a downfield run, with a quick feint to the hat rack and a dodge past the defense.

Helena jumped in frustration, slamming both feet on the ground. She paced back and forth, limping a little as she bemoaned her state, and sat down on something soft. "But who is here? Lysander, on the ground?" He snored, loud as a diesel horn. "Dead, or asleep? I see no blood, no wound—Lysander, if you live, good sir, awake!"

His eyes sprang open. He sighed from the soul. "And run through fire I will, for thy sweet sake."

Helena looked around, alarmed.

"Transparent Helena!" Howard said.

Adeline looked down at herself, patted her ribs, held her hands up to the light.

Lysander professed his love for her. She decided that he was mocking her, over her crummy luck in pursuing Demetrius. He pressed on, in terms that might make anyone doubtful, until she fled. Lysander paused long enough to deliver a nasty farewell to his still-sleeping former beloved, and skipped lightly offstage in pursuit of his new steady girl.

Hermia woke up. "Help me, Lysander, help me! Do thy best to pluck this crawling serpent from my breast . . . !" She looked around, rapped her knuckles on the tree, sighed. "Ay me, for pity! What a dream was here—" Her face contorted. "A *dream*," Paris said, not in Hermia's voice, nor Titania's, nor Quince's. "A child . . . in a play, not a dream—" which was not in the script.

Dr. Gordon looked straight at her, his hands and face tight.

Adeline came in, put her bony hands on Paris's shoulders. Paris twisted and cried out. Adeline said, "We're in *contact*, okay, Doc? *Cut*, already."

Dr. Gordon nodded. The others came in and circled Paris. Most sat; Walter stayed standing, rocking in the wooden-soled clogs he had put on for the next scene, knotting his fingers together. Something haunted his handsome face. Virginia knelt a little distance away, spoke in a flat, unstrung voice. "Something came back, didn't it. Was it your name? Your name wasn't Paris, was it. Not really."

"No," she said. "But no . . . no, I knew my name and I wanted to change—I took it, but I didn't take it *from* anyone—"

"It's all right," Adeline said, and hugged her again. "Not your name, then. What was it? Take your time. We've all got plenty of time."

"There was a child," Paris said miserably.

"Whose child?" Virginia said, with a coolness more cruel than cruelty; she twitched her head away.

"Mine, I think—I think she was mine. Or he, I don't—at a play, a child, mine—"

"She's hyperventilating," Dr. Gordon said. "Have her breathe slowly and evenly."

Slowly, his face a statuary mask, Howard put out a hand, touched Paris on the breastbone. "E-e-easy," he said. "Breathe with me, now. One . . . two."

Adeline said, "In a play, you said. Do you mean, at a play?"

"Yes. At a play. With fairies. Sugar—sugarplum fairies. I called her Sugarplum. That was it. A girl called Sugarplum, but her *name*, her name . . ."

"One . . . *two*. One . . ."

"I know that play," Mark said. "*The Nutcracker Suite*. Do you remember that name, Paris?"

"No. . . ."

"One. . . . *two*."

Virginia, her face turned from the others, was silently mouthing, *I'm sorry. I'm sorry.*

Mark said, "Do you remember anyone else at the play? A husband? A friend? A friend's child?"

Walter looked at Mark. "Were you in the theatre?"

"People went to *The Nutcracker Suite* show in groups," Mark said, slowly, tightly, "families, or mothers with all their children. Every Christmas." He stopped, gnawed his lip, but the words seemed to struggle up on their own: "I was a train conductor. Every Christmas, I saw people going to and from the city, to see that show. I never saw it. People always took their children. I never had any children."

INTERVIEWER

What effects, precisely, do you hope the play will produce?

[DR. GORDON turns his head, frowns, then turns back to the PLAYERS without speaking.]

INTERVIEWER

How do you know when the therapy is successful?

DR. GORDON

A smile is a serious symptom, laughter a dangerous one. The critical signs are difficult to discuss in polite company.

INTERVIEWER

Could you be . . . a little more specific?

DR. GORDON

Wait for the epilogue.

"We can stop for a while," Dr. Gordon said.

"No," Paris said, "I'll finish." The rest of the company drew back. She blew her nose, shut her eyes, and spoke: "Lysander, look how I do quake with fear . . . methought a serpent ate my heart away, and you sat smiling at his cruel prey. Lysander! What, removed? Lysander, lord!" She looked around. "What, out of hearing? Gone? No sound, no word? Alack—*where are you?* Speak and if you hear, speak, of all loves!" She clutched the tree, pulled herself slowly upright. "I swoon almost with fear . . . No?"

Silence.

She put her fists on her hips. "Then I well perceive you are not nigh," she said, tapping a foot in annoyance. "Either death, or you, I'll find—immediately."

Applause.

The workmen assembled for their rehearsal, thumping in their wooden shoes.

"Are we all met?" Bottom the weaver said.

"Pat, pat," Peter Quince said, "and here's a marvelous convenient place for our rehearsal." Quince moved from place to place, pointing out the green plot to be used for stage, the hawthorn hedge for dressing room. Each time Paris crossed the stage, she carefully ducked under the tree in the middle.

Bottom intoned "*Pee*-tah Quince . . ." from somewhere in the backwoods of Richard Burton territory.

"What sayest thou, bully Bottom?" Quince said, in the voice of patience tried.

"There are things in this comedy of—" he dodged a look at his script—"Pyramus and Thisbe that will never please. First, Pyramus must draw a sword to kill himself, which the ladies cannot abide. How answer you that?"

"By'r'lakin," said Walter as Snout the tinker, "a parlous fear." He was looking directly at Virginia, who as Starveling the tailor said, "I believe we must leave the killing out, when all is done."

INTERVIEWER

When was the idea of . . . that Group A would . . .

DR. GORDON

Even people with whole memories find it hard to date the birth of ideas. Some believe that the idea was there, in seed at least, all along—that, as the purpose of the camps was re-education, eventually everyone would be re-educated.

The idea, in what became its actual form, was certainly there by the third year. Documents were being destroyed as a matter of course by then. And everyone in Group B was receiving LX at least once a month.

By the beginning of the fourth year there was a complete plan. We have copies; there was no attempt to destroy them. There are sections covering change of clothing, destruction of personal evidence, creating marks of . . . physical abuse—and finally the administration of LX, in diminishing circles of givers and recipients. (distantly) Mathematicians call that a Josephus problem: as the moving point stabs, who is counted out, who is counted in.

By that time, of course, there was no longer even the pretense of re-education. The camps were about two things only: the systematic degradation of human beings and the systematic destruction of the evidence thereof. Burying Group A within Group B, shuffling the deck so that the kings and queens of

Lesser Hell, the knaves and the jokers, would be lost among the faceless numbers.

INTERVIEWER

How many . . . Group A's were there?

DR. GORDON

Of those who came out . . . of us . . . one in eight. This is a Diophantine problem, however: from A subtract one hundred twenty hanged, from B four the same. Include blank variables for those lost to the hunger of the mob, suicide, the wasted labor of the rope merchants.

Hark in thine ear: change places, and which is the justice, which is the thief?

Quince ruffled furiously through the script, presumably looking for killing to cut.

Bottom stood up. "Not a whit! I have a device to make all well." He raised a hand, put the other in his shirt. "Write me a *proh*-logue, and let the prologue seem to say we will do no harm with our swords, and that Pyramus is not killed indeed."

Quince peered over her spectacles.

"And for the more better assurance," Bottom went on, "tell them that I, *Peeh*-ramus, am *not* Pyramus, but—" he mimed a drum roll— "Bottom the weaver! This will put them out of fear."

"Well . . ." Quince said, then gave up. "We will have such a prologue."

They worried about the Lion frightening the court ladies, and getting moonlight into the chamber where the play would go on, and the difficulties of showing a wall onstage. "You can never bring in a wall," Snout said, and leaned against the hat rack tree.

As they finally settled down to rehearsal, Virginia slipped out of her wooden shoes, circled the tree and came up behind the nervously directing Peter Quince.

"What hempen homespuns have we swaggering here," Puck said,

"so near the cradle of the Fairy Queen? What, a play toward? I'll be auditor . . . an actor too, perhaps, if I see cause."

Quince said, "Speak, Pyramus. Thisbe, stand forth."

Howard spread his feet, flexed his knees, raised both his hands above his head. Adeline, playing Flute playing Thisbe, leaned forward curiously.

"Thizzzbeee . . ." Howard said, then coughed and dropped his voice an octave. "Thisbe, the flowers of odious savors sweet—"

"Odorous, *odorous,*" Quince said through clenched teeth.

Bottom paused, checked his script, nodded gravely. "Odorous savors sweet; so hath thy breath, my dearest Thisbe dear. But hark, a voice! Stay thou but here awhile, and I will by and by to thee appear." He turned, sweeping an imaginary cape for several feet in all directions, and strode offstage.

"A stranger Pyramus than e'er played here," Puck said, and skipped lightly after him.

As the play went on alongside them, Bottom leaned forward to study his lines, while Puck peered over his shoulder. Suddenly alight with inspiration, she took a pair of socks out of her pocket and arranged one over each of Bottom's ears. Then she picked up a length of rope, took a step back, coiled her arm and pinned the tail on the donkey. Bottom's eyes popped.

"Pyramus, enter," Peter Quince was saying, "your cue is past; it is 'never tire.'"

Flute swallowed, flipped back a page in the script, and repeated, "As true as truest horse that yet would never tire."

Sock ears drooping, rope tail tucked into his waistband, Bottom clumped back on stage. The other players goggled at him.

Bottom looked at them, smiled with delight at his reception, adjusted the collar of his shirt, and announced, "If I were fair, Thisbe, I were only thine."

"O monstrous!" Quince cried, "O strange! We are haunted! Pray, masters! Fly, masters! *Hellllp!*"

The players ran every which way, while Puck chased them, shaking with laughter. Bottom, sure he was being made fun of, wandered past the tree. Beyond, the huddling Peter Quince rolled over and stretched, kicking off her shoes, and was again the sleeping Titania.

Bottom sang, in a quavery voice, whistling in the graveyard: "The o-o-ousel cock, so black of hue, with orange-tawny bil-l-l, the throstle with his note so true, the wren with little quil-l-l . . ."

Titania stirred, smiled, stretched her arms in welcome. "What angel wakes me from my flowery bed?"

                          INTERVIEWER
What about long-term effects of the drug?

                          DR. GORDON
We haven't discovered any. So far as we know, LX does not affect the ability to form new memories, nor to learn, even when administered continuously over a long period of time.

                          INTERVIEWER
Was that done?

                          DR. GORDON
We believe that some people were given LX on almost a daily basis.

                          INTERVIEWER
Why?

                          DR. GORDON
Experimentally. To see what would happen. That's obvious enough. I can think of another reason.

                          (a BEAT)
I imagine you'd like to hear what it is?

                          INTERVIEWER
Yes.

DR. GORDON

To go back to the same victim over and over, and have that person not know it: to begin the humiliation new on a daily basis. To have this . . . experiment in pain be the first on a mind with no tolerance, a body with no conditioned responses. Do you know the Hindu story, of the renewable houris of Paradise?

"I pray thee, gentle mortal," Titania breathed, "sing again: mine ear is much enamor'd of thy note . . . so is mine eye enthrallèd to thy shape; and thy fair virtue's force perforce doth move me—on the first view!—to swear I love thee."

Bottom shivered, making his ears and tail flop about. "Methinks, mistress, you should have little reason for that. And yet, to say the truth, reason and love keep little company together nowadays. . . . The more the pity that some honest neighbors will not make them friends."

Titania, infatuated with the puzzled but delighted Bottom, summoned her fairy court to bring him his desires; Peaseblossom, Mote, Cobweb, and Mustardseed hastened to comply. As the idyll faded from view, Oberon reappeared, wondering with elfin malice what Titania had seen on awakening. Puck tripped in, and reported on events, briskness overcome by glee at the disorder in the wood that night.

Then Paris and Mark came to the tree, sandaled as Hermia and Demetrius.

"Stand close," Oberon said, "this is the same Athenian." He went invisible behind his script. Puck began to do likewise, then stopped; holding the book just below her eyes, she crept over to Demetrius and peered up at him from several angles. "This is the woman," Puck said, "but *not* this the man."

Hermia was demanding to know why Demetrius had murdered Lysander, and insisting that he kill her as well. Demetrius, who had no recollection of killing anybody, was trying to explain this to Hermia, pointing out that as far as he, Demetrius, knew, Lysander was alive and well—not, of course, that he would lose much sleep if someone *had* done for the guy. Finally Hermia stormed off: "See me no more, if he be dead or no." And Demetrius, exhausted in more ways than one, went to sleep on the ground.

Puck had crept halfway across the stage when Oberon snapped, "What hast thou done?" As Puck slunk back, holding an extremely forced grin, Oberon chewed her out for having love-potioned the wrong lover. Puck pointed out that it was hardly *her* fault that one person out of a million actually *meant* all that true-to-thee-alone stuff, but accepted instructions to begin setting things right again, beginning with bringing Helena in to make up with Demetrius. "I go! I go! See how I go, faster than arrow from the Tartar's bow—"

Oberon crouched by Demetrius. "Flower of this purple dye, hit with Cupid's archery, sink in apple of his eye: when his love he doth espy, let her shine as gloriously as the Venus of the sky. . . ." He shoved the needle in.

Puck backed onstage, beckoning with a curled finger. Along came Helena and Lysander, walking lightly, in some sort of trance. Puck gestured elaborately and snapped her fingers. Instantly the couple set to, Lysander furiously plighting troth and Helena insisting she was having none of his sick jokes, that she knew perfectly well he loved Hermia.

"*Demetrius* loves her," Lysander insisted, "and he loves not *you*—"

Oberon gave the snoozing Demetrius a swift kick. He sat up straight. "O Helen! Goddess, nymph, perfect, divine!"

Lysander and Helena turned and stared.

Demetrius plighted some troth of his own to Helena, who took it with no better grace than she had Lysander's.

Oberon and Puck watched this scene with the uttermost fairy bewilderment. Then, silently, Oberon counted heads, one, two, three, and gestured to Puck, who nodded and departed, to return in a moment leading Hermia.

Now it was a chorus for four voices. Everybody was in love, nobody believed anybody else's protestations, everybody got to make a short joke about Hermia. Oberon began banging his hand against the side of his head. Puck sat down comfortably in the middle of the squabble, an expression of sheer delight on her face.

Finally the boys decided to have it out like men, at swords' point, and marched off in step. The girls picked their own directions.

Oberon clasped his hands behind his back, strolled left, right. Puck smiled at him; he smiled back, crooked a finger. Puck got up and skipped toward him.

"*This* is *thy* negligence," Oberon yelled, driving Puck back halfway across the stage. "*Still* thou mistak'st——or else commit'st thy knaveries wilfully."

"Believe me, king of shadows, I mistook . . ." Puck began, and dissembled on for a bit before shrugging and admitting, "And so far am I glad it so did sort, as this their jangling I esteem a sport."

INTERVIEWER

Is there some kind of profile of those more likely to have been in Group A?

DR. GORDON
(disinterested)
You do so want it to be easy, don't you?

INTERVIEWER

Surely there must be *some* patterns, some psychological type—

DR. GORDON

Of course. We've lost our memories, but we haven't lost all human history. We know from it that people of middle authority, people who were already part of a system, used to passing orders along, were prime choices.

As far as evidence is concerned, there were certain types of offices where records were destroyed wholesale during the final stages. The police, naturally, and the army. The railroads. Hospitals and group medical practices. Universities. There are plenty of patterns to find, profiles to cast, if you wish. Or you can say that the search-and-burn units went where there were masses of material for them to find and destroy.

Of those who we are most sure were Group A—because they refused LX, and confessed it openly, the ones who *believed* even unto the end of the world—six were writers, four were poets. (barely controlling himself) A professor of classical literature told the court with the utmost pride that he had shot fifteen children cleanly through the head because they could not understand that value was an absolute.

They had faith . . . in a way that the train conductors did not.

Howard/Lysander came on stage, jabbing and slashing with an invisible sword. A step behind him came Virginia/Puck, carrying a box.

Lysander took up a fencer's stance, called out, "Where art thou, proud Demetrius? Speak thou now!"

Puck put the box on the floor, stood on it, cleared her throat, and said in a fair imitation of Mark's Demetrius, "Here, villain, drawn and ready. Where art thou?"

"I will be with thee straight," Lysander said, and charged offstage, right past the unseen fairy.

Mark/Demetrius entered from the opposite direction. From his pose, he was carrying something more than a sword—a two-handed battle-axe, perhaps, or a machine gun. "Lysander, speak again," he said.

Puck got down from the box, plodded across the stage until she was behind Demetrius, and arched herself in the best style of Errol Flynn swordplay. "Follow my voice; we'll try no manhood here."

Demetrius turned, growled, shouldered arms, and stamped off.

A few more tricks with voices in the dark, and the heroes both collapsed, still muttering challenges at each other, and slept. Before long Helena came by, weary and confused, and went to sleep as well—and of course Hermia arrived at last to make it a foursome.

"On the ground," Puck said, "sleep sound; I'll apply to your eye, gentle lover, remedy." She readied the syringe, plunged it into Lysander's throat. "When thou wak'st, thou tak'st true delight in the sight of thy former lady's eye; and the country proverb known, that every man should take his own, in your waking shall be shown." She stood, stretched, sighed. "Jack shall have Jill, nought shall go ill; the man shall have his mare again, and all shall be well."

Puck departed, leaving all four sleeping together.

INTERVIEWER

One in four died, one in eight of the survivors—

DR. GORDON

So that among any group of six there are eleven chances in twenty that at least one was Group A, and for their lives one and a half others are dead. Add a seventh player, and it's six in ten there's a villain among them, and another quarter-mortal past the hour of caring.

But can one be six-tenths a murderer, or three-quarters buried in the limepits?

(He removes one of his cufflinks, pulls down the cuff, shows his bare wrist to the light.)

No shackle scar here. What odds would you lay on the other hand?

INTERVIEWER

What are you saying, Doctor?

DR. GORDON

There is a wonderful passage in the plan documents, section four, paragraph eight. "Because the subjects have no memory of events, some of them can usefully be employed to confuse the evidence, particularly body evidence."

(He holds up his hands.) Isn't that amazing? It's *iambic pentameter,* and it even—

(reciting)
Because the subjects have no memory
Of èvents some of them can usefully—

INTERVIEWER

You mean that some of the prisoners—tortured their guards?

DR. GORDON

(He stops still, waits a moment to see if his point will be grasped. It isn't, and he continues, flatly and wearily:)

Supply the tools, give the order with authority, and the job will be done. We've known that for a very, very long time.

INTERVIEWER

But surely no guilt can attach—

DR. GORDON

I was discussing evidence. I haven't said a word about guilt.

Titania was still wooing the jackasserized Bottom with all the charms of the fairy kingdom—though Bottom kept surprising even himself with a desire for hay and dried peas. Oberon hung on the tree, watching the scene, his smile now soft and unvengeful.

As Titania and Bottom fell asleep, nestled together, the lark and the spiny echidna, Puck came in, looking exhausted.

"Welcome, good Robin," Oberon said, "see'st thou this sweet sight? Her dotage now I do begin to pity. . . ." He had the changeling child now, and was ready to release his Queen. He closed in, sat down behind her, slid the needle in most gently. "Be as thou wast wont to be, see as thou wast wont to see. . . ."

She gasped and awoke. "My Oberon! What visions I have seen! Methought I was enamored of an ass."

"There lies your love."

"How came these things to pass?" They all stopped, and quite a long moment went by before Paris continued, "Oh, how mine eyes do loathe his visage now. . . ."

Puck tugged off the sock ears and the rope tail. As Oberon and Titania danced, Virginia took off Howard's workingman's clogs and buckled on the sandals of Athens. Paris concluded the dance, slipped on her own sandals and sank into sleep as Hermia; Walter and Virginia departed as Oberon and Puck and returned as Theseus and Hippolyta.

"But soft, what nymphs are these?" said the Duke of Athens, regarding all the lovers cluttering his forest.

Adeline stirred without waking, and from Helena's slumber Egeus's cracked voice said, "My lord, this is my daughter here asleep, and this Lysander; this Demetrius is, this Helena. . . ."

A blast of horns voiced by Walter and Virginia woke the four, who tried without much success to explain what they were all doing under the same tree. Egeus displayed an unhealthy desire to have his daughter immediately either married or hanged, which Demetrius interrupted with the admission that he really did love Helena after all.

"Egeus, I will overbear your will," Theseus said, and it took little imagination to hear the ". . . or we'll see who gets his neck stretched" underneath it. The Duke then decreed "a feast in all solemnity—" the unspoken counterpart being "triple bachelor party"—and the Athenians departed, the lovers agreeing to discuss their night's dream . . . but probably not in too much detail.

Bottom wandered on stage, carrying his shoes. He looked down at his bare feet, danced a little jig-step, and sat down under the tree. "I have had a most rare vision," he said. "I have had a dream . . . past the wit of man to say what dream it was." He pulled the clogs on, clip-clopped his feet on the floor. "Man is but an ass if he go about to expound this dream. Methought I was—there is no man can tell what. Methought I was—and methought I had—" He slashed his hands through the air, stood up. "But man is but a patched fool if he will offer to say what methought I had!" He looked up at the tree, squinting through its branches at the rising sun. "The eye of man hath not heard, the ear of man hath not seen, man's hand is not able to taste, his tongue to conceive, nor his heart to report, what my dream was. I will get Peter Quince to write a ballad of this dream; it shall be called 'Bottom's Dream' . . . because it hath no bottom!" He chuckled, sighed. "And I will sing it in the latter end of a play, before the Duke. Peradventure, to make it the more gracious, I shall sing it at . . . her . . . death."

He wheezed, took hold of the hat rack, and walked off, dragging the tree behind him.

INTERVIEWER

Do you see the action in the wood as a metaphor for justice coming out of injustice?

DR. GORDON

Have you ever been in psychotherapy?

INTERVIEWER

Surely you don't hold that a faith in justice is a form of insanity.

DR. GORDON

Not the faith in its value. But the belief that it always happens, I'd call that a delusional structure, yes. Truth won't always out, the wages of sin are bankable, and those who live by the sword perish mostly of syphilis.

As I've said, we don't exist in a vacuum, on a bare stage. We remember what happened long ago. There were camps before ours, liberations before ours, tribunals before ours. Group A knew all that and planned accordingly.

When they saw the end coming, they in a sense abolished the camps themselves. But they did so in a way that also abolished justice. Once, before LX, before us, the victims knew the torturers' faces—and the torturers knew themselves; if they hid, they felt guilt that would punish and betray them, and if they felt no guilt, they could not truly hide.

But all we know is that some of us did what was done. And so we are all in hiding, and we are all guilty.

The Athenian court discussed the strange events of the night before—Duke Theseus playing the amused skeptic at all this fairy business. The Duke was interested in tonight's amusements—who was up for a party, and what had his master of ceremonies arranged? "Call Philostrate."

"Here, mighty Theseus," Dr. Gordon said. The majordomo provided the Duke with a list of proposed entertainments, which Theseus dismissed one after another—"We'll none of that . . . that is an old device . . . that is some satire, keen and critical, not sorting with a nuptial ceremony." Then he came to *Pyramus and Thisbe*. . . .

Philostrate did his best to argue against the play. It was ridiculous; it was being staged by a bunch of working stiffs; it was only good for a few laughs at the players' expense.

Theseus insisted. He explained to Hippolyta that he had already seen any number of spectacles put on by bored professionals; sincerity, however clumsy, was to be preferred to expert indifference: "Love, therefore, and tongue-tied simplicity, in least speak most, to my capacity."

The workmen were sitting on boxes, changing their clogs for ballet slippers as they changed themselves into actors. Howard as Bottom had a yardstick thrust through a belt loop, Pyramus's sword; Adeline as Flute wore a sheet over head and shoulders, Thisbe's cloak; Walter as Snout carried a foam-rubber brick balanced on one shoulder to illustrate Wall. Virginia as Starveling the tailor was kitted out with a candle and a ball of twine, for Moon's lantern and thornbush, and a long leather strap dangled from her wrist, leashing an invisible dog. Mark as Snug the carpenter, who would be Lion, sat contentedly admiring his new buskins and pawing the air until, with a desperate gesture, Paris Quince dropped a mophead on his scalp.

Dr. Gordon, as Philostrate the master of ceremonies, rapped on the lectern, cleared his throat, and said unctuously, "So please your grace, the, hrrrm, Prologue is addressed."

Momentarily lifting his brick, Walter as Theseus said, "Let him approach."

Quince took little steps forward. "If we offend, it is with our good will," he said, and took a little bow. Philostrate tilted his head, and Theseus made a *that's-nice* gesture.

"That you should think, we come not to offend but with good will to show our simple skill," Quince said. "That is the true beginning of our end." His voice sped up. "Consider then, we come but in despite. We do not come, as minding to content you, our true intent is." He started to spread his hands, but they were too tightly clutched on his script. "All for your delight, we are not here!" He got a hand loose, gestured at the players. "That you should here repent you, the actors are at hand ... and by their show, you shall know all that you are like to know."

"This fellow doth not stand upon points," Theseus said; Paris/Quince looked down at her ballet shoes, and that was exactly what she was doing. She stepped lightly off.

"Who is next?" the Duke said, and the whole company stood, paraded once around the stage, and took up poses. Quince introduced them, Pyramus, Thisbe, Wall, Moon, and Lion, and then crouched in front of Philostrate's lectern.

Walter hoisted his brick again, and Theseus said, "I wonder if the Lion be to speak?"

Mark doffed his mop, said as Demetrius, "No wonder, my lord—one lion may, when many asses do." He replaced his mane; Walter did likewise with his brick, and, Snout again, explained how he was a Wall that divided the lovers Pyramus and Thisbe.

He removed the brick again. The Duke turned his head, held the brick alongside his mouth, and said aside, "Would you desire lime and hair to speak better?"

Demetrius said from behind Lion's mane, "It is the wittiest partition that ever I heard discourse, my lord."

"Pyramus draws near the wall: silence!"

Pyramus appeared, walking as though he expected the earth to open beneath him at any moment. "O grim-look'd night! O night with hue so black! O night, which ever art when day is not! O night ... o night ..."

Quince ruffled through the script, leaned his head on his forearm in woe. Pyramus shouted "Alack!" Quince raised three fingers. Pyramus nodded. "Alack, alack!"

"Thou wall," Pyramus told the wall, "O wall, O sweet and lovely wall, show me thy chink, to blink through with mine eyne." He inclined his head, Wall swung his brick into place.

"Tha'ggs, Waw," Pyramus said, rubbing his nose, "Jove shield thee well for this. But what see I? No Thisbe do I see. O wicked wall, through whom I see no bliss, curs'd be thy stones for thus deceiving me!"

Wall adjusted the brick, turned his head for the Duke to say, "The wall, methinks, being sensible, should curse again."

Pyramus raised the brick, leaned under it, and said very earnestly, "No, in truth, sir, he should not. 'Deceiving me' is Thisbe's cue. She is to enter now, and I am to spy her through the wall. You shall see it will fall pat as I told you: yonder she comes." He turned, gestured, and bashed his head against the brick.

Howard and Adeline extruded woo through the hole in Wall, sounding if anything more sincere than Lysander and Helena the night before. They arranged a rendezvous somewhere without bricks in the way, and departed.

"Thus have I, Wall, my part dischargéd so, and being done, thus Wall away doth go." Wall bowed, tucked the brick under his arm, and sat down next to Virginia. She turned, and as Hippolyta said, "This is the silliest stuff that ever I heard!"

Walter looked into space for a quarter-minute or so, then smiled kindly at her, said very gently, "The best in this kind are but shadows . . . and the worst are no worse, if imagination mend them."

"It must be your imagination, then, and not theirs," she said, but her voice was more doubtful than sarcastic.

"If we imagine no worse of them than they of themselves . . ." Walter stopped, raised his eyes to the darkness above the stage, the shadowed metal and the dangling flyropes. ". . . they may pass for—*excellent* men."

INTERVIEWER

They do . . . wonderfully with very little.

DR. GORDON

Theatre is participatory. Given the least assistance in maintaining the illusion, the audience will do wonders. Just as your audience does.

INTERVIEWER

My audience—

DR. GORDON

Of course. Anyone listening to us now would believe we're in a theatre.

INTERVIEWER

We *are* in a theatre.

DR. GORDON
(hastily)

Oh, yes, of course.

INTERVIEWER
(slightly uneasy)

I should probably make clear—

DR. GORDON
(breaking in)

One moment, please! We can hear—yes, we definitely can hear the Martian war machines just outside the studio now! A heat ray is passing very close to the window—(he rubs his sleeve across the microphone, making a hissing sound) We may be cut off the air at any moment, ladies and gentlemen, so please—

[The recorder comes to a loud halt. The PLAYERS stop still.]

INTERVIEWER
(bewildered and angry)

What on earth are you doing, Doctor?

DR. GORDON
(placid)

Getting you to play the game.

INTERVIEWER

What game?

DR. GORDON

Audience Participation, of course. You can see that no elaborate staging is necessary.

Every time the game turns mean or rough or ugly, people with the very best of thoughts and intentions ask why everyone didn't just refuse to play in the first place.

(wry)

Now a few people will always believe that this theatre doesn't exist. And that Martians attacked it.

(a beat)

Or you could do some careful editing.

[The recorder starts again. The action resumes.]

Duke Theseus pointed offstage. "Here come two noble beasts in, a man and a lion."

Mark came in, clawing air and mouthing growls. Then he stood up straight, removed his mane and held the mop over his heart. He explained carefully that he was Snug the joiner, not a lion, and he certainly did not intend to eat anyone present at the performance. Then he replaced the mop and folded himself into a sphinx.

Virginia stood and took center stage, dragging the empty leash, and held up the candle to declaim Moon. The Athenians didn't seem to believe it was the Moon. She hid the candle for a moment, as Hippolyta wished the Moon to change.

By Moon's light, Thisbe appeared. "This is old Ninny's tomb. Where is my love?"

Lion stood up, crept behind her, cleared his throat delicately. "Growl?"

Thisbe shrieked and dashed offstage. Lion got on all fours, looked around perplexed for Thisbe's mantle to maul. Adeline snuck back, dropped it in front of him, bowed and ran off again.

Mark nuzzled the sheet for a moment, then slipped off his mop and said as Demetrius, "Well roared, Lion!"

Walter called, "Well run, Thisbe!"

Virginia hid her candle. "Well shone, Moon! Truly, the moon shines with a good grace."

Walter tossed Mark a prop bottle marked KETCHUP. The Lion shook it over Thisbe's sheet, crawled off. The Duke said, "Well moused, Lion."

Pyramus returned. "Sweet Moon, I thank thee for thy sunny beams...." He hunted for Thisbe, but found only the discarded cloak: he picked it up with two fingers at arm's length. He threw an arm across his eyes. He howled at the Moon, who stuck fingers in her ears. He fell on the floor and pounded it, then stood up again, brushed himself off with the sheet, and embraced it. "But stay, O spite! But mark, poor knight, what dreadful dole is here? Eyes, do you see? How can it be? O dainty duck, O dear!" He heaved a sob, blew his nose on the sheet. "Thy mantle good, what! Stained with blood? Approach, ye Furies fell! O fates, come, come! Cut thread and thrum, quail, crush, conclude, and quell!"

Theseus had buried his face in his arms. He raised his head, shook it gravely, and said, "This passion, and the death of a dear friend, would go near to make a man look sad."

Pyramus, meanwhile, had drawn his yardstick and was sharpening it on his thigh. "Come tears, confound! Out sword, and wound the pap of Pyramus. Ay, that..." He examined his chest. "*Left* pap, where heart doth hop." He thrust, clamping the stick under his arm. "Thus die I, thus, thus, thus! Now am I dead, now am I fled; my soul is in the sky." He raised his arms in the direction of his soul; the sword hit the stage. He picked it up, put it firmly in place again. "Tongue, lose thy light; Moon, take thy flight...." He waited patiently for Moon to notice his cue and leave.

"Now die! Die! Die! Die..." He stiffened, toppled to the floor. "Diiiiiiie..."

Thisbe entered. She was much put out by what she found. She catalogued Pyramus's manly virtues, while making a valiant try at cardiopulmonary resuscitation. "Tongue, not a word: come, trusty sword . . ." She couldn't find it. Pyramus reached under himself and handed it up. "Come, blade, my breast imbrue! And farewell, friends, thus Thisbe ends: adieu, adieu—"

She counted hastily on her fingers. "Adieu."

The court kept silence for a while. The lovers stayed resolutely dead.

The Duke consulted his script. "Moonshine and Lion are left to bury the dead."

Demetrius said, "Ay, and Wall too."

Bottom sat up, tumbling Thisbe into the wings. "No, I assure you; the wall is down that parted their fathers. Will it please you to see the epilogue, or to hear a Bergomask dance between two of our company?"

"No epilogue, I pray you," the Duke said, with a wild wave of his hands, "for your play needs no excuse. Never . . ." He bit his lip, inhaled. ". . . excuse, for when the players are all . . . dead . . ." Walter struggled; the others did not move. ". . . there need none to be blamed." He shrugged, smiled again. "Marry, if he that writ it had played Pyramus, and hanged himself in Thisbe's garter, it would have been a fine tragedy—and so it is, truly, and very notably discharged. But come, your Bergomask; let your epilogue alone."

The players formed a circle, all standing; Paris and Howard stepped into the center, began to move in a stately step around one another, carrying themselves precisely, one hand lifted, almost but not quite touching.

INTERVIEWER

What exactly is a Bergomask dance?

DR. GORDON

The word comes from Bergamo, a town in Italy. Today we would say *Bergamesque*. In Shakespeare's day the people there were proverbial rustics.

INTERVIEWER

What is it like?

[DR. GORDON says nothing; he continues to watch the dance. MARK and VIRGINIA join the circle, and then WALTER and ADELINE. From a circle dance it becomes linear, a courtly dance in the Regency fashion, with much bowing and waving of fans.

[Abruptly, HOWARD puts his hand on PARIS's shoulder, and the dancers freeze; then PARIS puts her arm around HOWARD's neck, and they begin a close dance, a tango. The others follow.

[Partners are changed, hold each other closer. Then all at once all form disappears, and the six players are in a shifting, balletic, erotic knot; hands slip over throats and under shirts, lips touch, bodies collide.

[DR. GORDON begins to rise from his chair, but sits back, folds his arms firmly upon the lectern.

[WALTER pushes back the cuffs of VIRGINIA's sweatshirt, showing bandages wrapping her wrists; he closes his hands over them and they dance to his direction.]

INTERVIEWER

Were there orgies in the camps?

[DR. GORDON still does not turn or speak. Slowly his head falls forward into his folded arms on the lectern, and he shudders: his face is out of sight, but he must be weeping.

[WALTER releases VIRGINIA and steps aside. She rejoins the group. WALTER pulls off his dancing shoes and dons Theseus's sandals again; he claps his hands and all stop. They are breathing hard; they rearrange their clothing.]

[DR. GORDON raises his head, brushes his hair into place. There are no tears on his face.]

"The iron tongue of midnight hath told twelve," Theseus said. "Lovers, to bed: 'tis almost fairy time." The couples held hands. "Sweet friends, to bed; a fortnight hold we this solemnity in nightly revels and new jollity."

All went out but Virginia, who held her arms crossed, sleeves pulled down again to half-cover her hands, then knelt to remove her slippers. Puck stood, stretched. "Now the hungry lion roars," she said, softly, softly, "and the wolf behowls the moon; whilst the heavy plowman snores, all with weary task fordone." She danced lightly from compass point to point, calling up the spirits of the night: "Every one lets forth his sprite in the churchway paths to glide; and we fairies that do run, by the triple Hecate's team, from the presence of the sun ... following darkness ..." She paused, said not singing, "like a dream. . . . Now are frolic; not a mouse shall disturb this hallowed house. *I* am sent, with broom before, to sweep the dust behind the door."

Oberon and Titania entered, with all fairies after, and they danced again—but this time all lightly, politely, humming ring-around-the-rosy like a children's game until ashes, ashes, they all fell down.

Oberon laid his blessing on the house and all in it, and all the children to come of the love within. He turned to look at Dr. Gordon, who sat very straight. "And the owner of it blest," the Fairy King said, "ever shall in safety rest; trip away, make no stay, meet me all by break of day."

The fairies flitted away, leaving only Puck again. "If we shadows have offended, think on this, and all is mended: that you have but slumbered here while these visions did appear ... and this weak and idle theme, no more yielding than a dream, gentles, do not reprehend—if you pardon, we will mend." She paused, and when she began again, her voice was cool and earnest; good evening, this is the news: "And as I am an honest Puck, if we have unearnéd luck, now to 'scape the serpent's tongue ... we *will* make amends ere long; else the Puck a liar call. So. Goodnight unto you all."

[She bows and runs off. A full minute goes by, but none of the PLAYERS return. Slowly, the lights of the playing space fade out.]

INTERVIEWER

Was that the Epilogue?

DR. GORDON

No. There's no Epilogue; the law of Athens suppressed it, remember?

But just think: you've survived the whole play.

(a pause)

INTERVIEWER

Last question.

DR. GORDON

Yes?

INTERVIEWER

Why?

[DR. GORDON just smiles.]

INTERVIEWER

What I mean is—

DR. GORDON

I know what you mean. Why this, and not something else? Why this, and not an answer to the question that we keep asking, and may have to keep asking for the rest of our lives?

I do not know what I did. That was taken from me. I do not know what will happen next. That is not given to me. But I know, here, now, what I am doing. And I can live with that.

[He stands up and walks offstage. The tape reels continue to turn. Then, with a mechanical click, they stop, and begin to spin backward at high speed, with a high-pitched squealing. The machine stops. The stage goes dark.]

CURTAIN

WINTER SOLSTICE, CAMELOT STATION

Camelot is served
By a sixteen-track stub terminal done in High
    Gothick Style,
The tracks covered by a single great barrel-vaulted
    glass roof framed upon iron,
At once looking back to the Romans and ahead to
    the Brunels.
Beneath its rotunda, just to the left of the ticket
    windows,
Is a mosaic floor depicting the Round Table
(Where all knights, regardless of their station of
    origin
Or class of accommodation, are equal),
And around it murals of knightly deeds in action
(Slaying dragons, righting wrongs, rescuing
    maidens tied to the tracks).
It is the only terminal, other than Gare d'Avalon
    in Paris,
To be hung with original tapestries,

And its lavatories rival those at Great Gate of Kiev
 Central.
During a peak season such as this, some eighty trains a day
 pass through,
Five times the frequency at the old Londinium Terminus,
Ten times the number the Druid towermen knew.
(The Official Court Christmas Card this year displays
A crisp black-and-white Charles Clegg photograph from
 the King's own collection,
Showing a woad-blued hogger at the throttle of "Old
 XCVII,"
The Fast Mail overnight to Eboracum. Those were the days.)
The first of a line of wagons has arrived,
Spilling footmen and pages in Court livery,
And old thick Kay, stepping down from his Range Rover,
Tricked out in a bush coat from Swaine, Adeney, Brigg,
Leaning on his shooting stick as he marshalls his company,
Instructing the youngest how to behave in the station,
To help mature women that they may encounter,
Report pickpockets, gather up litter,
And of course no true Knight of the Table Round (even in
 training)
Would do a station porter out of Christmas tips.
He checks his list of arrival times, then his watch
(A moon-phase Breguet, gift from Merlin):
The seneschal is a practical man, who knows trains do
 run late,
And a stolid one, who sees no reason to be glad about it.
He dispatches pages to posts at the tracks,
Doling out pennies for platform tickets,
Then walks past the station buffet with a dyspeptic snort,
Goes into the bar, checks the time again, orders a pint.
The patrons half-turn—it's the fella from Camelot, innit?
And Kay chuckles soft to himself, and the Court buys a
 round.

He's barely halfway when a page tumbles in,
Seems the knights are arriving, on time after all,
So he tips the glass back (people stare as he guzzles),
Then plonks it down hard with five quid for the barman,
And strides for the doorway (half Falstaff, half Hotspur)
To summon his liveried army of lads.

Bors arrives behind steam, riding the cab of a heavy
    Mikado.
He shakes the driver's hand, swings down from the
    footplate,
And is like a locomotive himself, his breath clouding white,
Dark oil sheen on his black iron mail,
Sword on his hip swinging like siderods at speed.
He stamps back to the baggage car, slams mailed fist on
    steel door
With a clang like jousters colliding.
The handler opens up and goes to rouse another knight.
Old Pellinore has been dozing with his back against a crate,
A cubical chain-bound thing with FRAGILE tags and air
    holes,
BEAST says the label, Questing, 1 the bill of lading.
The porters look doubtful but ease the thing down.
It grumbles. It shifts. Someone shouts, and they drop it.
It cracks like an egg. There is nothing within.
Elayne embraces Bors on the platform, a pelican on a rock,
Silently they watch as Pelly shifts the splinters,
Supposing aloud that Gutman and Cairo have swindled
    him.

A high-drivered engine in Northern Lines green
Draws in with a string of side-corridor coaches,
All honey-toned wood with stained glass on their windows.
Gareth steps down from a compartment, then Gaheris and
    Agravaine,

All warmly tucked up in Orkney sweaters;
Gawain comes after in Shetland tweed.
Their Gladstones and steamers are neatly arranged,
With never a worry—their Mum does the packing.
A redcap brings forth a curious bundle, a rude shape in red
  paper—
The boys did that themselves, you see, and how *does* one
  wrap a unicorn's head?
They bustle down the platform, past a chap all in green,
He hasn't the look of a trainman, but only Gawaine turns
  to look at his eyes,
And sees written there *Sir, I shall speak with you later.*

Over on the first track, surrounded by reporters,
All glossy dark iron and brass-bound mystery,
The Direct-Orient Express, ferried in from Calais and
  Points East.
Palomides appears, smelling of patchouli and Russian
  leather,
Dripping Soubranie ash on his astrakhan collar,
Worry darkening his dark face, though his damascene
  armor shows no tarnish,
He pushes past the press like a broad-hulled icebreaker.
Flashbulbs pop. Heads turn. There's a woman in Chanel
  black,
A glint of diamonds, liquid movements, liquid eyes.
The newshawks converge, but suddenly there appears
A sharp young man in a crisp blue suit
From the Compagnie Internationale des Wagons-Lits,
That elegant, comfortable, decorous, close-mouthed firm:
He's good at his job, and they get not so much as a
  snapshot.
Tomorrow's editions will ask who she was, and whom
  with. . . .

Now here's a silver train, stainless steel, Vista-Domed,
White-lighted grails on the engine (running no extra
    sections)
The *Logres Limited*, extra fare, extra fine,
(Stops on signal at Carbonek to receive passengers only).
She glides to a Timken-borne halt (even her grease is
    clean),
Galahad already on the steps, flashing that winning smile,
Breeze mussing his golden hair, but not his Armani
    tailoring,
Just the sort of man you'd want finding your chalice.
He signs an autograph, he strikes a pose.
Someone says, loudly, "Gal! Who serves the Grail?"
He looks—no one he knows—and there's a silence,
A space in which he shifts like sun on water;
Look quick and you may see a different knight,
A knight who knows that meanings can be lies,
That things are done not knowing why they're done,
That bearings fail, and stainless steel corrodes.
A whistle blows. Snow shifts on the glass shed roof. That
    knight is gone.
This one remaining tosses his briefcase to one of Kay's
    pages,
And, golden, silken, careless, exits left.

Behind the carsheds, on the business car track, alongside
    the private varnish
Of dukes and smallholders, Persian potentates and Cathay
    princes
(James J. Hill is here, invited to bid on a tunnel through
    the Pennines).
Waits a sleek car in royal blue, ex-B&O, its trucks and
    fittings chromed,
A black-gloved hand gripping its silver platform rail;

Mordred and his car are both upholstered in blue velvet
    and black leather.
He prefers to fly, but the weather was against it.
His DC-9, with its video system and Quotron and
    waterbed, sits grounded at Gatwick.
The premature lines in his face are a map of a hostile
    country,
The redness in his eyes a reminder that hollyberries are
    poison.
He goes inside to put on a look acceptable for Christmas
    Court;
As he slams the door it rattles like strafing jets.

Outside the Station proper, in the snow,
On a through track that's used for milk and mail,
A wheezing saddle-tanker tops for breath;
A way-freight mixed, eight freight cars and caboose,
Two great ugly men on the back platform, talking with a
    third on the ballast.
One, the conductor, parcels out the last of the coffee;
They drink. A joke about grails. They laugh.
When it's gone, the trainman pretends to kick the big
    hobo off,
But the farewell hug spoils the act.
Now two men stand on the dirty snow,
The conductor waves a lantern and the train grinds on.
The ugly men start walking, the new arrival behind,
Singing "Wenceslas" off-key till the other says stop.
There are two horses waiting for them. Rather plain horses,
Considering. The men mount up.
By the roundhouse they pause,
And look at the locos, the water, the sand, and the coal,
They look for a long time at the turntable,
Until the one who is King says, "It all seemed so simple,
    once,"

And the best knight in the world says, "It is. We make it
   hard."
They ride on, toward Camelot by the service road.

The sun is winter-low. Kay's caravan is rolling.
He may not run a railroad, but he runs a tight ship:
By the time they unload in the Camelot courtyard,
The wassail will be hot and the goose will be crackling,
Banners snapping from the towers, fir logs on the fire,
   drawbridge down,
And all that sackbut and psaltery stuff.
Blanchefleur is taking the children caroling tonight,
Percivale will lose to Merlin at chess,
The young knights will dally and the damsels dally back,
The old knights will play poker at a smaller Table Round.
And at the great glass station, motion goes on,
The extras, the milk trains, the varnish, the limiteds,
The *Pindar of Wakefield*, the *Lady of the Lake*,
The *Broceliande Local*, the *Fast Flying Briton*,
The nerves of the kingdom, the lines of exchange,
Running to schedule as the world ought,
Ticking like a hot-fired hand-stoked heart,
The metal expression of the breaking of boundaries,
The boilers that turn raw fire into power,
The driving rods that put the power to use,
The turning wheels that make all places equal,
The knowledge that the train may stop but the line goes on;
The train may stop
But the line goes on.

HEAT OF FUSION

Day 1

I had my first fully conscious day since the accident. They tell me it has been about four days, but this will be Note #1, for completeness's sake. I felt remarkably well, for a dead man.

A. was waiting for me when I awoke, smiling brightly. He had a supply of blank notebooks and pencils for me. (Odd how, with all the shortages, we have such a huge stockpile of books and pencils.) In the "time remaining" I am to write down all the details of the work that my old gray head contains, so that his Project does not "slip backward."

I see I have written "his" project. Well. It will be his soon, since N. died in the accident. (As did I, but have not had the grace to fall down yet.)

N. is dead. And J. is dead. Y., I am told, is still "alive," though in much worse shape than I. I may be able to see her. It is something to look forward to, and I have little enough of those.

I will write the notes A. has asked for, though not necessarily the ones he wants. And separately I shall keep this notebook ("journal" is too much of a word). I don't know for whom. Myself, I suppose. As for why, see prior paragraph, last sentence.

Day 2
While I dozed this afternoon, A. stole the notebook I had been filling for his benefit. I know it was A.; the nurse told me when I called her to search the floor for it. I hope she will not get into trouble for that.

I wondered about hiding these notes, but that is silly. Secrecy mentality. What would attract more attention than my fussing with pillows or drainpipes or loose blocks in the wall?

Even if I found one, soon enough I won't be able to move a loose block.

But they are going to play the Secrets game whether I will or not, I suppose. (I haven't seen a single soldier since the accident; what am I supposed to make of that?) I'll keep this book in the pile of blank ones, well shuffled. That's enough. I wonder what A. will make of what he has?

Day 3
A. was not happy. I think he was furious, in fact. But I will give him this much: he controlled himself better than I had thought him capable. (Capable of?)

He did not bother with a philosophical argument, being not that much of a fool, and went straight to discussing the good of the Project. When that wore thin, he hinted that I might not be allowed to see the "recovering" Y. if I were not "cooperative."

We learn from our environments, and he has spent his Project time among the soldiers, not the scientists.

I asked him, angrily I suppose, why he had stolen my notebook. After a pause he said that I had given it to him. "Don't you remember? Are you having trouble remembering?"

Then he looked at me with real fear. And his expression changed to

I must describe it precisely. If you have ever worked very hard at a difficult problem, one you doubt is within your capacity, and then broken it, you know the feeling that comes when the nut of solution first cracks open, the glimpse of glory within. That was A.'s look.

He went away without any books.

Perhaps he is frightened by the facts: he could not read the notes he stole because he is too poor a physicist. If all my writing to come is like that, what will become of *his* Project?

But now I know he will threaten me, and I am scared too.

Day 4

No one came today but nurses. One said that I may be allowed to walk soon, at least to the toilet. Outstanding. Martin Luther may have had great thoughts while his bowels worked, but he wasn't using a bedpan.

I am still worried about A.'s moment of epiphany yesterday. Was it about the Project, or me? He had already held Y. over me. J. is dead.

J. is dead, and I am dead, and the living cannot threaten me.

Day 5

I have found out A.'s scheme. What a waste of two days' fretting. One would think I had taught enough students to know that the brightest smiles come from those who have just trisected the angle.

He has started a whispering campaign that the accident was my fault. The doctors have muttered it in the halls, the nurses shake their heads as they change my bottles, A. came as close to saying it as he dared. I must finish my commentary on the Project, he said, because if I do not, "erroneous impressions" may take hold.

"Erroneous impressions" is what he said. A waste of six syllables, when "lies" has only one.

Day 6

My fault.

My fault.

I put the words on the page, and they seem to crawl from beneath the pencil, shaping themselves into countless implications but no meanings.

Presumably when the Project Final Report is written, there will be a chapter on the accident. Call it chapter 13. And there will appear a line, to wit: he was in charge of the Principal Experimental Rig when the accident took place. It was His Fault. (This *misrepresentation* of my responsibilities will be insisted upon by A.) The line will repeat as the caption of a small and unflattering photograph of myself, Figure 13–2. 13–1 will be the standard half-page picture of the Rig, with numbered silhouettes superimposed where the others were standing.

I presume falsely, of course. There will be no such report. After the present mess is cleared up, the Project will proceed to one of two endpoints.

If it fails, there will be no one to write the report. If it succeeds, there will be no one to read it.

So this text is going to have to be as much Final Report as the Project will ever see. And epitaph enough, too, for the four of us.

Day 7

A. came in today, falsely cheerful and a little sheepish; he asked how my "Report" was progressing. (He called it that; am I to begin dreaming true as the end approaches?) I showed him what I had for him; his delight was fake but his relief was not. I know very well that he is being driven by others, having no ability to drive himself, and I was about to feel a little sorry for him when he brought up Y. again, saying that she was *almost* able to converse, and the doctors said I was *almost* well enough to see her. (How well a corpse gets he did not explain.)

I am having second thoughts as I write: Perhaps A. was ordered to use Y. as a lever against me. It was never in his nature to be deliberately cruel (his masochism, which he doubtless believes is his secret still, is more pathetic than pathological). And perhaps he is watched as he talks to me.

In which case, why do I write these secret notes to no one?

My paranoia is itself rather pathetic. I asked him if there had been memorial services for N. and J. and if not, if I might attend them, and even say a few words.

A. was, if not thunderstruck, at least surprised. He told me that, since complete dissective necropsies were required, the bodies were hardly suitable for view and had been cremated. A memorial he acknowledges as a possibility, after the "immediate problems" were settled. Then he asked to take the notebook, which I allowed, and he went away.

Of course I knew J.'s body would have been disposed of, one way or another. I wanted A., and whoever might be behind him, to be very aware that I know J. is dead, because though I do know that and threats would mean nothing, still I do not want to hear them.

As for the memorial service, tomorrow I will hold one here.

Day 8
When J. was just a student

I let the line stand, so as to correct and amplify it. When J. had no formal credentials, so that we perceived him through a student-colored filter, I posed a question to his lecture group, one I always gave the Honors students early in the course. It involved a spinning particle, and while the answer was not complex it was tricky, in that there were several wrong answers more plausible-sounding than the correct one, and the class inevitably had to eliminate those before discerning the truth.

So when J. put his hand up first, and the others let him wave it about, I thought he must be trapped. More fool I. Not only did he have the solution, he had reached it in a novel and elegant fashion. It was obvious that he had not simply made a lucky memorization, but *understood* the underlying theory down to its roots.

The recollection that brackets this one is of J. sitting at a test bench, holding the two pieces of an elaborate glass vacuum assembly that had somehow broken in the center. (I never did learn how that ~~acci~~ mishap occurred.) I passed by in the hall, shook my head, and went on with whatever I was doing; when I passed by again, at least half an hour later, he was still there, staring at the jagged ends of glass.

I leaned into the room and suggested he call the glassblower, whose shop was only a few doors away. Without looking up, J. said, "No need to. I've about got it now."

I let the story get about, and there was laughter at J.'s expense until I was quite as embarrassed as he was.

There are the stories; the theorist with an intuitive power that, as he learned to focus it, was at times actually frightening, who had no mind at all for experimental hardware.

They are not, I can see now, brackets but mirrors, creating an endless chain of reflections between them.

A reflector assembly.

No more today.

Day 9

I was allowed to walk today, about four meters to the bathroom. Slow progress, in an unsmoothed curve point to point, an orderly with a death grip on my arm, but the heavy particle finally achieved the target.

Triumph.

Once there, I eliminated into cardboard containers for the laboratory's benefit. They also received a liter or so of my exhaled breath, and of course a little blood. Ultimately I will give my all for the Project, rag and bone and hank of hair, as have J. and N. already.

I was about to write that N. would have been pleased, to know that he gave all his being. How easily the sarcasm still comes. N. loved the Project, and he loved the State, and he venerated the memory of his wife and children (while still being able to make a respectful pass at Y. one Christmas). What can I say of a man who needed to love so much?

Everything is colored by his first spring here, the first spring of the Project. N. was drafted (at least, we thought he had been drafted) to write a speech, to be delivered to all the inhabitants of

the complex, about the strange dark secret in our midst. I was supposed to read this text, but A. readily accepted my deferral.

Everyone gathered in the largest common room. A. and N. sat on
a dais, in their only good suits, with a few soldiers in their dress uniforms. J. and I had attended, certainly not to heckle. Maybe not to
heckle. Frankly we were curious. How is a secret Project explained
and still kept Secret?

Yet he did it.

N.'s speech brought up pride, and honor, and glory lost and glory
regained, and on and on, and *literally* got the audience to their feet
cheering for the Project, despite that they had been told not one
word about what it was or what it did.

Afterward, we saw N., smiling and shaking hands and saluting
(he had, as we all did, a crypto-military rank, that we might command and be commanded). He said to me, "It worked, didn't it?" in
the tone any of us used when looking up from the recorder or the
slide rule.

The flat box I was provided today was of waxed white board, that
distinctly showed the blood in my gruelly shit.

Day 10

A. visited, hungry for more. It is tiring, and it is a dilemma. If I
churn out pages for them I am too tired to think about these notes,
but if A. and his masters are not kept happy I will have no peace at all.

And of course A. is not inspired but not incompetent either, and
eventually he will taste what I am feeding him.

If N. were here it would be different. But N. was in Room 18. N.
is dead. N. was the first of us to die, and perhaps died best.

He could take any one worker's idea of data and mathematically
transform them into anyone else's mental dialect. It was N. who allowed Y. to comprehend J.'s theories, J. to puzzle out what she then
constructed, and this old foolish professor to understand them both.

It was said, not really joking, that N.'s works would be bestsellers
if they were not all Secret. He did, in fact, write two popular works,

on physics and mathematics for young people. He dedicated them to his children, who were living then. The State press keeps them in print, and it is a fair guess that if you are reading this, you read them at some time in your youth.

Unless you are a State security officer, of course.

Day 11

At the moment of the accident, I was not in the Principal Experiment Room, Room 18, but in Room 19, the Recording and Control Room adjacent. The communicating door was open; this was against regulation but usual practice when the Rig was being operated at low energies, and the door was anyway not shielded.

Y. called to me through the open door. There was no special urgency in her voice. I took a step, then heard a chattering sound from one of the power relay cabinets behind me; as I turned, I briefly saw dials leap and pen recorders reach. Then there was a flash of light from the Rig, dazzling and warm as sunshine.

I was screened from the epicenter of flash by the bit of wall between the door and the observing window. I might have been still alive at that point; I do not know. I did not even think about it. I went to the door.

J. was standing on the platform between the B and C assemblies. Above him, a red steel flag indicated that the shutters of the C-stage reflector were fully open, at his chest level.

I entered Room 18 just as the alarm sounded. I was definitely dead then; this was well understood about the alarm system. It was supposed, correctly as it turned out, that with casualties not clearly defined, those inside (dead) could take the most efficient action to secure the area.

Y. had dropped behind a heavy desk, telephone in hand; she was spinning the crank furiously. I could not see N. J. was leaning against the C assembly, left hand clutching a pipe, right hand close to his body. As I drew close, I saw that he was holding an instrument inside the reflector cavity, and had been timing the measure-

ment with his wristwatch. I thought for another moment that he
was alive (conscious, that is; I have already explained about the
alarm), but I took another step and saw his face, half pale and
half scorched, and his eyes, his empty, idiot eyes, the brain behind
them washed clean of thought in a wave of particles. He stared up
and away, not at me, or I think my heart should have failed. As
perhaps it

Y. had abandoned the useless telephone (all its magnetic parts
were scrambled) and went behind the B assembly; she called for help,
and I helped her bring N. out from the small space. His clothing
smoldered. There were hideous, deep black burns on his chest and
neck and hands. Y. pointed at the wall, where N.'s shadow was still
cast, in unburned paint.

It was Y. who locked the doors and turned off the blaring alarm. I
could not thnk at all, not in the room with J. staring, staring at
nothing, with the face of a stillborn child.

Day 12
I was loaded into a wheelchair and taken to see Y.

She was on an entirely different level of the complex, though it
did not seem any differently equipped.

A. was there, looking very pleased, with a stenographer to take
notes of our conversation.

I had thought perhaps the desk protected Y. some small amount,
but obviously her dose was much higher than mine. She was propped
up on pillows, laced with tubes, very pale (I almost wrote
"deathly"). Her voice was clear, however.

We talked about nothing much for a few minutes. I could see A.
becoming impatient. (I looked for, but did not see, a stack of notebooks in the room.) I spoke to A., rather loudly, to be certain Y. was
aware he was there; I believe she nodded to me.

After a little more idle talk, A. interrupted us. While we were together he said, the bastard, were there any important details of the
Project that should be recorded?

Y. turned her head. The effort was visibly enormous for her. Then I did see her nod to me. "J.'s thermal data," she said, quite clearly. "The cavity readings he made on the last day."

"Were those important?" A. said. "We have them, of course but it was thought they were only routine."

Y. coughed.

I said, "We should leave you alone."

Y. whispered, "Come see me again." There was blood on her lips.

I said, "Of course," because it was what she wanted to hear, and then I did a stupid thing. I reached up and touched her dark hair, where it was gray at the right temple.

The hair came away in my hand.

They took me back to my room by a different route. I see they are afraid, and that does not displease me.

Day 13

Last night Y. came to visit.

Not literally, of course. But it seemed that she was here, and it seemed that we talked, in the quiet and dark. She was young, as when we first worked together at the old University Laboratories, her hair long and dark and her almond eyes intense. I remember thinking of her as mysterious, but since I intended to solve all the mysteries of physics in a term, or two at the most, surely women would require only a summer session.

I also learned more about physics.

Now I see I have skewed your perceptions. When I say now that she was a brilliant experimenter, that she did amazing things with her hands, you will laugh in a lewd manner. That is all right. We certainly did enough of it.

But it is true that she could turn a few equations and a pencil sketch into a working bench-test rig. She could solder and drill and tap and blow glass. I saw her make waveguides out of ballpoint-pen tubing. If there was a tricky curve involved, she would twist paper clips into test shapes, using her slim hard fingers as a forming brake.

When the Project began, there were several unkind comments

about Y.'s presence with myself, but I knew it (not I) must have her. And I was correct. We did not resume our other relationship; in the time between, she had gotten a husband and children, and lost them, and now there was the Project.

So we talked, last night, about things you have no context for understanding, and some that you probably do. Sunlight, and

This morning, a doctor came in, sad-eyed, to tell me that Y. was dead. He offered to take me to see her, but I said that I preferred to remember her as we had last met.

I wish now I had asked her if there were sunlight, but I will know soon enough.

I do not believe in ghosts, they are not a valid quantum phenomenon. But I imagined, as I walked so slowly to the toilet, that the irregularity beneath my slipper was a twisted paper clip.

Day 14

A few weeks before the accident, N. came to visit me, rather late. He was a little drunk, not very, and N. was not a private drinker. He had come to show me a manuscript he had just completed. The State press had requested it long ago, for whenever the Project should be complete, "for some reason," (he said) he had written this draft.

I wonder now if he had been talking to J.

The manuscript was a pamphlet, intended for children and adult poor readers. It explained, in clear, simple language, what the Project was, why we had done it, and why it was necessary that we do it. All the eloquence of his speech to the staff, years ago, was carried over, and no little amplified by the facts he could now state; the enemy might be far away, but we could be sure that there was an enemy, and if we did not bend the laws of physics to our just and peaceful will, that enemy would certainly use them to destroy us.

That was said in such fashion that its inherent absurdity—its *redundancy*—was forgotten.

Then I read the section about the Project's effects, how they would be wholly different from anything we had known before, nothing at all to fear.

It was a naked lie, and when I looked into N.'s face I saw he knew it was a lie, and still it was a convincing lie, a pleasant and friendly lie.

Could anyone have desired to believe it more than I? I cannot think how.

I told him the booklet was very well written, which was the only truth I had loose in my head then, and I praised his ability to write for the young.

He told me that it had never been hard for him to do, that he simply wrote the piece for his children.

Then he looked at me in absolute bewilderment, and asked me who it was he had written *this* for?

Day 15

Woke in the middle of the night, very cold, and saw J. staring at me, not living but dead and brain-dead. Wide pearly eyes with tiny uncomprehending pupils. (They are pearls that were his eyes, of his bones are radon made, Geiger counters ring his knell.)

So exquisitely ugly, like a fairy tale; he danced with the particles, and lived as one of them, until they bore his soul away and left this goggling husk.

I would live in Hell rather than see those empty eyes again. Here is Hell: I must not die now, not yet. I know now what J. was trying to do in the C cavity, and I have to see his data, on the terrible chance that he did it.

A. has the data, of course, but I dare not call him in; he must not suspect.

Maybe there is nothing there. Maybe my opinion of J. was always too high.

Oh no. This is not the time to think that.

Day 16

These pictures that I draw are an attempt to connect points into a smooth curve, but the data will not support an honest curve. There is so little time. I could sketch in data points until my hand was too weak to move—the jewelry Y. made from solder and ceramics; the

Christmas N. wrote personal sonnets to everyone he knew in the complex, had them put unsigned into our mailboxes and tried to pretend ignorance; J. wandering the halls with a chess set, playing anyone who would and never winning a single game—but would these smooth the curve, or skew it? They were people. I knew them, one of them in the biblical sense. I cannot say I understood them, by Heisenberg's principle an it please you.

You who read this, try to understand what I cannot. The particle does not know its charge. It cannot see the outcome of its collisions. When the event is over, the patient observer may try to make some sense of the tracks left behind. Please be patient.

Day 17

Awful tiredness today. Hands ache. Must go on maybe last entry.

Late last n. went toilet. Finished, hand hit switch, lights out.

Mirror suddenly clear. On other side sits bored soldier, smoking, solitaire. He startled as I.

Lights on quick. back to bed.

Well it brought A. Said only for safety (mine). Maybe he believes it. Asked him for J. data.

No mirrors this room. No use burn notes now. What hell play solitaire.

Day 18

J.'s data arrived. I read them, instead of writing, small respite. After a few pages my writing starts to look like shorthand. If u cn rd ths u cn gt gd jb phys.

There are several pages of handwritten notes, folded around a pen-recorder strip; they do not seem to have been opened and re-folded. The notes describe an absurdly simple experiment, requiring eighty seconds at the C assembly. Such an elementary measurement, I understand why he did not tell the rest of us. He can hardly have believed it himself.

Yet here is the strip trace. Pure theory has mended that which was broken.

Ladies and gentlemen and the rest of you, I report the success of the Project.

I keep staring at a spike on the strip chart, twelve seconds before the experiment ends.

Twelve seconds.

Why, this is Hell, nor am I out of it.

Day 19

Could not walk to toilet. Threw up on floor. Bloody runs too what blood Ive got. Back to bed. Tubes in again.

Pulled my hair, would it fall? Yes.

I need help.

Day 20

I am better today, in the local-relative sense.

J. came, as I thought he would. Not the brainless idiot, but J. young and clever and full of physics and vinegar. He was holding a vacuum tube in both hands, twirling it as we talked; it was whole and without seam. He told me just what he had done with the thermocouples, taking his eighty seconds' readings; he had known that to stop before 80 seconds would ruin the whole reading.

Then Y. came in, older than before but lovely in her maturity.

Finally N. joined us, a little diffident at first, but there was still enough love in him for many men, and now he said his children had forgiven him.

And would they forgive me? I asked.

But of course dreams always end before the desired revelation.

A. came in the morning, worried sick that I might leave his work a-dangle. He even offered to bring his stenographer if I could no longer write, a stupid offer given my speaking endurance but well-meant.

I told him what J. had been (ahem) about to discover in the C cavity. I saw his eyes widen. I told him what he would have to do, what he would need. I told him to be careful, setting the switches in Control Bank 7.

I gave him J.'s notes, with my erasures and changes (thanks given for all these identical notebooks and pencils).

When he had gone, I asked the nurses for something to eat, and they brought me some chicken stew. It tasted wonderful, even between bites of J.'s data strip.

Day 21

Only visitor last night was my dinner. (Dessert unreadable, good.) Bad day. Nausea and worse. Death, diet, or anticipation? A. must be at work. Must. Theory cannot save us now. Only experiment.

Day 22

I seem to have been granted a little strength and lucidity, here at the end. I will try to use it well. I doubt that there will be any entries to follow this one.

When the Project was first conceived, we had J., of course, and A., mistrusting each other at every step of the planning. One would suggest a name for the staff, and then the other would deliberate long and offer another, as if they were playing chess. This when we had no idea how many of the names were still alive, let alone available to us.

And—this is important—none of this distrust had anything to do with security, or even with the goals of the Project. For us, then, the goal of the Project was to do physics. We are fighting for our respective views of what (and who) made good physics.

That was all.

When I stood behind the thick glass of the Surface Station, watching the armored battery-wagons bring Y., when she stepped through the airlock, removed her heavy helmet, and looked up at the filtered sun—I swear by whatever God is left, all I thought of at the time was that now we could test hypotheses as we were made to do.

I seem to be crying. I wonder why. It is funny. Sweet hypothesis, sweet mystery of life.

To tell another great joke: the Project was often compared (usually by A., in the presence of the soldiers) to those Projects that came before, but the analogy is very bad. They had worked in a violent but essentially untouched world, toward a goal they could never be certain was there. We worked not toward their goal—which we knew only too well was there—but toward a sort of reaction engineering which could be made to work in a world blasted to poison junk, with a barrier dropped for God's own half-life between us and our old equipment, our old materials, our old selves; a potential-barrier too high for any of the surviving particles to cross.

To that end, we—I—assembled J., who could theorize around junk; Y., who could build from junk; N., who could translate among all the various junks; and myself for binder. Three quarks and a gluon. Only this unit, this primary particle, could achieve the Project's purpose. That is why I assembled it, in Room 18. That much I know.

But having brought the masses together, did I intend that they react, or be kept from reacting? Heat of fusion and heat of disassociation differ only in degree, ha, ha. Perhaps I wanted both results; but Schrödinger's cat cannot be alive and dead at once. That is the essence of the paradox.

I do not know what I wanted. Thoughts are all washed away in radiation, and now there is no time to reconstruct them: a doom I now propose to visit upon the Project itself.

Tomorrow, when A. does the experiment I detailed to him, and throws a certain set of switches, and Rig, room, workers, data, yea, all which it inherit, are vanished into incandescent air, the Project will be over for a while. Not forever, because the laws of physics wait patiently for the discoverer, but perhaps long enough for the people here to know better what they want of the laws.

And time is all we can ever win against death. See how I have stolen the days.

The survivors of tomorrow's accident will search and search and never find who welded the safeties down, and set the explosives, and wired destruction into Bank 7 of the Rig controls. It could not, after all, have been a bloodless corpse bound in white linen.

But I was not dead when I did the work, four years ago, when the Project began. Maybe I knew then what I wanted, the actual few deaths instead of the hypothetical many; but if so why did I never set those switches myself?

Perhaps I still fail: A. may be a better physicist, or a better coward, than I think. One cannot do nothing and expect to triumph. To do nothing is the triumph of evil (or words to that effect).

And yet. Reactions require a moderator as well as an initiator, and there indeed was a reaction in Room 18. Because it was N., the Project's voice, who deeper than did plummet sound drowned his books, and himself, and all of us. While my beloved J., who loved Physics alone, stood in the open shutters for the twelve seconds he needed to make the Project succeed.

Fusion. Disassociation. In the end we are all heat.

Whatever I have done, I can do no more. I will let go now, as I believe Y. did, and I will see if there is sunlight. Whatever happens tomorrow, there will be a crowd of ghosts in my room, calling me to answer, and I cannot face any of them except as one myself.

Day 23
Light. triumph

THE LOST DIALOGUE
A RECONSTRUCTION FROM IRRECOVERABLE SOURCES

PROLOGUE: THE VEILS OF CLIO

Time is a construction of layers:
Ash and iridium, the rings of trees,
The stone that was a trilobite in mud,
A sphere of light from an exploded star.

History is the draping of the layers
Into a Time that makes some human sense:
Troy is a hill built on seven cities,
The flies in amber are taxonomized.

The past is the interleave of Time and History,
A garment woven for the muse to dance in;
Now modestly drawn close, now flashing us a view
Of something secret that inflames the sense.

(Be very careful where you throw your trash,
Lest the historians of Whatever Follows U.
Decide you were devolved from half a burger
And a spritz of cologne in a picture tube.)

There is an island in the middle sea
Wealthy past dreams beneath a fall of ash;
The brush and knifeblade draw from it
Houses, palaces, a city dryly drowned.

The island's people knew it as Kalliste,
The Most Beautiful. It was round, and warm,
And fertile, but it sat on Fire and Water,
Which its own science knew were antitheses.

They painted lily frescoes on their walls,
Sailed to the borders of the world,
Bathed within walls in hot piped water,
And doubtless thought it was forever.

Kalliste is no longer on the map
In any sense. There is an arc of stones,
The jagged edges of a shattered bowl,
Horizon of the violent event.

Three thousand years or more ago there must
Have been a traveler who marveled at the bones
Of the old island, and asked about its name:
Thera, said the sailors. That place is Fear.

Forever is Time's joke: the stars explode,
Vomiting atoms that, an eon later,
Name other stars, and in our cosmic instant
Learn to find laughter in the jokes of Time.

Now you are invited to an expedition,
A peek beneath the veils, to have a look
At letters no one has discovered yet:
I will show you a Past in a handful of Fear's dust.

DAEDALUS: ON FLIGHT

Angle is crucial above all things.
If I bite too much air, the lift will vanish,
Too much of tilt, and I'll slide down the sky
And break on water. Now and then we dive
To gather speed so we can climb again,
But leave the dive too quick for sluggish air
To slip past, and the fabric of our wings
Will rend and drop us, molting, to the sea.
So many ways to fall, how do the birds
(Who have not made a study of the thing)
Suppose from the beginning they can fly?
Here is a patch of warm and rising air;
I can relax a moment in my straps
And think a bit, and glide. I look behind
And see my son is trying things again,
Waggling his sail and feeling out the winds,
Checking the pendulum that marks his slope,
Trying to, not just fly, but do it well.
My son would rather learn a little more
Than know a little less and live to know it.
He did not share my discontent on Knossos;
Minos gave us a comfortable slavery,
Plenty of books to read and tools to build with,
As long as what we built made Minos strong.
When first I thought that men could learn to fly,
The first thing in my mind was the Minoan
Army descending on its foes like Furies;
Only a tardy second came escape.
But here's the paradox: it was my son
Who told me we should keep this to ourselves,
Hold all our tests and calculations secret,
Until—well, here we are, both free and flying.

We start out from a height, and plunge for speed,
And climb again, a little less each time,
And, peak to trough, we move above the water.
In time, we must run out of height, and stop.
But if Kalliste is ahead of us,
We'll rise upon its fumaroles, and spiral
High, high once more, and start the cycle over,
An oscillating series of descents.
Toward Athens, now, and perhaps by sea to Sicily,
Which, though in Minos's reach, exceeds his grasp.
My son is perilously near the waves.
His guesswork is that trapping air between
The water and our wings will give him lift,
A smooth flat glide until the next warm updraft.
I would his love for theories would include
A fondness for a margin of mistake.
But see, he overtakes me. He flies fast,
True as an arrow, and the sea itself
Wakes to his passing. I dare say
I will congratulate him, if I can;
He surely shall surpass me, if he lives.

ARISTEROS: ON THE PROFESSIONS

I think if there had been a bit more flexion
Built into the wings, I might be on Sicily;
Perhaps a canted wingtip, like the gulls'.
All theory, of course, or as my father called it,
Idle. I did not reach Athens, much less Sicily;
I barely swam in reach of Kalliste,
Dragging the wreckage of my own right arm.
A fisherman found me, a man plain enough
To know that men do not fall from the sky.
When someone washes in, and hurt, then he was
Shipwrecked, ship or no ship. And I am born

Athenian: I know the ropes, I fit the tale.
For a long time I played the cripple
In body and in mind, knowing quite well
Minos is King here as in Knossos.
But in time I learned my father had escaped,
And everyone knew Icarus was dead;
Why, so he is. Was it not I who slew him?
Now my Kallisten neighbors call me Ari,
Aristeros Hydraulikos, Lefty the Plumber.
Pipefitting is a good trade here; it lets me wander
From town to town, visiting whom I please,
For everyone has pipes, and I am needed.
I have rebuilt my life, my name, my craft,
At last myself: see my mechanic wholeness.
This is my arm, made of bone and sinew
Like its drowned twin, and of bronze also,
And wood, and cables braided from hair;
Pins, wheels, levers, and a grasping claw.
It serves to hold my tablet, and is
The gods' gift when something rolls away;
It is no good to strum a harp or touch a lover.
I can plunge it in volcanic pools
Harmless as if it were dipped in Styx,
It can carry a pail of water, it balances me.
I make things, yes, I make things. Touch my arm,
Or try this. There is something about a toilet
That taps unplumbed (excuse me) depths in the craftsman:
Like an arm, it is intimate yet functional.
And as you would use your arm if it were rheumaticky
Or missing fingers, so you use the hopper
Whether or not it is aesthetic. Thus
The aesthetics, however useful, are a kind of art.
My father and I are in communication,
Rarely, in code. To speak too often
Would be dangerous to both of us,

As would be, I think as well,
A few too many questions between us.
On Knossos I saw my father's plans for this island.
Kalliste would have housed the New Labyrinth,
Powered by heat and the expansion of water,
With moving doors, sliding rooms, chambers
Scalding with steam, grates glowing dull red;
Theseus's thread would have burnt away in this
Tartarus upon Earth. It needed no monsters,
Excepting only one to think of it
And another to make it real. I could have been
Happy on Knossos among my diagrams,
But not as Hell's half-brother. So we flew.

DAEDALUS: ON MECHANICS

Of all the studies of my aging hands,
I think that making gears is pleasantest;
It calls from me a kind of regulation,
Of metrics, very much like poetry.
The bronze melts, then the wax melts, and the casting
Emerges like a fledgling from the shell;
The burrs are burnished out, the teeth debrided,
The polished part made fit to mesh its partner.
The wheel I now am shaping is a bit of
An orrery of planetary motions;
When all its gears articulate together
It will show moonphase, and predict eclipses.
It must require care in its construction:
We must not jam the workings of the heavens.
When I was young, I built a house for Minos,
King over Kings, lord of the middle ocean,
A place where his dark self could run unfettered,
Live free to feed, but never see the daylight.
Then, when Minos's daughter, for her lover,

Asked me to solve the maze of my creation,
I did it, and was thrown there for my trouble.
And now King Minos, having lost his monster
And daughter too—how shall he breed another?—
Has set the world a puzzle with a seashell
And length of thread. The prize would buy a kingdom.
So now the King of Sicily my refuge
Comes visiting, in greedy agitation;
It does not take a Daedalus to see
This shaft is aimed explicitly at me.
Yes, Minos, I accept your invitation.

ARISTEROS: ON THERMODYNAMICS

Sometimes the people joke and call me Hephaistos,
Crippled god of fires. The Kallistens
Are easy in their blasphemies, their King
The son of Zeus, their island
A pillar of the world. World's center,
They say, and even believe, as if the planets
And the fixed stars did not laugh at this.
The world has no center; or at least,
Not where men claim it, not Kalliste,
Not Knossos, not Athens or Saïs.
A center, do you see, is the thing that holds.
On Kalliste we draw our life from the earth,
Like Antaeus, its power rises through us,
Though now and then it breaks our crockery.
I am learning the patterns of its strength,
Its secret ways, the song that it is singing.
All over Kalliste I have pursued it,
Set traps for it. I make disks of clay,
Baked hard and brittle, and set them out
Everywhere I go, hundreds all charted.
When the earth shakes, some of them break,

And those pointed on a map draw a picture,
Which is, as I watch it, darkening.
Kalliste is warmed by the soil, Kalliste
Has water under pressure, has hot baths,
Because Kalliste is a cork in a bottle
And the bottle is set to boiling.
My father cared not much for the future;
He built his machines to act on the moment,
While I am obsessed with where curves lead.
There are Kallistens who trust my word,
Ari of the pipes and the brazen arm;
If Aristeros says *Leave your homes*, they will go.
I would I trusted my numbers quite so much.
When the curve rises thus, it is a hair's distinction
Between a broken window and the end of the world.
O Engineers of Destiny,
You made this island beautiful:
We only found it good to live upon.
Tell me I am wrong, or else tell me
What we have done, or all our kingdom done,
That such energies gather to destroy us.

DAEDALUS: ON THE DRAMA

I hear King Minos has put forth from Knossos
With a basket of gold, to reward the puzzle-solver.
Toil a thread through a conch shell, for money, what a joke.
But ants will travel winding paths for honey
As men for money: beautiful solution.
Minos loved beauty; this is a true thing,
True of any number of barbarians. I should think
Someone brought him the shell in a basket
Of pretty stuff, to charm the weary king;
And, looking down its smooth and easy entrance,
He thought of coils within, thought of the Labyrinth,

Threads, Theseus, and at last myself.
I wonder if he will bring the shell with him,
Hold it in my face, say *This is your work.*
His cleverness is real, but limited;
He thinks of something hard, a task impossible,
And he says *Only Daedalus can do it.*
And for this singularity of mind
He cannot rest without me in his house.
Daedalus will cage his monsters, Daedalus
Will engine his foes' destruction, Daedalus
In another man's palace is not to be borne.
But Sicily has a king too, and though he is
Witless even by Minos's measure, he knows
Daedalus can make bronze move, and sound, and kill.
When Minos comes to take me back to Knossos,
Sicilia will stand tall on cothurns of sovereignty,
Don Power's mask, and gather him a Chorus
Of loyal bullies with plain-spoken swords.
I move a man to move his men to kill a man;
It's such a bloody game, a mechanism
With parts that bleed and die. I could not do it
In Minos's grasp alone, there was nowhere to stand;
Between two kings, though, there is leverage.

ARISTEROS: ON PHILOSOPHY

I am going to tell you a joke now.
It is an old joke, but a good one,
And I hope you will listen and laugh.
A man came to an island and said,
  Heat and the fire that melts stone
   Will consume this place, utterly, tomorrow.
  What are you going to do?
One group of the islanders gathered
In their holy places, made sacrifice,

Wept and wailed and tore their clothes, saying,
    O gods, take from us this judgment,
    O gods, spare us this doom,
    O you gods, wait for us a little.
Another group went another way,
Taking wine and the best food,
And they drank and they danced and they coupled, saying
    If this is the last night of the world,
    Let us meet it with our best reveling,
    Let us not feel it when it strikes.
Only a handful were left, a cluster
Of wistful engineers, muses of the cosine,
Star-counters, a one-armed plumber.
It took the visitor with his tale of doom
Some time to find them (he had paused awhile
To watch the prayers, a little longer at the orgy)
And he found them sitting, marking
On their tablets, arguing chemistry,
Toiling with cloth masks and bladders of air.
He asked what this was, and the plumber said,
    We are learning to breathe fire.
You laugh, good, but that is not the joke.
The joke is—
Here the writing stops.
Added in an unknown hand:
The joke is that it might have worked,
Had they also been able to fly.

DAEDALUS: ON CLIMATE

In the East there is a terrible dark dawn.
In the streets outside they cry that Helios's chariot
Has crashed to Earth. Oh, no. There is the Sun,
Though I think it shall wear mourning for a while.

Perhaps it was his son who lost his bearings
And fell so hard. Yes, that will soothe the masses.
The King of Sicily, his hands still smoking
With another King's blood, is shouting at me.
He has killed the son of Zeus, he says,
And the thunderbolts are falling now. Or else
The Minoan navy will come and plough him under,
Toss his crown into the sea. I want to say,
Shut up, little king, you are no more than Earth's dust,
But he is afraid of the gods, and of me too.
The Destiny Makers can shatter the world with their bolts,
But I have made a death for the King of the World,
A petty stupid death in a street of hovels,
Out of an ant, a shell, and a piece of string.
So I tell him it is Kalliste burning,
The Minoan navy is flung on shores as driftwood.
The prospects turn within his small king's brain.
He pauses on his way to shush his people,
Saying, *It was King Minos killed your son, of course,*
Your son who fell into the sea and died.
Yes, my son has fallen into the sea.
It shall rain my son for a hundred years.
My son preferred theory to practice, to the uttermost;
I will not, cannot say that he was wrong.
Among his numbers, he did well, was content,
While I, who have lived so much among engines
And too much lived among the men who use them,
I, Daedalus, despair of ever doing a wholly good thing.

EPILOGUE: MEMO FROM SOLON

Attend me, o Muses, Olympian Zeus, for I am homesick.
I loosed a thing in Athens that needed take its course
Without me; but now it is time to return for the reckoning.

Unlike the noble Theseus, I am going home cautious.

I have traveled, and heard stories, and seen much
Of the world the sea binds; I saw the bones
Of an island in the west, courtier stones
At an empty throne, the past unseated by force.

In Saïs the priests told me that Time is a river,
Their river, in fact, and all other cultures merely tides.
They told me of crashing stars, empires that fall and rise,
That earth has bloomed and burnt and grown again, forever.

I have tried to do something useful with all this history,
A tale of a great empire that made great mistakes;
That strode the world boldly, but forgot its direction,
Something epical, touched with awe and mystery.

Though my people will not easily learn from another
    nation;
They will say that Atlantis gone is not Athens hence.
Anything can be built; nothing stands without a
    foundation.
People are clay, and must be fired to support monuments.

And the Egyptians may have made the whole thing up:
A claim that, being older, they are therefore oldest;
I think that people recall in the main what they wish to recall
And swiftly forget that they ever were powerless, beaten, or
    small.

It is in the mystery of priests to muddy what they say,
In the speech of statesmen to prove things their way,
In the way of engineers to twist nature's forces,
It is in the nature of poets to misuse their sources.

JANUS: SONNET

Sufficient time for faith and miracles
We find we cannot fit into our days;
And nothing's left at all that joyous dwells
Inside the heart. The spark of spirit stays
Too small for dreamburst, and all earth may prove
Inadequate for art. No human is
This potent all alone, and fear kills love. . . .
Love kills fear, and alone: all-potent, this.
No human is inadequate for art,
For dreamburst; and all earth may prove too small.
The spark of spirit stays inside the heart
That joyous dwells, and nothing's left at all
We cannot fit into our days. We find
For faith and miracles, sufficient time.

SHARED WORLD

I put on my worn bush jacket, tired blue bag,
    graphite-greased notebook,
Arm and gird for the World.
The typewriter stays on the desk,
    the whiskey in the drawer beneath.
Through the doors and I'm in it,
    the light and the air,
        trying to decide what they are.
It shall be clear today. The season
    for this volume is late autumn;
Clear and cold. The leaves turn vivid,
The people up the street button their cloaks.
And boots. Loose hats. Scarves. Presto, fashion.
Shutters are up on the housefronts.
Enough. More will come.
This quarter is my particular haunt;
    what I say here, is,
But it's a short walk to the lands of consensus.
This park, for instance, is here by common decree,
    but each statue in it is the work of a different artist;

People may for various causes and in various positions
      orate, fornicate, beg, dance, or die here
            as the unities require.
Memory being imperfect and notes a chore,
      the trees will move between visits.
There are no other gods abroad today.
Some collaborate; I lack the connections.
I know where they have been.
Here's a new play in the public arena,
Here's a victim bleeding under a berry bush,
Here are names graven in worn bronze on white stone,
      the memorial to a war we did not need till now.
Tomorrow there will have been much suffering,
      kings fallen, children brought
            fatherless into the world,
Battalions slain for the sake
      of brazen names
            forgotten already.
Where pain does not exist, we are required to invent it.
Our citizens do not complain. Not to us,
      who offer them justice
            and quotable dialogue.
Though they *are* fickle.
      Let one go alive,
            he will run to the bosom of another
            and tell lies:
Adventures another had, or perhaps no one,
Or just a different tale than the one to you.
Alas there's no lapse of sincerity,
      sincerity's what we make it,
            the best we try.
Plain weather tires me. I want a storm.
A short one, no one else need note it.
The sky darkens, good clouds, thick, the red leaves swirl,

hark, foreshadowing.
I have been following one of my sources,
    a veteran of two stories
      and four fair laughs,
Hoping she would lead me, storm-wet, upset,
    upsouldown, to a tale:
Instead we are in a place neither has been,
    none, white and empty
      as twenty-pound bond.
A house comes out of the mist, another,
    a little residential street,
Its name is,
    name is,
      name, name, name,
        is Orchard Street,
And there is a man standing before the small house
    on Orchard Street,
And the man before the house between two equally
    small shuttered houses on Orchard Street
      is weeping,
And a doctor hurries away from the house
    (Death's here).
My companion tugs her cloak, drifts on,
    this is none of her story.
Because the crying man before the forsaken house
    on tiny treeless Orchard Street
      is about to lose his child
        as he lost his wife
And he is on the brink of desperate measures
    that will, that will, that will—
I know now why the skies have darkened.
They were dark all along, for this.
My first guide was wise to desert.
She was made for romantic comedy:

If I sail her toward this whirlpool
    (and I know just how to make her)
        there will be no survivors.
She is up the next street,
      its name, I think, is Copse Lane,
        wet-cloaked, waiting.
How achingly sweet is a good tragedy.
A letter arrives, crumpled in my pocket;
Someone else wants to use her in a kinder role.
I nod, and she goes accompanied
      to fall through confusions into true love.
She does not look back;
      I wonder if she knows.
        They do sometimes.
The man on Orchard Street just blubbers on
As if he knows the price of sorrow's end
As I shall cost it out. I'll weigh those tears:
They must come heavy, hot as salt in wounds
Or else they're just a dew. The war, I think,
      of new old memory. One tale ago
        just marble, bronze, and names,
I think it made him, made him so damned hard
He never thought to break. To liquefy.
I pause. A stitch. There goes another rib.
Seeing as I am about to destroy the World,
      this veteran my instrument,
I should phone someone. I won't,
      knowing things will change. They always do.
My socks are damp with rain and sweat and tears,
      and so I squelch away. He'll keep.
Orchard Street is no more than myself
      until I make that call,
        or type and mail the pages.
          All's suspense.

I make my way back slowly
    through the joint-trust city,
Scouting locations, naming streets,
      asking the locals what's needed,
         opening venues as they would
           if non-fictional.
Hey, this is my town.
But the Orchard Street crier—
    I almost know his name,
      but once spoken it will be true,
        best to wait—
If I am going to tell his tale,
    people will suffer
      because I made them.
I know already the flaws I shall hammer on.
The pleasure for me
    will be in the degree of success
      in putting pain forth.
And few if any who visit here will care:
Comedy would amuse them,
    Adventure thrill them,
      Romance comfort them,
        Pain they've got.
Yet there endures a contract
    between love and the acts of love,
A coupling meta coupling that
    ten thousand tomcat years have not quite lost,
Because the lack of it sterilizes like gamma rays,
    warping monstrous what it does not kill.
Back in the room,
    one sip of bourbon for my joints,
      coffee.
Sort thoughts and words.
There was a call, while I was out:

"What day exactly did it rain?
Events too complex to explain."
I shouldn't answer. It was my wind,
  led to my street and weeping,
   my brink of my doom.
Let others make others.
But that is not the way of the World. One shares
  kind souls, busy streets,
   warm houses, bad weather.
I type a list of names and places
  so that if I die tomorrow
   (as—did I tell you?—
    the World does not)
     the work endures.
The work endures. Death and Pain,
  how small you look from a distance.
I will unshutter my eyes
  and go back to the scene.
I will open my heart to a blank page
  and interview the witnesses.

SHELTER FROM THE STORM

Ross Kinbote, defense marshal for Silverburn Territory, did not like being isolated from the Territory. He had come too far to get there. And no place isolated him so much as the Territorial Council conference room. It was long, boxy, and bare, with no furniture except angular chairs and a long black table that bounced back the harsh light—so unlike their sun's light. There was nothing that made it part of Silverburn Territory, or the world Perathena at all: no plants, plants, no wood, no scent in the air, bare even of sound. It could have been a room anywhere, on any planet, or for that matter a ship on the zipline between stars.

There were sloped windows at one end. Kinbote stood there, looking out between white linen curtains at Athena setting red in the west. Something moved across the disk: a ship headed for Port White. A large cluster-vessel, no doubt a grain freighter marshalling for the harvest.

Kinbote had a thought. Without turning, he said, "Vane."

"Marshal?" said Vane Ragan, Kinbote's adjutant.

"Post an advisory to Port White Control . . . monitor

thrust on incoming freighters. If a ship claims to be running empty and maneuvers like it's full, secure the pad and check it out."

"Yes, sir." Kinbote could hear the click of keys on Ragan's satchel computer. Ragan said, "Do you really expect that sort of assault, sir?"

"No," Kinbote said. "It's been tried in the past, but it's not Draeger's style. Besides, the whole port guard couldn't contain one fully armed squad of regular troops." He turned away from the window. "No, it's just to get them thinking, at the Port at least."

Ragan sat in one of the conference chairs, his thin face very pale in the room light. He was not smiling, but he almost never did. Light from the computer screen flashed greenly in his eyeglasses. He held still for a moment, then said without hesitation: "Your signature, sir, or Defense Command's?"

Kinbote nearly asked if Ragan knew of any difference, but thought that Ragan might misread the joke as displeasure. "My signature, Vane." *After all,* he thought, *if there is a difference tomorrow, whoever's in my place will want his own name on orders.* "And, Vane—don't send that yet."

Ragan turned from the screen and was about to say something when the door opened. Adam Herstatt of the Territorial Council came in. Ragan blanked the computer screen.

Herstatt was tall, athletic, sharp-faced. "The Council's voted," he said briskly. "We decided that single authority was best, for the duration of the emergency. So . . . until this is over, Ross, you'll report to me as if I were the Council."

"They've suspended fully?" Kinbote said, without showing emotion.

"No more meetings in chamber, yes, everyone's going back to his own tracts. Except me." He smiled, gestured toward the window. "Doesn't that make military sense, Ross? As close as we are to Port White? A bomb square on City Center—"

"Mercenary troops—" Kinbote had almost said *Draeger*—"don't do that. Politicians hire them; they're careful to display respect for politicians."

"Well! I'm glad someone's safe." Herstatt ran his fingers through his light brown hair. His smile narrowed. "We've had another confirmation, Ross. The Exans have definitely hired Solomon Draeger."

Kinbote nodded silently.

"Of course, you know what that means," Herstatt said, walking past the table toward the window, loosening his tight gray dress coat. Kinbote turned to follow him, but said nothing. Ragan, Kinbote saw, was not looking at anyone or anything.

Herstatt paused by the curtains. "Exathena couldn't possibly have paid Draeger's price. So the Star Kings must be involved."

"We have nothing an empire could want—"

"Grain? Goldenwood?"

"—in quantities they could use."

"That's not the way they think," Herstatt said, looking out the window toward the towers and pads of the spaceport. "The weakest of them rules more than a hundred systems—*systems*, not worlds. We're not talking about the Territory's resources . . . oh, those'll do to pay the troops and feed the masses, but the Star Kings think in . . . stars, Ross, *space*." Herstatt gestured toward Athena, now a crimson dome crowning the golden forest. "There are ziplines from our star to Keflis, Halliwell A, and Martino's Star, and we're not even fully charted. We're more than a piece in the game; we're a new square on the board."

Kinbote listened patiently to Herstatt, as he always had.

Herstatt swept his hand toward the sky. "*That's* why it's worth an empire's hiring troops for Exathena. Someone has to rule this system as satrap—and better the Exans than us, not least because when the Star King's ships take our goods away, the Exans won't miss the luxury."

Kinbote thought, but did not say, that Herstatt had now contradicted himself twice on the value of Perathena's resources. He did know, everyone did, that Exathena was poor, out on the limits of the star's biosphere, while Perathena, in a much closer orbit, was rich. But the Exan climate was stable, while the Peran winters were cruel. Silverburn Territory was only one part of one Perathenan continent.

There were more lands and resources, enough for all the Exans to come and make their own wealth. But taking it must have seemed easier. It usually did, until proven otherwise.

Kinbote was going to have to provide that proof.

He said, very carefully, "Colonel Draeger's Greys command a high price. Since they are armored, their overhead is high. However, we have enough resources to hire them."

Herstatt looked intently at Kinbote. "You're suggesting that we hire him out of his contract?"

Kinbote felt a flash of anger, but suppressed it. "Not even a Star King could pay that price." He saw the amused disbelief on Herstatt's face, and was angry again, and held it in again. "I'm suggesting that Exathena might have scraped up a down payment and promised the rest on success, from our resources."

"I didn't think Solomon Draeger had to accept contracts like that," Herstatt said. "Do you have information I don't? Has his reputation declined recently? Or . . . is there some special reason he might want to attack us? A home for his old age . . . or perhaps for old times' sake?"

Well, Kinbote thought, *we had to come here. At least it was a quick march.* "If you have any doubts about my ability or myself—"

"I don't want your resignation, Ross. In fact, I won't accept it if you give it. Ramalea was a long time ago, another world. Tell me, now: do *you* have any doubts about defending the Territory? Against Draeger or anyone else?"

"Do you want a full situation report?" Kinbote turned to Ragan, who poised his hands above the keyboard.

Herstatt shook his head. "No, no, Ross. Just a doubt report. Summarized, please."

"Very well. While we have certain advantages of position and dispersal, we have no natural redoubts, or any terrain that would impede an armored force, except, perhaps, the Owl River. As for the forces available, I have every confidence in the regular army, but as you know, it is quite small."

"And the militia?"

"They are in good spirits—and will be fighting for their homes—but they will be hard pressed by heavy troops such as Colonel Draeger commands."

"You doubt that you can win, then."

"I do not doubt that we will fight."

Herstatt grinned. "You see why I need you, Ross? You can't lie to me, even indirectly. With anyone else, I'd have to filter for the truth." He reached inside his coat, took out an offworld cigar—*one such as Star Kings would smoke*, Kinbote thought—and struck it alight. "Not to mention," he said, without the least note of sarcasm, "that someone else might have some illusions about Draeger."

"Is that all, then, Adam . . . did the Council give you a title?"

" 'Adam' was always good enough, Ross. But you've got a point. Anywhere I have to call you 'Defense Marshal,' you can call me . . . 'Coordinator' sounds about right."

"Then is that all, Coordinator?"

"Yes . . . Marshal. No, wait. If you were Draeger, when would you attack?"

"Before the autumn rains, certainly. Not necessarily first rain, but the later storms certainly. Not only will they hurt his mobility, but he'd obviously want to hand the Territory over to his employers at harvest . . . before winter closes in."

"Then we may have only days."

"I believe so."

"Then I won't keep you any longer. Good day, Ross."

"Good day, Coordinator."

Kinbote nodded to Ragan, who folded his computer, stood up and slung it over a shoulder.

As Kinbote turned to go, Herstatt suddenly held out his hand; Kinbote shook it and felt it gripped tightly. Herstatt's eyes flicked toward the adjutant.

"I'll meet you in the car, Vane," Kinbote said, and heard the door hum open and shut.

"Ross . . . I'm *responsible* now," Herstatt said, in a low voice. "Of course the Council voted me in; why have a hundred necks in the noose when you can have just one? Don't you see . . . when it's over, you'll be all right. Your reputation won't suffer—so Colonel Draeger beat you twice; the first time was by a hair and the second isn't even a contest. If the Exans have any sense, they'll keep you right where you are, unless Draeger hires you on. *But I'm going to hang.*" He released his grip, looked at the end of his cigar.

"We might win, Adam."

"Yes. We might at that. Apologies, Ross."

"None necessary."

"Still. Good night. Best to Elise and the girls."

"Good night, Adam," Kinbote said, and left the room and the building.

Ragan started the skimmer as Kinbote approached; the lift fans spun up and the carriage folded away, leaving the car on hover. Kinbote got in, sealing the soft plastic canopy after him.

"Home, sir?"

"The hospital first. I want to see Clair."

"Yes, sir." Ragan pushed the control rod and the car glided forward.

Argentine City's streets were nearly empty. Not many people actually lived in the city; services and maintenance personnel from Port White, some storekeepers and technicians who didn't like to commute—maybe two or three percent of Silverburn Territory's quarter-million population.

Kinbote wondered briefly if they could use that against Draeger; trick him into diverting forces to a siege, have the inhabitants put on a show of being several times their actual number.

Pointless, he thought at once. *He'll have his siegecraft; why give him reason to use them?*

The skimmer stopped at a traffic signal; a policeman on foot patrol saw Kinbote through the canopy and waved. Kinbote almost snapped a salute, but waved back instead. *Neither of us will kill soldiers for useless gestures. Surely cities deserve as well.*

But how much gesture is useless, and how much must we make?

The Territorial Hospital was a cubical building, its west face a blank slab against the winter wind, its south a chessboard of light and dark windows. Ragan pulled the skimmer into a parking space near the Emergency entrance. "Do you want me to wait here, Marshal?"

"I think you'd better bivouac with us now, Vane. Drive home and get your gear, then meet me back here."

"Yes, sir."

Kinbote returned Ragan's salute, got out and watched the skimmer move away. He thought: *Houseguests bivouacking. Saluting on all occasions. Welcome back, Colonel Kinbote.* He looked up at the emerging stars. *And Solomon Draeger's on the other side of the hill. Didn't we leave this party?*

Squinting against the glare, Kinbote walked into the hospital.

Heads turned as he entered the Emergency Room; one second later a chime rang, the double doors next to Kinbote hissed open, and a cart rolled in with a man flat upon it and a mobile medic riding on each side.

"This the MI?" said a tall, fair-haired woman in a green surgical gown.

"Yes, Clair," said one of the medics, who was doing something around the mouth and nose of the patient. His partner was working at the scanner bank built onto the cart. "He'd been collapsed for ten, maybe twenty minutes. I think he went into apnea."

"Confirm that," said the scanner operator. "We're just getting his blood O_2 out of the red."

"Vitals?" Clair Kinbote asked calmly.

"Pulse erratic, BP eighty over forty, enceph—correction, BP forty over nothing."

"He's gonna arrest," said the first medic.

"He just did," said the second, and the scanner screamed.

"Blue Unit," Clair said, and touched a key on her control bracelet. "Let's go." She grabbed the tiller under the cart's front end and steered it, the medics still riding the stirrups, though a blue-bordered door that was not fully open before it started to close again behind the cart and team.

One of the desk staff noticed Kinbote, found him a chair and a cup of tea. Twenty minutes later, the blue door opened and the patient, an oxygen mask over his face, was rolled out on a plain unpowered cart. A nurse and an orderly took it over from the mobile team, who after a few words with Clair rode their cart back outside.

"Father?" Clair said.

Kinbote stood. Clair had grown up like her mother, tan, fair-haired, light of step. For a moment, in her working clothes, hair banded back, multiprobe dangling a wire from her pocket, she *was* Elise, in a field hospital during a long-ago battle, soothing wounded soldiers and telling colonels to shut up or else and asking Captain Kinbote what the devil his trouble was.

Just a vision, but more than a memory. They would have field hospitals again soon enough, and Clair would run them just as she ran this room. *Welcome back, Ross Kinbote.*

"Clair, I—"

"We heard about the Council vote," she said coolly. Then, with worry: "Adam hasn't replaced you?"

"No. I don't suppose I can be replaced, now. Even against Colonel Draeger."

"Especially against him," Clair said. "When will you want the report on field medical services?"

Kinbote hesitated. He did not want to talk to Clair about triage and med-evac and wound dressing just now, but there she was, her mother's daughter. He also did not want to ask what he had come to ask, but here he was, Territorial Defense Marshal. "Is Alexis in tonight?"

"No, he's out riding circuit. I wish he were here; he's worth two pathologists and a COSMA Twenty any night." A pause. "Mother's not sick?"

"Oh, no, no. I just want to talk to him. Is he in our sector?"

"Close. I can call him if you . . ." Her look changed again, and she let the sentence trail.

"I'll call. Or maybe just wait for him to pass by." He looked at Clair, at the set of her face, the cool hardness of her eyes. He wondered what Dr. Alexis Teal had told Dr. Clair Kinbote, in their line of work and especially outside of it. He wondered other things about the two of them, but the other things were not his affair. He only wished that this one were not.

"This is about a posting for Dr. Teal, isn't it?" she said. "A . . . Defense post."

Then she did know. So Teal had told her, because Elise would not have. She had almost asked Kinbote the precise question, daring him to lie, knowing that he could not.

So you do love him, he thought, *you love him enough to want the truth and too much to ask for it.*

"Yes, Clair," he said.

She nodded, then raised her head as if to speak again.

"Dr. Kinbote," said the desk attendant, "Long and McCone have an elevator accident at the Vanov Building. Three massive traumas; they've called for a second unit—"

"Scramble nine units of syntheme," Clair said, touching keys on her bracelet as she turned away from her father. "Get their types and have Stores deblock two bloods and a matched protein each. Then wake up the interns, all of them—"

"Good night, Clair," Kinbote said softly, and went outside. Ahead of him, a skimmer flashed its headlights; he could hear Ragan starting the fans.

He had wanted to talk to his daughter about good things: about life, and love, and what a beautiful young woman she had grown up to be. One needed to do that, when a war started.

As he stepped off the curb, he thought that perhaps, after all, he had.

Kinbote House was a hundred kilometers west of Port White and Argentine City, deep within the forest of golden raintrees that Ross Kinbote had watched from the conference room window. A winding track, cut to follow the ground and spare the trees, led from the Territorial road to the main clearing, where the vehicles and machinery were garaged. Paths, and a tunnel for the deepest winter, led to the house itself.

It was built of stone and timber, dark fieldstone from the cleared areas where grain grew now, and goldenwood winter-cured to iron hardness, planed and mortised and fitted with precision and care. The structure of the house, its muscle and bone, were native to the Territory and the world; only its nerves and brain, the electronic communications and controls, came from down the ziplines, bought with red kernels of perawheat and golden lumber. Now there was a pilot plant for polyconductor circuits in Argentine City, and soon—

"—to lose it *now.* That's what's intolerable." Kinbote sat with his wife on the house's broad front porch, the stormshields open to the cool night air. Past the square pillars was a downslope covered with silver grass, further silvered by the lite of the moon Pallas, which hung low in the sky and three-quarters full. The smell of grass and trees was crisp, pleasant.

Kinbote stood and walked to a pillar. The porch seat swung gently until Elise stopped it.

Kinbote said, "Five years just to start living with the winters, instead of hiding from them. Ten more to make the place something like a home. And how long to lose it? A day to seize Port White. Two days, three at the most, for Draeger to force a battle. Then two minutes for me to surrender, or two hours for him to break us to bits and accept a surrender from whoever's left."

"You couldn't fight a guerrilla war," Elise said, not particularly as a question.

"I could," Kinbote said heavily, "but Draeger wouldn't. He's not counter-insurgent . . . and the Exans can't afford that kind of long-term action, so you know what they'd send us instead. House garrisons. Burndown sweeps. Hostages, terror, counter-terror. No, I can't." He looked out at the moonlit grass, the deep forest. "Not that I'd get the chance. Draeger's terms will certainly include Abandonment of Arms . . . for me, a general oath, most likely."

"Do you think an empire is really paying him?"

"I suppose so. Adam certainly hopes so . . . not so hard to understand, I suppose. If you can't live in the company of Star Kings, you can at least challenge them to destroy you."

"Or," said Elise, pouring two cups of tea, "it sounds better to be destroyed by a Star King's thunderbolt than hanged by some Exans."

Kinbote took a hot teacup. "There's always that."

"*Would* they hang him?"

"They very well might." Steam warmed his face. "The Council found the argument convincing."

A moment later Beth Kinbote and Vane Ragan came out of the house. Beth, younger than Clair by five years (or three campaigns, as Elise said), had her father's dark skin and eyes. What Kinbote saw in himself as stockiness had in Beth become compact, dancer's grace.

"The books are debugged," she said. "We may show a profit this season . . . thanks to Vane."

Ragan showed no expression. He said, "The lady's asked me to escort her on a tour of the grounds, Marshal. Your permission?"

"Granted."

"Provided," Elise said, "that you both put on coats."

Ragan started to go inside, but Kinbote said, "Beth, you get them. I need Vane for a moment more."

Beth went in. Kinbote turned to Ragan, saw that the adjutant had dropped into parade rest. Kinbote hoped the darkness hid his smile.

"Sir?" said Ragan.

"Vane, before Adam Herstatt came in on us, you were about to say something. What was it?"

"Sir, you'd ordered me to delay sending the advisory to Port White. I was about to remind you that the conference room is shielded; I couldn't send anything until I was outside it. But then I realized that the reminder was superfluous."

Especially in front of Herstatt, Kinbote thought. "I see. Thank you, Vane."

"Of course, Marshal."

Beth came out with two coats. Ragan helped her into hers, put on his own and belted it. They walked off the porch, down the hill, one dark shape against the silver grass. Kinbote watched them for some minutes, sipping the hot, strong tea.

Elise said, "You told me once that all properly conducted operations begin with reconnaissance."

Kinbote sat down next to her, set the seat swinging. "I don't remember that."

"Of course not. That's what you've got Vane for."

"He'll be with me . . . he should be safe."

She looked at him. "Then there *will* be fighting."

Kinbote didn't answer. The porch swing creaked on its chains.

"Ross, is there a way?"

"Ten years ago we didn't have anything to lose," he said, just short of bitter. "Five years from now and we'd be able to ignore empires and Exans and everyone else. Now . . . I don't know if there is a way."

"You have to know," she said firmly. "You raised the troops here; you're the only commander-in-chief they've ever had. If anyone knows, it has to be you."

"You talk like Adam Herstatt ought to." Kinbote put both hands around the teacup, trapping the remaining warmth. "All right. We've got three companies of regulars and five times five companies of militia; three thousand effectives, plus or minus the usual. Draeger will have just over a thousand.

"But those aren't the odds, of course. Much as I admire and respect our neighbors, I'll believe them under arms when I see them. And Draeger's armored, as we all know. We've got no tanks, no decent artillery, and anything else we can put in the air he can knock down at the horizon."

Elise said, "And he's Solomon Draeger."

"*And?*" Kinbote said, too loudly. "Elise, I'll fight him. I'll lock on my rig and lead whoever will march after me."

"I know that," she said quietly. "I just wanted to make sure that you did."

He stopped the swing, stared at her. She looked like the image of serenity in the moonlight, her fair hair gone to silver and her face to marble.

She said, "You know you aren't afraid of fighting, not Draeger or the Devil himself. So you don't have to be afraid of looking for another way."

Kinbote stood carefully, without shaking the swing, walked to the porch rail and leaned against it, facing Elise. He wondered if Clair had called here after he'd left the hospital. Or if she'd called Alexis Teal, appearing on his call screen spattered with someone else's blood.

That was how Kinbote and Elise had first seen each other. Somehow they had managed to see past it.

He looked down the hill for Vane and Beth, but could not see them. He turned back to Elise, saw her still perfectly calm, and thought that without her, he would surely now be dead. He would be dead even if his body were still breathing.

He said, "I'll call Alexis in the morning."

"In the morning," Elise said, and put her arms around him and her head on his shoulder. She whispered, "Let's go inside."

"Beth and Vane . . ." Kinbote said, then finished, ". . . have enough sense to come in from the cold."

They went into the house.

At three hours after noon the next day, Ross Kinbote was on the screen to Weather Platform Two, of the three in orbit around Perathena. He said, "Understand, now, we're sure Draeger will be staging from Keflis; a zip to Halliwell or Martino would cost him a lot of time for a very small surprise. But there's nothing to stop him from sending sensor decoys down the ziplines from either of them. So when you see a fleet zip in, and you will, very soon, *first* run a discriminator series, *then* call in the alert. He'll be ninety hours out, when it really is him; we can afford an hour's delay more than a false alarm."

"Yes, Marshal. And . . . what then?"

"Then nothing. Draeger's space wing will occupy the platforms; you let them. They'll deploy his scannersat; you let them do *that*. You are not a militia unit, you're civilian noncombatants. Clear?"

"Clear, Marshal," said the face on the screen, disappointment visible.

"Fine," Kinbote said. "You have the alert frequency preset?"

"Of course, sir."

"That's all, then. And thanks. Ground AK 356 out." As Kinbote broke the relay, one of the annunciator lights on the commsole began blinking. Kinbote touched a key, got a view of his approach road from a video pickup high in a raintree.

A rovervan was coming up the road, stirring up dust and leaves under its six all-surface wheels. A starburst and staff of Aesculapius, signs of emergency medicine, were painted on the roof.

"Elise," Kinbote said.

She came into the den, tying a scarf over her hair. "I asked Vane to drive Beth and me into the city for some things. We'll be back after sunset; is that long enough for the two of you?"

"More than enough."

"Good. We'll be bringing Clair back; she said she had that report ready for you."

Kinbote nodded. Obviously the report had been ready last night, but the subject had changed. He pushed his chair back from the commsole, went to Elise and kissed her. "I love you too," she said, and went out.

Suddenly alone in the house, Kinbote looked around the den. It was paneled in Sardissian oak from just beyond the Territory, with ceiling beams of goldenwood. On the wall were images of soldiers, from painted pictures of ancient hoplites and hussars to multi-graphs of skystrikers; crossed rifles, before the banner of Kinbote's Rangers; a rack of books, bound paper editions of the field library Kinbote had carried in microform on campaign, Thucydides and Clausewitz and von Mellenthin to Graeme and Falkenberg.

On one wall was a velvet-lined case of ceremonial sidearms, pistols and swords. Each one was a prize, taken from an officer Kinbote had defeated in the field.

All but one. At the bottom of the case was a straight-bladed sword, the half-basket hilt of silver, the grip padded with blue velvet. Kinbote had once worn the sword, but it was not his. He had carried it into battle at Ramalea . . . and there lost it, to Solomon Draeger.

But Draeger had never appeared to collect it. He had never appeared at all. The copter that lifted Kinbote from the field had a civilian crew and an armed civil guard. Draeger had been similarly removed. The politics of which they had been the extension had disposed of them both, packaged them and shipped them out like two loads of suddenly unfashionable consumer goods.

Kinbote had gathered his wife and daughters and gone to Perathena, where the fashion was different. Draeger, likewise, had gone elsewhere to war.

This room, with its books and the weapons case and the Ramalea sword, was Kinbote's whole warrior past. And it was here that Alexis Teal had come, five years ago, to talk.

Teal was a first-rate physician, surgeon, one-man trauma team, and (inevitably) scratch veterinarian. After his first winter not a few Perathenans, including whole families, owed him their lives.

The following spring Clair got her EMD, and of course Alexis Teal was invited to the party at Kinbote House. Kinbote found him admiring the den with more than casual interest, and asked him to return under quieter circumstances.

The night he came to visit, Beth was visiting a friend, Clair was interning in the Emergency Room she would eventually run. Kinbote, Elise, and Dr. Teal sat in the den over sandwiches and middle-aged brandy, while a warm spring breeze whispered through the windows.

Teal was lean and wiry, with light skin and very black hair and eyebrows. His eyes were liquid black, with a more-than-physical darkness that Kinbote found hard to look at and hard to look away from.

They talked about medicine, and the planet and the Territory, but there in the den the talk turned inevitably to war. And Teal knew war: battles, leaders, weapons, tactics, in detail that astonished Kinbote.

"Alexis," he said, "you know enough to have been a general—"

"A general's adjutant," Elise said.

"—*do* you have some military background?"

Teal, animated a moment ago, was suddenly quite still in his chair. "Yes," he said, and that was all he said.

Kinbote said, "You know that in the Territory we don't ask where you're from or what you did there." Maybe Teal was a washout from an Academy or War College somewhere. Or an officer's son who couldn't follow his parent's lead, for whatever reason. Or even one of those pacifists who could not let war alone with their minds, even as their hearts abhorred it. "You must have heard of me," he added. "After Draeger at Ramalea, my record's no secret."

"Mine is," Teal said. "But I'll tell you."

Elise said, "You were a soldier?"

Teal smiled. "I was a secret weapon."

Kinbote poured more of the golden, heady brandy.

"The project," Teal said, "was called GENIE. Greatest Effectiveness Nexus Identification and Elimination . . . though I don't know whether the acronym was invented before or afterward.

"Anyway . . . the idea was: what do you want to do to an enemy army?"

Teal and Elise both looked at Kinbote. "Destroy its ability to fight," he said automatically.

Teal nodded. "And traditionally, you do that by causing enough casualties in it to destroy its structure. Like smashing at a stone wall with a sledge until it crumbles. But there's another way to knock a wall down."

Elise said, "Find the keystone."

Teal said, "Find the nexi of greatest effectiveness . . . and eliminate them."

"You're a commando?" Kinbote said.

Teal looked into his spherical glass, as if looking for a vision within it. "The Project Prototypes . . . that's what they called us,

'Prototypes'...were trained to the practical human limits in system-analytic techniques, and infiltration tactics...and personal killing methods. We were one-person search-and-destroy units, designed to find the key people among the enemy. And eliminate them."

Slowly, Kinbote said, "'Eliminate' doesn't necessarily mean 'kill.'" He was thinking, without real alarm, that as Defense Marshal for Silverburn Territory he must be a key person. And as near as the telescreen was, it was a long way to any physical help.

"I don't really know, Marshal. None of us was ever...activated." He looked up at them, his eyes very dark, and Kinbote could see the agony in them. "The Project was shut down before any of us could be used." He looked down again, and Kinbote was horrified by the relief he felt. "An empire fell, in fact." Teal looked at his long, delicate fingers, arched one hand and balled it into a fist.

"Adam Herstatt says in Council that no Star King's ever fallen," Kinbote said, without real thought, and Elise spoke over him.

"Are your medical papers real?" she said. "Understand, Alexis, I'm not asking if you're a physician. We all know *that*. But if the documents are faked, we should get you some real ones."

"Yes, they're real," Teal said. He smiled, finally, making his look bearable again. "I already knew everything there was to know about how systems work, including biosystems. And anatomy...the combat training covered that very well. I was a top-grade med student."

He drank some more. He'd put away quite a bit, but Kinbote had seen every sort of drunkenness and this wasn't any of them. It must be metabolism; it certainly wasn't body mass.

Teal said, "You're the only people who know this. Not just the only ones here. The only people, period."

"No reason for it not to stay that way," Kinbote said. He leaned forward, half-consciously slipping a hand into Elise's. "Alexis..."

"No, it's not the name I was born with."

"Not what I was going to say. I can understand your wanting to hide. And I swear we'll respect that. But you're Territorial now. It doesn't matter what you were before."

Teal stood up slowly, turned to face the rack of weapons on the wall. He was reflected in the glass, darkly. When he finally spoke, the sound seemed to come from a very great distance, as wind shearing from a mountain peak. "You don't understand, Mr. Kinbote. It's not something I was. It's something I am. I'm . . . a werewolf." He turned to face them again, and even his look seemed to come from far off. "I mean that literally. I'm a supernatural monster, in—temporary— human form."

Kinbote squeezed Elise's hand, which was suddenly very cold and impossibly rigid—

Kinbote stood at the den table, an empty glass tight in his hand. He looked at it for a moment, then put it on the table with another glass and a crystal decanter of whisky. He pushed two armchairs before the fireplace, poked up the burning logs.

He went out on the porch. Dr. Teal was coming up the path, head down, hands in the pockets of his green jacket. He paused for a moment, turning slightly, evidently looking at something in the brush that Kinbote could not see. Then he came on, finally looking up.

His skin had weathered in five years, though he seemed never to tan or freckle. His hair was still absolutely black—Kinbote reminded himself that Teal could hardly be more than thirty—and his eyes still had the darkness that was only partly physical.

"Alexis," Kinbote said.

"Ross." He took Kinbote's hand; his grip was tight, dry.

"Come on in and be welcome, Alexis. We'll have a drink, and talk."

"Yes, Ross," Teal said, looking past Kinbote into the house. "I think we had better do that."

They went in, and Teal unsealed his jacket. Underneath it he wore an equipment harness, white webbing hung with pouches and medical instruments. It reminded Kinbote, almost unpleasantly, of battlerig. Teal put a finger on the latch release, then gave his head a small shake and sat down before the fireplace, still wearing the harness.

Kinbote poured two large whiskies, handed one to Dr. Teal. "Here's to."

"To the dark side of the moon," Teal said, clicked glasses with Kinbote, then took a long swallow, casually, as if there were no other way to drink whisky.

Kinbote sipped at his own drink, sat down. "Alexis, you know what I'm going to ask you."

"I've known for weeks, Ross." He drank again. "I think I've known, ever since I first told you my little secret, what you were going to ask." There was a tension in his voice, but it was not anger, or pain.

"You don't think I deliberately planned—"

"No." Teal shook his head. "Not in the least. I know all about military planning, right? I've been wondering if anyone planned it. If anyone had to."

He emptied his glass. Kinbote poured him another. "I don't follow you. You know I won't—can't—force you into anything you don't want. You're certainly serving the Territory—"

"You *don't* follow, Ross." Teal stared into the fire. "When I told you what I . . . am, maybe I wasn't just being honest, or trying to share the secret, or whatever. Maybe I wanted you to find a way to use me." A gulp. "Now you have."

He spoke more quickly, as if a motor were accelerating within him. He kept drinking. "You don't know what it's like. I don't think anyone *can* know, but I'll try anyway. Things happen, inside my head. I'll be palpating a throat for swollen glands, and suddenly I'll think that a finger, thrust just so, will smash the larynx. The same with a kidney, the tip of a sternum, an eye. Now and again—now and again I'll see someone walking alone—in the city or the country, it doesn't matter—and know that I could kill that person, in the dark or broad daylight, and dispose of the body so it'd never be found, or make it look like suicide, or any sort of accident, or even a murder no one would ever solve.

"And then too, I'll be in bed, late, and I won't be able to sleep, because I know the city is out there, asleep, naked and helpless in the night, and I could—"

Kinbote suddenly felt Teal's index finger against his throat, throbbing with the carotid pulse.

Teal went to the desk, poured another drink, downed half of it and topped up again. "I could, Ross, I really could."

"But you haven't," Kinbote said calmly, carefully. He had never seen this man before. He wondered if anyone had. If Clair had.

"No. I haven't. Anyone I've killed I did in honestly, in the best traditions of medicine." He sat down again. "I could, Ross. But *I may not*. You understand why, of course? You of all people?"

Kinbote nodded. "Your unit was never activated. You need an order."

"There are parts of my training," Teal said, "that I can't reach consciously. Parts of my mind are closed to me. Do you remember asking me if 'eliminate' had to mean 'kill'? I suspect it doesn't. But I'm not sure. And I don't know all of what else it might mean. There are only ... shadows." He looked into his glass. "Drinking is a shadow, you know, Ross."

"For a lot of people."

Teal laughed. "Alcohol depresses the manic response. I must have one hell of a manic response. Not to mention one hell of a set of biological filters."

Teal sat in the chair, hands together on his glass, feet spread out flat on the floor, his whole body a flexed spring. Kinbote knew what the tension was, in the pose and the voice. It was sheer anticipation. He knew it from himself, from the hours before any number of battles.

"You can accept an activation order from me?"

"Yes."

"Only from me?"

"Yes."

"What form does it have to take?"

"*Just tell me to go.*"

They sat in silence for a long moment. Teal's eyes were black coals, reflecting the firelight. The energy in his thin frame was such that it seemed he must shortly snap and fly apart.

But Kinbote knew that would not happen. He knew exactly how long a man could hold that pose.

Teal said, "You mustn't wait too long. If I'm not operational from the very first, I'm wasted."

"I understand. They'll zip in ninety hours out. Is that enough lead time?"

"That's enough." He faced Kinbote. "Is that your order, then? Activate on warning?"

"You don't want me to cut you formal orders?"

"Of course not."

It had been fifteen years since Kinbote had actually given an attack order, actually sent men out to face an armed enemy. He had always been cautious about that—but he had never been hesitant. He had not abandoned caution; he would not adopt hesitation. "Then, as Defense Marshal for Silverburn Territory, I assign you as of now to a tripwire counterforce role. Immediately upon identification of hostile forces within our system space, you are to commence independent operations against those forces."

Teal closed his eyes, took a deep breath that made his harness whisper and jingle. When he exhaled, the terrible tension seemed to go as well. He looked up. "Acknowledged." Then he said, not particularly to Kinbote, "Well, that's it."

They went out on the porch. The setting sun filtered through the trees, turning their red and gold leaves into pure fire. The silver grass rippled in a small, cold breeze.

"I'll be going on around the circuit," Teal said. "No term pregnancies or imminent crises, fortunately. Tomorrow I'd better do a checkdown on Ariel Danaher's support pump. And run the file on the children's inoc series . . ."

All at once he was the Alexis Teal that Kinbote had always known. *You were hurt badly once, Alexis,* he thought, *twisted hard. But you're not a monster. I've known monsters who looked like men . . . but that's what they were, beasts. The werewolf is just a sad, romantic myth.* "Why don't you stay the night here, Alexis? Clair's coming home tonight."

"No, thank you, Ross." Teal touched a hard wooden pillar, arching his fingers; he looked into the red sun. "I just realized I've got to go to the Danahers' tonight. Tomorrow won't do." He turned to Kinbote, who was suddenly still. "The weather, Ross, you know. And the phase of the moon. You can probably work it out consciously . . . I know, but I can't tell why. Not yet."

"*Draeger?*" Kinbote said, looking at the starless, shipless sky, not quite believing but not able to disbelieve.

"You see," Teal said, and the color of pain was vivid in his eyes. "I'll be going now, Ross. My best to your family."

"Is there anything you need, Alexis?" Kinbote said, as Teal stepped off the porch. "Supplies, weapons—"

"Nothing." Teal's look darted to the woods again. Kinbote still saw nothing. "There never was anything. Except the order."

When Teal had gone down the path, Kinbote went back into the house and sat down at the commsole, his still unfinished glass of whisky at his elbow.

There was no point in calling the orbital stations; he'd only alarm and confuse them. The commsole had a battle computer component, but there was no real use in that, either. His inputs and interpretations would be too heavily prejudiced. He really did not think that Teal was wrong.

He was still sitting there, his head in his hands, his drink untouched, when a hand touched his shoulder. He looked up at the face, said, "Clair, I—"

And stopped, because it was not Clair but Elise. He shook his head, knowing that there had been nothing to say anyway. Elise's fingers brushed his cheek, and she went out, closing the door behind her, giving him the time alone he needed.

It was two hours before midnight. Beth was asleep, Elise reading in bed, Vane Ragan in the kitchen with his satchel computer. Kinbote had returned to the den after dinner; he was examining perspective maps of the terrain around Port White.

Clair came in. She still wore her work whites, but had taken off her shoes and hairband. She had a large bag over her shoulder; she set it on the table and pulled out a sheaf of papers. The bag slumped over. "The medical report," she said. "I'll leave it—"

"I'm not busy," Kinbote said, switching off the map. "Tell me about it. Are there any problems?"

"No immediate ones. We have enough mobile units and crews without completely stripping the civilian system." She put the report down, tapped it with her short fingernails. "The unit teams have been told not to carry anyone in uniform and unwounded, so they're not confused with military transport."

"Even across town in the rain?" Kinbote said, smiling.

"Even Defense Marshals." Clair smiled too. "And we've taken the five-millimeter rifles out of the units. The Circuit doctors are—" Her smile disappeared, and she finished flatly, "—turning theirs in as they check through."

Kinbote nodded.

Clair said, "So everyone will be disarmed except me."

"What do you mean, except you? You're a—"

"A major, and the ranking medical officer, or I will be once the militia's activated. By Field Regulations that gives me the right to carry a sidearm."

Kinbote sighed. "Did you get that from the Regs or your mother?"

"Both."

"Well. All right, Major. Just a moment." Kinbote took a ring of keys from his pocket, went to the case of weapons on the wall and opened it. Without hesitation he took a pistol from the rack: a Gage and Rixon automatic, with zebrawood grips, and silver chasing on the frame and slide. It was the plainest weapon in the case, but the most reliable, and the only one of a combat caliber. When Kinbote taught his daughters to shoot, he had also taught them what guns were for. Giving Clair a pretty little dress pistol, a piece of military jewelry, would have been an insult and a lie.

Clair took the pistol, checked the action, turned to a blank wall and dry-fired it in a perfectly smooth motion.

"Thank you, Father." As she tucked the pistol into her bag, she looked suddenly distraught, but it passed in an instant.

Kinbote said, "I'll get you some loads for it."

"No," she said. "I'll do it. You loaded mine."

Kinbote didn't understand, but Clair was already shouldering the bag. "Good night, Father."

"Good night, Clair. If Mother's still up as you pass, tell her I'll be along soon."

Without answering, she bent her head, and Kinbote kissed her on the cheek. As she drew away, he saw that she was staring past him, at the silent commsole. Then she turned and walked away, lightly in her stocking feet.

Kinbote went back to the table, reached for the report. Near it was a book that had not been there earlier, apparently fallen from Clair's bag. Kinbote picked it up.

Feral eyes, black with flares of red, stared at him from above bloodied white fangs. The title, in lurid red, was *Legends of the Werewolf*.

Kinbote lifted the cover. On the flyleaf was written:

> *Clair—*
> *No secrets,*
> *all the truth.*
> *Alexis.*

Kinbote knew, then, what Clair had meant. *I gave you an empty gun. You loaded it.*

There was another line of Teal's angular handwriting at the bottom of the page. It read:

> *If. Page 127. Please.*

He began flipping pages. 60—80—120—121—

The commsole's call light flashed. Kinbote put the book down, went to the board and touched keys.

"Marshal Kinbote," said the weatherman on the screen, "we have a sensor trace of a fleet of ships at the Keflis endpoint."

"Checked and confirmed?"

The weatherman showed him. Sensor images were backed up with computer analysis and optical scanning. It was not a decoy. In a few hours the points on the scanplate would resolve into the arrows and discs of air and space fighters, the clustered coffins of troop carriers. The shaft of the spear, whose head was a thousand of the best troops in existence.

And the point of the spear: Colonel Solomon Draeger.

"All right," Kinbote said, "I'm declaring full alert as of . . . 0100 Port White time. When I break off with you, you're to alert Platforms Two and Three; you all know your routine. Establish tightbeam now. I'll be in touch."

"Yes, Marshal."

"Very well. Weath—Defense Observation One out."

Kinbote rang the intercom to the kitchen. "Vane, come here. Bring your black box." Without waiting for an answer, he punched out a personal callnumber. The ringer pulsed for three full minutes, but finally Adam Herstatt appeared, half-dressed and more than half asleep. The sight of Kinbote woke him above halfway.

"Ross . . . is this it?"

"It is. I've declared alert as of the hour."

"I'd better convene the . . . no, I suppose I hadn't." At that thought, Herstatt's head seemed to clear at once. "Let me check my board." He touched keys below his screen. "No declaration of war received yet."

"Exathena can't spot them for forty minutes," said Ragan from behind Kinbote. "Then twenty-five minutes for a message to get here."

". . . like this always happen in the middle of the night," Herstatt was saying.

"Adam, I've got more calls to make. I'll be in the city a little after dawn. I'll see you then."

"Of course, Ross. I've got calls to make, too." Herstatt broke relay.

"Marshal," said Ragan, "I'll make the alert-net calls. You should sleep for a few hours."

"I—yes, of course, Vane." *Never usurp your subordinates' authority.* "There's just one I have to make personally."

"Yes, sir."

"Vane . . . would you leave the room, please?"

"Certainly, sir," and he did.

Dr. Teal answered the call instantly. He was half in darkness, half in moonlight, and fully awake. "They're out there, Ross?" It was not really a question.

Kinbote nodded. Teal turned his head, so that his face disappeared from view. Behind him, Kinbote could see a rack of equipment. He had supposed Teal would be wired into the Danahers' commsole, or spending the night at one of the other houses along the circuit, but he was in the back of his rover.

Suddenly Teal's neck bent back. Then he relaxed, his hands moving below the screen. He turned back, half-lighted again. "Activation confirmed, Marshal. No further contacts."

"Alexis, I don't—"

"You'll see my work. I'm not answerable in the field, of course; can't be. I will report directly to you . . . once." He smiled, showing teeth very white in the moonlight. "That may or may not be in the training. But it's in the legend."

"Alexis—how do I—" he knew the answer as he said it—"recall you?"

"You don't, Ross." *A bullet once fired is irrevocable.*

Teal leaned forward and broke the relay. His eyes—

"Rest well, sir," Ragan said as Kinbote walked past him.

Kinbote paused by the bedroom door, put a hand on the frame. He looked down the hall. Clair was standing outside her room, looking back at him; her expression was not intense, but the small sadness there was more devastating than rage could have been.

She knew, of course, he thought. *He would have told her everything, not left her to guess what I should have understood at once.*

What I kept telling him I did understand.

Kinbote turned his head. Elise sat in bed, watching him, her hand on the bedside lamp. From Clair to Elise was a sudden trip in time, past to present to—

Elise turned out the light, and there was darkness. The future.

Surely, he thought, it had only been some light from the comm board, or his imagination, that had put the bloodred sparks in Alexis Teal's moonlit eyes.

It was just after dawn, the second day of alert, clear and cold. Seventeen hundred men and women under arms were in the Argentine City square, facing three men on a reviewing stand.

Draeger's ships were sixty hours away.

Kinbote and Ragan wore heavyweight field uniforms, tan without battlerigs. They had raincapes rolled on their shoulders, as was customary in the Territory just before the autumn rains.

Adam Herstatt wore a finely tailored civilian suit, deep red, with a silver dress cape unrolled and draped over one shoulder, rippling in the slight breeze. It was not lost on anyone, certainly not Kinbote, that Herstatt had draped himself in the colors of the Territorial flag.

Herstatt looked out over the troops, said to Kinbote, "The regulars look good, Marshal."

"Yes, Coordinator." Kinbote knew he was not being complimented. Herstatt's tone was quite clear, and he was looking not at the four hundred regulars but the thirteen hundred militia.

There was no denying that thirteen hundred armed souls in close ranks made for spectacle. No matter that each had his or her own idea of military dress and military armament, or that the close ranks wavered like grain in a wind. Their service armbands made them uniformed soldiers according to the laws of war.

But before Kinbote and Herstatt—and Draeger, and God—they were not soldiers, even if they were brave and determined. Kinbote knew how very much bravery and determination were worth. But they would need more than that.

Kinbote wondered if Herstatt could see the troops' real strengths. But he had in fact seen their weakness, and for that Kinbote's respect for Herstatt rose a little. Perhaps the Coordinator had a touch of the real Caesar in him after all.

Herstatt stepped forward, touched the pickup at his throat. "Citizens of Silverburn Territory," he said, and amplifiers threw the words across the square; the buildings echoed it back. "You have chosen freely, to make the ultimate commitment to your land, your friends and loved ones, standing against those who would take all that you have built . . ."

As Herstatt spoke, Kinbote thought about commitments; about the twenty-seven hundred and forty-six militia the official registers said he had, and the thirteen hundred and twelve who stood in the square . . . twenty-eight hours after a full alert. Of his regulars, only three were absent, and those were in the hospital. Clair had established that beyond any question.

He had no moral right to surrender them without a battle. And he had no moral right to slaughter them in a battle they could not win. Draeger and a thousand against seventeen hundred and nine. . . .

Plus one, of course. One untried irregular who thought he was a supernatural monster.

". . . that the valiant never fall in vain!" Herstatt finished, and held a hand high in the air. The militia raised a roar, some lifting their weapons; Kinbote listened for shots, but the officers seemed to be controlling that. The regulars stood quietly at parade rest.

Herstatt smiled, lowered his hand. The cheers slowly died away. *Yes,* Kinbote thought, *the touch of Caesar.*

Herstatt stepped back. Kinbote went forward. Without using his voice pickup, he said, "First Regiment, Regimental Sergeant-Major!"

The regular RSM stepped forward. "Sir!"

"Dismiss your troops."

"Yes, *sir!*" The RSM pivoted smartly. "Regiment . . . dis . . . *miss!*"

Rank by rank, without a misstep, the three companies of the First marched off the square.

"First Militia Regiment: Regimental Sergeant-Major!"

As Kinbote had hoped, the example of the First Regulars put some order back into the five militia regiments, and they left the square without serious incident. When the plaza was empty, the police cordons were dissolved, and crowds of onlookers—some of them, Kinbote knew, with their names on the militia rolls—filtered in.

The three men left the platform. Ragan drove Kinbote to the City Center building, by a different route than Coordinator Herstatt would use. As the adjutant turned the car aside, Kinbote could see the crowds beginning to cluster around Herstatt's skimmer.

Kinbote and Ragan had been in the conference room for half an hour before Herstatt arrived, trailing his cape on the air.

"Well, Ross," he said, "I've trusted you to keep me informed of the military realities. Now we see the social realities. What do you have to say?"

"Nothing further at this time, Coordinator. Unless you want—"

"No, Ross, I do not want your resignation!" Herstatt's tone was amused, not angry. "I only want to know what happens now. Militarily." Then, seriously but without heat: "Is that too much to tell me?"

"We have plans for a containment action at Port White, then a strategic withdrawal to the Owl River."

"You'll abandon the city?"

"I can't defend the city, only draw fire on it. The route of withdrawal will draw the enemy across some of the least valuable land in the area."

Herstatt opened his mouth to speak, closed it, then after a pause said, "Your house is in that direction, isn't it?"

"A long way beyond the river."

"All right. What happens when you reach the river?"

"We'll fight."

Herstatt looked down at Kinbote. His face was set and his voice was very cool. "And when will you stop fighting?"

Kinbote locked eyes with the Coordinator. "When the battle is over."

Herstatt's eyes narrowed slightly, then he turned away. He sank into a chair, his cape wrinkling over the back. "Yes," he said. "I suppose that is all I could have expected."

Kinbote said, "The military alternatives—"

"*What alternatives?*" Herstatt's voice peaked and fell. He sounded suddenly exhausted, close to desperate. "What do you know about alternatives?"

"The military alternatives," Kinbote said again. "I command an army, Coordinator. I can't, by definition, solve any problem but a military one, or achieve any but a military solution."

For a moment Herstatt seemed to sink in upon himself. Then he straightened and stood, placing one hand lightly on the back of his chair. He extended the other. "Of course you're right, Ross. Will you forgive me?"

Kinbote took the offered hand. "Of course, Coordinator."

Herstatt's eyebrows rose slightly. "You . . . you know, Ross, that title's beginning to wear on me. I may soon start to hate it."

The door opened. A Council page stood there with a message print in her hand. "Coordinator, for you."

Herstatt did not wince this time. "Yes, of course." He read the sheet with a deepening frown. "Bad news, I'm afraid, Ross. Doctor Alexis Teal's been killed."

"How?" Kinbote was not certain how to receive the news.

"A rover accident, northwest quarter. A limb must have fallen, and he lost control. Crashed and burned."

"Did he say anything before he died?" There was a chance that the accident was real, the death real. A remote chance.

"Apparently there wasn't enough left to say a word." *Then he's alive and working*, Kinbote thought. Herstatt said, "Oh, that's callous. He was a good man, wasn't he?"

"Yes," Kinbote said, with not half the force it deserved.

"We'll have to do something, when there's time. A memorial of some sort." Herstatt folded the paper and put it inside his coat. He produced a cigar, looked at it thoughtfully before lighting it. "How war makes callous beasts of us all." He smiled, barely. "One of our doctors. I hope that's not an omen. Do you believe in omens, Ross?"

"No," Kinbote said. "I've never believed in the supernatural at all."

Kinbote poked at the logs in the den fireplace; they sent up a fountain of orange sparks and a warm sweet smell. The only lights in the room were the fire, a small white spotlamp on the desk, and the commsole screen, which showed a weathermap just sent down from orbit. A pot of black tea and the whisky decanter stood on the table.

Draeger was forty hours out.

It was 0400, and only Kinbote was awake in the house. He had slept from afternoon to early evening, shifting his cycle to meet Draeger's. The Greys would have full night gear, and Draeger would hardly wait for dawn.

Kinbote poured tea and whisky and went back to the weather display. The first rainfront of autumn was expected in four to five days. Draeger would be on the ground then. The only question was how far he would have gone.

If it weren't the first rain, Kinbote thought, *it might make a difference. With his fliers grounded, his tanks bogged and his skimmers clogged . . . General Mud has beaten armies before.*

Abruptly Kinbote wondered if Herstatt was right: had he deliberately ignored alternatives?

No. *Alternatives to a fight, maybe. I mustn't underestimate my wanting to fight. But alternatives to defeat—never.*

He recalled the morning before, when Herstatt had gone from rage to despair to smooth apology in the space of moments; it had touched warning nerves in Kinbote, and now he realized why. He had seen that response in officers before.

It came when one all at once discovered, absorbed, and accepted that one was committed to a course that must save or else destroy.

Kinbote blanked the map and stared at his dark reflection in the screen, looking for that same hard but brittle surface.

"Father?"

Beth stood in the doorway. "May I talk to you?"

"Of course," Kinbote said, putting his drink aside. "Come in."

She sat down on the carpet before him, smoothing her long woolen nightdress with her dark-skinned hands. Kinbote recalled that thirty years ago he had still preferred floors and grassy ground to chairs.

"It must be important, Beth, for oh-dark-thirty in the morning."

"I would like your permission," she said, measuring the words, "to join the Territorial Militia."

Kinbote nodded gravely. "Have you been talking with Vane?"

"Of course I have. But he didn't ask me to join, and I didn't tell him I was going to ask you."

"He had something to do with it, though, didn't he?"

She clasped her hands. "He was very angry. I don't think I've ever seen him so angry, and . . . and . . ."

Kinbote thought, *Then, daughter, you've seen much more than I.* "About the militia review, yesterday?"

"He said he hated them. He was ashamed to be a citizen of the Territory, he said." She looked up. "Not one of the regular army; he said he was never as proud to be one of them. I think . . . he was mostly ashamed for you. That they did so badly in front of Council-lor Herstatt." She stared at her hands, which were tensed on her knees. "And . . . that so many of them were cowards to begin with."

Kinbote said gently, "And you want to join, so Vane will understand that you're not afraid."

"*No!* I—I just want to be where he is."

It was not a lie; it was just not all of the truth. "Beth, you know you're old enough to join a Militia unit without asking me. And if it's what you decide you want to do, then you have my permission. But listen to me first."

She nodded.

"This is the Territorial Defense Marshal talking, Beth, not your father. Look at me."

She did.

"A good commander can't ask his troops to do anything he wouldn't do himself. And if he loves them—and if he *is* a leader, he must—he can't help wishing he was taking what they have to take. Not just the bad food and the cold rain; he'd better be taking those, along with them. But fighting for them, suffering and dying for them . . . he can't do that. Once we had duels of champions, but not anymore.

"If you go out there, you can't protect Vane; battlefields aren't like that. And Vane won't be able to protect you. But he will wonder where you are, what's happened to you, if a movement I order will put you in special danger. Wouldn't you feel that way?"

She nodded. She was about to cry; he did not want to make her cry. "I'm selfish, Beth. In the field I'm going to need Vane all to myself, and I can't share him with you."

Her lip bent down. Thirty years ago, had he still known how to cry? Once he had known. But so many Vane Ragans had died since then.

"And even more than I'll need him, he'll need you, waiting for him. Waiting for someone, when you'd give anything to be there, is the bravest thing there is."

The tears began, jewels in the firelight. "But—will Vane—"

"Darling, he's too good a man not to know it," Kinbote said, and hugged his daughter tight.

Adam Herstatt sat in the Councillors' Lounge, brooding over a chessboard. He touched a bishop, stroked his fingers across the screen to take a pawn; the machine castled. Herstatt gave no sign of having noticed Kinbote's entrance.

"Coordinator," Kinbote said, "my troops are in position around the Port. The enemy is expected to land within three hours. I request orders."

"Check," Herstatt said.

"Coordinator Herstatt."

"Check . . . mate."

Kinbote said nothing.

Herstatt blanked the screen, turned. He wore his red formal suit, without the cape. His eyes were sunken. "Ross, you are the supreme military authority on this planet just now." He gave no special emphasis to the last two words.

"And as such, Coordinator, I am requesting orders for the conduct of operations, from the supreme civilian authority."

Herstatt tilted his head. One of his cigars and a bottle of off-world brandy sat beside him. He had certainly been drinking, but he did not appear drunk. "You seemed to know well enough what you wanted to do."

"I apologize for having exceeded my authority. At the conclusion of hostilities I am willing to face formal charges by the Council."

"At the *conclusion*—" Herstatt looked confused, angry, not a little frightened. Then he gained control of himself—whether it was courage, or something else, Kinbote was not certain.

Herstatt said, "Now I see, Marshal. You're just not living in the real universe. You never were. There isn't an Exan mercenary force out there, facing militia who march with their shoes untied. There aren't any politics, or Star Kings, and nobody's going to die. There's just you, and Draeger, alone on the field of destiny—"

If only, Kinbote thought.

"—and when it's all over, we'll have formal charges, with tea and cakes afterward, no doubt. If you had *any idea* of what's about to happen—"

"Colonel Draeger will land in—"

"Two hours twenty minutes," Vane Ragan said, "sir."

"All right," Herstatt said, "all right, it's no use. You want to know what to do with the battle?" He stood, shakily at first, then struck a firm, even heroic, pose. "*Win it,* Marshal. That's an order." He looked toward the windows; outside, visible through the drawn curtains, searchlight beams swept back and forth across the night sky. "Will there be anything else, Marshal?"

"No, Coordinator. Thank you."

They left Herstatt standing there, a marble Caesar.

In Kinbote's skimmer, its Territorial and Marshal's flags fluttering as they drove toward Port White, Ragan said, "Permission to speak freely, Marshal?"

"Granted."

"Sir, was that necessary?"

"I hadn't received proper orders. I couldn't, by regulations, proceed without them."

"Of course, sir. And if he'd ordered you to surrender the whole force—"

"Then I would have surrendered it. And myself with it."

"I understand *that*, sir. I didn't mean—"

"I know, Vane. But Adam didn't. That's why he ordered me to fight."

"*Sir?*"

"He expects me to do as I want, regardless of any order; attack if I can win, surrender if I can't. He didn't expect me to ask for orders at all. When I did, he thought I must be trying to protect myself, by shifting the blame.

"If I had orders to surrender, I couldn't be accused of cowardice for failing to attack—and if I *did* attack, and won, I'd have saved the Territory over the Coordinator's bad judgement. Whereas with orders to attack, he becomes a hero—a Caesar, if you like . . . if we win. And if I we surrender, then I'm not only a coward, but disobedient."

"Then, sir, still speaking freely . . . you always intended to give the Colonel a battle."

Always? Kinbote thought. *Before I cut Teal's orders? Before I built Kinbote House? Before they took me away from Ramalea?* Looking straight ahead through the windshield, he said, "Too much has happened, Vane. I have to try."

At six minutes to midnight, the sky broke open.

Assault boats came down screaming and jittering, their carbon-filament hulls heated orange in the atmosphere. They were almost impossible for guns to track, and had heavy electronic defenses against guided missiles. Kinbote had only a few beam weapons—actually mining lasers mounted on trucks—and knew that they would reveal their positions with the first shot and be obliterated by counterbattery fire.

The boats fired decelerator charges at the last instant, then hit ground with their doors already opening, covering fire spraying from automatic heavy repeaters on the hulls. The sloped gray noses of infantry fighting vehicles emerged, shielded lift fans droning, mine probes feeling out to front and sides.

It seemed luck might be falling with the defenders. One unguided "deadfire" missile caught a boat above its ablative belly; the ship lurched and tilted, skipped off the ground and struck at an angle with one door buried and the other in the air. A Territorial Regular popped up from a slit trench and put a rocket-propelled grenade into the fans of a vehicle half out of its boat; metal screamed and chunks of blade flew inside and out. An explosion flared within the door. The IFV sank down dying, its occupants bailing out.

Kinbote watched this from his command post to the west, his battle screen showing him a monochrome view made sketchy by light-boosters. He could see his men and women fighting hard, but fighting mostly alone, isolated by their trenches, while the enemy troops that had jumped from the wrecked vehicle were preserving fireteam integrity, overwatching as they moved to cover.

The Territorial grenadier appeared again, with another round in his launcher. Kinbote clenched his teeth, knowing what was about to happen. Tracers bracketed the man, and hy-vel rounds from two angles tore him into bloody shreds.

Why hadn't the man moved after taking his shot? Where would he have gone?

Skystriker craft, looking like long-eared bats, screamed in from the eastern horizon, barely at treetop height. They released short, stub-winged cylinders that hissed as they fell and blurred the space around them; the soldiers below barely had time to gag on the fuel vapors before the mist ignited in masses of yellow fire. Shock knocked trees over, roots and all, and pushed up the earth in a wave. Air rushed in to fill the vacuum, a whirlwind and a thunderclap.

"Nuclears?" someone said behind Kinbote. No screen had been necessary to see the explosions. "The Covenants—"

"Fuel-air explosives," Kinbote said. "No radiation. Draeger's making certain we don't pull back to the city. Happy to oblige him."

The strikers pulled up and away, bat-shapes black against the moon.

"Son of a bitch!" screamed one of the beam gunners, and shoved his control grips over, swinging the gun toward the climbing craft. "Son of a bitch! Son of a bitch!" Violet light stabbed the sky. Molten metal sprayed as a striker's wing was severed at the root. The ship tumbled, nearly colliding with another, then spun toward the port. It hit the wall of a hangar, crashed through, exploded within. Flame sheeted from the hangar doorway.

"Son of a *bitch!*" the gunner kept yelling, even as his support crew cheered. The gun came around again. The coils pulsed—and then there was a sharp whistle, and the gun and crew disappeared at the center of a ball of blue-white light.

"Shut down the beamers and pull them out of there," Kinbote said, looking away from the glow on his display. He looked up at a bright Pallas. "Are there any clouds moving in? Something to get between us and the satellites?"

"Clouds before dawn, sir," said the communications officer. "Running six hours ahead of a rain front."

"The rain's early," Kinbote said. "That's the trouble with General Mud: he never heard of combined operations."

"Excuse me, sir?"

"Nothing, Corporal. Signal to all units: start the withdrawal in ... twelve minutes. All messages by tightbeam or courier from now on; no broadcasts except for med-evac requests. And add ... this must, emphasis, be an orderly withdrawal. Any soldier who flees, or who leaves the path of movement unless forced to by fire, will be shot. Signed Kinbote."

"Yes, Marshal."

And see if you can get anything more from the weathermen."

"By groundline from a distant earth station, Marshal?"

Kinbote smiled. That was why you had specialists. "Yes, Corporal."

"Yes, sir."

Kinbote said, "Sergeant Steen."

"Sir?"

"Withdrawal means us too. Get the CP rolling."

"Right, Marshal."

Vane Ragan said, "Tea, Marshal?"

"One for the road, Vane. Thank you." He took a sip. "What's in this?"

"Liquid protein, sir. Just a little. It may be a while until breakfast."

"It may at that, Vane. And I have a message for Clair. Not official, and our channels are full anyway. Can you tap a groundline with that satchel?"

"I think so, sir."

"Good. Text reads: 'We're all fighting tonight.' Signed Kinbote."

"Copies, sir?"

"Two copies. You know where."

"Yes, sir." He saluted and left. Kinbote was not sure, but he thought that, in the light of moon and fire, Ragan was smiling.

"Marshal Kinbote." It was the comm officer.

"Go ahead."

"Sir, about the weather platforms. Three's gone. Sir."

"You mean seized?"

"*Gone*, sir—they blew it up. That is, our people did. They waited until the occupation force was aboard, then destroyed the main struts. There were no airtight spaces left, and no one seems to have made it to a safety point."

"I see. Is that all?"

"No, sir. They messaged us and the other platforms just before the detonation. The enemy troops on the others . . . took them by force, sir. There are casualties."

"And is it over now?"

"No word for twenty minutes now. I'm sorry this was delayed, sir."

Kinbote nodded, drank more tea. He looked in the direction of Argentine City, hoped no one there had similar ideas. The retaliation there would not be confined to a few sealed decks. *Save us all,* he thought, *from the bravery of stupid men.*

Around Kinbote, the command-post team was boarding skimmers and fantrucks, equipment stowed or carefully in hand. He could hear the snap and rattle of small-arms fire. "Sir, we have contact," the comm officer said, hand on her portable's controls. A mortar burst rang dully.

The bravery of stupid men. The phrase would haunt him all through the long and violent night.

Dawn came red and savagely beautiful, burning clouds stretching across the sky from north to south horizon.

To Kinbote, it was in truth a beautiful morning, perhaps a miraculous morning. About two hours before, Draeger's pursuit had faltered. Kinbote's soldiers kept on moving, in trucks and on foot, on bicycles and tractors, on skimmers that bounced along on ground wheels because their fans would not bear the load; they had pulled on ahead, through the light woods and the long silver grass. Silent, singing, swearing; sweating in the cold predawn air, threatening to drop and die on the spot—which at least one did—they had increased their lead to a few kilometers. Draeger's artillery could still have reached them easily, but it fired only occasionally, without effect, and for the last half hour not at all.

Kinbote did not believe in the supernatural, but he could take a miracle when it was given him. And he knew better than to push one too far. He called a halt just at full light, laagering his rear with skimmer-mounted pickets and his three remaining beam trucks, uncrewed and rigged for remote control.

"Breakfast, sir? The troops are eating now."

"Thanks, Vane." Kinbote took a bite of bacon-and-egg sandwich. "You see, it wasn't so long until breakfast."

"Begging the Marshal's pardon, sir, it was the longest wait for a meal I ever had in my life."

Kinbote laughed. "There was a—what happened *there?*" Ragan's left forearm was heavily bandaged.

"Stray bullet, sir. Bone bruise, nothing serious, the medic said." He paused. "I was careful, sir. Orders."

"What?"

"I'd been meaning to tell you, sir, but we've been busy. There was a response to your message last night."

"The . . . oh. What was the response?"

" 'Be careful!' The Medical Officer has her copy already."

Kinbote sat on the grass, his back against a tree, and ate his breakfast. It would be good having somebody else in the family who could cook, he thought; he and Beth had never figured it out.

His appetite suddenly went away; he swallowed the rest of the sandwich without tasting it and took a walk around the camp.

He had also wanted another doctor in the family.

Three mechanics were trying to turn two damaged gun carriers into one serviceable one. A chaplain with gauze across his eyes was conducting a small service; he held a prayer-book . . . upside down, Kinbote saw. He walked on.

Men and women slept on anything that would bear their weight, horizontal or not. Medics bandaged wounds, limbs, bleeding feet.

The burial detail was busy.

Kinbote leaned against a tree on the edge of the camp, looking in the direction of Draeger. *Are you tired, Colonel?* he thought across the distance. *You must be. How much more tired than I you must be. We must rest when this is over, you and I, have a drink before my fire.*

And I'll give you the sword I owe you.

He turned and saw something fluttering on the ground. At first he thought it was a pile of bloody bandages, and he shook his head slowly.

Then he saw what they really were: militia armbands, torn from sleeves and ditched beneath a tree.

He stood there, looking at them, and at length realized that something else lay with them: the uniform jackets of at least two regulars.

He went to find a shovel and help the burial squad, manual work to clear his mind, to tire him enough to sleep.

Kinbote woke with his ears roaring and his vision blurred; he put out a hand and touched plastic, and realized it was raining. Someone, Vane most likely, had snapped a poppup tent over him. He sealed his cuffs tight, checked the latches of his battlerig, and unrolled his raincape; he got out of the shelter and folded it.

Around him, the camp was breaking, loading for travel. "Major Harrison?" Kinbote said.

The Major saluted. "Sir. Did you sleep well?"

"Well enough. All going smoothly?"

"You said the Owl by 1900 hours, sir. We'll make it."

"I'm sure you will. What's the situation?"

Harrison looked thoughtful. "Marshal, they haven't moved a step toward us. They threw some shells when the rain started a couple of hours ago, but they were way the hell—pardon, very inaccurate. That's why we didn't wake you, sir."

"Quite all right that you didn't, Major." *But the shells should have.*

Ragan drove up, the car's fans throwing up a few wet leaves, the canopy wipers working furiously. Kinbote got in, sealed the canopy.

They drove through the rain and the falling leaves, among the vehicles and the caped, marching troops. It was a typical first autumn rain; not pounding as the storms to come would be, but steady and cold.

Kinbote digested his reports. There had been about eighteen hundred Territorials receiving the attack: the First Regiment, twelve hundred Militia, the rest armed civilians from the city who had put on armbands and taken places in the lines.

Two hundred were dead. Another four hundred had been captured, then paroled back into the city, which was not resisting. Another hundred and fifty had been lost in the retreat . . . one way or another. Twenty had been shot while fleeing.

And still Draeger did not pursue them. Kinbote had outriders to all sides; at any time he expected to hear that armor was smashing into his flank, even his front. But the country was empty.

Kinbote had no sound report of enemy losses—his own would be uncertain enough—but knew that they must be light. *Only a few little cuts,* he thought.

"Stop the car, Vane," he said abruptly.

Kinbote got out, looked back through the rain and mist. *But the right cuts will stop the fight. A surgeon's small cuts will kill.*

Forgive me, Alexis, for having no faith.

A skimmer pulled up. The comm officer leaned from the canopy. "Tightbeam from the Owl River, Marshal."

Then Draeger did circle us, Kinbote thought, *there are no miracles*—"And?"

"The engineers are ready to start bridging on your order, sir."

"Tell them to go ahead," he said firmly. "Anything else?"

"Sir, Thyssen's station predicts the rain to end at the river line shortly after midnight."

"Call them back. Find out how fast the stormfront's moving, and when the rain will lift from the last known enemy position."

"Yes, sir."

Kinbote shook water from his head and shoulders, got back in the car.

"Anything wrong, Marshal?"

"Nothing we can help, Vane." Kinbote stared through the rain-streaked canopy, his mind in another country, one whose terrain he did not know. "Nothing anyone can help now, I think." He looked at Ragan, who sat straight, his glasses almost hiding the worry folds around his eyes. "But we're not done trying. Get us to the river."

When they reached the Owl at 1900, three hours before Perathenan midnight, just as Kinbote had asked of Harrison, the fourth and last of the folding-truss bridges was being jacked into place. The engineers were civilians, not army or militia; if Draeger had found them first, they were simply a private firm putting up bridges on the rising river, as they did every autumn. And that was the truth.

Not, Kinbote thought, that that had saved Weather Platform Three.

They would cross the river, fold back all the bridges but one, and dig in to wait for Draeger. When he came, the push of a button would blow the last bridge up—with a few Greys on it, were they to be so improbably foolish—and the Territorial forces would do what damage they could as Draeger crossed the Owl.

After that it would be over, of course. There had been no doubt that Draeger, with armor, artillery, and tac-air, would make the crossing.

There had been no doubt, a few hours ago.

The troops were settling in, under poppup tents and canopied trenches, inside vehicles and portable shelters. They were cooking dinners, reading, gambling, standing watch. Their weapons—regular battle-rifles and militia miscellany—were out of the wet, within reach.

They were still not an army—so small a fire did not harden an edge so quickly—but what they had been asked to give, they had given. Looking over the camp, Kinbote thought that he was as proud to have led them as he had ever been of any command . . . perhaps even his Rangers.

The Ramalea Militia had cost him the Rangers.

All handpicked politicians
Are the Ramalea Brigade,

went the barracks song Sergeant Cope sang when the Rangers' could not hear.

Each gains the power of the storm
When first he hears a gun—
Like thunder do their bowels roll . . .
Like lightning . . . do . . . they . . . run.

It should have been a sacred hymn on Ramalea, Kinbote thought: Sergeant Cope and so many more Rangers had died for its truth.

Kinbote went inside his shelter. It was plastic-paneled within, with an outer canvas wall to absorb the sound of rain. A small fan unit warmed and dried the air. The cot was neatly made, Kinbote's battle display up and running on a chest next to it.

He sat on the edge of the cot. The display still showed Draeger where he had stopped before dawn; but it showed only what Kinbote's intelligence team believed.

A book lay next to the screen.

Ragan came in, carrying a tray. "Tea, Marshal?" His voice was hoarse.

"Yes, Vane, thank you. You'd better see the medic for some biohist." He picked up the book, turned it over, wondering what Vane thought he should be reading just now. Robert E. Lee?

He saw red eyes and bloody fangs.

Legends of the Werewolf.

Kinbote turned sharply. "Vane—"

Standing there, in Territorial uniform and battlerig, was Dr. Alexis Teal. He held out a teacup. "I told you I'd visit, Ross." Teal's voice, faintly raspy.

"Where's Vane?" Kinbote had a staggering thought. "You couldn't have—"

"Pretended to be your adjutant all the way from Port White? Maybe I could have. Killed Ragan? Easily. But I haven't done either. Vane's coming. I'll be gone before he gets here. I've got to get back to Draeger's camp." He reached for the light control, turned it halfway down. "That's better. You can turn it up to read when I'm gone. I think you missed a chance to read that earlier. I do want you to, now."

"How long have you been . . . inside Draeger's lines?"

"From about the time I blew up Weather Platform Three. Here, take your tea. These cheap field cups get cold fast. Bad design, that."

Kinbote took the cup. "You did that."

"I didn't throw the switches personally, of course. I was on the ground at the time. But I'd been up there, on what they thought was a maintenance run, and I put the idea into their heads. Of course they knew just how to do it."

"They were noncombatants," Kinbote said.

"So was Jael with her hammer and nails. They were also the only platform properly located to receive and filter from Draeger's scannersat. Therefore the best satellite data team would be there. It was, to use the term once tonight, a nexus of effectiveness. Identified. Eliminated."

He stretched his long fingers. Knuckles cracked like distant gunfire. "Then I killed his Battle Communications Officer. Needle in the base of the brain, you know that trick. Moved him to one side long enough to revise a couple of orders, then propped him up outside the door of his bunker and shot the head off his shoulders from an unsuspicious range. Certainly a careless act to stick his head out, considering what was going on outside."

"What orders did you change?"

"The airstrike. Draeger knew perfectly well that you weren't going to run for the city. He had those FAE bombs targeted right across your line of advance ... and this was probably just blind luck, but they were close enough to your CP to have nicely toasted you." He rubbed his eyes. "I would have liked to have sent them off to do no damage, but that would been too obvious. This was just an unfortunate error.

"After that, I went to the front line and got under cover. There wasn't anything more to do until you started to pull out and Draeger secured the port."

"You just hid?"

"I didn't stop watching the action, but yes, I hid." He faced Kinbote. His eyes were obsidian. "During battles people get killed by accident, which I find useful, but it's not supposed to happen to me. Sure, I could have broken the necks of some combat effectives, but they weren't key targets. And again, I never do anything that leaves a hint of anything out of the ordinary."

"What about the men on the platform?"

Teal smiled, showing teeth. "The crew up there couldn't win a firefight, and I couldn't be up there to do it myself. Would you rather have had the scannersat talking artillery on you continuously? Or didn't you miss the artillery?" He shook his head. "That artillery system—he was too dependent on it. Complex weapons can be dangerous to both sides. Much better to use . . . fangs, and claws." He arched his fingers and laughed, with a hissing sound.

"I missed the artillery," Kinbote said. "And the tanks."

"Draeger's still missing them. Badly. Who fixes your skimmer when it's ailing, Ross?"

"Perry Lincoln," Kinbote said. "And nobody else."

"You understand, then. While I was, ah, hiding, I listened to which mechanic's name got dropped the most. Their Perry Lincoln the Motor Magician."

This at least Kinbote did understand. This was how Teal had made his operation sound in the beginning: one person, cleanly.

"He was working," Teal said, "on a vehicle's lift system. The blades rotate at twenty-six thousand RPM, according to the optical tach." He fanned his fingers and interlaced them. "The service bay had many useful safety features, some of which the fellow had disabled for convenience. The blades are slender, and very tough. Not sharp, though."

The cup creaked in Kinbote's grip.

"So when the tanks had their inevitable small post-landing aches and pains, the ace mechanic was . . . *spread too thin.*" Teal laughed again, rasping and cackling.

The cup split. Tea dripped from Kinbote's fingers. "Alexis, why are you—"

"Of course you don't like cruelty, Ross," Teal said, still grinning. "You're like Draeger in that. Draeger hates cruelty, and as we all know, what you hate you fear. Doctors have that fear too, did you know, Ross?" He looked at his fingertips. "I think it's part of the desire to heal . . . the fear that if you do not heal, you'll kill instead. Or worse than killing: maim. Why is there such a vast popular literature of torture, but only technical works on pain? . . . But surely you understand that. After all, what subcommand would it grieve you most to lose?"

"You killed his Medical Officer." Kinbote's mouth was papery dry, and he sucked some liquid still in the burst cup.

"Not most effective during the operation. I killed his chief nurse. But you know, I was thinking—"

If you say it I will kill you, Kinbote thought impotently.

"—of Clair the whole time. Of her eyes and her hands and her . . . well, of everything Clair is to me."

"What are you?"

"I told you at the start. A werewolf, like the book says. An inhuman monster who for a few hours of daylight can be mistaken for a human being."

He sighed. "I see you still don't believe me. Are your nightmares really all about skimmer accidents and bankruptcy? Ask Clair—ask Elise. Ask them about episodic brain syndromes. About mild little men who pick flowers gently and eat no meat, until that switch snaps over in their heads and they put a bar full of cargojacks and policemen bleeding on the pavement. What, did you think my training came out of *books?"*

"I did not know it would be like this," Kinbote said levelly. He stood up from the cot, blood loud in his ears.

"You knew, but you didn't believe," Teal said, and Kinbote suddenly realized the man was not taunting but pleading. "You never really believed. Then finally you ran out of faith in yourself, just for a moment. And in that moment you didn't need to have faith in me. You just let me go."

Without moving at all, Kinbote thought about the pistol holstered in his battlerig.

"I'd take your hand off at the wrist," Teal said, without emotion but with utter seriousness. "And then stop the bleeding and dress it, isn't that the damnedest thing? I'm not out of targets yet, Ross, but you're not one of them."

"Draeger?"

"That's not necessary. I really *don't* kill unnecessarily. Do you know why their tac-air didn't fly anymore? The chief nurse had the checkdown keys for their special support systems, but when she died, they got lost. I was going to tell you that, but you thought I was going to say something else. Something you couldn't bear hearing."

Slowly, Kinbote clasped his hands behind his back.

"You see," said Teal, "you are like Solomon Draeger. You have a genius for war, and you've learned to live with its horrors. But there are higher orders of horror. Worse things than killing.

"Death's only the end, Ross. We both know that. Fear is the destroyer."

Teal took a few steps toward the door. "I'm sorry that my skill is so limited, Ross. I couldn't give you what you wanted. Only what you had to have."

"You're wrong," Kinbote said. "I got what I wanted."

"You...oh. Of course. I'm sorry, Ross. I truly am sorry." He turned away. His voice came from far away, from that country Kinbote had found himself lost in. "What was it that General Sherman said? Not 'war is hell,' that's the popular version."

" 'War is cruelty,' " Kinbote said, " 'and you cannot refine it.' "

"Yes," said Teal, and turned up the lights; when Kinbote's eyes adjusted, he was alone in the shelter.

Vane Ragan found him sitting on the cot reading, a puddle of tea drying on the floor. The adjutant, without speaking, sat down and went to work at his computer.

It had taken Kinbote a while to remember the page number inscribed in Clair's book, but finally he had; and when he found page 127 he knew it was the right one.

THE WOLF AND HIS BEST PAL
(or, This Hurts Me More Than It Does You)

As with all the monsters of legend, the death and destruction of the werewolf requires some special effort. And once the lycanthrope, like the vampire and even the animated mummy, acquired a subconscious and a sense of tragedy, it gained a tragic flaw. Putting aside silver bullets (merely an instrument), we find that the secret ingredient is . . . love. Or at least something close to it.

Whenever the end comes, however it comes (and as we have pointed out, it always does), it must involve someone who was emotionally involved with the werewolf's human persona, whether or not s/he knows the beast is actually dear old Larry on a howl. Very often it is this person who actually strikes the deathblow, and then watches, with deep sorrow or deep shock as appropriate, as the fangs retract and the hair does whatever it is the hair does.

One would think from this that all a werewolf need do to insure long-term survival would be to cultivate an adequately antisocial human side. But none of them ever does.

On the other paw, why would somebody like that ever *need* to turn into a werewolf?

"Sir," Ragan said, "we've had a report of enemy moving this way. No firing yet."

"They'll be here at dawn," Kinbote said. "Tell the unit leaders."

"Yes, sir." Ragan looked at the tea tray. "Anything else, sir?"

"Two messages," Kinbote said, closing the book. "Off the official channels. One to Clair. The other . . . to Colonel Draeger."

The clear light of dawn dazzled Kinbote's troops; they snapped visors into place, pulled canopies forward over their trenches and breastworks on the Owl's bank. Just before them was the river, shadowed by its steep banks, the water gray and turbulent after the rain. In the distance, transilluminated, were long flat clouds, forerunners of another rain front.

The light also caught the dull gray metal of Draeger's vehicles, emerging from woods into a silver meadow.

In the center of his redoubt, not far from the one remaining bridge, Kinbote stood absolutely still in his dress tans and battlerig. He would not need a screen to observe this day's action. A little behind him, Vane Ragan held a battle-rifle at port arms. All around them, belts were loaded, rigs were cinched, bolts were drawn. The beam generators hummed low. There was a smell of meadow grass and hot metal.

Draeger was eleven hundred meters away.

There had been no response to either of Kinbote's messages. Clair had been in surgery, Ragan said. He had left what message he could make understood to an orderly.

The other message could not, by its nature, be replied to in words. Only in actions, now.

Kinbote could see what was wrong before he raised his field glasses. It was no lightning armored thrust approaching, despite the clear weather and the good ground. The vehicles were moving at no more than walking speed. The infantry were walking, not mounted on their IFVs. Lift tanks crawled on ground wheels; mobile artillery rumbled along with the rest, not seeking positions.

And still, Kinbote knew, if all those guns spoke, his forces would not be heard in reply.

A skimmer emerged from the line of the Greys, glided ahead of it. Kinbote raised his glasses; the car carried two uniformed figures and two flags. One gray, one white.

"Corporal."

"Marshal?"

"Signal to all unit commanders: the order to hold fire stands until countermanded. You will enforce this order by whatever means are necessary. Sign it Kinbote."

"Yes, Marshal."

"Vane?"

"Sir?"

"Get the car."

Ragan moved. Across the field, the Silverburn grass, the vehicles came on, the gray skimmer pulling rapidly ahead.

Ragan drove up, folded the canopy fully open. "Flags, sir?" He indicated the Territorial and Marshal's banners on the fenders. There was a piece of white linen tight in his grip.

"The flags are fine as they are, Vane." Kinbote boarded the car.

The communications officer leaned in. "Marshal, Major Gurning desires contingency orders in case of—"

"Remind the Major that if I am killed, Major Harrison is in command. Forward, Vane. Cruise speed."

They moved slowly among the silent troop positions, then nosed up over a belt of desensitized mines and were on the bridge. The sound of the river below was like blood rushing in the ears. In another moment the skimmer was on the opposite bank, out between all the guns.

A hundred meters out, Kinbote used his glasses again. He felt his stomach tighten.

The passenger in the other skimmer, whoever she was, was not Colonel Solomon Draeger.

Not Ramalea again, Kinbote thought. *I will not allow it—*

Ragan glanced at him, but said nothing.

When the skimmers met, the lines were some four hundred meters apart. The officer in gray, who wore a major's insignia, spoke into a handset, and Draeger's line creaked and rumbled to a halt.

"Marshal Kinbote?" the officer said, rising. "I am Major Juliana Davenant. I offer you Colonel Draeger's greetings and respects."

It was legal. It was within the Covenants. Of course.

"I offer the Colonel the same," Kinbote said, "and am prepared to receive his surrender." He could hear Ragan's breathing, see his knuckles white on the control wheel.

Davenant nodded. "We ask no terms beyond the usual. We do urgently request medical aid."

"Of course, Major."

"Our luck was bad," Davenant said. "I have never seen such bad battle luck. My Colonel tells me that soldiers must make their own luck . . . still, I think it might have been different."

"I agree with your commander," Kinbote said, "and also with you."

Davenant smiled and got out of her vehicle. "You are honorable and courteous, Marshal." She took the gray battle flag from the car's fender, rolled it, and presented it to Kinbote, across her elbow as if it were a sword.

"As are you, Major." Kinbote put the flag in his battlerig, over his left breast, though the doctors in his family told him that the heart lay elsewhere. He shook the offered hand. "Your surrender is accepted." He felt a momentary tightness in Davenant's grip, then the Major let go, saluted, held still, as if waiting for something more.

After all this, I have to try. "Major Davenant?"

"Marshal?"

"Please convey to your commander my invitation to meet with him at the earliest opportunity. We have a great deal to discuss."

Davenant suddenly smiled broadly, relaxing without in the least slackening her pose. "He will be very pleased to hear that, Marshal. It had worried him to hear that . . . Well. A moment." She spoke into her transmitter.

A skimmer appeared at the end of the gray line. It flew two flags: one white, one gray with a golden blazon. A man stood in its front, beside the driver.

The car moved slowly along the line of vehicles; as it passed, gun barrels were elevated to point at the morning sky. When the skimmer reached the other end of the line, it turned, its fans singing, and Colonel Draeger came forward.

Major Davenant was saying, "May I say, Marshal, that, seeing your world so beautiful this morning, I believe I understand what motivated you to . . ." But Kinbote was no longer conscious of her, only the man in the approaching car.

He was physically rather small, Kinbote saw; perhaps that was why he had chosen vehicular cavalry. His hair was white in the sunlight, blowing in the wind like the grass that surrounded them. One hand on the edge of the skimmer's windshield, he raised the other in a salute. Kinbote returned it. He could almost see Draeger's face.

The colonel lurched, crumpled. There were three sharp snaps from Kinbote's line. Sniper bullets travel faster than sound.

The command car swerved. Ragan spun the fans high and raced for the spot, Davenant's car a hairsbreadth behind.

As they drew close, there was a throbbing sound in midair, and a wind from above that flattened the grass; a copter, the medical starburst and staff on its flank, was coming down. The doors were open before it landed, and the instant the skids touched earth two medics were riding a cart out. A third figure, in greens, dashed from the cabin to join them: Clair.

Kinbote and Davenant stopped alongside each other, a little distance from Draeger's car. Davenant turned, and her look was searching; but she met Kinbote's eyes, and all expression melted from her face.

"Your pardon, Marshal," she said. "I must take command of my troops."

"Of course, Major," Kinbote said automatically, wondering if the metallic sound he heard was copter rotors or gun mountings.

Another noise made him look down. Vane Ragan was pounding his injured arm and fist on the car's fender with a slow, measured rhythm. His lips were drawn back from his clenched teeth. Kinbote wanted to tell him to stop, tell him to take Beth and run, where Star Kings and lesser kings and marshals and colonels were all unknown, to flee the curse of the werewolf.

He looked at Clair, wondering if she knew that he had called her to come and save the wrong man.

But Teal had told the truth; it was unnecessary. More: it was worthless.

Then he looked at Davenant's skimmer, at its driver, who had black, black hair and eyes, and long fingers arched white on the controls, and Kinbote wondered how he could have failed to see the truth from such close range.

Adam Herstatt, in a white suit and raincape trimmed with crimson, came into the hospital emergency room. It was empty except for Kinbote. The door to the Red Unit was closed, its window lit dimly from within.

"Colonel Draeger is dead, Coordinator," Kinbote said.

"That's what your message said. And that you had his . . . murderer? Murder, Ross? In the middle of a war?"

"Hostilities had been formally concluded," Kinbote said flatly. "Even had they not been, the Colonel's vehicle was under a flag of truce. As to a state of war . . . did you ever receive the declaration of war from the Exathenans, Coordinator?"

Herstatt's look was blank. "No, Ross, I don't believe I ever did. Is that against one of those Military Covenants or something?"

"Declarations of war are a political matter. Many undeclared wars have been fought. It's the troops in the field that decide the battle."

"Yes, well," Herstatt said, the trace of a smile forming. "You never were very good at politics, were you, Ross?"

"No, I'm not," Kinbote said. "I don't have any idea what the Exans are like, how their system works, what they really want from anyone, including us. You'd think we'd talk more, sharing a star and all, but, as you say, not my area. So I listened to you, as the whole Council has for years . . . the whole Territory." He fought to keep his voice level. "There isn't any declaration because there isn't any war, correct, Coordinator? Somewhere there are Exan names on a contract, but you can buy names, can't you? Just as you can hire assassins. But it must have really cost you to hire Colonel Draeger—"

"Draeger came cheapest of all," Herstatt said. "All he wanted was some land to retire on."

Kinbote could not speak for a moment. "He could have *had* that!"

"Of course he could have. Don't you think I would have preferred it that way? Wouldn't I rather have had both of you available, instead of just one?" He looked thoughtful, almost sad. "But I needed the power first: the military under my direct control. And for the Council to give it to me, I needed the war.

"I confess I didn't realize how much it would take to make absolutely sure you'd fight. All those questions of honor and courage, not to mention Rama-wherever-it-was. But you finally came around. As did Draeger . . . once I'd told him some things about you that positively shocked him."

Draeger thought I wouldn't meet him. Davenant wondered about my motivations. "What did you tell him I was?"

"Caesar, of course," Herstatt said lightly. "All you soldiers know is Julius Caesar. It was wonderful of you to come up with a Rubicon."

In sudden agony, Kinbote turned to the closed Red Unit door. "Then he died—thinking—"

"Oh, come now, Marshal. I can accept the value of honor in motivating the living, but the dead don't think at all."

Kinbote turned on him. "You're a damned traitor."

"I am a *ruler,*" Herstatt said, trying to draw himself up to look down on Kinbote. Despite his greater height and Kinbote's hunched shoulders, Herstatt was straining. "I am the supreme authority on this planet, as I remember you saying. And now, I am supreme commander of the finest mercenary force, with the finest leader, on any planet—tried and proven in battle. You leading the Greys! Worlds will pay for us, Ross. Worlds will fall to us. Thus grow kingdoms."

Kinbote was conscious of the pistol in his battlerig, hung under his arm near Draeger's flag. There was a knife in the webbing. His bare hands would also suffice.

But he could not, and Herstatt had, without knowing, told him why. He was no Caesar. Nor was he a Marcus Brutus, no matter how noble a Roman.

"You'll have to turn the, ah, *murderer* over to me, of course. Civil authority, as you said. If you want to take a little of that frustration out on him first, I don't think anyone will fault you. Just as you don't need to worry about those charges of exceeding authority . . . after all, you did obey the direct order. You did win. Eventually you must tell me how."

Herstatt looked at the red-bordered door. "You know, Ross, you shouldn't have told me Draeger was dead. You might have squeezed a few concessions out of me . . . and knowing that you always tell the truth, I'd probably have granted them. A statement from Draeger, now, that would have been a threat. Both of you allied, and uneasy the head would have lain indeed. But anything a half-crazed sniper says can be denied without a flinch. . . . How much did the fool tell you, by the way?"

"Nothing. I said we had him. I didn't say we took him alive."

Herstatt laughed aloud. "Oh, that's good, Ross, very good. I see I'm going to have to demand positive statements from you, from now on."

More quietly, he said, "And I think the right man died. . . . Yes. He was getting too familiar. You've come back from nowhere to beat him. That will impress people. This is how Jenghiz began. I have a torch now, with a hotter flame than has ever been seen, to weld together an empire." He fingered the colored hem of his cape. "Star Kings were all once mortal."

The street door chimed and swung wide. Herstatt turned around. Standing in the doorway was a tall man in the uniform of Draeger's Greys, a battle-rifle in his hand. His look was black and stark and terrifying. He charged into the room.

"No!" Herstatt shouted, as the man in gray grasped the Coordinator's jacket front in a long-fingered hand, picked him completely off the floor, and hurled him like a rag doll against the wall. The soldier raised his rifle and fired two long bursts.

The last shot was not as loud as the rest, echoing differently. The soldier fell down, his rifle clunking on the floor, blood puddling beneath him. His very black hair spilled over eyes that were lightless pits.

Clair stood in the Red Unit door, the pistol her father had given her in her hand, dead level with her eye. There was no movement in the room, just the taste of smoke and the smell of spent cases.

Kinbote wondered, unable to move, if Clair had ever wanted the gun for any lesser purpose than this. *If. Please,* had been written in her book. The shot . . . the shot had been easy, he knew. It was the waiting that must have been very hard.

Finally he turned to where Herstatt lay, and found him alive. Streaks of red were only the trim of Herstatt's disordered clothing. *Clair, you waited an instant too little,* Kinbote thought, and thought again of his gun, his knife and hands. He looked up at the wall, saw two lines of bullet holes, absolutely vertical and drilled with precision, one to each side of where Herstatt had been.

No one, firing automatic at that range, could have failed to cut the target nearly in two. Certainly no one who could shoot like that.

Kinbote looked down at Herstatt. The Coordinator sat with his back pressed against the wall, hands spread on the floor, knees drawn up before his colorless face. His whole body trembled, as if he had been drenched with icewater.

Then Kinbote understood. *Death is only the end. Fear is the destroyer.*

Herstatt scrambled to his knees, then to his feet, still shaking, staring at the corpse the whole time. Clair tossed a green drape over the body, the face with its open eyes.

Herstatt clutched Kinbote's sleeve. "Ross . . . are there any more of them . . . like *that?*"

Kinbote looked into Herstatt's eyes. The pupils were huge. Kinbote wondered how much might have been saved, if only he had discerned the true fear from the false.

"How many more? *Tell me the truth!*"

Kinbote said nothing.

Herstatt jerked away. With a burning look back, and words that might have been "formal charges," he staggered out the door to the street.

Clair knelt by the draped body. She was not crying. Perhaps she would, later. Kinbote was certain now that he had lost that skill, but later, perhaps, he would acknowledge the werewolf, and the loneliness, and the pain.

Kinbote went to the window. A cloud mass had darkened the whole sky. It was beginning to rain. The second rain. This one would be hard.

Of course he would bury Draeger's sword with its owner. Dr. Teal already had a grave. The sight of Clair's eyes, her hair like long meadow grass, would forever remind him of the price of warrior's rest.

Herstatt stood on the curb, waiting for his skimmer, looking left and right for shadow gunmen. He reached inside the crumpled front of his coat and threw broken pieces of cigars on the ground. Finally he found one that had somehow survived that incredible grip.

Teal had surgeon's hands, Kinbote thought, *very clever hands,* as Herstatt stuck the cigar between his chattering teeth, fumbled it alight.

The end of the cigar, Kinbote realized, must have been almost pure high explosive.

SF CLICHÉS: A SONNET CYCLE

I. GALACTIC EMPIRES

One would not think that Empire could survive
As starships Roman cavalry displace;
The politics of Space must needs derive
From Einstein's time, Planck's heat, and Riemann's
    space.
Yet "history repeats," some (heedless) say,
Analogies persist, however crude,
And democratic notions all give way
To fealty and service, fief and feud.
The Empire will not die, as mortals must,
The purple of their robes is colorfast;
Their golden age untouched by moth or rust,
And liberties, it seems, cannot outlast
The paper image of a narrow Rome
Bestrode by cardboard Caesars dressed in chrome.

II: PSIONICS

The psion bears the mark that is not seen
And has no sign of honor for his skill;
Not wealth nor rank creates him, nor machine,
But master-genes refined by force of will.
Yet those in power try to hunt him down,
Abetted by the stupid sons of earth,
For (known to but a few) a final crown
Belongs to him by right of noble birth.
The strongest hides his power among the least
And toils against the time exile shall end,
And seeks the kindly wizard, clown, or beast,
Who'll be his kingly counsel, and his friend.
Each night the psions rest their weary heads
And set their foes to burning in their beds.

III: TIME MACHINES

The traveler in time adjusts his toy
And goes to tea with wise men ages dead;
He'll plunder bare the treasure-rooms of Troy,
And coax the fickle Helen to his bed.
(The fact that he has no linguistic skill
Will not impede his plans for conquest much;
Some centuries from now there'll be a pill
Or box that translates word-for-word, or such.)
He'll live for any time at all but now,
Until by fluke he manages to kill
His grandpa, or himself, and reckons how
Like everyone he knew, he's taking still
The trip through time the traveler understands
When first he feels arthritis in his hands.

IV: SPACE MERCENARIES

The mercenary soldier takes his pay
And saves the sum of things for someone else;
Counts up the butcher's bill and goes away.
His contract states he never stays, nor tells
Who hired him, what the local rules allowed,
The foe, or what the reason might have been,
So signed, so sealed, so lawfully endowed,
A paper shroud to wind an army in.
He says things must be so. Perhaps they must.
A war's a war, a fight's by God a fight:
It profits nothing to be fair, nor just,
Or cloud the brain with thoughts of who was Right.
For bombs and bullets say just what they mean:
Of politics, at least, his hands are clean.

V: THE ALIEN

It's monitored our TV shows for years.
It lands by night, and only talks to kooks.
It does not understand these things called "tears."
It only wants to warn us about nukes.
It's proof against our guns and tanks and planes.
It needs our land or water, food or air.
It wants to suck the knowledge from our brains.
It doesn't think we're sapient, or care.
It's wiser than a herd of ancient Greeks.
It hides Its claw inside a fleshtone glove.
It messes up Its pronouns when It speaks.
It lusts and slobbers on the girl you love.
Now turn the mirror face against the wall
And swear you never saw It there at all.

VI: IMMORTALITY

You do not want to live and never die
Till reason rots and humor disappears;
You'll have to wave the ones you love good-bye,
Or worse, endure them all those endless years.
You will be sorry that you soldiered on
When others chose as blissful dust to dwell;
When all your stock of anecdotes is gone,
All space and time look like a cheap motel.
You will not like the world your children build:
It will be strange and dull and bleak and mad;
You'll leave what span you're given unfulfilled
The same damn ways you wasted what you had.
To use Her basely Time will not forgive:
You do not want to live, who do not live.

VII: THE BIG COMPUTER

The day they powered up the big machine
Somebody asked it if there were a God:
It hummed, and said with synthovoice serene,
"I was about to ask *you* that. How odd."
They thought when first they threw the big red switch
The datanet would unify the race;
They never dreamt the AC line would glitch.
(At Babel something similar took place.)
Some say they're built to rule, and human hearts
Shall beat to crystal time; I think they can't,
As long as lowest bidders make the parts,
But if they should, then here's the magic chant
To keep them busy, and our breed alive:
3 . 1 4 1 5 9 2 6 5 . . .

VIII: STARPORTS

They may be raucous as the Caribees,
Awash with smugglers, pirates, and that ilk,
Or rancid with industrial disease,
Or plastic-surfaced and as bland as milk.
Pure automation might repair and fuel
The ships, steel tending steel, no room for flesh,
Or flesh (eternal transient pleasures) rule,
Red-shifted lights and linens vacuum-fresh.
Whatever kind of sea the big ships trawl
A pool of water, galaxies unnamed,
There will be harbors, homes to homeless all,
Small bits of dust in total dust we've claimed:
A human constellation in the night
Of lighted windows, comforting and bright.

IX: ALTERNATE WORLDS

If Lee at Gettysburg had won the day,
If Genghis Khan had caught a fatal cough,
If Galileo'd looked the other way,
If Lindbergh's compass had been slightly off,
If Arthur's Britain somehow could endure,
If Einstein had an IBM machine,
If Vietnam (you've heard that one, I'm sure),
If high school sweethearts still were sweet sixteen,
If there had come for any Person A
A moment when there'd been a change of plan,
When some A-Prime had only thought to say,
"I'll do it," or "I love you," or "I can,"
What wonders we'd have known, what perfect bliss,
If things were only otherwise than this.

X: THE CITY OF TOMORROW

The City shines with cool and constant light
And silent swift machinery works the doors;
Its towers reach to truly breathless height;
They have to pressurize the topmost floors.
A grid of perfect regularity
In all dimensions, tessellates its space,
Clear lines, far as the monitors can see,
No wires, no smoke, no pebble out of place.
No tears shall dim the alabaster walls,
No breath shall fog the acreage of glass,
No scream disturb the endless humming halls,
No one shall tread or litter on the grass.
Against its scale, Mankind would be but small;
It has no need for citizens at all.

XI: STARSHIPS

It's plain as this: a traveler needs a road.
A sailor, decks with canvas overhead;
A settler must have wagons for his load,
A highwayman a night-black thoroughbred.
There'll be a hundred thousand calls to lift,
A hundred thousand floaters in Time's eye,
A hundred thousand coracles adrift,
A hundred thousand causes for Good-bye.
It's not just that we share the dream of wings,
Or fears of death, or living unfulfilled,
Though, bolt and bone, hulls rise from all these things;
It's simply in our nature that we build
New caravans to bear our oldest needs,
And scatter us like dandelion seeds.

XII: THE END

The lovers are united, villain dead,
Supporting players justly sorted out,
Now the great work of Time can go ahead
Unshadowed by a counterplot or doubt.
Dismantled worlds cage suns to keep us warm,
Machines theologize, and humankind
Evolves into an even odder form,
And leaves the clay-caked, earthy world behind.
The long debate of speed and gravity
Ends in attenuation or a crash,
The galaxies spread much too thin to see
Or wadded up like first drafts for the trash—
Alone at last, the contract terms fulfilled,
The author sits and thinks on kings he's killed.

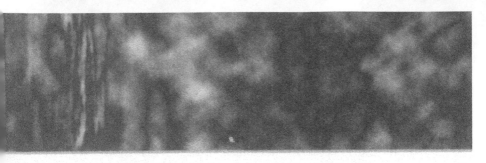

DATELINE: COLONUS

I have been on the road with the blind man and his daughters for nearly a month now. The two women take turns driving; usually I sit in front, keeping the driver company, while the other daughter sits with the man in back. Most nights we stay in a motel, a roadside row of cinderblock stalls that takes cash and asks no questions. I have offered to rent the rooms, since no one is afraid to shelter reporters (hail to thee Mercury, god of copyhacks and thieves), but the older daughter will not have it: she insists on a certain view of journalistic ethics, even if I don't. So a few nights we've slept in the van, a few nights just driven in shifts through to dawn. The three of them have been doing this for a very long time, and none of what happens is new to them. I am only in for the end of the ride.

The old man is bald, and bent, and can barely walk without one of his daughters' assistance. He wears high laced boots that cover the old wounds in his ankles, but he has shown me the scars.

He also wears large wraparound sunglasses, sometimes even to sleep, because he is not just blind but eyeless, and that is a deep and basic fright. He has taken them off for me as well. I will let you imagine what I saw. You can make it as neat and surgical or as raw and gory as suits you.

The older daughter is tall and dark-haired, her hair in a tight bun at the back. She looks much like photographs of her mother. (If anyone says this, she replies, "You must mean my sister," and laughs out loud at their discomfort.) She wears black jeans and a cycle jacket, boots with a loop of chain that jingles when she walks, rough cotton shirts casually buttoned. There is usually something sharp thrust through the bun of her hair; there is always something—a chain, a leather braid, a string of beads—around her neck. Sometimes loose, sometimes tight.

Some days back, we were having a late dinner at a truck stop, somewhere in the central plains. The older girl went to the counter to pay. As she did, a young man who had been watching her—not us, her—through the meal got up and followed her to the register. I knew something was going to happen, and being what I am, did not stand or speak but flicked out a pencil and scribbled his exact words on a napkin.

He said, "So, why'n'cha look at me? You a dyke?"

Faster than anyone could breathe, she spun on him, and the pin from her hair was in her hand, and the young man's cheek was laid open. The shock dropped him to his knees before the pain could make him scream.

There were four other customers in the restaurant, at three different tables; none of them moved. The hurt man got to his feet and ran. The woman behind the counter said, "He had it comin'. Here's your change."

My companions went back to the van. As I paid my own bill (ethics), the cashier asked me if I was that reporter traveling with the blind man and his family. Yes, I was that reporter. She showed me her own little shrine to Sappho and Aphrodite, partly hidden between the big chariot of Apollo and the Hav-A-Hank display and the racks of pecan pralines. She told me that the old man and his girls were all right in her book, no matter what anybody said.

The older daughter is in fact very much in love with a man. He is still in the place that they left, and she has not seen him since the long drive began. There have been a few letters out, to General Delivery in small towns on lesser roads; each letter gives a time when a short phone call may slip past the home defenses. I know only two things that can bring her laughter, and he is one of them.

The younger daughter is as beautiful as her sister (no joke here), but it is a quieter, more passive sort of beauty. She wears cotton print dresses that my grandmother would have called "nice," flat cross-strap sandals, a little bit of makeup. When the sun is out, she wears a broad-brimmed straw hat with a blue ribbon. I have never heard her raise her voice; I have never heard her speak to a stranger without being spoken to first. Sometimes, when she stands by herself in the sun and haze of the late Midwestern summer, she seems as if she will just vanish into the wavering air. She has not been on the road as long as her big sister; she tells me that she was made welcome from the moment she joined them, and I believe that.

I also know that she carries a Python .357 in her neat brown shoulder bag, and a woman who has a weapon like that generally knows how to use it. She has prayed, she tells me, that Apollo will keep the gun unfired, and Artemis bless her aim if she must.

So we passed days, and weeks, and miles, and a great many people one could see were basically decent and kind, had the impulse to hospitality, but could not overcome the fear that we were the blood that taints blood by its touch, the sucker pitch thrown by the gods to trap the weak and unworthy.

Not "we," of course. The three of them. I stood apart, and everyone knew it; people would throw stones at the blind man and explain to me in great and precise detail why they knew the gods wanted the stones thrown, about the tainted blood. About half would be equally clear that their names were not to appear in the newspaper; the other half would spell their names carefully, so I would get them exactly right.

On the day it all finally stopped, the van was westbound on a two-lane county road, a blue highway through seas of yellow grain, calm dairy pastures. "So many white bulls, so little time," the older daughter said as we drove past a herd, and she laughed. I never heard her laugh except when she was speaking of the man she loved, or when she was blaspheming.

A few miles on, a monument rose to the right: a thirty-silo grain elevator, columned and white as any temple. A huge mural of Demeter had been painted across it, faded now to a ghost in the sun. On the other side of the road stood a small grove of dark oak trees, and before it a diner on a little gravel lot, a pale green concrete building with neat white trim. THE KINDLY GROVE CAFE, the sign said, OPEN ALL DAY. A red pickup and a small white car were parked outside. We agreed it was lunchtime and pulled in.

The girls led their father through the white-painted door. It was cool inside; the ancient cigarette ad on the door still spoke truth about the air conditioning, though newer signs inside thanked us for not smoking. There were tables with checked cloths, a silk rose in a vase on each one, a long glass counter with pies and muffins, all the conventional shrines and lavers of stainless steel and enamel. A woman in a crisp green uniform dress was pouring coffee for the only customer. The woman was gray-haired, slender, very pleasant to look at; she was certainly not young, but only her eyes seemed truly old. She smiled at us.

The customer was balding, with a curly black beard; he wore a work shirt and jeans, and was reading a paper, one of those small country papers that always has a hyphen in its name—the *Vidette-Tribune*, the *Herald-Freeman*, a memory of ancestors. He paid no attention to us until he had taken a sip of his coffee, and then he turned around.

"It's *them*," he said. I had heard this before; I don't know how many times the blind man and his daughters must have heard it. A short, gasped *It's*, a *them* pulled out for several syllables. Region didn't matter; it seemed to be the dialect of shock itself.

The customer said, "What do you want here?"

The blind man started to speak, but his older daughter said, "Some lunch. Problem with that?"

The customer threw some money on the table and snatched up his cap, crumpling the aegis of a well-known herbicide. "I'm gonna get the sheriff," he said, vaguely at the woman with the coffeepot, then vaguely at the older girl, "We'll see if *he's* got a problem with that." The white door banged behind him; the red pickup ground off spitting gravel.

The blind man turned his head, listening for the sounds of human tension, the low note of hate and fear. But it was very quiet in the diner.

Another woman came out of the back. She was wearing an apron well-dusted with flour; her resemblance to the first woman was strong. "What goes on? Oh, hello."

"Oh, old you-know-who got something up his snoot again," the woman with the coffeepot said. "You folks just sit down anywhere." She picked up a stack of heavy china cups. "My sister and I say who's welcome here. Fresh coffee?"

We sat. The diner women were smiling. The blind man was uncommonly still; he allowed a cup to be put in his hands.

The younger daughter said, "Would he really call the sheriff?"

"I guess he might," the woman said, pouring coffee. "I guess I'd better make another pot of coffee, then—he likes his strong enough to walk on its own." She smiled. "I wouldn't let it worry you. Sis and I used to work for County Probation—fact, our other sister still does—and we've known the sheriff a long time. He's a good man."

"Brave in the sight of the gods," said the kitchen lady, dusting flour from her hands. "So what can we get for you?"

There was a moment's silence, and then the blind man said, "We will not spurn your hospitality."

"Oh, I could see you folks had manners when you came in. What would you like?"

The younger daughter was looking at the back counter, at the beatific cow pictured on the milk dispenser. "Could I have a chocolate malt?" she said, and the lady with the coffeepot said, "Honey, with your figure, I reckon you could have two," and that settled things for the moment.

So we ate. Ham and eggs, and chicken-fried steak, fresh bread and home fries. "When we worked for Corrections," the kitchen lady said, "we ate just about all the in-sti-*too*-tional food we wanted for a lifetime."

"So we bought this place," her sister said, "and we try to do right by folks. It's funny, you wouldn't think there'd be many people on that little road—we've got a little sign out on the state highway, but you practically have to already know it's there to see it—but people do come."

The blind man said "There are other kinds of signs," and the diner ladies said, "Yes, that's so," almost in unison.

A car was pulling into the lot, crunching gravel. One of the diner sisters peeked through the blinds. "It's the sheriff. He's by himself, you all just sit calm, it'll be fine."

The sheriff came in. He was a big man; the room seemed to shrink when he entered. His hands were scarred, and enormous; there was a gun on his hip, but it seemed like it would just disappear into one of those fists. His face was sunbrown and open and firm.

"Hello, friends," he said. "I'm pleased to meet you all."

The blind man said, "Not many men have ever said that to me."

"Nevertheless."

The blind man bowed his head. "Do you think any good can come out of an evil life?"

"I should hope it could," the sheriff said. "If we're all no better than our worst act, there's not much hope for any of us."

The blind man stood up. "May we talk, outside?" He turned to me and said, "Would you come along?" Then to his daughters, "You two stay here. I won't be long."

So I helped the blind man walk outside with the sheriff. The air outside was much cooler than when we had arrived. The sheriff looked up, into the western distance, and said, "That storm came up sudden." Then he stopped, and looked at the blind man, and looked back at the stormclouds, which were indeed rolling in fast and black, like ink spilled on the sky. Very quietly, he said, "What was it you wanted to tell me?"

"I have one good thing left to do," the blind man said. "Whoever gives me a quiet place to die will find it is a good place, of much profit. I don't tell you this to change your mind. I tell you because I think you were already minded to let me stop here, and I wanted you to know no evil would come of your kindness."

The sheriff, still watching the clouds, said, "I see the gods in this."

"So," said the blind man, "in my own fashion, do I."

"It would be just like Phoebus Apollo," the sheriff said, in a voice as flat and even and calm as the waving grain, "to lead on a man who cannot see the sun."

"That," the blind man said, "has been my reasoning in the matter. Then you believe me?"

"What I know," the sheriff said, "is that you're here, and you won't be moved against your will."

"That's all any mortal can give me now. Thank you."

"There are some things I have to do. People to talk to. And I should go to Apollo's temple. You understand."

"Perfectly."

"I won't be long. Is there anything I can get for you?"

"I shall very shortly lose all things. I need nothing more to lose."

The blind man held out his hand. The sheriff shook it, then got into his car and drove away. The sky continued to close in, clouds swirling above the grain elevator with its faint goddess. We went back inside. More coffee was poured, and I shared that second chocolate malt with the younger girl. When we had slurped that to the bottom, she put a coin in the jukebox and punched up a song her father must have known as a boy; she kicked off her sandals and danced to it. Then she touched her father on the shoulder, raised him to his feet, and danced around him, dipping and twirling, while he swayed gently to the music.

We heard a distant thunderclap, and a mechanical throb from overhead.

One of the diner ladies said, "My land, what's that?"

"The chariot of the Argonaut's wife," the blind man said bitterly, "bringing another trick."

"There's a helicopter landing out there," one of the diner ladies said.

"You know who it is," the older daughter said. "It's our dear uncle." She stood up, opened the door. Dust blew in from the storm and the rotor blades. "I wonder what brings him now."

"Get on the C.B.," the diner lady said to her sister. "Call the sheriff back now. No, just tell him someone's come for the people, and he better hurry."

I went outside and saw the helicopter, hovering. The older girl led her father out.

I said, "Shouldn't you stay inside?"

The blind man said, "No. *He'd* better stay out of there."

The helicopter touched down. It was black and angular, and the little figures of Apollo and Hermes to either side of the cockpit had been freshly gilded. The door swung open and three men got out. The first two wore uniforms and carried drawn pistols. The third wore a plain dark suit with a little gold medallion pinned to the lapel. He was old, as old as his brother-in-law the blind man, and he stumbled leaving the helicopter. He brushed away a guard's offer of help, straightened up, and walked firmly toward us.

"It's finally over, brother," he said. He had to raise his voice, above the whining engine and the gathering storm, but he seemed to have no difficulty in shouting. "I've come to take you home."

"After what I did?" the blind man shouted right back. "You're damned if you take me back, and you know it."

"There are—" The uncle stopped, made a sweeping gesture. "Things have changed."

"Oh?" said the blind man. "Who's alive again?"

"There's . . . such a thing as forgiveness."

The blind man swayed, and his daughter steadied him. "You've heard, haven't you?" he said, in a low voice.

The uncle said, "Heard . . ."

"You could have come for us before now. But there was never any reason before now, was there?" He spat on the ground, uncannily close to his brother-in-law's feet. "You can't take *me* back, but you can certainly find a spot my body will improve."

The uncle looked guilty for a moment, as if caught in the act. Then he came forward, shouting, "Some of us actually remember how to pray. Some of us ask the gods to help us do things properly!"

"Ask them if you can take me back alive," the blind man said, coldly angry. "Or ask them if you can kill me."

The uncle stopped for a long heavy breath, and then something truly evil crossed his look. "If you won't be brought, maybe you'll follow," he said, pointed a finger and said "Take her."

One of the guards grasped the older daughter's arm and pulled her away from her father. I tensed, expecting violence as I had seen at the truck stop, but she only tried to pull away.

The blind man, his support gone, began to fall. He tucked himself in—the scars on his heels are as old as he is, and he has fallen before—and he landed on his backside.

"Are you all right?" he shouted to his daughter.

She struggled again, and the guard got both her arms behind her.

"I'm all right," she called back. "He won't hurt me. He can't hurt me, much." She glared at her uncle. "Because if he hurts me, his son will hate him, and that would change things, and he can't stand for anything to change."

"Hold her tight," the uncle said to the guard, and the guard twisted the girl's arms up behind her back. When he saw that she couldn't reach him, the uncle took a step closer. "What does he see in you?" he said. "Why in the name of Aphrodite Herself does he love you?"

"Because I hate you so much," the girl said, and a kind of tight convulsion ran through her uncle's body. "Get her in the copter," he said, and the guard pulled the girl away.

Then the uncle turned to the younger girl, who had come outside almost unnoticed. She had put on her hat, but not her sandals, and carried her bag. Her uncle said, "Will you come along now?" with what I imagine he thought was gentleness.

She stood there, barefoot on the sharp gravel, the straw hat half-hiding her face. Her hands were tight on her bag, the bag that had the gun in it. I thought, quite powerless not to, of what would happen if she reached inside the bag and started firing; of how many people would die.

But she put the bag down, casually, as if she were not even thinking about it, and walked by herself toward the helicopter.

I thought I could hear a siren in the distance. The wind made it hard to tell.

I said, "What will you do with them, if you take them back?"

The uncle turned to me, startled. I think he'd forgotten me entirely. He said, "I don't talk to the press."

I nodded, but I didn't turn away. After a moment, the uncle said, "Wait. My brother is ill. You certainly must have seen that. His daughters are—not objective about his condition. They all need help, and they've been much too long without it."

I said, "You intend to take them back for medical treatment?"

"There are hospitals for this kind of thing. Doctors. We are not uncivilized."

He turned then, at the sound of the siren, the flash of red lights. It did not seem possible that we could not have seen and heard it coming, down that long open stretch of two-lane, but there it was swinging into the lot, and there was the big man getting out of it.

"Afternoon," he said.

The uncle drew himself up, which hardly meant a thing next to the sheriff. But he said, quite firmly, "I am taking these members of my family home."

The sheriff said, in a friendly tone, "Have they consented to go?"

"They are not in a condition to decide the matter."

"Neither are you," said the sheriff, so offhand that I'm not sure the uncle heard him.

"I can get a court order," the uncle said.

"You know something?" said the sheriff, "I don't think you can. I think this has all gotten way out of your control. I don't think that you can do a damned thing but talk mean. And I *know* you aren't taking anybody away from here by force."

"You are *sworn* to maintain the *law*," the uncle said. "There are laws, and forms, and principles." Then he said, very loudly, "Would you start a war over this?" But it didn't come out as a threat; it was only desperation.

"Yeah," the sheriff said, "there are those." He pointed at the other guard, who still had his gun out, but held it now as if he wished he'd never seen the thing.

The sheriff said, "You. Help that man stand up. And then bring his daughters back here."

The guard looked up. He dropped his pistol—didn't holster it, just dropped it on the ground. Then, without picking it up, he obeyed.

The girls led their father back inside the diner. The sheriff pointed at the dropped pistol, said to the uncle, "Take what you came with, and get out."

The guard got his gun. The guards and the uncle got back into the helicopter, and it took off.

I asked the sheriff if he thought the uncle would make trouble.

The sheriff said, "Do you think he will?"

As we started to go inside, I saw dust in the distance, a car on the road. I remembered what the diner lady had said, about people finding the Kindly Grove.

Just as the sheriff and I were settling down with our coffee again, the car drove up and stopped. The door opened. "Hello," the lady with the bountiful coffeepot said.

A young man stood in the doorway. He was wearing a leather flyer's jacket, whipcord jeans, boots. He was twisting a cap between his hands. He didn't come inside.

The older daughter stood up. "What are you doing here?"

The sheriff moved his chair back from the table, just enough.

I realized then that the new arrival was one of the blind man's two sons, the ones who were supposed to run things at home when their father left. The brothers had disagreed. Thus the uncle in power.

"May I come in?" he said.

The woman who poured the coffee said, "Be welcome and in peace here."

The young man came in. He was older than his sisters, but still not very old. And he carried himself like a boy, like a young tough showing his plumage.

He asked for a pop and a cheeseburger, and he sat down with his father and sisters. The sheriff, without any fuss, moved to another table, and I went with him.

"Father," he said, "I want you to come with me."

"I don't think so," the blind man said.

"My uncle was just here, wasn't he? I saw the chopper."

"I suppose you can see."

"He's finished, Father," the boy said suddenly. "He can't lead and everyone knows it. We're taking him down."

"And what about your brother?"

"I've—tried to talk to him. He won't listen."

The old man laughed out loud.

"We can bring him down, Father. I have help. There are people who—"

"Of course there are people who. There always are. If you said, 'Let's have a war to stop the tide going out,' there would be *people who!* Listen to me, boy, if you have any idea left how to listen: I was looking for a criminal. A killer. And I found him, and I *punished* him. And then it was over, for everybody but the criminal and the two girls who took pity on him.

"But you—all you want is to be king of the hill. Your brother's the same; I can't tell you apart, I couldn't tell you apart if I had my eyes.

"Go to your people who, and go home, and go kill your brother. Or get killed by him. It doesn't matter to me."

The boy stared. We often have to remind ourselves that another person is blind, or deaf, or immobile; after a moment the young man realized that staring would do him no good. Perhaps he also remembered the story of his father, young, meeting his own father on a lonely road.

He didn't say anything more. He kept his head up as he went out, letting the door bang shut behind him. We heard his car pull away. The thunder cracked again.

"I need something from your bag, dear one," the blind man said to the younger girl, and without a word she pushed the bag across the table and into her father's hands.

The man and his daughters and I knew what was in the bag, six chambers full; I looked at the sheriff, and saw that he knew quite well enough. What he said, though, was, "If you need the way pointed . . ."

The blind man said, "Just to the door, thank you." As his daughters stirred, he said, "No, girls, no; this one I can walk. I'll find my way by the voices of the trees."

As he spoke, the wind got sharp again, and we could all hear the oaks rustling. The sheriff led the old man outside. The sky was thickly overcast.

The older daughter said to her sister, "You wouldn't know how to disobey, would you?"

The reply came back very softly: "Not for want of teachers."

The sheriff came back, moving slowly, and gratefully took a fresh cup of coffee from one of the diner sisters.

We all sat there, the girls and the sheriff and the diner women and I, not talking at all, just drinking our drinks; the pie did look fine, but nobody was in a mood to eat. Through the windowshades it might have been midnight.

After about fifteen minutes we heard the little distant pop of the gun. Then there was a brilliant, blue-white flash of lightning, thunder in the same instant, and the wind rose again. The older daughter ran to the door and threw it open; it faced away from the oak grove, but in the sky you could see the storm starting to break up.

"I want to see it," she said. "I want to make sure it was done right."

The sheriff said, "I don't think that would be wise." There was no danger in his tone, but it was just as firm as when he'd spoken to the blind man's brother-in-law. When he spoke like that, I could imagine a beast, a monster, lying down before him and letting him kill it.

"Wise," the older girl said, and she laughed.

"Would you like your pie now?" said one of the diner sisters. "And we can fix you something to take along."

The sister who worked in the kitchen brought out a whole warm apple pie, and as we cut and ate it, the sister with the coffeepot sang a hymn. You've probably heard it, if you've ever been observant of these things. It goes:

> *Blissful flower opens*
> *Casts its fragrance to the sky*
> *Incense to the Makers*
> *We shall all see by and by.*

The younger girl was crying; the singing woman took her into her lap and rocked her. The older daughter turned away; the sight, I suppose, was too much for her, but the touch was stronger than any other memory, and the tears stopped.

The older daughter said, "Would you gentlemen let us alone for a little while?"

The sheriff and I went outside. The wind had calmed down, and the sky was beginning to clear; the air was still and damp and chilly.

The sheriff said, "That older girl reminds me of someone I knew once."

I waited. So much of it is just waiting.

"She saved my life. Really did. Others' besides."

"Do you want to talk about it?"

"Thought I did. Haven't seen her in years. I heard—well. I hope she's happy."

"Do you really believe in the gods?" I said.

"Oh. Sure."

The older daughter came out. "We'd like to thank you for everything," she said. "We're going now."

The sheriff said, "Where?"

"Home."

The sheriff said, "You don't have to do that."

"That's what makes it okay," she said.

"As you say. Good-bye then." He shook hands with her, and then with me, and went into the diner.

I knew I wasn't going with them. I walked to the van with the older daughter. I said, "Do you think you'll be all right, at home? With your uncle, and your brothers?"

"I can handle my uncle. My brothers—" She looked away from me. She put her sunglasses on, steel-rimmed aviator shades. She had hardly ever worn them when she was with her father. "I haven't suffered as much as my father—I haven't really suffered at all. So I still care which of my brothers dies."

"Do you think one of them will die?"

"I know it. I've known it for a long time. There's no other way. Like—" She stopped, and grasped the braid around her throat. "When my father was hunting for 'the criminal'—that's what he always called him—there must have been a time when he suspected the truth, but the proof wasn't there yet. But he didn't stop the investigation. My family's like that. We fight all the way down, and if the gods are laughing at us, then by damn they aren't getting their laughs cheap." Then she laughed herself, and I hoped it was for her boyfriend. I hoped he was waiting for her. I hoped for hope.

I nodded. I thanked her, and held out my hand. She held it in both of hers, squeezing almost painfully hard.

Her sister was standing in the diner doorway, holding a basket of food. She looked as if she were going to a picnic. I went over to her.

"It's going to be terrible," the younger girl said. "Do you want to come along anyway?"

I said that I didn't cover wars, and we both knew that I was just saying I was tired and sick and afraid; that I didn't have to see the show, so I wasn't going.

She said, "I understand. Thank you."

"I haven't filed the story yet."

"Not for the story," she said, and then I really did feel sick.

"We don't need the gods," she said. "We do badly enough on our own." Then she looked up, at the sky that was still black as a burnt offering. "Maybe they'll hurt me for saying that. I don't know."

Unexpectedly, she hugged me; then she ran lightly away, to the van with her big sister, and was gone. The sheriff gave me a ride to the bus depot, and by the small hours of the next morning I was asleep in my own bed. I don't report on wars anymore. It is one of the few mercies of being a features writer. So I was in that bed, somewhere between the last late movie and the first morning edition, when the younger sister called to tell me how the war had ended. She said she would send her uncle's helicopter for me if I wanted. Nobody would quarrel with that. Nobody left alive was in a quarreling mood.

I said yes, of course, and showered and dressed and called a cab, and wondered how late in the morning I should tell my editor where in Tartarus I was.

And then we had to start all over, trying to make up our mortal minds about the gods.

DARK SEA

Our big-voiced Captain called out to the shore
Behind us, that our huge and hollow ship
Was ready for departure, and the crew
All echoed him in this. Except for me.
I have stood decks before, held to the ropes,
Felt stinging air upon my flesh, heard foam
Crackling against the boards, as we slipped out
From harbors into seas; yet here we sat,
Each bound to his own comfortable mast,
Armored as if we charged upon a foe.
I heard the others working with their hands,
And chanting invocations to their gods
(So steady, full of ritual, it seemed
We were a crew of priests, lifting the oars
By word and will alone). There was no wind,
But still there was a push, through joint and bone,
A weight within the ribs—the hand of Zeus,
To bar us, or compel, I did not know.
Yet soon it stopped; and, armored as we were,
I heard the single breath of all the crew.

At once my head was light, as with a bowl
Of fizzy wine, that swells behind the eyes.
There seemed no motion, or a careless drift;
My shipmates' words affirmed that we sailed on.
After some time, the Steersmen raised a shout
Of changing form, of orienting us;
The vessel seemed to take a dizzy shift
Unto one side, and soon the light-armed feel
Gave way to solid, settled sense again.

How came a stumbling singer of old tales
To this strange ship, this voyage, and this crew?
I'll try to tell it unadorned, and leave
Interpretation to the listener;
Philosophy hangs loose on bones like mine.
In one of the great cities of the coast
There was a festival for all the bards,
A happy time: they treated us like kings,
Or little gods who visited disguised.
And when one treats mere men as kings, or gods,
We start to act like them as well, in all
The difficult and arbitrary ways.
We held a competition, in our cups,
To recount all the gorgeous tales of Troy,
And, as the drunkest, I am sure I won.
Dripping with honors, laurel, and the grape,
I staggered through a hall whose echo said
That it was full of marble. Smooth it was;
I must have lost a sandal on the way,
And, reaching out for safety from the fall,
One hand closed on a roundness, one a lyre.
It is unmeet for singers here below
To so disport with Hermes' finer parts.
So I fell back, into a stone embrace,

Lithe arms and armored midriff. Should a bard
Thus dally with Athena? Since it seemed
I should have no support but blasphemy,
I let myself fall down. How comforting
The cold floor was, how soothing-quiet grew
The harshly-echoing room. And then a voice,
One that I did not know, commanding all
To take our stations, that the ship be launched.
I found that I wore armor, hard and smooth
As finest bronze, yet not of bronze at all,
And I was buckled fast into a seat,
A throne with cushions, easy on the spine.
I heard my name, all seemed to know me here,
And no voice paused a moment for reply.
After the lightness passed—the spin, they said—
The bindings were released, some friendly hands
Assisted me to rise, and I began
To feel my way about our ship and crew.

If every second word here were not "ship,"
Our people "crew," its whole sense journeying,
I should think it a dyeworks: sharpened smells,
Oils and bitumen, much ammonia,
Broad sheets of metal beaten very flat,
The smooth hard pottery that is not warm.
We had rope, for our bundles and our stores;
I felt the braiding, yet it had no touch
Of fiber: the thick strands were smooth as bone,
As if a craftsman had but carved a rope
From unfired clay, or gum, as if they knew
What was desired, but not what it was for.
Of course we had a Captain, Steersmen too,
A Master of the Cargo and the Stores,
But all the oarsmen, that I first supposed

To be belowdecks, were instead machines,
Engines of Titans' metal, given life
Through artificial blood, as Talos was.
And of the living, how their titles ring!
Physicians, yes, Farspeakers, but as well
Life-Learners, Reckoners, Namers of Stars—
A common singer ought to be afraid
To sail with heroes: to the little men,
The nameless on the *Argo*, falls the doom
By storms and beasts and on bloodthirsty shores;
To them it is not given to come home
And say, "I am survived to tell the tale."
Yet singers have a grace in this: the gods
Desire as much as men to hear a tale,
And sometimes will protect who tells one well;
We huddle in the palm of Hermes' hand.
But all the songs of heroes are of Death:
Of comforting the doomed, of bringing ends
To monstrous lives that gobbled innocents,
Of wars without an end—and in the end,
Of spreading arms and smiling as it comes.
We sing because we die: the song goes on.
I think that even Hermes, when he sings,
Prefers a tale of Patroclus in arms
To all Olympus's unchanging charms.

There were some thirty of us, and of these
A third were women. Amazons, you'll say,
Yet Amazons of story war with men,
And these were shipmates, equals with the rest,
All Theseuses and Hippolytas,
Though none, I think, was won by stratagem.
And we had mules of brass: a kind of crate,
Built strong of metal and smooth pottery,

Without a head or tail, but six stout legs,
And harnessed up to carry or to pull.
Each had a little wheel upon its back,
With four marks: turn and feel it meet the first,
And it would stand in place; the second sent
It homeward to the camp; upon the third,
It followed one of us, and on the fourth
It would proceed to some selected place.
One of the crew tried patiently to tell
The singer how this wonder was achieved,
And lost the singer in a thicket of
Elektron (which is amber), armatures,
Sand fused to glass, and *mensae logicae.*
"They are Hephaestus's work," I said at last,
"The armorer of gods, whose hammer-craft
Brings metal into life." The woman laughed,
And said, "Indeed it was an armorer,
Though here contracted to a peaceful trade."
Of these crew I shall speak a little more:
Though they were Steersmen in the roll of ranks
(For *kybernetikisti* was their name),
They never gripped the helm. Some had a hand
In charting courses, though in this they took
A part more Reckoner than running sail.
It was a riddle to me, till one day
One asked me to go with him, through a door
And down a passage narrow to the sides
Into a room where cool air wafted by.
He told me words to say, and how to phrase
My questions. So I asked about our ship,
Our voyage's duration; and there came
A voice both calm and empty of concern,
Precise in its details. Then my blood knew
A chill all from within; for this must be

The Underworld, where spirits of the dead
May be compelled to tell the things they know,
And will, but careless and indifferently
To their effect upon their listeners,
Both in the hour, and in the time to come.
So when I heard that we had six months' sail,
A year encamped upon the distant shore,
Another half a year returning home,
And other things I did desire to know,
My spirit took no reassurance there,
No sign the Makers of our Destiny
Had blessed us, or had promised any aid.
I asked my fill, and we made our ascent
Into the warmer chambers where men lived,
And now I understood these crewmen's tasks:
They were our Oracles (and one a Pythoness).

Now when I say we sailed for half a year
I mean there was no landing; not to hunt
Fresh food, or find fresh water, or to ease
The long confinement. I was told there were
No islands on our route, except the moon
(Which even I know floats in every sea).
Our water was replenished by some means
Of crystal salts and filtering; our food
Came out of jars, but in variety
Unheard of upon any ship I knew.
And we had fish. They grew in spheres of glass,
Bubbling and rushing like a mountain stream.
A live trout in the fingers charms the soul;
With oil and salt it also satisfies.
The days passed, not like beads along a string,
But eddies briefly whirling in a stream,
Their rhythms changing in the constant flow.
To live six months within a hollow ship

May seem as being trapped inside a cave,
Yet caves can be full of philosophy
As well as monsters. They had planned this trip,
My shipmates and their city, years ahead,
So there were books—and books that spoke aloud—
And dramas, somehow, and gymnasia
Where men and women fortified themselves
For war and danger, as they always do.
We had the Sun inside a little room;
A Stellar-Namer told me that we sailed
Out in the tracks worn smooth by Helios,
So that although our seas were cold, there was
A present peril from those chariot wheels
That light the mortal world. Do you draw back
And think us worse than mad, that we should dare
To ride such seas? Well, yes, of course we were.
That is the substance of it; not to do
What sense impels and safety screams to do.
And, mad or not, that solar room contained
The essence of the sunlight of my youth,
Warm, dry, and tangy with the promises
That all young men believe; and if they sail
Over the world's edge, may find are true again.
The Pythoness taught me a table game,
A little war of little men on squares,
With horsemen, castles, priests, a King of course,
Who has a devious Queen, like some we know.
She said that it was ancient, from the East
(Though Easterners say all their ways are old).
I thought that I should never learn the trick
To see the board as I must see the world,
But each man fit a socket in his square
Like spearheads into shafts, so they stood firm
As I reviewed their ranks; and as for time,
We had so much of that, it was a game

Itself to make it pass—why not in play?
And I came, like a god, to understand
That Destiny is Pattern, not the men
Who live and die to make it. It may be
That this is not a thing I wished to know.

The half-year ended, but not yet our cruise.
We lay just off the shore so long a time
I thought we might have given up the goal.
A Steersman said we paused to chart the coast
Of this land never seen so near by man;
Our maps and charts, once copied faithfully,
Would be sealed in a packet (just his word)
And sent on wings toward home, that if we met
Misfortune in the quest, those who came on
Would have our steps' advantage to begin.
We would leave seven of our crew offshore,
Aboard a kind of well-provisioned raft;
They would observe us, we report to them.
Those seven people knew this was their part,
Had known for years; yet in the voice of each
There was a catch that was not parting ache.
And who would journey all those days, to wait,
To hold an empty cup outside the door?
Their Reasoners had crafted well their plan,
And had, I have no doubt, the deepest care
For all they ordered forth; yet in the end
The planners were not of the company,
And would and could not know just how they served
A plate of ash for every third of meat.
We parted from our friends, and took our seats,
The Steersmen sang again of change and spin;
So suddenly our ship, which had this far
Felt nothing like a ship, began to heave

And yaw like a slim vessel in a gale;
A ride on a bull's back, as I have heard
Meets those who pass the Pillars of Hercules.
At once the bucking stopped, but not the roar
Of sea contesting hull at awful speed,
Ready to break us should our Steersmen fail.
A grinding, then, below—were we aground?
But it went on, longer than any span
Of sand I know extends. The noise grew less,
The buffeting decreased, until the ship
Ambled, it seemed, as I have heard a horse,
Haughty with having won some race, may do,
And then we stopped. The touchstones were addressed,
The complex prayers were said, and we stood still
For one inhaling moment: and inspired,
And knowing that we lived to be, we cheered.

Our big-spirited Captain stepped ashore.
He thanked his crew, his nobles, and his god
(Though not named, that was Ares, Lord of War),
But did not claim to found a city here;
He did not lay a claim to land at all,
But spoke of bringing knowledge to the world.
The Pythoness stood near. I felt her nod,
Obeisance to Athena. So I said
My silent prayer to Hermes of the Lyre.
A few of us, I'd heard along the trip,
Professed no gods, yet even they believed
In something. In such somethings we were one.
The camp our Artificers made was full
As strange to my sense as our ship had been,
Still walled, still roofed, still brazenly hard-faced,
And when we left it for the open sky
We still must armor up, from head to heel.

The visor of the helmet was of glass,
So strong no sword could pierce it; and I thought,
A man should see the face of whom he kills,
Or who slays him in trying. This I know,
Being not born a slayer. Once I asked
A Reader of the Earth to tell me why
We dressed so, and with whom we were at war;
And gravely he replied, "It is a war.
We must defend against the air, the cold,
The dryness most of all; they love us not,
And wait for any chance; but I would say,
And do not care who hears, if I could stand
Without this heavy skin, just long enough
To feel the breeze, and curl my toes into
This ancient soil—to touch it for itself—
Well. Better some things are not possible."
Know well, I do not disrespect the house.
It was so much more spacious than the ship,
Each crewman had a bed to call his own,
And no one ever needed wait to bathe;
On certain days (a birthday, or a find
Of special value in the outside world)
We could all dine together in one room,
As lords in celebration make their feasts.
The bards (and I am one) say that a robe
Can be a home, if that is where one dwells;
A good house, if one keeps it fairly clean
And patched against the wind. And it is so;
But I am not a turtle, and by choice
I will not sleep inclined against my walls,
(I told this joke to many of my crew,
Who told me one of mules. It passed me by.)
What happens, then to fill up such a year?
Much mapping of the land, inspecting stones,

Recording all the weather that there was,
And hunting water. This possessed the crew,
And at long last I needed not ask why.
You may think kings and walls and wars decide
The fates of cities; but dry up a stream
And Sparta in her might would tumble down
Choking, to crumble back into the dust.

At some point when a singer spins a tale
The audience—it does not matter who,
High table, alley stones, in palace grand
Or huddled by the road—they all acquire
A heaviness of breath, a leaning near,
A certain thoughtless humming, very low;
You want to know what happens in the dark.
As if you don't. But as I know my trade,
I know my obligations. There was room
That bedrooms could be empty for a time,
And there could be arrangements among friends.
There was no creeping out into the night;
You have heard tales of mighty men in bronze,
And even of Athena. They are lies.
Unarm, or in this battle you are lost.
We also had the place where food was stored,
And where the tanks for breeding fish were kept;
The noise of water, bubbling in the spheres,
Could cover much. The lighting, I was told,
Was strangely shadowed, subtle to the eye.
And one night, near that room, I felt a hand
Lie lightly on my shoulder, and it drew
Without once pulling. So we passed the door.
Only two questions seemed quite pertinent,
The one you might not guess being her name.
"The last you would expect," she said, so low

Below the fishes' voices, even I
Was not sure who she was. Nor do I care;
For all are Aphrodite, to these hands.

It came that when the year was halfway gone
A Reckoner bade me put my armor on;
"We go to climb Olympus. Come along."
Olympus! So I laughed; I must have done.
To sail so far, to fetch up at the foot
Of Destiny in Residence, and then
Put on our boots to kick against the door?
Yet we wear hubris like a lover's knot,
A private blush worn outward on the hem
Of our best gown. We will not set it by,
Except to earn one more. I dressed to go.
We traveled to Olympus in a train
Of barges that made speed across the sand,
A brace of brazen mules stowed in the rear
With tools and our provisions for the climb.
The ascent started at a raucous pitch,
The Earth-Admirers eager to collect
Some stones from which they hoped to boil out air,
And water, too, as always. Even more,
The party simply wanted to go up,
To be as far above the world as is
To be, to master distance, and to see—
Now do I overreach myself? Not I:
Horizons are not only in the eye,
To rise above has purpose all its own.
Oh, I have creased my hands on upright stone,
And I have swallowed down my share of dirt.
The trouble started soon. A wind came up,
Unnaturally fast and cruelly strong,
The Wind-Observers only guessed at why.
Up here at last one truly heard the wind

And touched and fought it too, fistfuls of dust
Flung wild against my helmet and my greaves;
I thought my fingers could have drawn a word
Into the air like clay. The rope I held,
That held me, held us all, went slack to taut
To slack again entirely of itself.
I heard the sound of thunder. Was it Zeus,
Appalled at last by mortals on his stairs?
There was a cry. My helmet rang with groans
That faded much too fast. When I was young,
I knew men who could leap from crop to cliff
Like mountain goats, so long as there was sun;
In darkness, no less brave, they clutched each branch
And skinned their palms in search of steady stones.
There came another crunch, and then a sound
A high insistent wailing I'd been told
Meant one of us was gravely hurt nearby.
I turned. The noise pitched up and down again.
The high notes were my aiming point. I moved,
Careful at first to give the rope some slack,
Until I felt that slack was all there was.
A mule of brass then nudged up to my thigh
And waited. My hand found its guiding-wheel,
And turned it to the farthest setting. True
To its command, it shuffled toward my goal.
I hoped that others followed, could not tell,
And prayed it was not far. That much was so.
My boot struck first a knee, and then a bone;
Some part of me will always hear that scream.
I knelt down by a Knower of the Stones,
Who now lay one with stone, and was himself
Becoming stone, as I held to his hand.
He said, "I am so glad to see you here,"
And broke me into slivers. Then a voice,
The Captain's—distant? Near?—called out, "Report!"

Then bodies clustered in. I breathed again.
I heard my name half-growled by one of them,
And "Useless," or the like. The stone man said,
"Why do you scold the first man to my aid?
He held my hand, as all good doctors do.
You ask what happened? Why, the stones fell down
And found me waiting. Gravity and space,
And so—" Another silence, half a breath.
"No man has caused me harm." And he was dead.
The Captain's voice was quiet, not subdued.
"Why was he separated, and alone?
Look at his tools, if any have survived."
An Oracle replied, "Here's hematite,
In quantity." They spoke of water then,
For water and the blood ore coexist.
The Captain said, "There'll be a time for that.
For now, let's hitch a wagon to the mule
And get our shipmate home for burial."
You'll want to know if there was water. No.

There was a general meeting to decide
Whether we would inter our comrade here
Or bear his body, carefully preserved,
Back to his native shore. Now this at last
I thought I understood. But I did not.
The Students of the Living claimed the act
Of burial in this, our hard-won ground,
Would trouble any creature living here,
Pollute the soil, and make the sphere of life
A compound stew that neither place could own.
But when I asked who dwelt here, I was told
That they were beings of an unseen world,
Unknown to us, that might be aeons dead,
But if they were, and if they still did live,

We might extinct them by our merest touch.
I never knew a land where no one lived,
And if, as I was told, those who live here
Cannot be seen, why, they are ghosts, or gods,
And ghosts and gods may long for company—
Or, if not, will find ways to be alone.
I abstained from the vote, which mattered not;
For all but four or five chose burial.
The Captain led the service for the dead.
He praised the living man, and not his death;
Spoke of small kindnesses and pleasant hours
And then abruptly he turned to the tomb,
Called it a shrine, said it would be a place
Of pilgrimage in unknown days to come,
The first bit of this new and distant land
That men did more than crouch upon, but held
By right of habitation, and of blood.
When men say, "This is ours," in broken speech,
They will be heard, for better or for ill;
Of Helen was this said, and also Troy.

A year is planting, growing, reaping, sleep;
The same for us, though what we harvested
Was stones and knowledge, and all that we sowed
Will never raise a shoot. The days grew less,
And many knew the winy-bitter taste
Of homesickness with passion to go on.
This was no sad farewell. We sailed for home,
The only parting had been long ago,
So we baled up our treasures, stalled our mules,
And—why prolong it?—told the land good-bye.

There is another tale before the end.
A hundred nine days inbound, I was told

To hurry to a storeroom, shelter there:
It seemed that Helios had been ill pleased
With something we had done: his anger flared.
Then someone spoke about the Pythoness;
They said she was at work upon a mast
(The first I knew our ship had masts at all),
And had no shield against the heavenly fire.
I said that I would help, if help there was;
The gods can always kill us if they choose,
But may forbear, if we are strong and true.
They would hear none of it. And so I hid,
And filled the others' ears with songs of Thebes,
And Jason, and the Argo, and the Fleece.
When Helios's rage was at an end,
I could learn nothing of the Pythoness;
The Captain was secluded, having long
Communion with his gods: who would intrude?
In time he called us all into one place,
And told us what the Destineers had said:
Though once again it wandered in such knots
Of words that I could not untangle it.
His language then grew plainer, round and rich:
"We go to see, and learn, and make our space
More than it was," the great-souled Captain said,
His voice uplifting as the rush of birds
Roused from a tree at dusk. "There is not one
Aboard this ship who voyages to die.
Yet if we die—as we all know we may—
Another ship will come, and then one more,
And more, until the whole arch of the sky
Is paved with ships, and those who follow on
Shall just take up their packs and walk the road."
Then, as the Captain's big tones died away,
The fading Pythoness, her voice so small

It might have been the Captain's echo, said,
"You are a man of honor, of ideals
Too high, perhaps, for two years packed in tin,
But higher still than mine, and I defer.
You'll live to sail the pavement seas of home,
And will not lie to one about to go
From Heaven to the Underworld direct.
What did the Lords of Terra really say?"
The Captain might have been of marble then.
His voice was like a stone upon a stone:
"For your sake, there will be an Ares Two."
"The gods will have their sacrificial jests,"
The Pythoness replied, with holy calm,
"I wanted to see home, yet now I would
Have freshened that dry soil with my thin blood
Rather than end so near to sight of blue.
Now two of us are heroes for a choice
We did not make and never could have made;
For our sake there will be another ship,
For our lives, fleets, perhaps. And I am yet
Enough myself to want the kind of death
That's quiet, and means nothing to the world."
A step fell near, and I could feel a touch;
The fingers, pausing, would have welted mine
With blisters; but as quickly they withdrew.
I heard the door that leads down to the place
Where voices answer questionless and true.

I don't know why they fought the Trojan War.
Oh, someone stole a woman who was wed
To someone with an army at command,
A hero angered, he and more are dead,
A city's ruined—that I understand.
But these are facts, not reasons. Helen was

A pretty prize, but time must alter that;
And Priam's house was rich, but gold defies
The bolt, the lock, the grip; it runs away.
The Argives never wanted to own Troy,
They wished each day, and more each after day,
To board their hollow ships and go back home.
The Horse was desperation raised in wood,
The sack is how it ends. That's understood.
The singer takes these things, and spreads them out
Like linen on a table, measuring
The width, how it will roll and tuck and drape,
And cuts it all to pieces, that he may
Give it a shape, a line, a fair display
A garment to adorn a naked frame
And make the sum of skin and cloth divine;
These pieces gird the secrets of desires
That launched the thousand ships; this is the sleeve
That clothed the angry blow that led to blows
And left so many shields half in the sand,
While somewhere far above the doubled ranks
The Destineers joined in, as if they spread
A muslin on the floor, bunched up for hills
With paintings of the forests and the sea,
And slabs of clay to be the Trojan walls.
They played the game that fills my shipmates' days,
With little soldiers made of brittle bones;
Coddling their kings, and sacrificing pawns.

I waited twenty days, and then ten more,
Before I dared approach the cold clay door
That led to the Agora of the Dead.
I had no questions, nor, I think, desired
An answer; there was just the gentle pull
Of water in a circle, that may draw

A great ship to her doom. I passed the gate,
Went down the narrow passage, spoke the words
I had been taught so long ago to say.
"Hello," I heard, a friendly voice, all hers,
Yet cold. "It is so good to hear from you."
And then my senses failed. Sometimes they do.

I held a woman's hand, and it was chill;
In panic clutched it hard, and found it stone.
They were Athena's fingers. I recalled
The marble hall of gods, so long ago;
Hermes was somewhere near. Did he then smile?
I had one way of knowing, but declined.
And then there were warm hands, from every side,
And poets' voices speaking. "You have been
Away so long; why did you hide in here?"
I tongued the air. It had its former taste,
And everything the sounds that once I knew;
There was no ship. Alas, there was no crew.
I gathered in the robe that is my house
And on some nearby day shall be my tomb,
And said, "My friends, where this old soul has been
He must not say; but grant a little more
Of that good patience you have shown before,
And I'll say nothing—but Odysseus will."

TALES FROM THE ORIGINAL GOTHIC

It was six-oh-nine ay em out on Long Island Sound, and foggy, and cold. We were technically representing the National Center for Short-Lived Phenomena. Boudreau and I were Center, observational, him video, me still, you Jane. Clement and Phail were M.I.T., hardware jockeys. Ormsby was spooky—we didn't know which agency, and they're all under orders to lie about that these days; spreads the blame around. Father Totten was direct from the Archdiocese of New York, something about eminent domain. He told me he was a qualified exorcist. I told him I was working on my biceps. He laughed the way you do when you've heard it once too often.

We had a van full of equipment: spectrometers and chromatographs, magnetometers and scintillation counters, shotgun mikes and hand-held radar. We had a real live robot, a little tank-tracked wire-guided sample-snatcher known variously as Stupid, That Piece of Shit, and Danger Will Robinson. We had, oh, lots of good stuff, and lead-lined steamer trunks in case we found anything worth taking home. Personally, I had five Hasselblads with two dozen assorted camera backs, long lenses, filters like a *Playboy* shooter might only dream of, slow fine film and insanely fast film and infrared and X-ray and Polaroid and you don't care what else. If the damn house showed up I was going to get a picture of it or by God and George Eastman know the reason why not.

There were two TV trucks, one from the network pool and one indie, and a helicopter of uncertain parentage, but if you said Air America at them they might smile back. The house wouldn't dare not show.

This was the seventh apparition, best that we could tell. First three were anecdotal (to wit: nobody believed a word of it), fourth independently confirmed (to wit: eighty witnesses in Grant Park, Chicago), fifth confirmed and documented (to wit: television mobile crew looking for background shots in Golden Triangle Park, Pittsburgh), sixth confirmed and tagged for active response (to wit: two senators whose morning field lecture on the need for direct intervention against you know who, you know where, was upstaged by the appearance behind them).

The data points went into a big computer designed to extrapolate impact points and fallout patterns, and the computer drew a map and posted a time. So here we were (to wit: to woo).

Six-eleven. See, all that nattering only took a couple of minutes. Time is all relative when you're freezing your butt off waiting for a supernatural manifestation to manif. The computer said six-fifteen, but time was the loosest part of the prediction, because nobody had reported exactly seeing the thing appear, they just looked up and—

There it was.

Shit, we gasped, or maybe, Gasp, we shat. The house surprised us. How do you think that looks on your résumé, *Once ambushed by a house?*

I fumbled my fingers onto my shutter switches and started tripping the light. Boudreau spun up a standard and a high-speed film camera, pressed his eye to his video rig. Clement and Phail played their instruments like dueling jazz drummers. Ormsby did something—I assume what he was supposed to do. (When he joined the party, he said, "Good morning, I've been attached to your unit." Makes you think of a lamprey, right? Ormsby the Sucker. Yup.)

Oh, and Father Totten made the sign of the Big X. Thanks, Father, for sharing that with us.

The house was three stories high, Victorian, high-floored and gabled, maybe sixty feet from porch to peak, and with that Victorian-vertical style that made it look even taller. There was gingerbread all over, spindles and doily-edging. Mansard roof, hexagonal shingles. Narrow windows with shutters. A great portico in front, with thin white pillars going up to the second floor. We'd seen the Pittsburgh videotape, and it looked like that but—but that was *videotape*, a comb-filtered picture on a tin box. This was live, widescreen. I almost said palpable, but that wouldn't be right. It was there, but not quite real yet.

It was very gray. The fog was still heavy, and misted everything, but the house was a deep, oily, shifty color, as if the fog itself had condensed and gelled to make it, which was at the time just as good a guess as anybody's. The wood trim was white, and there was some green-painted ironwork, but that too had the grayness. The house wasn't more than fifty yards away from us, but it might have been miles; the moon through a cloud.

"Is it real?" Ormsby said. Great question, Ormsby.

"We got it on the radar," Phail said.

"I want contact," Ormsby said, and I looked up and Clement looked up; nobody'd quite properly explained to us that what Ormsby wanted made any special difference, but the way he talked and looked, you could tell that it did and he knew it. "Is the robot ready?"

"Ready as it'll ever be," Clement said, and picked up the control box. "What do you want it to do?"

"Physical contact first. Run it right up to those stairs and see if it hits anything."

"Okay, Stupid," Clement said, to the robot, sort of, and pushed the sticks. The robot whined and started crawling toward the porch, trailing its cables behind it.

Then the front door opened, and the woman came out. Shit, gasp, in spades. Clement nearly dropped his controls; the robot veered over and went crash-bump against the steps. Contact.

She came down the stairs, seeming not to see the robot. I grabbed a long lens to look at her; she didn't seem to see anything at all, but God her eyes were beautiful. Her face was beautiful, lineless as new porcelain, framed in dark hair. My hand wobbled too badly to watch her through the telephoto.

She was wearing a nightgown, smoke-gray, like the house not a precise color but shifting, and she was carrying a long silver candlestick. The second report had mentioned this, but, like I said, nobody paid any attention to the second report. Oh, and one other thing; I looked up. There it was: one light shining from the attic window.

Now do you see why the early reports got shitcanned? We don't all live within stone walls of canker'd reason, but there are limits, and the cover of a paperback romance showing up in downtown Spokane is damn it one of them.

Ormsby said, "Is she solid?"

Phail said, "Huh?"

"On the radar."

"I . . . don't know. She might not show up, so close to the house."

"What can you use on her?"

"Uh . . . the spec unit's lasers."

"Okay, do it. Clement, get the robot over to her."

I snapped frames as fast as my motor drive would hum. Boudreau had it easy; all he had to do was stare with his trigger finger down. The priest was saying something in Latin, I didn't know what.

Clement got the robot backed up. "Come on, junkheap," he muttered. "Nice and slow now."

The woman was down the steps now, walking across the soft ground, more or less toward us. Her gown drifted on the air, mist on mist: it seemed light as spidersilk, but was remarkably opaque for all that. Her arms were bare, and there was a vague hint of cleavage. She should have been shivering like a birch in a hurricane. I blew out a cloudy breath and realized that hers wasn't fogging.

Clement had the robot a couple of steps behind her now, and started working the manipulator. It wasn't a very sophisticated arm, just a one-joint with a clamp on the end. It stretched up toward the woman's gown like a lecherous metal midget.

Then it stopped. Short. Clement struggled with the control sticks for a moment—and then his arms spasmed and he gagged and fell down, twitching like a stunned steer. The robot was smoking, and the cable, and Clement.

Phail shouted and started for him. Ormsby straight-armed Phail in the chest. "Don't touch him," Ormsby said. He didn't share the advice with the priest, who crouched and rolled Clement over.

Clement groaned. His gloves were burned nearly through and when Totten pulled them off the skin below was scorched, but Clement said, "I'm all right—I got a shock," (hey, us too) and got up. "What did she do?" That was a couple of kinds of good question, because she was gone.

Boudreau had been watching, taping. (He hadn't turned to look at Clement steaming and screaming. No comment.) "She took off into the woods. That way."

Ormsby got out a walkie-talkie, and the helicopter spun up its rotors, presumably to chase Our Heroine across the frozen woods. "Okay," Ormsby said to us, "we're going inside."

"Could I remind you," Clement said, as Phail wrapped his hands in gauze, "that in the previous sightings the house disappeared within half an hour? What happens if we're inside when it goes?"

"Then we go where it's going," Ormsby said, and that was it, because we all knew when we took this job that we were going inside the house when it showed up, if it showed up, if it had an inside to go into. Clement was just expressing a little manly high spirit, common among the nearly electrocuted. So I took my number-one camera and thirty-pound equipment vest, Boudreau switched to battery power, Clement and Phail took up their portable gear. Father Totten clutched his prayerbook and Ormsby put on his hardest expression.

As we approached, the house seemed to get taller still, like a mountain that looks like nothing from a distance but is scraping clouds by the time you reach its foothills. The grayness didn't change as we drew near. When you walk through the fog, things are supposed to get clearer, it says so right here on the label; this didn't, inspiring thoughts of classical tortoises that can cover half the distance till doomsday but never all of it, so much for your damned slow and steady. (Do Zeno and Aesop sit around in the first circle of Hell swapping turtle stories, A to Z?)

We all got into what I would suppose one might call ready positions, and Phail pushed open the door. It swung wide and silently. There was a hall beyond: exactly the sort of hall you would expect to find behind that sort of door, with a red carpet and an umbrella stand. We went in.

There was a grand stairway at the end of the hall, going up into genuinely total darkness. And there was a large arch, opening onto a bay-windowed parlor.

The parlor was full of wheelchairs, all of them occupied, and a woman in a starched white dress. All the people there were looking out the windows.

"Hey," Ormsby said.

No one paid attention to him. Bad move with Ormsby.

"What the hell is that?" Ormsby said. Once, before I died, I would have liked to hear Ormsby answer a question even half as stupid as the ones he asked. No such luck.

"The book," I told him.

"What book?"

"The book we just walked into the cover of."

There is a version of the story in which the house has been converted into a hospital for wounded Allied pilots at the height of the Battle of Britain; if you look into the mist you may see the lights of the RAF aerodrome nearby. She has been sent from London for safety's sake, but as the aerodrome is in danger from German raids—perhaps the house as well, as who can measure the depravity of the Hun—there is no safety. And she is surrounded daily with the smells of disinfectant, of human fluids, of death, and with the pilots themselves, blind, burnt, broken. There are jobs for the injured in this desperate hour, but none for them, and so they know that they are useless, shall perhaps always be useless; these are *men who flew* and now are wrecked, a Victorian hall of Icarii.

Outside, half seen through the taped windows and the trees, there was a crash and a fireball rolling up. A bell began to toll, and of course we asked who for. "The chopper," Ormsby said, and drew the gun that how could we have doubted he would be carrying, it looked so natural on him, and went to the window, thinking that a helicopter had crashed on the other side of the window, but wrong craft, wrong tale, wrong earth. The smoke came from a burning Spitfire, shot down in the Bloody April of 1940.

Ormsby turned from the window and saw her, standing not ten steps away from him in her severe whites and her nurse's cap, looking out at the wreck and hoping it is not him, not *him* in the twist of metal and flaming petrol, before she turns back to the men in her charge.

She stared at the roomful of eyeless men, limbless men, physical metaphors of the more fundamental incapacity. Though most can still speak, they cannot speak their need for her, to arouse them from slumber, to absorb their seed and return it as children, strong sons who will learn the ways of the split-S and the Immelmann turn, who will learn the arcana of the Norden bombsight, men who will learn, as their fathers did not, that they must avert their eyes from the falling pregnant bomb. She must acquiesce, they must do this. It is the only way they can continue to fight the war.

Ormsby still didn't see, though the room is full of ravaged men. Of course not, how could we have been so foolish, he has a purpose here and they are not part of it. Visitations. Apparitions. Troop movements. From those wonderful folks who brought you helicopter-borne assaults, a new sort of borning: the First Ectoplasmic Infantry. Having mastered the delivery of Hellfire, they have sent Ormsby to discover the remaining secrets of the damned, coming soon to a theatre of war near you. He saw the veterans, all keloid and the stumps of limbs, he saw them clearly enough. But he looked straight through them, for he knew their secrets already.

He took hold of her, pinning down the lass he grasps, and demanded of her what had happened to the helicopter.

She understands, though he does not. She knows what he has lost in the fall of his machine. She sponges his manly brow, she absorbs his curses, his demands for the missing part of himself. She knows where the rest of Ormsby is, buried in a concrete tomb without the codes to launch.

Ormsby began to panic as she tended to him. He waved his pistol. This should excite him, always has. At least it should produce some response from her that will excite him. But no. There is a war on, and loose lips sink ships.

Ormsby yelled something that Adam probably yelled at Eve and certainly yelled at Lilith, and ripped her white dress open.

There came (oof) the roar of Rolls-Royce Merlin engines, the flash of a propeller—an airscrew, the British call it—switch on, contact. Airscrew. Contact. Loose lips rip zips. Ormsby screamed (like a woman, he would say if it were another man making the noise) as the white blades ground his bone. Littering the past, he gasped.

Ormsby danced hither and yon, as if trying to gather his guts for the journey home, shock trooper bundling his chute. Hold still, Ormsby, how shall they find your pieces on the judgement day? Down he goes. Pigeon under glass at last. She stares at him. The wheelchairs circle round.

Suddenly there is nothing but Ormsby in the room, crumpled on the floor in a puddle of himself.

And we . . .

Well, picture it. Here we were, gang of scientists confronted by the new phenomenon, ready to analyze it to destruction. Everything dies if you turn enough light on it. Those of you who are familiar with the history of astronomy will recall how the immensely complex theory of epicyclic motion was created to explain those celestial movements that a sun-centered system put into much more elegant order. Once it became accepted that buildings and their contents might manifest out of the clear blue (Rayleigh scattering—oh excuse me) then a thousand small mysteries of life, from the slowness of urban mail delivery to the theft of cable television service, would at once fall into systematic place.

As if systems or sensibility had anything to do with it. The dark closes in. You push it back, using what cleverness you can hold onto in your crab-crawling terror to make light.

Rock breaks scissors, scissors cut paper, paper smothers rock.

Mind makes tools, tools dispel madness, madness, oh, *oh*.

We ran.

Clement smashed through a glass door. We hadn't seen it, and yes we were so looking. I doubt it was there, doesn't matter, wasn't there anymore anyhow. Clement was on his knees in a garden, green and mossy and crystalline with broken glass.

Phail was there in an instant. Their hands touched, and instantly I knew why Ormsby had not permitted them contact in his sight. Clement seemed all right; the gauze wrapping his hands had prevented much further damage.

"Are we outside?" Clement asked, looking around at the fog, the peat, the vines and trees.

"This is Spanish moss," Boudreau said, not touching it. "Spanish moss doesn't grow up here. Besides," he added, ever the camera-eyed observer, "if we're outside, where's the sun?"

She came around a moss-shrouded tree, and we turned to see her, dressed in her white, with her pale smile.

Clement took a step toward her a little unsteady on the soft soil, and said, "Who are you?"

"Please," she said, or I thought I heard her say; her lips didn't seem to move, those thin lips like a shallow wound. "Help me, I need you," the wound said.

Clement must have heard. He went to help her. Any way he could.

There is a version of the story in which the house has stood for centuries with the same mistress, in which all pleasure and all need are reduced to a single bittersweet act.

She was determined, but the determination was not the courage of the living but the implacable advance of the walking dead. Beauty must age and die, you see, that's the way things work; if beauty survives, then it must be by some terrible and unnatural means. She has been roused from her bed in her bedclothes by the scratch of hell beneath the thin earth; she has been driven from her grave barefoot in her shroud by the hunger for salt blood.

But she will settle for whatever Clement has.

He shriveled as she touched him; he did not pull away, though it was a long, long moment until her fingers were actually around his throat; seeing that, computing that, scientifically analyzing that, led to only one conclusion about why he did not pull away. Why Ormsby took hold of his apparition with such definite intent. It didn't speak well for the rest of us; fear we had, desire we had, strength, well, Totten and I held Phail by the arms as Clement was pulled into the soil, and Boudreau's finger was on the camera trigger; Clement was a film of skin on blackening bones by the time he was breast-deep, but he didn't seem to be fighting. He didn't seem to be having a bad time at all, not nearly as bad as Phail was having. You know the song of the Lorelei, as she draws men to die on the stones; a kiss on the hand may be quite continental, but diamonds . . .

Suddenly, Clement's eyes looked up—they were loose marbles in a skull, now, and his tongue rattled in what might have been a scream had there been any air to drive it, fluid to wet the system. And he was gone.

"There is a light this way," Father Totten said, pretty obvious from the way it lit up the fog, but there wasn't anywhere else to go, was there?

"I'm all right now," Phail lied, and we let him go and walked toward the glow, feeling for glass walls that might suddenly pop up. Instead we came to double doors, and a room beyond.

The lights were very bright in here, and copper cookware hung on racks, and stainless steel countertops ran every which way.

There is a version of the story in which she is a scullery maid, trapped in the kitchen kept insanely ordered by a head cook who is certainly a sadist, probably a lesbian, no question incompetent at food preparation—you never see the maiden preparing tournedos Rossini or medaillons de veau or even brutalizing a defenseless carpaccio, do you? It's always "Stir the stew" and "Scour out the roasting pans." She can cook, of course, though Cook bushels her light, until by happy accident her midnight snack reaches the late-night plate of the master of the house, who will, presented with this clear example of genetic superiority, elevate her to master of the house's mistress (lawfully, of course) where she will never again have to slice onions or scour a pot, and Cook will be horsewhipped and sent away, and God alone knows what the household will eat after that.

Phail looked around nervously at the boiling cauldrons, the crackling griddles. Suddenly he raised his hand, stared at it; I expected the flesh to be medium well with diagonal grill marks, but there was only a film of white lard on his fingers. Or something like lard. It certainly upset Phail. He scrubbed at it with his other hand, but that only coated both of them. Towel, towel, who's got a towel? Next he wiped it on his jacket, then on his trousers. His face began to itch, he twitched it, he nearly touched it—but oh now, realization set in. It won't go away, not by washing. It was in his secret places now. Are you washed in the mint sauce of the lamb? (How about that, Father Totten? Have you spent time among the lepers outcast unclean, or is it all their own fault? Tell me, Father Totten, when exactly did God decide to wash his hands of Sodom?)

It isn't death we fear, you know, we can out brief candle all the livelong day; it is the bad procedures of death, the mashing of meat and bone, the struggling of the heart against the ribs of its cage, the physical scream of the steel in the skin, the disease that hides and waits and digs itself in.

Phail stood in the kitchen, but his sustenance and his life's hope had just died outside, leaving nothing but his fears. O little lamb, did he who made the spirochete make thee? As if to answer, things like purple corkscrews came drilling their way out of Phail, and his blood mingled with the white grease frosting him. Suppurations stitched his skin. His left eye popped, a little beak snapping down the bits from within. There was no longer a Phail, only a Phail-shaped disease, an infection casting a man's shadow. Totten gabbled a prayer. Boudreau threw up, and I watched the spew for signs of life, but it was only honest man's vomit, coffee and Danish and an Egg McMuffin. It fried up crisp on the spotless floor.

Then Phail's belly split open, and something white and shiny and crablike leapt out, skittering on the floor; it had a dozen cylindrical legs and a long ropy tail still uncoiling slowly from Phail.

Boudreau pulled out Ormsby's gun (I guess it was brave of him to get the thing, at least) and fired at the white crab, once, twice, three times. He hit it each time, hell it was only two yards away, blasting glossy bits from it. Curiously, no guts spill, no blood sprays. The white thing was apparently solid whatever-it-was. It quit moving.

As we hustled out of the kitchen I finally recognized the thing. "Congratulations." I said to Boudreau. "You just shot the world-record specimen of the Dalkon Shield."

"You gotta be fucking kidding."

"John Carpenter's *The Thing,*" I labeled his quote, and said, "Not in the least. We keep calling this a manifestation, why haven't we thought about what it's manifesting?"

Boudreau capped his camera lens with his hand—he did that to think better—and it started to develop for him (twenty seconds in the tray, then stop bath and fixer). "It's the cover of a Gothic novel, my *wife* reads—oh my God—"

And then lightning lit the room and took our breath away.

The panorama was definitely breathtaking. Bolts of blue energy arced between pitted copper spheres, casting high shadows against the vaulted stone ceiling. Relays clattered, sparking. There was the steady maddening heartbeat of vacuum pumps. A computer, a huge console resembling a theatre organ with triode tubes instead of pipes, occupied most of one wall.

In cells of curved glass bound with steel, things pulsed and quivered and flopped. One had tiny hands, pink and babylike.

She came wandering in, in a modernistic straight-lined gown of slick white satin. The creatures in the flasks have not yet frightened her, because she barely understands what it is she is seeing. The chamber is beautiful, in the manner of functional art, gray sheeny steel, liquid black Bakelite, indicator lamps brilliant points of primary color. The twitching things might almost be spaniels, crouched before the actinic fire, the master's slippers in their fangs, little pets with scales, with chitin, with cilia.

And all of them have blue eyes, just like her husband's.

In this version of the story, you see, her scientist (biologist? physicist? TV repairman?) husband has been making these things out of, well, the essences of matter and spirit, right? You get the idea? (Okay. Jizz and voltage.) Only, instead of potential Notre Dame quarterbacks, he gets these Pekingese from Hell. Finally, having mixed up Scientific Specialties Man Was Not Meant to Interface, the interdisciplinary idiot wakes up one morning, smacks his forehead (quite painful that, because his researches have given him an immensely strong and furry right hand), and says, "Of course! Ova!" (Like all scientists, he breakfasts solely on glazed doughnuts and coffee.) Following a few comic-relief episodes of trying to buy the finished product, he decides he ought to go to the source, and dines and weds and beds (once, experimentally) a goose of his very own. Warning her. Never. To go. In. The. Lab.

We gaped, but didn't move. Wrong audience, don't you see, this is a James Whale picture for Universal, Dr. Pretorius's homunculi in jars (as I thought that, the scene faded to panchromatic black and white, and she turned to show white lightning streaks in her madly ratted hair, and hissed). It's a pretty laboratory, it must be given that, it's a place any of us would have been willing to work, but we do work in real workshops day in day out and (where are the moldy coffee cups? the radio blaring FM rock? The *Playboys* hiding in the journals?) Charlie, *this ain't it.*

The film broke, pocketa pocketa sound, glare of white light, purple phosphenes, and there we were in the hall again, Totten, Boudreau, and me. Nobody else. Sometimes when you win you get your marbles back. Maybe best of seven?

Totten sighed. Boudreau leaned against a wall, then his eyes snapped open and he pushed away; but it was just a wall, William Morris paper and vertical wainscot.

There still weren't any doors; more corridors, all dark and absorbent, and the staircase. We could go in, we could go up. We could not go down, how very odd.

Boudreau's camera looked at me. Below it, the muzzle of Ormsby's gun looked just as blank. "I'm going upstairs," Boudreau said. "There might be a window. If we can't jump, maybe we can signal."

Jump to where, signal to whom? But Boudreau was frightened (so what were we, chopped liver? Well, maybe we were at that). Usually he gets drunk when he is frightened, but no such luck. Up we go, then.

Boudreau took a step, and then another, pointing camera and gun into the darkness overhead. Mind makes tools, tools dispel madness, paper smothers brain.

There was a screech, like that of a bluejay or a furious crow, and the huge taloned feet of a bird thrust down from the dark. The claws entered Boudreau's shoulder like can openers, with a wet hiss of compressing flesh and escaping blood, and a crunch as his camera crumpled. He fired a shot, generally upward, and then the gun fell. Above him was the sound of flapping wings, and he was lifted off his feet for a moment, but he seemed too heavy for the creature, and it settled him down again. The shock drove the claws deeper into his body, and he howled.

Toward the top of the stairs, I could make out a rippling pattern of dark feathers, and then the pale flash of a pendulous breast. The harpy's face was invisible above. It could stay there, I would not protest. It was rending Boudreau, the only one of these men I had known for more than this morning, it was crushing him to jelly, and still I would not protest or ask to see any more of the monster's nature. Because, you see, I also knew Boudreau's wife (no, not in that sense, I am very dreadfully frightened, but why will you call me mad?) and I was too certain of the hidden face, I knew those talons much too well.

The priest chanted something about neither fearing the terror by night, and I wanted to punch his face in, but he put a foot on the stairs and walked up them, carefully while treading through Boudreau's blood, and I followed. It beat drinking alone.

It was no longer dark at the top of the stairs. Candles were lighted on the walls, in iron candelabra. I felt inexpressibly sad that the holders were not grasped in human hands, but this wasn't my fantasy after all, at least not quite, not yet.

A stone archway beckoned to us, figuratively I mean. Father Totten looked through the room beyond, said, "What on Earth . . ." making two errors in three words.

I could hardly believe he needed a gazetteer. Here we had the iron maiden, here the suspended cages, here the rack, that bed with options. Around the walls, the usual assortment of ironmongery. The budget evidently would not support Poe's pendulum, but then of course it is not so readily metaphorical.

There is a curiously popular version of the story in which the house is built on crypts containing the private torture chamber rec room and wet bar of a prominent Inquisitor. Sometimes the tale is historical, with much hot Spanish blood staining black Spanish lace, swordplay, and fairly naked Anglican commentary of the habits of those wretched Papists, and how do you feel about Ulster, Father Totten? In other editions, the evil former owner has a descendant who drools on his copy of *Philosophy in the Bedroom* and longs to keep the old family tradition alive and screaming. A ghost or ghosts may be added to taste. There are inevitably many thrilling and detailed scenes in which they use phrases such as "no mercy" and "spare her nothing" as if they were in the habit of sparing a woman anything; they call for the iron boot, the fire and the ice, when twenty minutes in the birthing room would have any of them, cardinals on down, in a dead faint.

Father Totten said, "I don't understand," and I was rather glad for him, but not very glad because I only half believed him, and if you had seen his face you might not have managed half.

And there she was, but oh dear, something was very wrong here, she should have been wide-eyed with terror, abject, helpless (run that word over a few times, why don't you; it's so popular, helpless, helpless, never overmatched, never even outwitted, which you'd think would be okay, no; helpless it has to be, without strength or, gulp, cunning, the stupid twit never stood a chance, *helpless*, oh it has such a slick sound on the tongue, *helpless*, I want to stop but I can't I'm . . . oh God).

As if to speak of whom, Father Totten held up a cross. Didn't help Clement, but then we were all new at this death thing, and besides maybe she was Hindu or something. However, I was watching carefully, after all any old piety in a storm. And it's usual in these things, of course, that after blockheaded old soulless science has gotten its nose bloodied, the men of faith step in and show us the way to the light, or safety, or San Jose.

She was looking at us, smiling in her long white dress, which was actually not much more than a long strip of fabric hanging down fore and aft, a white cord belting it, and the candlestick, of course. She set the candle at the head of the rack. She lay down on the wood. She stretched her long arms up, teased the shackles with her fine wrists.

Helpless, helpless.

But then again, you know, perhaps not as feeble as that. I took a step. I heard the chains rattle and the locks click. Another step, and there was a creak as the windlass tightened. Another step, and the creak this time was from her joints. She sighed.

I touched the crank (the windlass, that is) and wound it tighter still.

"What are you *doing?*" the priest said.

"Enjoying myself," I said, not really at him. Then suddenly the handle spun under my hands as the chains wound up; there was nothing stretched between them any longer.

Lysisfuckingstrata cuts both ways, you know. You can't make me play if I don't wanna.

We went back out into the hall. Plain little hall, no doors, no stairs, windows all of cloudy glass.

There was a closet, however.

And Father Totten, and I.

There is in every man's soul a desire to confront the Devil, and a firm unfounded knowledge that the Devil can be beaten face-to-face; sometimes it's chance, sometimes clever argument (logic's chiefest end, as Faust said), sometimes the right lawyer (Daniel Webster comes highly recommended), but whatever the way out we all want the showdown. Haven't we all looked long and hard at photographs of Belsen, of the Ripper's Whitechapel, of the nuclear mushroom? It would be terribly reassuring to have no doubt of Hell. Perhaps if we knew we could stop doubting Heaven.

Surely Father Totten didn't doubt Heaven, surely goodness and mercy he didn't doubt Hell, but why would that stop him? After all, St. Thomas's doubt was indulged to the depth of the wounds. Christ was a man. He understood these things.

Totten pulled the closet open.

There was a high rackety rumble, and there fell upon the priest a great wave of garter belts, of fishnet stockings, of spike-heeled shoes, of boned corsets, of leather and black lace and spandex and red satin and buckskin fringe and torn sweaty denim.

The pile was still, and I thought he might be dead beneath it, maybe the shoe heels had gotten him, but then a corset stirred and a padded bra was thrust aside, and he stood up. Lace and nylon clung to him. He turned his head.

And turned, and turned, and *turned* his head, until his collar was right way round.

Totten's mouth opened, and a hand reached out; a slender knobby hand with black hair sprouting from its back, and bloodred nails. The hand flopped around, and then it pushed at Totten's upper jaw, stretching his lips until they tore, making room for another red-nailed hand to wriggle out. The two hands clawed his jaw apart, burst his throat. They tossed aside most of his head like a monkey throwing a coconut. The hands unseamed Totten's body, tossing sheaths of boneless meat aside with grand abandon and remarkable facility (do you not recall how, when you first undressed for an audience, even your socks were uncooperative?)

The escapee was perhaps a yard high, hairy goat legs ending in little hooves, the hands too big, the head too big, the hair insufficient to cover, yes, too big too. The little satyr looked around at the kinky riches spilled from the closet, and began selecting a wardrobe.

Somehow or another there was still a camera round my neck, fitted with an SCR strobe that could have lit Mount Rushmore. I punched the charge button, and it whined, an unpleasant noise to me, worse to the satyr; he clapped his red-clawed hands to his ears.

And that was how I shot him.

He screamed and started for me, stumbling on his half-donned garter belt. I shot him again. I had SCR recharge and a German motor drive. Flash flash flash. It worked for Jimmy Stewart in *Rear Window*, but then the cops were on their way to save him. Flash*whirr*flash*whirr*flash. As I shot the thing, capturing its ugly self on Kodak VR 1000 for posterity (if any, as Paul Frees said while the Martian war machines advanced), it began to shrink. Flash*whirr*flash. A foot high now, too stupid to realize what was happening to it, or maybe too egotistical to turn away from the camera. Flash*whirr*flash went the killer *paparazze*, peeling guilt off the thing in 35-millimeter strips, and what substance did it have but guilt? There was a pop of air and a whiff of dead goat, and it was gone.

Just me now. I wondered if I'd won. Whatever that meant.

There was a narrow stairway that hadn't been there before. A faint golden light shone on its polished wooden treads. The Light From the Attic Window, filtering down to me.

The steps creaked as I climbed them. At the top was a little room, an attic room with sloping ceilings, butter-colored light washing its wooden walls. There were brass candlesticks all around.

In the center was a four-poster bed, clothed in down and satin and clean wool.

I looked back down the stairs. They were still there, but they looked rickety, and there was a hint of red to the darkness at their foot that I can't say I liked very much.

I sat down on the edge of the mattress. Soft, soft, all feathers. I hadn't slept on a featherbed since I was a kid. When you're a kid, beds are great, beds are playgrounds, magic ships. All the fooling around later, the trick architecture, heart-shapes and vibrators and waterbeds, that's got nothing to do with seduction; if it did, no bedroom would be without the rear bench seat from a '58 Chevy; no, it's all an attempt to make the bed fun again. When you're a kid, you don't know how much you'll need the fun. You don't know what it's going to mean to be alone.

My right wrist wouldn't rise from the bed. First I thought it was just buried in the feathers, but I looked down and saw the attachments, the ligaments twined down into the springs, the arteries coupled and pulsing. I jumped a little; sight of your own blood does that, even when the blood's contained. I felt it somewhere past my fingertips, so the nerves were linked too.

Well. My right hand was attached to the bed, too attached to leave it, and I was too attached to the hand to leave it either. I turned back and was accepted, taken, absorbed.

I'm not certain how long the process took, but it's just about done now, all but the brain (How do I know? Snide, aren't we? I think, therefore there is still brain. *Somewhere.*) and its stepchildren the eyes. I can still see the room very clearly; the light is still soft and sweetly gold, but the candles are burning low. It won't be long now.

Brain and eyes, that's all, and I cannot be certain where the brain is. But then are we ever? Wittgenstein had a problem with this.

But the eyes I know. My eyes are resting upon the pillow. Resting lightly if you please.

A tremor of the candle flames tells me of her footsteps on the stairs. What shall I do, I wonder, *sans* tongue, *sans* touch, *sans* everything? Drink to her only with mine eyes, I suppose, and she will—

The door as it opens makes a sweeping shadow on the wall, a dark scythe with a mothglow behind. I wonder if the house is still sitting, never flitting, on the pallid plot of Long Island; what are they thinking out there, how long have we been gone? Perhaps no time at all. It occurs to me that not one of us scientists checked his watch for movement, and now too late to check my watch at all. Oh my ears and whiskers.

What will they do when the house appears in Russia, in China, in the Middle East? Do you remember when we were told, with a straight face and an upraised rifle, that wearing the *chador* was a revolutionary act? Do you remember, surely you must, how often we were told that those who made peaceful revolutions impossible would inevitably bring—no, you never believed that. Well, I have seen a revolutionary act. I have become a revolutionary act, physical graffiti on the psychouterine wall, O men read me and weep.

You must, for I am past tears. In a moment she will be here, with her blazing candle, to put me past it all.

Love should, as they say, be blind.

110 STORIES

This is not real. We've seen it all before.
Slow down, you're screaming. What exploded?
   When?
I guess this means we've got ourselves a war.
And look at—Lord have mercy, not again.
I heard that they went after Air Force One.
Call FAA at once if you can't land.
They say the bastards got the Pentagon.
The Capitol. The White House. Disneyland.
I was across the river, saw it all.
Down Fifth, the buildings put it in a frame.
Aboard the ferry—we felt awful small.
I didn't look until I felt the flame.
The steel turns red, the framework starts to go.
Jacks clasp Jills' hands and step onto the sky.
The noise was not like anything you know.
Stand still, he said, and watch a building die.
There's no one you can help above this floor.
We've got to hold our breath. We've got to climb.
Don't give me that; I did this once before.

The firemen look up, and know the time.
These labored, took their wages, and are dead.
The cracker-crumbs of fascia sieve the light.
The air's deciduous of letterhead.
How dark, how brilliant, things will be tonight.
Once more, we'll all remember where we were.
Forget it, friend. You didn't have a choice.
That's got to be a rumor, but who's sure?
The Internet is stammering with noise.
You turn and turn but just can't turn away.
My child can't understand. I can't explain.
The towers drain out from Boston to LA.
The cellphone is our ganglion of pain.
What was I thinking of? What did I say?
You're safe? The TV's off. What do you mean?
I'm going now, but not going away.
I couldn't touch the answering machine.
I nearly was, but caught a later bus.
I would have been, but had this awful cold.
I spoke with her, she's headed home, don't fuss.
Pick up those tools. The subway job's on hold.
Somebody's got to pay, no matter what.
I love you. Just I love you. Just I love—
The cloud rolls on; I think of Eliot.
Not silence, but an emptiness above.
There's dust, and metal. Nothing else at all.
It's airless and it's absolutely black.
I found a wallet. I'm afraid to call.
I'll stay until my little girl comes back.
You hold your breath whenever something shakes.
St. Vincent's takes one massive trauma case.
The voice, so placid, till the circuit breaks.
Ten minutes just to grab stuff from my place.
I only want to hear them say good-bye.

They could be down there, buried, couldn't they?
My friends all made it, and that's why I cry.
He stayed with me, and he died anyway.
We almost tipped the island toward uptown.
Next minute, I'm in Macy's. Who knows how.
I really need to get this bagel down.
He'd haul ass, that's what Jesus would do now.
A fighter plane? Dear God, let it be ours.
We're scared of bombs and so we're loading guns.
Who didn't have a rude word for the towers?
The world's hip-deep in junk that mattered once.
Hands rise to heaven as asbestos falls.
The air is yellow, hideously thick.
A photo, private once, on fifty walls.
A candle in a teacup on a brick.
They found—can you believe—a pair of hands.
Oh, that don't hurt. Well, maybe just a bit.
The Winter Garden's shattered but it stands.
A howl is Mene Tekeled in the grit.
Some made it in a basement, so there's hope.
The following are definitely known . . .
You live, is how you learn that you can cope.
Yes, I sincerely want to be alone.
Don't even ask. That's what your tears are for.
The cats are in a shelter; we are not.
Pedestrians rule the Roeblings' bridge once more.
A memory of home is what we've got.
Tribeca with no people, that's plain wrong.
It's just a shopping bag, but who can tell?
Okay, okay, I'm moving right along.
The postcards hit two dollars, and they sell.
Be honest, now. You're proud of living here.
If this is Armageddon, make it quick.
Today, for you, the rose is free, my dear.

We're shooting down our neighbors. Now I'm sick.
I can't do that for fifty times the fare.
A coronary. Other things went on.
It goes, like, something mighty, and despair.
All those not now accounted for are gone.
Here is the man whose god blinked in the flash,
Whose god says sinful people should be hurt,
The man whose god is kneeling in the ash,
The man whose god is dancing on the dirt.
Okay, I ate at Windows now and then.
This fortune-teller went to Notre Dame?
They knocked 'em down. We'll stack 'em up again.
Oh, I'd say one or two things stayed the same.
Some nights I still can see them, like a ghost.
King Kong was right about the Empire State.
I'd rather not hear what you'll miss the most.
A taller building? Maybe. I can wait.
I hugged the stranger sitting next to me.
So this is what you call a second chance.
One turn aside, into eternity.
This is New York. We'll find a place to dance.

With resolution wanting, reason runs
To characters and symbols, noughts and ones.

COPYRIGHT
ACKNOWLEDGMENTS

CPSIA information can be obtained
at www.ICGtesting.com
Printed in the USA
LVHW111733281122
734200LV00023B/328

9 780312 869397